I0677956

# THE NATURE OF PLOTS

# Praise for *The Nature of Plots*

"K.M. Zahrt has created an intriguing literary mystery [...] studded with nuggets from literature's great classics."
                    —**Jennifer Porter,** *The Tishman Review*

"In *The Nature of Plots*, K.M. Zahrt makes the life of a hard-drinking literary scholar in Hemingway country seem pretty darn exciting. Inventively plotted and laced with romantic encounters that would make James Bond blush, this research thriller takes on the big questions of art, life, and the legacy of The Lost Generation—and delivers a genuine surprise ending."
                    —**Andy Mozina, author of** *Contrary Motion*
                    **and** *Quality Snacks*

"*The Nature of Plots* transforms the reader into the world of Samuel Schurke, a doctoral candidate, who embarks on an investigative journey that intertwines his family, friends, and research with the legacy of The Lost Generation. Using literary allusions like nourishing pieces of candy, [K.M. Zahrt] combines art, philosophy, mystery, and intrigue into a suspenseful plot that cleverly culminates to a surprise ending."
                    —**Jason Lee Brown, series editor of** *New Stories from the Midwest* **and author of** *Championship Run*

"Drawing its title from a passage in DeLillo's *White Noise*, [*The Nature of Plots*] blends the historical past with the kind of truths that only fiction can offer: that exposing the past sometimes serves the greater good, sometimes merely one's own ego; that mortality can be met with dignity; that the plot of what might be today's 'lost generation' is worth rewriting. Through a masterful self-referential parody of memoir and diary genres, [K.M. Zahrt] insists that we all be lovers of story first and last..."                    —**Mary Catherine Harper, author of**
                    *Some Gods Don't Need Saints*

ALSO BY **K.M. Z**AHRT

*Odd Man Outlaw*
*Thanksgiving with Pop-Pop*

# ~~The Nature of Plots~~

A NOVEL

# K.M. Zahrt

THE GRAND PRESS

GRAND BLANC, MICH

THE GRAND PRESS

GRAND BLANC, MICH

Copyright © 2017 Kenneth Michael Zahrt

All rights reserved. No part of this book may be reproduced in any form
or by any means without the prior written permission of the author,
excepting brief quotes used in connection with reviews.

This is a work of fiction. Names, characters, places, and incidents are
either a product of the author's imagination or are used fictitiously. Any
resemblance to actual persons, living or dead, is entirely coincidental.

Grateful acknowledgment is made for permission to reprint excerpts
from "Postmodernism and Consumer Society," published in *The Cultural
Turn* by Fredric Jameson. Copyright © 1998 by Fredric Jameson.

Cover and book design by K.M. Zahrt. He does his own stunts.

ISBN: 978-0692837047

www.kmzahrt.info

For Katie, of course

# THE ~~SCHOLAR'S~~
# SCOUNDREL'S GAME

# Part One

To "the numberless unknown heroes equal to
the greatest heroes known."
—Walt Whitman, "Song of Myself"

# 1

Everybody lives. Everybody dies. That's all we know for sure. But what I've come to understand is, as you'll see—and trust me, I've resisted this conclusion as much as anybody—lives are randomly forged from improbable combinations of opportunity, luck, and happenstance. The combinations compound and evolve ceaselessly until death and beyond. (And every last one—Emma's urging me to add—is, for better or worse, "a mosaic of miracles," as she puts it.)

To the point: John "Johnny" Lawrence just so happened to be born in 1982. He lived twenty-seven years. And he just so happened to die last summer, in 2009. It was an unfortunate accident—arbitrary and indiscriminate. Those are as formidable of historical facts as any you'll ever find.

Johnny was, as you know, the son of the now infamous automotive-industry executive, John Lawrence, who was in the news before Johnny's death and even more so afterwards. At the time, Mr. Lawrence was the face of his company and was under fire for their financial crisis and their contributions to the economic slowdown. When Johnny died, social media swooned over the odd circumstances—partly because of the interest in his father and partly because he'd left behind a manuscript known to you by now as *The Lines of Change*. Publishers vied for the rights to it with tenacity—a story that took on its own life in the media-sphere.

Even Johnny's closest friends, myself included, weren't allowed to read it until after the first editions were already on their way through the presses.

Johnny was more than a friend to me. We were members of what we now call the "Circle of New Voices," along with Tom Peters, Ashley Daniels, Gretchen Bech, and—to a lesser extent—Alexandria Lawrence, Johnny's sister. The Circle was a name we coined on the road trip the five of us took last July—the one that ended in tragedy, as you know.

Johnny's death signified the end of the Circle in reality, and his passing has lingered like a terrible hangover. His death left me in a state of reflection, and I'm without doubt as to the cause. I can't help but feel somewhat responsible for Johnny's end. And I'm not alone; the rest of the Circle feels the same way, on their own terms. We were there when it happened, and we share in the burden of guilt. It surrounds us as a dense fog.

So here we are. Alex's therapist suggested we write as a way to honor Johnny. Although I won't be writing of Johnny's death specifically (we've agreed Gretchen alone has the objectivity to tell that part of the story), this represents my contribution to our shared efforts to continue the work he began, with what now appears to be the future of the Circle—a bond forever solidified in word as once in deed.

Is it what Johnny would've wanted? I don't know. I know this is bearing down on me—a feeling I understand comes to me by lineage as I sit and scribble in the same way my grandfather once had done, at the same table, occasionally pausing to look out the same cabin window at Walloon Lake (hoping that writing this into physical existence will somehow support Johnny's legacy and add value to my life).

I'm reminded of the telephone game we used to play as kids. Sitting in a circle, somebody would whisper a secret into the next child's ear. The message would be passed around the circle until the last person would announce the message received. Without fail, the message inevitably changed in unimaginable ways. (Legacies are fickle and unforgiving; they require meticulous, impossible maintenance.)

At a major turning point in my life, which I'll get to here, I thought I'd quit the legacy preservation business once and for all, but then, Johnny died. (You see, legacies are also lives; the best of lives preserved in the best of light.)

Then again, everybody lives, and everybody dies, and that's all we know for sure—the who and some of the what. The where and when are simple enough; they fill in naturally with a biographer's precision—a matter of recording location and time, names and dates, once they've occurred. Then, of course, there's the why; hopefully we'll uncover some sense of the why.

Who: I am Samuel Leonhard Grundstein Schurke, born on July nineteen, 1982 (when), in Oak Park, Michigan (where). I know you'll recognize the name Leonhard Grundstein. I know you know me, too, and I'm not ashamed. (To this day, I regret nothing.)

Yes, Leonhard Grundstein was once one of the most famous authors in America, and the most well-known ever to properly come out of Michigan. Some say, "the German-American author," but they do so condescendingly. I don't accept that. Leonhard Grundstein was as good of an American as anybody; he just so happened to be of German ancestry. That's truth as much as anything.

And, no, I'm not named after him because my mother was a huge fan of him or his work. I'm not sure my mother thought much of him at all. My grandmother, on the other hand, was his biggest fan. I was named after Leonhard Grundstein because he was my grandfather.

If you ask my mother, she couldn't tell you why she decided to name me after him, but I know. I'm connected with him on a deeper, more abstract level. My mother sensed it when she first held me, looked into my eyes, and named me. He's my forefather, and I'm his namesake. He's part of who I am, part of the blood in my veins. My mother says I feel deeply connected to my grandfather because I was named after him.

At any rate, that's at least the beginning of my who, when, and where. When and where I end, I wish I knew; then I'd be able to do a better job of managing the gap in between. (I'm reminded of Johnny. "If we must accept our histories," he wrote in his memoir, "must we also take responsibility for our future?" I would not know.)

That leaves some of the what and the why.

The what we already know is birth and life. It happens long before self-awareness. We are not asked before our time, "Would you like to be born?" We are not asked as babies, "Would you like to continue on this life journey?" We are powerless to stop it, and we are nearly powerless to affect it. It's interesting how it happens, then, isn't it? How the what of one's life can be completed indifferent to one's will. Even if one attempts to do nothing, to sit in a chair and try to do nothing, not even think, then what did said person do? Said person sat in a chair and attempted to do nothing. That's what. We can somewhat change the general direction of our what by our decisions and our actions, but death alone can stop it from accumulating.

That is where the why looms overhead in the gloomiest of existential clouds. Why do we exist? What, in God's name, for? Tired, tired questions. But still, we believe it's reasonable enough to expect answers to be borne out of the natural course of our lives, don't we?

I can tell you some of the details of how I came into existence, but that's not much help with the why. Here's what I know according to family legend: I exist because my grandmother, Katerina Schurke, bore Leonhard Grundstein's illegitimate child, who would become my mother. Grundstein married two times, and sometime during his second marriage, he met my grandmother. When Grundstein offered to leave his second wife,

Ingrid, for my grandmother, Katerina said, "No, Leonhard. I love you, but we live in different times."

They did, of course, live in different times. Their who, what, and where lined up, for a brief period, but their when and why never would. Born in 1926, Katerina was nearly half his age—only twenty-four when my mother was conceived in 1950. By the time my mother was born, Grundstein was fifty-one years old, over the hill for anybody and over the hill for the century; he had already experienced a lifetime's worth of successes, mistakes, and failures.

As the story goes, when Katerina told Grundstein she was pregnant, she told him she intended to keep the child and raise the girl on her own. Grundstein said, "I won't have you raise my child as a bastard." Katerina smacked him across the face and said, "And how would marrying you be of any help?" Katerina was as hard-headed as he was. It's said Grundstein referred to her, always with that cunning smile, as "a woman half fox and half bull."

Grundstein's second wife, Ingrid Grundstein—the mother of my Aunt Gertrude—knew about their relationship and had no misgivings about the child, but she made it clear that she wasn't the kind of woman who was going to be divorced, not at her age. They would have to find ways to cohabitate. And so was their relationship from then on—cohabitation—and it lasted one decade longer. My mother was not yet a teenager when Grundstein died in 1961.

My mother, yes, like Katerina before her, was a single mother. I was conceived in a moment of passion between her and a stranger, and my mother has been wont to say of it, often as she ruffles my dirty blonde hair, "I have never regretted that moment, nor anything that came of it." (A sentiment, as I mentioned before, I better understand now.)

That's why I retain the name Schurke. I've never known my father. (And I never will as far as I can predict.) I have a hole in my paternal lineage—the line is blank on my birth certificate—a hole my illusions of Grundstein had once filled.

Again, that's all more of an answer to how I came into existence rather than why. *Oh, how our lives would change if we could only stamp out this infernal question.*

As for the legend I'm about to tell: At the time (when), I (who) was a doctoral candidate at Oak Park University, a nationally recognized liberal arts institution in Oak Park, Michigan (where), where I was finished with my dissertation and was waiting to successfully defend it in order to receive my doctoral degree (what).

Why? Why? Why? ~~To get a job. To get the girl. To move on with my life. To save my life.~~ I didn't know.

(If only time would've remained neutral, would've paused and waited until I was able to cross that finish line—*Oh, that ambivalent hell-scape between dissertation and defense!*—then perhaps I'd be telling a different story.)

But let us go then, you and I.

# 2

I was watching a squirrel scurry up and down a tree outside the classroom window. *That's what the squirrel does*, I thought. *The squirrel scurries. It scurries to gather food. It scurries away from danger.* On a limb, the squirrel met another, and they sat and jabbered at each other and, seemingly, at me. *Squirrels jabber, lazy and comfortable. That's all. They don't philosophize. They care nothing of logic, ethics, and reason. They don't pursue impossible questions. But we know what no other animal knows, that—*

An ill silence brought me back into the classroom. I turned from the window, from my scurrying friends, to see all of my students staring at me. Jack, one of my most difficult students, stood, speechless, behind the podium at the front of the classroom.

He was a bully. All semester, when he wasn't texting in class, he would interrupt me and make wise cracks to his friends.

He was now finished with the aimless, ad-libbed presentation he was delivering on Michael Jackson, in which he provided feeble evidence at best as to why the King of Pop should be hailed as an American hero, and he was waiting for me to dismiss him.

It was my fault; I asked for it. For the students' final assignment, I asked them to research and write a small biography about someone they considered to be a contemporary American hero. The assignment was lame. I was drained at the end of the term from the brain dump that was my dissertation and from all the planning and lecturing. It had taken a toll on me.

For the better part of a decade, literature was what I studied, what I researched, what I wrote about, but there I was, living my life under the burden of stacks of freshman composition essays to grade. On the verge of finishing the marathon, I was out of energy and in need of a break before the other side of that finish line projected onward into nothing but a life-long career sitting behind a pile of books nobody reads anymore. (The comfort and privilege of such a position is not lost on me.)

*God, I need a vacation,* I thought.

I'd been assured by Professor Stan Daniels, the head of the English Department, that funding was coming through for a new position in the fall, and pending conferral of my degree, I'd be a leading candidate, although that was hard to believe. At Oak Park University alone, there were twenty-four adjunct English instructors that would all give themselves non-fatal gunshot wounds if it meant they'd get a full-time appointment. My main competitor was Montgomery Grudge, another doctoral candidate who studied Hemingway and worshiped at Daniels' feet. We shared Daniels as our dissertation advisor, who would, as far as we knew, decide which one of us would get the open position in the fall. But I was told to be patient and wait, and the job would be mine.

(*Oh, but we don't get the jobs we want; we end up with the ones we're supposed to have.*)

The excitement I had when I first decided to pursue my doctorate and to write my dissertation on Leonhard Grundstein's life and work was long gone, and I had no choice but to remain true to my course (or so I believed at the time), however distant from my dreams.

With my dissertation complete and not having been scheduled to teach, I was ready to turn everything work-related off for the summer, except of course for preparing for that dreaded dissertation defense. That I would have to do.

When I drafted my students' final essay assignment, all of this was working against me. It was well-past midnight, and my mind was already committed to other things. At the last minute, I scrambled to get it together to get through the class, so the requirements were simple: write six-to-eight pages about someone you consider to be an American hero, and be sure to answer the "five 'W's"—the who, what, where, when, and why.

"Thanks, Jack," I said as I made a note in the grade book.

Jack stepped away from the podium.

"No, wait," I said suddenly. I'd been too passive all year. I wanted the students to give me good evaluations—for my portfolio, for the job market—but I couldn't resist this opportunity to take revenge.

"You forgot the why," I said.

"What?" Jack asked.

"No, why. Why is Michael Jackson, in your view, a contemporary American hero?"

"He's, like, the King of Pop, man."

I watched Jack squirm under the scrutiny.

"He's, like, a musical god."

"Why?"

"The dude's, like, been around forever."

"Charles Manson's been around forever. Is he a hero?"

"Come on, man."

I waited.

"Alright," Jack continued, "how about he's made music that millions of people have loved for decades—"

"Is that a statement or a question?" (It's clear to me now, in hindsight, how much of an asshole I'd become in the vacuum of that doctoral program.)

"He's made music that millions of people have loved for decades."

"What about the scandals in his personal life? Does that hurt his hero status in your view?"

"No," Jack said. "He's an American hero because of his contribution to music."

"Only the legacy of his work, music in this case, matters?"

"Yes."

"Okay. Then, why is music so important?"

"Everybody listens to music, man," Jack said, "and everybody knows his music." He grinned at his buddies who were sitting in the back of the classroom, who were laughing—at him, I hoped—which only fueled my fire.

"Everybody knows some things in his personal life were off," I said. "Doesn't that mean anything?"

Jack shrugged. "Maybe."

"By your definition, fame is the only quality necessary to be hailed as a hero. If everybody knows his work, regardless of how good or bad of a person he is, then he's a hero. Correct?"

"Yeah, man, sure." A statement that, again, sounded like a question.

"What about Ted Kaczynski, the 'Unabomber'? Everybody knows his work. Is he a hero by your definition?"

That wiped the smirk off of his face. (I'd lost all reasonable perspective on how to behave like a generally good human being.)

"Did you even do any research? Did you even—" I stopped midsentence.

The door opened unexpectedly, and Professor Daniels entered my classroom. He was of average size with a slight beer-belly, and he had unkempt, sandy hair with faint streaks of gray. He was wearing jeans and a corduroy blazer. His ambiguously formal-yet-casual appearance was symbolic of his personality. On one hand, he had a down-to-earth quality, a liberal sort of "we're all in this together." On the other hand, he had a dash of scholarly snobbery and arrogance. When he talked about literature, film, or politics, he rattled off heavy words like "postmodernity," and "pastiche," and "hegemony."

"Don't mind me," Daniels said, taking a seat in the back row. "Just visiting." He folded his arms across his chest and surveyed the room.

I nodded to Jack and said, "Alright, great, thanks."

As Jack sat down, I led the students in applauding for him.

I moved to the front of the classroom. At the podium, on stage and in the spotlight, I figured I'd better say something conclusive, something human: "Good job this semester, everybody. I want to say that, even though you may not take another class from me in the future, you will always be my students. Good luck with your future studies."

The students began to file out.

"Feel free to email me if you ever need anything," I called over the screeching chairs and hushed chatter.

Daniels didn't move an inch as my students shuffled past him.

"Hello, Stan," I said. "Is there something I can do for you?"

"There is," Daniels said. "I need to see you in my office."

I felt my jaw drop just enough for Daniels to notice if he was paying attention. He squinted at me as if to say, *I see your concern, Schurke. What's got you worried?*

He stood and checked his watch. "How about we meet in my office in ten minutes?"

"That works for me." (False bravado—we were all so full of it.) "I'll be right down."

"Good," he said, and without hesitation, he turned to leave.

When I thought he was out of range, I exhaled deeply, hoping my chest would relax. *Why would he need to see me on the last day of class?*

Daniels popped his head back into the doorway and said, "Don't worry. I only have a small matter to discuss with you."

*Why? Why? Why? Why would he come all the way down to my classroom, to catch me after class, "to meet with me right away," if it was truly a "small matter"?*

It was possible I'd done something slipshod without knowing it or I'd neglected to do something important. It was possible I was guilty of a slew of infractions. Countless times throughout the school year, whenever I had no idea what I was doing, I'd make something up. Assignments, lessons plans, interactions with faculty, answers to students' questions, grades even—all could be reasonably called into question. Somehow Daniels had finally figured me out; somehow he'd discovered I didn't know what I was doing. I wasn't a fraud so much as a poser. Professor Poser.

*God, he's probably going to give the job to Grudge*, I thought, torturing myself. *He's going to give me the news. I should assert myself before he has the chance. I should tell him how I'll study pedagogy and rework my lesson plans over the summer, how I'll be prepared this fall, how I'll dedicate myself to my research, and how I'll commit to this job, this work. If I'm able to get a little break, then I'll be able to rest and recharge.*

(In my mental state at the time, I wasn't even capable of the smallest leisure.)

*Oh, how I could get my life in order*, I thought, *if I could only survive this one day.*

# 3

As I affixed the flap on my satchel, I thought I might be closing my career as an English professor before it had ever gotten started. I slung the strap over my shoulder and jammed my hands into the pockets of my sport coat. I scuffed my feet across the floor as I ambled toward the door.

The feeling brought forth a memory—the time I'd been denied a chance to dance with my crush at the Sadie Hawkins dance. I turned around and looked over the classroom one last time, remembering how it felt to see Alex on the dance floor with her date, Tom Peters, with his hands far too low on the hips of her strapless dress.

(I would discover she'd asked Tom as a favor to him. ~~And I would discover there was nearly no limit to her capacity to favor Tom.~~ The first time I thought of Alex the way I thought of her at that dance~~, when she began causing me so much unnecessary heartache,~~ was on the last day of seventh grade. School was letting out for the summer. I was standing under the big elm on the hill that overlooked the baseball diamond, and I was kicking rocks around the landscaping with Ashley when Alex came by on her yellow Liberia bicycle. She was talking to Ashley about joining her on her fancy bike to go get some Jolly Ranchers at the pharmacy. There they were, Ashley and Alex, similar in so many ways—height, size, shape, hair and eye color. Ashley said she was going to walk home with me; she had music lessons to practice for. As we watched Alex peddle away, zigzagging aimlessly along the roadside, Ashley said, "God, I wish I was as pretty as Alex. Wouldn't that be nice?" I didn't answer. Hypnotized by Alex's hair flowing in the wind, I was already sailing away. Ashley punched me in the shoulder and started for home.)

I shook the thought out of my head, took a deep breath, and tried to see the classroom for what it was. It smelled of chalk, body odor, and mold. (I never thought I'd miss that smell, but I do.)

In an hour, I went from wanting the school year to end— wanting to get away from the students, the lesson plans, the grading—to fearing I'd never be allowed to teach again.

*Daniels must've known how I'd worry.*

I turned out the lights, shut and locked the door. I'd have to turn my keys over to Daniels; I'd have to stand there and fumble with my key ring like an idiot. I considered taking the keys off of the ring before going down to his office.

I could hear Alex's voice, saying, "Don't be so dramatic." She never seemed to have a care in the world—part of her allure. But now, her aloofness only seemed privileged. She could afford not to care about this kind of work or any other kind of work. She had more confidence in the importance of creating art than I did. She cared deeply about her painting. On this occasion, she would probably laugh and say, "You'll have more time to work now that you don't have to work. Isn't that ironic?"

(I can remember carefree times before I got caught up in this drama, before I learned to be too busy to enjoy time. My mother used to volunteer her free time at a nursing home. It wasn't much, just listening. She'd go and listen to folks tell their stories. Sometimes she asked me to join her, and I didn't mind either. I'd read to them from the Bible or from a book. I'm reminded of a Bible verse I once read to a dying woman. Emma has a Bible here, and I'm looking for it now. Here it is: "I know that there is nothing better for men than to be happy and do good while they live. That everyone may eat and drink, and find satisfaction in all his toil—this is the gift of God."[1] One old man had me read from *Shiloh* every time, and once I asked him why, and he said, "The way that boy loves that beat-up dog makes me feel better." That was nice. Simple and nice.)

I proceeded down the hallway with my hands tucked into my pockets and my head hung low. I spotted a penny on the floor and kicked it as I walked. The copper disc skidded down the hall, then rolled and spun to a stop.

*One penny will not help me*, I thought. *I will need thousands of them, hundreds of thousands of them.*

To prepare for the worst of accusations, I tried to think of all the possible things I'd done that might've been reported to Daniels.

I thought of Veronica. She was a good student, a teacher's pet, beautiful and young. She was my type: fit, yet curvy; effeminate, yet confident. She was like Alex, except she smelled of chamomile tea. Alex smelled of acrylic. Veronica was the kind of woman who would reject this very description of her, who would reject my gaze even if she was the object desired.

With Veronica, I had embarrassed myself. I should've known better. Veronica frequently stayed after class with me and came to my office. She asked me question after question. She didn't need my approval; she wanted "to get her money's worth," as she put it. But I didn't see that clearly. To her, I was only a teacher, but I'd gotten accustomed to having her around. Our conversations seemed flirtatious to me. We discussed personal topics as much, if not more, than literature. She was only six years younger than I was.

One afternoon, when we were alone in my office, Veronica told me she thought her roommate's boyfriend hated her.

---

1. See Ecclesiastes 3:12-3 (New International Version)

She tried everything to make peace and be friends because she thought her roommate would surely marry him. The night before he was watching a rerun of a popular sitcom, and she sat down with him and tried to enjoy it, too. The first few jokes were stupid and harmless, so she laughed along, but after two or three misogynistic cracks from the egotistical male lead, she couldn't stand it anymore. She told the boyfriend, "The women this guy brings home don't have brains because women with brains wouldn't go home with a dolt." And, she found herself in a heated argument that ended with her storming up the stairs to her room—"You don't even know what it means to be a *dolt*, you meathead!"—and slamming her door.

"Not my proudest moment," Veronica told me the next day. "He didn't like me before without reason, but now he has plenty."

I put my arm around her shoulder and squeezed her close to my side and said, "I like you."

She looked up at me with lips half pursed, which I interpreted as a look of anticipation.

I added, "I like you a lot."

That's when she pulled away and made a show of looking at the clock. She gathered her book bag and said, "It's late. I'm supposed to meet—" She paused. "—my boyfriend. I'll see you in class, Mr. Schurke."

*Mr. Schurke. Mr. Schurke. Mr. Schurke.* Her voice rang in my head like hell's bells.

She never called me that before, and she never called me anything ever again. She was gone before I had a chance to apologize or to explain myself. All of my "explanations" would've been lies anyway. After that, she stopped attending my office hours, and she showed up late for class, sat in the back, and left early.

That was the previous semester, the fall term. It would've come up before then, wouldn't it have? What would make her tell Daniels about that now? An allegation of making sexual advances on a female student would, no doubt, end my career at OPU.

I grunted as I kicked the penny again.

Then I thought of Jack. He could be so frustrating. How many times had I made condescending or sarcastic remarks that were obviously directed at him? There were multitudes. "Please, let's all feel free to make as many wise-ass comments as we like," I would say. Was it a coincidence that Daniels had appeared in my classroom at the exact moment when Jack was giving his presentation? At the exact moment I was razzing him?

"Dolt," I said as I kicked the penny as hard as I could, launching it down the empty hallway.

There was another incident, too—*God, how many were there?*—with a punk kid named Gideon, who had black hair as long and greasy as his faded-black jeans. On that day, Gid sat in my classroom, fiddling with his cellphone.

"Gid," I said, "I'm glad you found this important enough to share on your Facebook page."

The class laughed. As I went on with my lecture, Gid went back to his phone.

In the faculty lounge, I'd heard stories of professors victoriously confiscating phones with impunity, and Gid just so happened to be my first opportunity to exercise the power.

I dashed to Gid's side and swiped the phone out of his hands. "Let's see. We're texting."

"What the hell, man?" Gid said. "Gimme it."

"My class, my rules," I said with a nefarious smirk. It was such a stupid thing to do. Even as I was doing it, deep down, I knew I shouldn't have been.

"Let's see," I said. "Ruby says, 'Hey baby. Where are you?' "

The class laughed, again. It was empowering, so I continued.

"Gid replies, 'Stupid class. Hopefully, I'll get out early.' Hmm, at least your texts are properly punctuated. There's more.

Let's see. Ruby says, 'Oh, good. I can't wait to see you! I miss you, and I love you!' "

The class was roaring now. I said, in a sappy, lovey-dovey voice, "Gid says, 'I love you too!!' Two exclamation points."

Gid lunged forward to snatch the phone from me. I let him take it, and I walked back to the front of the classroom. I said, "If you want to text in my class, be prepared to text in my class."

The penny came to rest near the men's bathroom.

It was becoming obvious why Daniels wanted to see me; I would be dismissed for sure.

I worried about what I would tell Alex. She would probably surprise me—she always surprised me—and say I was selling myself to the man in the first place. Maybe she'd say, "You're being institutionalized, indoctrinated, brainwashed, and you don't even know it. This will be good for you." Mr. Lawrence would think I was planning to be a leech. He would think I had my eyes on Alex's inheritance. Losing my job wasn't going to make that choppy sea easier to sail.

(We weren't even dating at the time. Alex always said, "The modern woman, in the way of the modern artist, need not be bound by the shackles of tradition.")

*Would I really lose my job? Would I really fail to get my doctorate after all these years? After all this effort? ~~For no reason? Because I made an advance on a female student? Because I was an occasional asshole to students?~~* Because all outcomes lead to ends. That's truth.

I picked up the penny and put it into my pocket. I didn't know when or from where my next paycheck would come.

I went into the bathroom and stepped into the same stall I always used when I was on campus. I shut and locked the door behind me and hung my satchel and sport coat on the hook.

After getting seated, I took the opportunity to check my phone. No messages. Alex must've been getting ready for the party:

Who:   Alex, her family, her parents' (rich) friends, and her friends (me)

What:   Art gala

Where: The Ballroom at the The Lakes Yacht Club

When:  Tonight, Thursday, April 30, 2009

Why:   ~~To promote her art. To sell her art. To make her parents happy. To be the belle of the ball. Because that's what she does.~~ I don't know why.

(Emma's asking me about all these strikethroughs. I told her I'm just getting ideas down; I'll come back to them later.)

At the time, I expected Alex to put me to work on preparations. She had me at her service then, but my only charge was to pick her up and deliver her to the yacht club fashionably late.

I looked at the photo of Alex on my phone. Those blue eyes. That bright smile. She was standing with her arms out at her sides as if she was Vanna White showing off a solved puzzle, but there was nothing behind her except a plain white wall. The wall represented our relationship—undefined. That was something else I hoped to straighten out over the summer break. I wanted her to be with me, and I wanted her to want to be with nobody else. That much I thought I knew.

(I was being a fool. She wanted me to be in her trance more than in love with her. Only once I escaped would I fully understand how much nonsense it was.)

On the stall door in front of me was a message written in big block letters with a thick black marker that read: STALL PONG? SEE BACK WALL. I looked behind me. There was a message on the back wall written in the same handwriting that read: STALL PONG? SEE DOOR.

Restroom graffiti always struck me as odd. I imagined leaning over with my pants around my ankles and my butt cheeks bare, going through the effort to write a message to no one in particular. What a ridiculous thing to do.

Jack would do something like that; he would waste his human potential to trick people while they shat.

To my left, there was a message carved out of the paint on the stall wall with the ambitious hope of lasting in perpetuity. The care taken to etch each letter with such precision suggested the message was of great import. It read: WHICH WAY DOES YOUR BEARD POINT TONIGHT?

I was struck first by its boldness. The question was specific, yet random.

Alex would've been enthralled by it as "bathroom art," acting as if such a genre had long-been established and legitimized.

To my right, by contrast, in hasty scratches, was another message: THE JOKE IS IN YOUR HANDS.

I folded a section of toilet paper into a neat square. *Origami?*

Finished, I walked the remaining distance to Daniels' office, thinking, *What's one capable of if one has no constructive pursuits? Pursues no achievements? One must believe in something. And, in what do I believe? America? Academia? Alexandria?*

*Oh, how I could sort it all out,* I thought, *if I could only get a single moment to pause and think!*

# 4

The door to Professor Daniels' office was ajar and a stream of light was escaping in a tall, thin beam that sliced through the darkness of the hallway. Along with the light came the smell of stale bread and the sound of a ticking clock.

I knocked.

"About time," Daniels said stern enough to knock me off balance. Daniels' consistency was off kilter. He was hunched over his desk scribbling something on a pastel-yellow legal pad. He was writing with such energy that the reading glasses on the end of his nose shook, barely hanging on for dear life.

*You and I both*, I thought.

He pushed the reading glasses up his nose, leaned back in his chair, and looked over what he'd written. "Hmm," he said, stroking his beard. "Hmm."

"You wanted to see me?" I said.

"Yes. Get in here." He put down the legal pad and looked up at me at last. "Move the books to the floor and have a seat." He pointed to a canary-colored chair that was stacked high with tomes, then started scribbling again.

I cleared a spot, sat down, and waited.

The office was no more than six-by-eight feet with cinder-block walls painted a tawny hue. His desk nearly reached from wall to wall and was covered by a collage of papers and manila folders. A bookshelf spanned the adjacent wall and was home to another organizational wreck. Books were crammed vertically and horizontally into any available space.

I noticed the ticking sound I heard from the hallway was not that of a clock, but of a Newton's cradle—the toy featuring a row of steel balls that take turns swinging back and forth—in motion on Daniels' desk. The ticking accented, like the score of a horror film, the tension I was feeling.

During my tenure under Daniels' tutelage, I never saw décor of any kind in his office, but now there was a new poster crudely taped to the wall above his desk. It was a vintage image of the inside of a European train station with crowds of patrons walking among the parked trains.

Daniels caught me looking at the poster. "*Gare de Lyon*," he said in a French accent, "*à Paris*."

I nodded.

He spun his chair around and gazed at the poster. "The end of the line," he said, not exactly to me.

Then he said, "There hasn't been word yet for next year. I'm not in charge of the funding. I certainly hope there's a full-time opening."

"Okay," I said.

"If it comes through, I'll let you know."

"Thanks." I straightened out my jacket. "I appreciate it."

"In the meantime," Daniels continued, "I have a course for you to teach this spring. 'Modernism' by the catalog. 1920s and 1930s. But you can, of course, stretch the reverberations of modernist tendencies more broadly, as you see fit."

I shifted in the hard plastic chair as I prepared to answer.

Before I could respond, Daniels added, "You're a good teacher."

In the five years I'd been in the program, the first time he'd ever set foot in my classroom was earlier that day. Why was he blowing smoke?

"I read your dissertation again last night," he said.

It certainly looked and smelled as if someone's pants were burning.

"You've done some excellent research here." No, Daniels was dumping gasoline on a liar's fire. "You've defined an entirely new reading of Grundstein's *The Son Down* with substantial evidence."

"Thank you, Stan," I said. *Please stop with the flattery.*

"But you've raised some big questions, some of which have gone unanswered."

*Here we go.*

"Why aren't there records on him from the World War I era? How can someone just fall off the radar in modern times? There must be something. What about afterwards, the time period between the wars? Why did Hemingway and Grundstein have such a bitter falling out during the height, arguably, of both of their powers? Was it because Grundstein was a Nazi?"

"No," I said.

"I think you should review that period again. Ask some more questions of your family members. The right clues need to be rearranged and realigned, followed to their bitter ends. There must be some answers left to find."

"I agree, Stan, but we've discussed this. This train has left the station for now. We're looking at a lifetime's worth of research. I'd never finish my degree if I waited for everything to be answered."

The Newton's cradle reluctantly came to a halt at last.

"Yes, yes." Daniels waved a hand at me. "That's not what this is about." His gaze returned to the poster before he continued: "What I was going to say was that you've set yourself up nicely for a full career's worth of leads to follow. Like I've always told you, since most scholars aren't willing to touch Grundstein, you've got a unique opportunity, and I think you've positioned yourself to take advantage of it."

"Yes, Stan. I agree. We've been over this."

"Okay. Well, teach the course for now, and we'll see how everything turns out."

"I don't know. You see—" I paused to considered my options. "—I've already made some plans for the summer." Ever since we graduated from high school, the Circle has taken an annual Fourth of July trip, but I wasn't quite sure where I'd intended to go with that line of reasoning.

"Yes, yes. The summer thing with Ashley and the others?" Daniels asked, removing his spectacles.

Sometimes I forgot Ashley Daniels, my best friend next to Johnny and Alex, was also Stan's daughter because I hardly ever saw them together. It seemed to catch up with me at the most inconvenient moments.

"That's not until July, correct?"

"Yes, but you see, I have the dissertation defense to—"

"That's not a problem," Stan said, interrupting me. "This will be over before the end of June, before your defense. And I can tell you, I've heard from Dr. Whittle and Dr. Ami-Peutetre; the committee seems generally pleased. For now."

"I was looking forward to a break. I want be fresh for the defense. I don't know if I'll have enough time to prepare; I've never taught this course before."

"It's only six weeks. A couple books. A couple papers." Daniels waved his pen at me as if it was a magical wand that made the job easy. "If you can't do this on autopilot by now, when will you ever?"

I nodded, and looking at my shoes, I noticed for the first time how warn and cracked the patent leather had become.

"Look at this as practice for your defense. I want to give you something more to put on your CV in case the funding doesn't come through."

"What's the schedule?"

"Class starts the first week in May so you have two weeks to prepare, and like I said, you'll be done in time to do your defense at the end of June and to take your trip in July." Daniels leaned forward on his elbows and looked down at me. "You should have plenty to celebrate at that time."

"Can you give me an example syllabus at least?"

"Look, Sam, you're over-thinking this." Daniels rose to his feet, put his fists knuckles-down on his desk, and lowered his voice an octave. "Like I said, it's a special-topics course on modernism for majors. Grundstein was an American modernist, so it's a good fit. Grab a couple of your grandfather's books off the shelf, something 1920s, something 1930s. Have them read *The Son Down* and draw a contrast between it and the early works."

Daniels turned and ruffled through the mess on his bookshelf. "You honestly can't manage this in two weeks?" He turned back from the bookshelf with books in each hand. The cover of one of the books was bent; he didn't bother to straighten it out. "Here we go. *The Timepiece*, published in 1925, and *West of Home*, published in 1932. Perfect. I know you must have copies of these, but maybe my notes can help. It's been years since I really studied Grundstein, and I probably should take another look at him, but your class will be over long before I get a chance." He forced the two books into my hands and stood over me. "Like I said, this isn't rewriting the Constitution here. It's just a six-week course on modernism. Read the books. Discuss them. Have the students write papers on them. Et cetera." Daniels pronounced "et cetera" like *et cet-tra*—three syllables instead of four.

There was only one thing Daniels wanted to hear from me. "Okay," I said.

As soon as I gave my verbal consent, Daniels' mind was elsewhere. He made a strange gesture, pointing to his chin with his thumb extended, which made an "L" from my perspective.

*Was that an "L" for Leonhard?* I thought.

Daniels snapped back into focus. "Look, Sam, can I tell you something? When I began my career studying Hemingway, I was looking at a subject matter that had already been under the microscopes of scholars for years. Hemingway lived his whole life in the literary spotlight. There were and are limited leads available on which to make a name. But, I had a hunch about something."

"Hemingway's lost manuscripts," I said.

"You're familiar, I know."

"Yes, of course."

Everybody knew the story: In Paris in 1922, Hemingway's first wife, Hadley, packed up his early manuscripts, including the only carbon copies, and boarded a train to take them to him in Switzerland. But, she left the train briefly before departure, and when she returned, the travel case was gone.

"See, I believed— I still believe—" Daniels was fluttering his hands at me. "They were, are, out there. Somewhere. They didn't get lost. They were stolen. They should've turned up. They should've found their way into a collection or onto a bookshelf. *Somewhere.* I've spent my whole career, a distinguished career I might add, following leads, traveling on granted funds, presenting my findings at academic conferences, giving prestigious keynote speeches, everything. All I was doing was eliminating possibilities, believing I'd strike literary gold if I only eliminated enough wrong leads, perhaps just one more, until all that was left was the right one." He slumped back into his chair. "But I have been made so miserable by what has been kept hushed."

(Emma's on my case about these references, asking me if these comments are true in the truest sense. They are true to the essence of it as far as my memory is concerned.)

"Would it have been better," Daniels continued, "to find what I was looking for in the first few years of my career? While I researched my dissertation? Would my career have been as good? Maybe. Probably not. I would've ridden the wave of my discovery as long as I could've, but it would've petered out. By thirty-five, I would've been a has-been. No. I've lived my career in that sweet spot, pressing ceaselessly against the current. You know?"

("Fitzgerald is low-hanging fruit," Johnny would say.)

Daniels waited in the overbearing silence again.

"Yes," I said.

"But no matter how good it's been, no matter how many times I read the end of *The Great Gatsby* and try to convince myself it would be better to stay here, to never have my fantasy, my green light, destroyed, I'm disappointed. Here I am, facing retirement. Looking at what, passing my life's work on to Monte to finish? No, I won't have my dreams mocked to death by time."

(Okay, the Hurston reference here is mine, Emma, but this is for Johnny, and that was our game; he'd pick it up. If I could stump Johnny just once, he'd appreciate that. And, what use comes of nearly a decade of literary studies if I'm not allowed, at the very least, to play this game? "That's fine," Emma says, "but you need to admit it. I want citations." I'll make some endnotes.)

Daniels spun in his chair and looked to the poster again. Without turning back, he said, "God, now would be the perfect time. At the pinnacle of my career. I have a small window to achieve perfection—a long, fruitful growing season that yields the harvest on time. Will Opportunity open her unforgiving doors to me?" He sighed and looked me in the eyes. "After all these years, I only have one lead left."

I waited for him to say more, resisting the urge to ask. (Scholars don't ask scholars to reveal their hunches. It's the first and most important unwritten rule. They snoop, prod, suspect, conspire, but they don't ask. Not directly.)

I began to fidget in Daniels' stare.

"That's all," he said. "For now."

I rose to leave.

"Show the films in class," he added. "Always show the films."

"Do we have them?"

"I don't know. We almost never do, but you'll find them."

He got up and shut the door behind me, leaving me alone in the dark and empty hallway with eight more weeks of purgatory to endure.

Who:    Samuel L.G. Schurke
What:   LIT 371: Modernism
Where: Oak Park University; Oak Park, Michigan
When: May 18-June 24, 2009
Why:    ~~Because Daniels asked me to. Because Daniels said I should. Because it's good experience. Because it's what I've always wanted to do.~~ To be determined.

(Let's face it, Emma, I'm never coming back to these strike-throughs. They're a part of this now.)

# 5

I pulled my car up to the iron-rod gate with LAWRENCE forged across the top. A vine-covered brick wall enclosed the property. I punched in the access code that I'd been issued by Mrs. Lawrence with noticeable reluctance from Mr. Lawrence.

Like Alex, Mrs. Lawrence possessed a unique kind of beauty—the kind that grew on you—and she knew how to use it to get what she wanted (for the most part).

Growing up, Mr. Lawrence treated me with ambivalence, just like he treated Johnny, but during the summer after seventh grade, that all changed for the worst. He had a sixth sense about my feelings for Alex. Then he began blaming me for his son's "frivolousness," as he called it. Ever since we were teenagers Johnny wanted to be a writer, and he carried out his life with nothing but that in mind. That had nothing to do with me, but Mr. Lawrence didn't see it that way. He didn't want me hanging around with his son. Now he didn't want me to be his son-in-law. He didn't want some academic schizoid to drive his foreign car into the family line. But I was convinced, once I received my doctorate and secured my position at the university, I'd have his respect.

Unlike Mr. Lawrence, the gate opened with a smooth precision and welcomed me without an unwanted wiggle or whine.

I parked my car—my fire-orange Volkswagon Karmann Ghia—in the driveway. The car was a sporty little round-nosed coupe. It was given as a gift to Leonhard Grundstein from Ingrid on his birthday in 1955 as an attempt to break him out of a depression that had lingered on for three years since the critical and commercial failure of *The Son Down*. Ingrid had the car imported and delivered right to the cabin at Walloon Lake. When I turned eighteen, my Aunt Gertie—Tante, as I call her—handed me the keys and said, *"Es ist dein Erbe, mach damit was auch immer du willst, aber nimm es aus meiner Garage."* I was confused as to what she thought I was heir to and what she wanted me to "get out of her garage," but when I saw the iconic VW on the keys, I knew she meant Karmann. I didn't argue with her. I usurped it before she could change her mind. I had Ashley tinker with the whole engine, replacing fluids and belts and checking this and that, before we drove it for the first time. It was in phenomenal condition, inside and out. Grundstein had put less than 1,000 miles on it before he passed.

(I drove it every day for nearly ten years and put more than 100,000 miles on it, until it found its final resting place; I swear it would've lasted forever if that spring hadn't been so tough.)

Clean shaved, combed, brushed, suited, I looked over my reflection in the glass of the front door—sharp, only a few wrinkles—and glanced at my gilded gold watch. I wasn't ready for the evening; I didn't have the energy for it. Thanks to Daniels, I was thinking about modernism and Grundstein instead.

*Open bar at the gala*, I thought. *Free whiskey. Can't wait.*

I rang the doorbell, and "The Victors"—the famous fight song of the University of Michigan—chimed inside the door. Mr. Lawrence was a staunch "Michigan Man."

Ilsa, the German housekeeper, answered the door. "Ah, *Herr Schurke*." She took pleasure in pronouncing my named with a heavy accent. "You've been instructed to vait in dee foyer."

"Thank you, Ilsa," I said. "Call me Samuel."

Ilsa looked down her long, pointy nose at me. "Anything I can get for you, *Herr Schurke*?"

"No, thanks," I said. Once I heard Ilsa making noises in the kitchen, I wiped the moisture from my head and from the back of my neck with my hand.

Then, there she was.

At the top of the stairs, she appeared in an alluring apple-red dress. I couldn't take my eyes off of the shimmer as she floated down toward me.

"Wow," I said, and as soon as the word escaped my mouth, I realized the dress was not on Alex, but on Mrs. Lawrence.

"Thank you, dear," she said, advancing upon me. She hugged me and held on too long. "Good luck tonight," she whispered in my ear, her breath tickling my neck. She smelled of cinnamon. She caressing my back, then broke the embrace and departed from the room as quickly as she'd arrived.

As if on cue, with the scent of Mrs. Lawrence's spicy perfume still hanging in the air about me, Alex appeared at the top of the stairs in a long, form-fitting black dress and glossy stilettos, both either designer or designed by a friend. Her heels could, and would, be used to break hearts. With each step, the high-cut slit of her gown revealed a teasing glimpse of smooth, tanned legs. Her top was open in a plunging "V", which traced on both sides deliberately exposed slivers of a lacy black bra. Her auburn hair was up and curled with the exception of a few perfectly placed stands that framed her face.

"Wow," I said again—a weak replication of the reaction I gave her mother.

"Samuel," Alex said, taking my hand as she completed her descent. She cupped my face in her hands. "You're early, my love."

"You look stunning," I said.

"Have you seen my mother?" she replied.

"I—"

"*Nein*," yelled Ilsa from the kitchen.

"I guess, I haven't. No."

Alex rolled her eyes. "Let's get out of here." She grabbed my arm and dragged me out the front door.

It was quite a sight to see—me and the gorgeous Alexandria in formal attire, running hand-in-hand from the massive front door of the mansion, left ajar, toward Karmann. (If you showed me a picture of that moment at the time, I would've said, "How fun." Today I'd say, "What a fool was I.")

We split at Karmann's grill. She hopped down into the passenger seat, shut the door, and pounded her fists on the dash. "Let's go, let's go, let's go."

I got in and turned the key over in the ignition; the engine sputtered.

Alex pulled her dress up, almost revealing all, and before I knew it, her leg was on top of mine. She slammed her foot down on the gas pedal. The engine caught with a jerk, and we were off, tires squealing and smoke rising in our wake.

On the expressway, Alex settled down. She drew a compact out of her purse and began powdering her nose as if we hadn't left the house in flourish.

"What's going on?" I asked. "Is everything okay?"

"That woman can be such a—ugh. She and daddy can't stop arguing about the finances. It's been going on for months. They're both tired and stressed and undersexed, and she's out of control. She tries to cope by controlling me. Ridiculous."

She put her compact away and turned to me. "No," she said, patting my thigh. "Everything's fine. Just take me to the ball, my stallion of the eve."

At the yacht club, we drove through the parking lot, passing BMWs, Mercedes, Land Rovers, and Porsches. Alex pointed out the Bentleys.

A valet attendant waved me on, directing me to pull up behind a Rolls-Royce.

"There's daddy," Alex said. "Good timing!"

I got out and handed the keys to Karmann to an attendant

along with a ten-dollar bill.

The attendant said, "Let me get you some change, sir."

"You're all set."

"Thank you, sir."

I followed Alex around to the driver's side of the Rolls-Royce where another attendant was holding the door open for Mr. Lawrence. He barely got out of the car before Alex jumped into his arms.

"Good evening, Alexandria," he said, pushing Alex back to a socially acceptable distance. He extended a hand to me only as a public act of civility.

"Good evening, Mr. Lawrence." I shook his hand firmly.

"Schurke," he said. He offered Alex his left arm, and he reached into his pocket with his right and pulled out a $100 bill. He handed the bill to the attendant.

The attendant said, "Thank you, sir."

Inside the yacht club, I lost Alex immediately. Mr. Lawrence took her off into the crowd, and I had no intention of following. I headed straight to the bar and ordered whiskey on the rocks.

As I waited, someone slapped me on the back. "There he is," the assailant announced. "Man of the hour." It was Bill McGill. His face was flushed, and he was with a group of middle-aged men with blood-alcohol levels high enough to emit the scent of scotch from their pores. Bill was a high school friend of Mr. Lawrence's, not an executive like the rest of the group. He was a mid-level lawyer for a firm retained by Mr. Lawrence's company. Neither of us belonged in that crowd, but the difference was that Bill relished in it. (I've abandoned that scene forever.)

"Did you find a compact-only for that foreigner of yours?" Bill asked loudly.

"From what I could tell," I said, "I'll be lucky if there's room for mine among all those foreign cars in the lot. I wonder who drives those."

A man to the right of me ignored Bill's interruption and said to the group, "But I told him, 'I've worked hard for every penny so why don't you investigate your ass, buddy.' They've already gotten their take, am I right?"

Another man chimed in, "That's damn right. The other day I had one of these reporters shoving a microphone in my face, saying, 'First, you sent American jobs to Mexico, then you ran the place into the ground, and now you expect the American people to bail you out.' I said, 'Look lady, I didn't send any jobs to Mexico, and I didn't run this place into the ground. That's not my call. I go to work and do my job like everybody else.' And then, get this, she says, 'Yeah, that's what the Nazis said at Nuremberg.' Now, I'm mad. So I said, 'At least we pay the Mexican's a living wage.' And, of course, that's the cut that makes the news. They didn't show her getting me all worked up."

The men raised their glasses and tipped them back.

My drink arrived—*thank, God*. I said to the group, "Good to see you."

As I walked away, I heard another man say, "Enjoy the party while you can, boys, before the Feds confiscate all the expense accounts."

Keeping a lookout for Alex, I expected to see her on her dad's arm, schmoozing with business associates or family friends. She often said, "With this crowd, it's as much about selling me as it is about the art."

I saw Mr. Lawrence standing around with a group of old men in suits engaged in a serious discussion—another old boys' club.

Then, I saw her, with him: Montgomery Grudge.

Grudge was standing at the base of the expansive, curved stairway that traced the wall of the oval ballroom up to the balcony. Per usual, his thick head of brown hair was heavily gelled in a wave from right to left. He wore glasses with thick, black frames and a plaid shirt under a corduroy jacket. Grudge tried hard to look like a Hemingway scholar, but the martini in his hand gave him away. He was never going to be the rugged out-doorsman Hemingway was; he came from an upper-class family from Birmingham—more longtime friends of the Lawrences.

Alex was on a step above him. I hated the way she smiled when she talked to him, the way her eyes danced when she looked at him, and the way she patted his shoulder compulsively when she stood next to him.

As a competing scholar, Grudge rubbed me the wrong way, but seeing him with Alex made me furious. (Fear is a powerful blindfold. This would all change in time.)

Alex looked up, and we made eye contact. I could only hope my face didn't betray my thoughts with a scowl. She smiled and waved.

Grudge looked over his shoulder, and when he saw me, he flashed that smug smirk of his. I raised my glass in return. He turned back to Alex to show me he wasn't going to give me a second thought. Alex said something to Grudge and walked the rest of the way up the stairs.

On the balcony, Mrs. Lawrence was chatting with a circle of women who were wives to these kind of men.

When I looked for Grudge standing alone at the bottom of the stairs, I was surprised to see he was gone. I took a big pull from my drink, but it was underwhelming; I would need more.

At the bar, waiting for my next round, I could see out to the bay. The doors of the yacht club—tall, broad, and made of glass—were open to the warm spring evening and to the view of Ford's Cove. With clear skies, I could see across Lake St. Clair to the Canadian shoreline.

Something told me Johnny, Ashley, Tom, and Gretchen would be out on the deck somewhere along the shore; this was as much their kind of crowd as it was mine.

Drink in hand, I stepped out of the fluorescent light of the ballroom and allowed myself to be enveloped by the dim, nat-ural glow out in the courtyard, where the clang and chatter of the formal event inside gave way to the calm solitude of the night. Torch-lit pathways sprawled out from the landing, leading through thick foliage to separate, private decks. A sign pointed me toward the gazebo; I was sure the Circle would be there.

Finding myself alone as I moved deliberately along a brick pathway, enjoying the fresh air on my skin, I suddenly wanted the solitude to last forever. I stopped to sip on my whiskey in perfect silence, the only sounds being the randomly consistent white noise of nature—birds chirping, leaves and grass shuffling—and I looked up. Through the branches overhead, the dusk sky was gradually revealing faint stars. I took a moment to inhale it all, such grandeur. The air filling my lungs recharged my body and my soul, and I felt as alive in that moment as the rays of light that were finally reaching the surface of the Earth and taking their chance, at long last, to dance on the caps of the waves.

I raised my glass. *To what? To God? To the Universe? To Grundstein?*

"As if the dead really do persist," I said, "even in a glass of whiskey."

Just then, a bee stung my face, on my chin below my lower lip. I smacked my mouth in an act of violence with murderous intent, sacrificing self-inflicted pain for the cause. But when I checked my hand for the insect's blood and guts, I saw nothing.

I hurried along the rest of the way, railing against any further attacks. Gradually, familiar voices began to emerge in the darkness. I rounded a corner and a gazebo that opened up to the water came into view. I could see two figures standing together on the deck, talking—hushed and fervent—like conspirators. As I inched closer, rolling my feet heel to toe to silence my approach, I recognized the shadows enough to identify them as Johnny and Gretchen.

"Are you sure?" Johnny said.

"You know how she is," said Gretchen. "A friend of mine is good friends with her; he confirmed it."

"How long has this been going on?"

"I don't know," she said. "A week ago, I saw them together so I made some inquiries."

Johnny shook his head. "Does he know about it?"

"At the very least, he has to know she's involved with other—" Gretch connected eyes with me. "Ah, Sam," she said. "You spooked me."

Johnny whirled around and stood, stiff as a board.

"I hope I'm not interrupting," I said. "I can come back later."

"No," Gretchen said. "We're discussing a small matter. About someone else. Something else, I mean."

"Yes," Johnny said, giving Gretchen a look as if to say, *We'll need to talk about this more.* "Come drink with us, Sam."

"I'll go track down Ash and Tom," I said. "I thought they'd be out here already."

"They ran to the bar," Gretchen said. "I'm surprised you missed them. They'll be right back."

Johnny jumped off the deck and landed next to me. He put his arm around my shoulder. "Come on, buddy. Join us. Let's drink."

"What are you drinking?"

"Scotch." Johnny raised a generously filled tumbler.

"Daniels on the rocks," Gretchen said. Backlit by the moonlight, I could see the icebergs in her glass struggling to stay afloat in an ocean of amber liquid.

I held up my glass in solidarity.

Approaching footsteps came from the direction of the ballroom. Although I knew Ashley and Tom were set to return, my heart leapt at the thought of Alex appearing in that dress. Tom, instead, turned the corner with a snifter in one hand and a burgundy bottle in the other, and Ashley followed on his heels with a flute of champagne.

I took a long sip.

With all eyes on him, Tom couldn't help but smile. He pointed to the bottle. "Tonight we drink Cognac—the drink of the stars."

"Good," Johnny said. "Tomorrow, rainwater."

Gretchen asked Ashley, "Did you get the... cigarettes?"

Ashley held up a package and removed a joint as long as a cigarette, as thick as a cigar.

We settled into the Adirondack chairs on the gazebo and looked out over Lake St. Clair. The founding members of the Circle—Johnny, Ashley, Tom, Gretchen, and I—had convened. We drank our drinks and the Cognac, and smoked, and watched the waves come in, pitter-pattering up against the bank, providing the soundtrack to our lives.

Karla joined us at one point. She walked up in silence and sat on Johnny's lap. She was Johnny's girl for as long as I could remember—on-again, off-again, nobody ever knew which. She should've set her sights on safer shores, but couldn't—a shame.

Later, soft, rhythmic rustling sounds reminded me not to look too closely in their direction.

That night—the air pregnant with reflection and urgency—I thought of Daniels' approaching retirement from a career of unresolved leads and unfulfilled promises.

*Am I, too, walking down a path to obscurity?*

I tried to gather the twigs of my life into some kind of nest. When I was trying to decide what to do after high school, was it not my mother who wanted me to meet with Daniels in the cafeteria at the university to discuss my educational options? She never talked to me about it. What did Daniels say? *"Did your mother ever take you to the library? Wasn't that fun, exploring all those books? That's what I do for a living, you know. Doesn't that sound like fun?"* Was he already selling me on this career?

"It's time to get out of there," Johnny was saying to Gretchen. "The dude snaps, kills five friendlies. It's not even an isolated incident. It's happened before, and it's going to happen again.

And, now that gas prices are back down to reasonable levels..."

With a quick glance, I noticed Karla had left unannounced.

"It's too fast," Gretchen said. "It's going to be a wreck. That's what all my friends reporting from oversees are saying."

I grew up with Daniels. He was a father figure of a sort, wasn't he? I first met him when I was six years old, when Ashley had invited me over to her house to play. No, that wasn't it, exactly. How did Ashley phrase it? I thought it was odd at the time, and now I sensed a flutter of what could've been a memory: *"My dad says I should invite you over to play."* Does his influence go back that far? That'd be one hell of a long con.

"*Slumdog Millionaire* was great," Ashley was saying to Tom. "Inspiring story. Loved the music. Loved the concept."

"It's interesting," I chimed in, "how our experiences inform our worldview, and vice versa, whether we're conscious of it or not."

"It could've been executed better," Tom said. "The Oscar should've gone to *Milk*. It's a film of substance. And Sean Penn. Do I need to say more?"

Ashley and Tom continued on without me.

I thought of how my summer break would be deferred until July because of Daniels, conning me again into another class and more work on Grundstein. *This work*, I thought, *sags like a heavy load. And, Alex? Will it explode?*

It was getting late; you could feel it in the night air. We rose to our feet—each of us stumbling in our own way. The trek back to the ballroom was burdensome and longer than I remembered. The pathway, once a mosaic of brick, now created an obstacle course of cracks to be hurdled, and the courtyard had lost all of its romance. The doors to the ballroom were closed. The room was empty except for staff, who were cleaning up.

Johnny motioned to a waitress to let us in, and we walked silently through the ballroom.

There was no sign of Alexandria; only her works remained.

# 6

My head was tight. My limbs were warm. The earth beneath my feet was pleasantly unstable, rocking me into a stupor. I was happy. (I remember that—being happy then—as a remarkable and elusive feeling from that period of my life.)

I wanted nothing more than to go home and sleep until the morning sun arose and declared, "Here it is, another day." But, the distance between me and my bed was as indefinite as marking a generation on the timeline of history.

An attendant was waiting for us at the valet stand in front of the yacht club. "Club policy," the attendant said, handing out tickets. "You're too drunk to drive. Taxi's on its way. Don't lose the tickets. You must have them for your cars to be released to you."

"There's time," Johnny said. He ran back inside, yelling over his shoulder, "Don't let them leave without me."

As we stood in a line at the curb, I became fixated on the ticket. *Don't lose the ticket.* It was feathery in my hand. *Must have the ticket.* I couldn't get a firm grip on it. *Lose the ticket, lose Karmann.* I struggled to get it safely into the breast pocket of my suit.

Johnny returned with a bottle of grappa.

The attendant faced Johnny—hands on hips—and scowled.

"It's sealed," Johnny said, pointing to the bottle's cap. "And we paid for the bar. Everything's on the up-and-up."

The cab arrived, and Johnny made a show of giving the attendant a handful of bills. "That's from all of us," he said, "to all of you."

"Thank you, sir." The attendant slipped the bills into his pocket and busied himself with the papers on the stand.

Johnny, in the front seat, spoke with the driver while the four of us squeezed into the back.

"Are you sure?" the driver said.

"Yes," Johnny said.

The cab driver made a left out of the yacht club.

Tom leaned over Ashley to roll down the window and light a cigarette.

"Where are we going?" Gretchen asked.

"We'll lose it," Johnny said, "if we talk about it."

"Nowhere good," I said to Gretchen. Nothing good ever happened after Johnny made an obscure reference to Hemingway.

The driver didn't get on the expressway, but took East Jefferson Avenue toward downtown. We passed the lush, green, landscaped and gated properties of Grosse Pointe, then the cemented wastelands of the industrial complexes, then rows of blighted homes. To my left, I could see glimpses of Belle Isle, the island oasis in the middle of the Detroit River, lit against the night.

Soon the skyline of the city came into view. The Renaissance Center, the tall cylindrical centerpiece of the Motor City, was incessantly broadcasting General Motors' iconic royal-blue square from the top as if it was a lighthouse for the world. A century seemed to pass from the moment I saw it to the moment we were under it. A collage of buildings, sports complexes, and casinos rushed by, barely giving our retinas time to transmit what we saw to our brains, capturing only the city's aura.

Our driver turned, and the cityscape went dark. Unlit buildings and boarded up windows gave way to large vacant lots. We passed a huge American flag flying overhead, and at the base of the towering pole were mounds from rubble.

"Tiger Stadium," the driver said. "They're taking it down. Can't be Tiger Stadium no more. Don't make nobody no money. Comerica now."

Busy rubbernecking, we didn't respond.

"It's their wealth," the driver added, "that allows them to waste so."

He turned again, drove a few blocks, then stopped. The meter read: $19.26. Johnny handed him a hundred.

"Come back and get us in an hour," Johnny said.

I didn't recognize where we were standing until the cab's headlights were out of sight and my eyes adjusted to the night. Michigan Central Station, like a haunted museum, stood before us. What was once revered as architecture was now a warehouse of windows.

"Let's go," Johnny said, taking Gretchen by the arm and hurrying toward the building, bent low to the ground.

Tom hesitated. "Guys, come on, for real?"

Ashley and I followed suit.

"Guys, don't leave me alone out here."

Johnny and Gretchen held open a gap in a chain-link fence. We went through one at a time, then Gretchen, and at last, Johnny.

Johnny led us to a broken window. "Once we get inside, it's going to be dark. Hold hands and stay together." He went in first, then helped Gretchen through.

Inside, it was as dark as the deepest depths of the sea. I could hear shards of glass crumbling underfoot at each step. It smelled of burnt rubber.

Ashley was ahead of me. Her hand was warm, rough and calloused. Tom was behind me. His hand was cold and smooth.

We scurried through two or three rooms that were pitch black. Our footsteps echoed back to us, and like a bat, I could sense the grand size of the man-made cave.

"Here," Johnny said louder than I'd expected.

I turned and saw moonlight at the end of the corridor. Suddenly we were running toward the light. The corridor opened into a great room, three-stories tall, encased in carved marble and topped off with an arched ceiling.

Gretchen spun, whimsically, around and around. "It's too much," she said. "I can't take it all in."

"*Gare de Lyon*," I said, thinking of the tacky poster on the wall in Daniels' office.

"It's like a cathedral," Johnny said.

"I'll bet there's more spirits alive in here than in a cathedral," Ashley said.

Gretchen stopped spinning to hit Ashley on the top of her head. "Why would you say that? Why?"

"All my ideas of cathedrals come from the movies," Tom said, "and this is nothing like how I imagine a cathedral."

"There's more," Johnny said. "Follow me." We followed Johnny into the base of a stairwell, held hands again, and climbed several flights of stairs. "Good enough," he said, at last.

We entered the floor and found ourselves standing at open-air windows overlooking Detroit.

"We recently ran a piece in the paper," Gretchen said, "about these artists who are coming from all over the world to see Detroit right now. Not real Detroit, but this Detroit."

"What for?" Johnny asked, who was sitting on the ledge of one of the windows with his feet over the edge and was kicking his heels against the exterior of the building.

"To quote-unquote, 'capture what urban decline looks like,' as if our city is some kind of found-art garbage bin for late capitalism."

"You're starting to sound like an academic, Gretch," Ashley said.

"We already have Schurke," Tom said. "Lord knows, we don't need another one."

"There's no need to ruin this beautiful night," Johnny said, producing the grappa. "Cabbie's going to be here in an hour so let's get started right." He took a pull from the bottle and passed it to Gretchen.

We stood upon the gravestone of the old city and looked at the resilient but tired Detroit of the day.

"Newton's cradle," I said.

"What are you talking about?" Tom asked.

"Don't listen to him," Johnny said, pointing an unsteady finger at me. "He's drunk."

The bottle was no more than half finished, but I was way beyond gone. "Remember Karmann," I said. "Can't lose my ticket."

I became tired and wandered off by myself. I went to a separate window, and leaned and loafed on the ledge, and saw the freckled lights of this American city. I saw the networked highways commuting individuals with car payments to credit-card houses of commerce and casinos, to bars and mortgaged homes of the stars, and back again. And I was comfortable, and I didn't want to get up. I started to doze off when I heard—*BANG!*—and I rose up and listened, and heard it again. *BANG! BANG!* And I knew what was happening.

(The conversation that follows, I must confess, is a hybrid of my memory of the evening, which was being formed under the influence of alcohol and cannabis as well as many internal and external stresses, and Johnny's account of it in *The Lines of Change*.)

I walked back over to the group, where Johnny, struggling, stood and said, "Have the greatest feats of civilization not already come and gone?"

"Greatness is subjective," I heard myself say. "Subject to time and place, to the whims of those present, then and now. It's a living thing—manifests, exists, gets preserved, lost, or destroyed—all under constant revision. Ebbs and flows."

"Is not everything produced today," Johnny continued, "some sort of hodgepodge of bits and pieces stolen from something past? The greatest *original* feats of civilization have already come and gone."

"If something is great," Gretchen said, "regardless of the factors Sam mentioned—time, place, audience, whatever—there's something inherently great about it, even if no one else ever sees it or thinks it's great again. It retains its greatness. It's intrinsic."

"Johnny, you put too much stock in originality," Ashley said. "Something can be great even if it's pieces are borrowed from this or that. Like rebuilding a car. Musicians do this all the time, too. Doesn't diminish the new arrangements."

"Novel and film adaptations," Tom offered. "*Gone with the Wind.* Lots of people view the film as a great work of art, but does the fact that it's adapted from a book make it less so? I, for one, don't think so."

"Greatness is largely contingent on time and audience," I said. "How long people care about it. That's why the literary canon evolves so much."

"I'm afraid," Johnny said solemnly, "I think I agree with that."

"Many greats have seen the greatness of their work recognized in their lifetime," Gretchen said, as if she could read Johnny's mind.

My buzz was wearing off so I took the grappa from Johnny and finished it.

"It's all a collection of fragments," Tom said, "that have all happened before. If you look into history far enough, comprehensively enough, like film scenes, it's all pre-recorded. A collection of seemingly significant signifiers that, taken separately, amount to nothing. Edited together, you have significance—history, film, life."

Ashley said, "Any melody that emerges is merely coincidental. It just happens."

"Not for art," Johnny said. "Art is the tool we use to make the patterns. Even complicated art is a neat, little package compared to life."

"Nothing is a neat, little package," Gretchen said. "See, two guys break into a farmhouse in the middle of nowhere, some desolate corner of the Earth, and murder a whole family—father, mother, daughters—the whole lot. It turns out the guys were hoping to rob the place; they were told the family was sitting on cash. There wasn't any. The guys didn't intend to murder the family, but when it went down, things happened. There could've been an infinite amount of variables that factored into the reason why the trigger was pulled—bad childhood, emotional instability—maybe they were only tired or hungry. Nobody knows what all went down. Even if you sat down with the murderers countless times and asked them over and over what happened, the story would change. Memory forgets and reconstructs. It's all unreliable. And incredibly frustrating. I don't like to think about it too much."

"What in God's name are we to do?" I asked.

"Capote puts the story together as a 'nonfiction novel'," Johnny said, "and tries to help us understand, and we take it for what it's worth."

"Next thing you know," Gretchen said, "articles will be coming out with evidence that Capote's story was all wrong."

"Scholars can already confirm," I said, "that at least one scene was embellished, if not fictionalized."

"Made for one hell of a book," Tom said, patting Johnny on the shoulder, "and a great film."

"There's probably a story out there somewhere," Gretchen said, "about two twisted teenagers who read the book or watched the film, got motivated, and committed a similar, but very, very different act. Life to art; art to life. The cycle continues. That's why true journalists don't want to tamper with any of it; we just try to write it down."

"You're in on it, too," Ashley said. "It goes all ways. All and none. Both and more. Everything is, at once, a copy and an original, a construct of reality. No matter how original we want something to be, it's always going to be a sum of variables that coalesce around a rhyme or rhythm of something."

"Newton's cradle," I said again.

"That's why I don't understand academics," Johnny said. "Studying and scrutinizing every little aspect of these old things, while not caring in the least about what's ahead. At what point do we say, 'What's the point of knowing anymore about these dead things, when people in general don't care anyhow? Why not study what's now? That's what'll make up the future.' Sam, how often do you worry about coming up with something new about dead things?"

"I don't," I said, laughing, "but Grudge sure as hell does."

"At least journalists try to preserve and track it," Johnny said. "Artists try to take it all and construct it into something. That's valuable, I think."

"I better tweet this right now," Gretchen said. "These are stunning insights. I better capture them."

"What's the point of creating new fiction, Johnny, when it's all already been done?" I said as a feeble attempt at a rebuttal.

Johnny jumped to his feet and began to dance and swing like a boxer. "Fiction is reality, man, because reality is fiction. Fiction is more real than the reality most people are living on Earth today. Think about it. Everything about society is made up. Make-believe. From the most basic forms of human relation-ships, forming primitive social tribes and languages, to modes of production—clothes, habitats, food. Even ideas. Think of ideas. All ideas are human constructions conceived of by the imagi-nation. Once we buy into an idea and time lapses long enough, it becomes something so instinctual that we have trouble think-ing in different ways. Think of today's ideas of race, class, and gender. They've been around too long; they're hard to change.

We start to have so much conviction that these ideas are bigger than what they are and how they got started, but at some point, they were simply made up. God, think of the idea of sitting at a computer sending emails all day from a cubical. What? That is our destiny? No, man, that's made up. It's a fictional idea of the human existence, but it doesn't have to be our reality. It doesn't have to be our final destination. It's all our fiction; we can re-write it."

"What's next, then?" Gretchen asked.

"We're already seeing it. What's next is a period of inevitable decline. Look at the billion-dollar bailout going on—the largest banks in the world now dipping into daddy's pockets to get out of a jam. And, give it enough time, our kids will probably learn about these same people in their textbooks as captains of industry as if most of them weren't the same assholes who ran that ship into the ground in the first place."

"You better watch it," Gretchen said. "Everything you say is on the record somewhere. Your daddy's probably listening to us right now."

"That's another issue all together," Johnny said, sparring at Gretchen. "But what I'm saying is, we just so happened to come of a age at a point in society's development when disruption must take place in order for us to revise it, improve it. The overall arc of civilization, when looked at with a long-zoom lens, will demonstrate progress. But when you focus in on our time, it will show a period of general decay. That's okay. It's necessary. We're at a point in the history of civilization when constructs need to be destroyed in order for better ones to take their places. The economy, the health system, education, marriage—all are being disrupted right now for the sake of progress. It's going to be hard on us, but we're the stretch marks. It'll be better in the long run. Think of it. What if all the cubical robots just stopped typing—disruption—and starting thinking like, 'Okay, now, with all the progress that we've made, what do we want to keep, and what should we change?' Here's an idea. How about we delete the notion of the eight-to-five, forty-hour work week? What if we said, 'That was a great innovation in Ford's day and it gave us great results, but now, since the technical renaissance, is that the best we can do? Are the ideas of office structures and cubicles still relevant?"

"I don't work the eight-to-five," Ashley said.

"Neither do I," Tom said.

"That's because you guys are artsy bums," Johnny said.

"I don't," I said. "Other than my class schedule, I can work my hours whenever I want."

"I work way more than forty hours per week," Gretchen said without looking up from her phone.

"Gretch, you work like it's the only thing keeping you alive," said Johnny. "Like it's more important than breathing. You're off the other end of the spectrum."

Gretchen looked at Johnny and said, deadpan, "I'm not on the spectrum."

"You get my point," Johnny continued. "We'll never know if we don't go through some disruptive times first. With all the recent advances in technology, haven't we also come to a point when we don't have to live in a way that was constructed by our predecessors? Isn't it our time to make this our society? We have enough people to spread work around. Maybe we all do four- or six-hour days? And we all can benefit from the amenities of modern society better, while having more time to enjoy them and pursue our passions. Don't you think that'd put us all in the best possible position to achieve the greatest successes any society has ever seen?"

"You are living in a fiction," Gretchen said.

"I thought the greatest feats of civilization have already come and gone," Ashley said.

"You're contradicting yourself now," Tom added.

"You talk as if disruption inevitably leads to good," I said.

"Progress. Improvement. What if disruption only leads to de-struction? Look at this train station. Is this good?"

"If we gave the right person the right opportunity," Johnny replied, "someone would turn this into something even greater than a train station."

I threw my hands into the air. "I surrender to Newton's cra-dle."

"Like a writer's studio?" Ashley said, ignoring me.

"How about we turn it into an office building," Gretchen said. "Don't worry about tenants. If we build cubicles, employ-ees will come."

"How about a hovercraft refueling station," Tom said, "for when we're all driving hovercrafts that all run on engines that burn carbon dioxide and emit oxygen?"

"I would turn it into housing for Detroit's homeless," Gretch-en said earnestly. "Turns out, if you give housing to homeless people, they're no longer homeless. Utah's doing it, and it's working."

"That's what I'm talking about," Johnny said, delivering an uppercut to a phantom opponent. "If we're going to be the best we can be, we're going to have to come to terms with some hard truths." Johnny spun and looked at me. "Here's a hard truth: You look too closely into the life of any hero and you're going to find out they were a douche bag in some way. The Founding Fa-thers, Carnegie, Rockefeller, Whitman, Twain, Hemingway—all douche bags in their own way. I'm telling you. You keep looking too closely into Grundstein, and you're going to find the same."

"So, you're an aspiring douche bag, then?" I said, smiling.

Johnny flopped down onto the floor. "Right hook," he said. "I'm down for the count." He sat up. "That was cheap, man. You know how I feel about the word 'aspiring'."

"What is it then? Are you or are you not a douche bag?"

"You're disrupting my worldview. I'm probably too much of a douche bag already, and if I don't do something about it, that's all I'll ever be. See, progress. All I'm really trying to say is, take the good and leave the rest. Our society needs some editing. That's all."

We sat and drank some more, but suddenly it was all so tiresome.

*Don't lose the ticket*, I thought. *Must have the ticket.*

Then a faint flicker of light, like a campfire in the distance, appeared below us.

"The cabbie's back," Gretchen said.

Johnny stood and offered a toast: "Let us raise our empty glasses to those who don't look up to or down at nobody, who had dreams before debts, who'll survive this depression and will feel like people again."

# 7

I lost the whole next day—the Friday after the gala. The sun was already threatening to rise when the cab dropped us off. I was still tipsy then, but things got much worse after that. There was an email from Alex in my inbox that was sent after midnight. Frightening. Alex rarely sent me emails, and she'd never sent one at any time of night. The subject line didn't help. It was simply titled: TONIGHT. There could've been anything waiting for me inside.

I faced my fate, and it read as follows:

> I hope you had a fun time. I had a fabulous time with M! What a surprise!

I re-read the email two, three, four, maybe ten times. *M? Who the hell is M?*

My memory drew up the image of Montgomery Grudge looking at me over his shoulder.

*What was Alex trying to do to me with this message?*

"Dolt," I said. "What does it mean?"

"Cram it," Johnny shouted from the couch in the living room downstairs.

"Go to bed," Ashley added from her room next door.

I got the urge to respond, and I clicked "compose" and started to type what was sure to be a scathing email, but when I did so, my fingers were on the wrong keys. I looked up and saw: 'qo3wk 2yq5 5y3 r7di';

I needed to calm down and think. And I needed a drink.

From the bottom drawer of my desk, I pulled out my secret stash: Maker's Mark. Countless times I'd seen men down whiskey in a fury on television; they'd tip it back and pour it down. I removed the red, wax-covered cork, raised the bottle to my lips, and turned it upside-down. I managed two large gulps before I choked. Bourbon poured over my face and my nice suit. I grabbed at my chest, the liquid burning in my throat. I fell to the floor in a puddle of booze.

It didn't take long for me to go from buzzed to bombed. After that, all I remember was rolling around on the floor laughing and shouting nonsense, my roommates pounding on the walls and yelling at me, and Ashley taking care of me.

On Saturday, I awoke mid-morning, my only suit soaked in whiskey and covered in vomit, and the first thing I did was send Alex a text message.

ME: I had a fine time, but I'm not feeling well today. Was there a lot of interest in your work?

ALEX: Good! As far as I could tell, it was well received. It'll take some time to find out if anyone is going to purchase. When you feel better, stop by!

I finally started to feel normal again after I slept in the cab on the way over to the yacht club to reclaim Karmann (walk of shame), but I was still too fatigued to face Alex.

That evening I officially began my break. I needed to close my previous course by submitting the final grades online, but I was already beyond it, consumed by thoughts of the next assignment Daniels had given me. As far as I knew, it was unprecedented; nobody in academia was teaching an entire course on my grandfather's work. That was partly due to the fact that Grundstein was a slippery character. A full-volume biography, authorized or otherwise, had yet to be published.

In graduate school, Daniels had suggested I leverage the lack of scholarship surrounding Grundstein as a gap waiting for me to fill it, a niche out of which to make a career.

*God, Daniels was always there*, I thought, *prodding me. "Who else would have easier access to records than a relative?" he'd said. Damn you, Daniels.*

Although many scholars may view biographical criticism as a fool's errand, in some ways, it can't be avoided. A necessary evil. From the start, I was skeptical, but Daniels encouraged me to let my research dictate the final product, which is the most dangerous game. It was hard enough for me to hunt down information about my biological father, much less my grandfather.

At the time, half a decade ago, the young scholarly interests in me were piqued enough to get me past the point of no return. Now I was tired of everything—Daniels, Grundstein, literature, existential questions, Grudge. The thought of getting away, getting some sense of solitude, would do me good.

That's when I got the idea to call my mother.

ME: "Mom, it's Sam. How are things at home?"

MOM: "It's Saturday night, Sammy. What's wrong?"

ME: "Nothing is wrong, Mom."

MOM: "What do you need? Money? Do you need money again? Are you in some kind of trouble, Sammy? You know, I never much liked that gang of yours."

ME: "Mom, no. I'm not in any trouble."

MOM: "What then?"

ME: "How are you?"

MOM: "My card group is meeting soon. It's the weekend, Sam. Shouldn't you be out? How's Alex?"

ME: "Mom. Everything's normal. I'm getting ready to teach a class on Opa, and I wanted to ask you—"

MOM: "Goodness, Sammy, not more questions. Not now. Is this class for your new position? Did you get it? You didn't tell me you got it. You don't tell me anything anymore."

ME: "Mom, no. Not yet, but this might help. Listen, I'm going to be teaching a class on Opa's work. It's a specialty course on modernism, and—"

MOM: "Sammy, that's great. That's what you've always wanted."

ME: "Mom, I have two weeks before the class starts, and I want to go up to the cabin—"

MOM: "Honey, you've been down that road. You've checked so many times, haven't you? You've never found anything."

ME: "I know, I know. I thought it'd be nice to spend some time up there. To relax."

MOM: "I don't care. Gertrude has the keys. Call her, dear. I have to go."

ME: "Okay."

MOM: "Love you."

The line went dead.

The conversation reminded me that there were two other good reasons why little was known about my grandfather; his closest living relatives were my mother, who didn't know much and didn't care to know more, and Tante Gertie, who was a recluse and a steel trap.

Tante was Grundstein's legitimate child, born of his wife, Ingrid, unlike my mother, who was born of Katerina Schurke, Grundstein's mistress. Like their mothers before them, there was a generation's worth of difference between the ages of Tante and my mother. Tante had always, not so much in word as in deed, made sure my mother and I were aware of the distinctions. She often used me as an excuse not to address my mother directly, a thing to this day she has never done in my presence. Instead, she says things like "tell your mother" this or that, and "ask your mother" this or that. She's always been kind to me, especially when my mother wasn't around, but she's rough around the edges. Grundstein always said Tante took after her mother, but my mother says she gets a lot from him. To her credit, Tante's never held my grandfather's misdeeds against me—the heir apparent to the family line.

I called Tante.

TANTE: "The cabin is a mess right now."

ME: "That's no problem. I could help take care of the place, pick it up a little bit."

TANTE: "*Ja? Frag deine Mutter.*"

ME: "Mom said it was okay with her if it was okay with you."

TANTE: "*Hast du deine Mutter wirklich gefragt, bevor du mich gefragt hast?*"

ME: "*Ja hab ich, also ist es okay?*"

TANTE: "Okay."

ME: "*Danke, danke, danke.* Can I come get the keys tomorrow, about noon?"

TANTE: "Okay."

ME: "*Danke schön. Bis morgen.*"

The line went dead.

Motivated by the trip ahead of me, I rushed to get last semester's grading done, laboring over tough decisions that might impact my students' academic standing. *Is Jack's 73% enough to justify the passing grade of a "C" or not?* After submitting all the grades, I emailed Jack to make sure he knew of the grace he'd received, ending the email with my favorite factoid: "Only about one in four Americans have the privilege to obtain a bachelor's degree, and you're on the verge of squandering it. Apply yourself." It was three in the morning when I finally closed my computer, feeling satisfied with my work.

At dawn, I was up and dressed in my modern professor uniform—Dockers khakis and blue Oxford button-up. After going through a McDonald's for coffee, I stopped at the library. It didn't take me long to get in and out of there. I didn't have to check the library catalog to find the books I was looking for; I knew right were to go. OPU had an extensive library for a university of its size; however, there wasn't much room for celebrated-but-fading-in-popularity modern American novelists, so the selection was sparse. I checked out *The Critical Companion to Leonhard Grundstein*. It was a thin, black volume, edited by none other than Dr. Stanley P. Daniels, Ph.D. I also checked out the only novel they had in stock, Grundstein's sixth and last published work, *The Son Down* (1952). The image on the cover depicted a disheveled, bearded man standing next to a barrel containing a blazing fire. Together, with Daniels' copies of Grundstein's early works, I would have enough reading material to get started.

I tossed the library books onto the passenger seat of Karmann and drove to Tante's house. Tante, as eager to get the deal done as I was, handed me a ring with three tarnished, little keys attached, none of which were labeled. She said, "*Schlüssel für die Kabine,*" and nothing more. She shut the door in my face as I did my best to offer my gratitude.

Next, I drove to Alex's house in a flourish, tailgating slow vehicles, passing when possible, and running red lights. When I pulled up to the gate, I punched in my access code, not even fretting about running into Mr. Lawrence this time or accidentally flirting with Mrs. Lawrence. On a whim, I was going to invite Alex to come with me for the two-week retreat.

(I had a delusional vision of me tooling out in the rowboat while Alex stood on the shore at an easel with her palette, painting me.)

I cruised up the driveway with extra pep at first, but then kicked the brakes and screeched to a dead stop. Parked at the end of the drive was a yellow Pontiac GTO Judge.

"Grudge is here," I said aloud.

I proceeded cautiously. The second I stepped out of Karmann, the front door opened, Grudge appeared, and I felt as though I accidentally showed up for class in my underwear. The moment in time froze except for my pounding heart, which beat on like a prisoner trapped against the inside of my rib cage.

Searching for something to confirm my suspicions, I analyzed him. He was fully dressed. Nothing there. His clothes were in order. Nothing there. His hair was slick and shiny, recently gelled and perfectly styled, per usual. Nothing there. His expression wasn't joyous, more of a tight-lipped frown actually. Nothing there.

Grudge shut the front door behind him.

I watched as my presence registered on his face, and that godforsaken smirk of his re-appeared. And he just stood there. A smirking dolt.

I made the first move. "Grudge," I said, nosing at the sky.

"Schurke," he replied. His grin broadened into a full smile as he walked toward me.

"What are you doing here?" I asked prematurely, showing my cards.

Grudge stopped next to Karmann and peered at it. "What are *you* doing here?"

I didn't answer.

"Going somewhere?" he added.

"Yes."

"Where to?"

"Up north."

He bent over and looked in the window. *"The Critical Companion to Leonhard Grundstein. The Son Down.* So, the rumors are true? You haven't finished your dissertation."

"Rumors, Grudge? Nobody's talking about me," I said, regaining my footing. "But, no, I'm done. Is yours done yet? Still working on that theory that Hemingway's evolving depictions of facial hair are somehow representative of his suicidal decline?"

"No." Grudge scoffed.

"If you must know, I'm preparing for a special-topics course

Daniels asked me to teach this spring. Are you teaching this term?"

"No," he said with a grunt. Then he smiled and said, "Alex is upstairs if you're looking for her." He flipped his hair as he turned and strutted toward the GTO.

Redemption, glorious redemption came when Grudge ignited the engine of his precious car to a chorus of ear-aching clicking sounds: *click-click click-click click-click click-click click-click...*

Suddenly I recalled Johnny and Gretchen talking secretively on the gazebo at the gala.

*I saw them together.*

*Are you sure?*

*I'm positive.*

Ilsa startled me, sticking her head out the front door. "Ah, *Herr Schurke, guten Morgen.* I didn't know you were here. You can come in, but Ms. Lawrence is—"

"No," I said, a knee-jerk reaction. "I have to go." I scurried back into Karmann.

I fetched a notebook from my bag and began to scribble a message for Alex:

> Dear Alex,
>      Stopped by to let you know I'm going up to Walloon Lake to stay at the cabin for a week, maybe two. Going to be doing some planning for next semester. Cell service might be unreliable, but try me by phone or email.

The closing gave me some trouble. My first instinct was to write "Love," but something stopped me, and I was unable to proceed. I considered using an informal, short-hand closing: SS. This would skirt the problem of defining my feelings for her in my closing while also implying my haste, perhaps explaining why I didn't stop in, but the sight of the two crooked letters placed adjacently in such a way would make my blood boil into a rotten stew of shame. Propelled by urgency more than decisiveness, I scratched out the generic closing, "Sam," tore out the paper, folded it down the center, and addressed the note, "To Alex."

The Lawrences had an old-fashioned tin mailbox next to the front door. I used the letter to prop the lid open so someone—Alex, hopefully—would see it.

As I was getting back into my car, Mr. and Mrs. Lawrence stormed out the front door, yelling at each other.

I froze.

As soon as they saw me, they both stopped and crossed their arms over their chests. Mr. Lawrence called out, "Schurke, if you bring that goddamned foreign car in my driveway again I'll have it towed."

Mrs. Lawrence said something to him, then stormed inside. Mr. Lawrence mouthed to me, *I mean it*, and flipped me off.

My tires burned as I sped away.

# 8

When I was clear of the Metro Detroit suburbs, beyond the assembly plants of Flint, over the swooping and curving concrete rollercoaster known as the Zilwaukee Bridge, and beyond the indistinct urban skyline of Saginaw, northbound I-75 opened and stretched before me. The landscape along the expressway, dull and dreary in an array of damp browns and grays, hadn't yet emerged from its winter-time hibernation. I rolled down my window to let the wind chap my skin and rustle my hair and to smell the promise of rebirth in the spring air. The rest of the trip was a dream that vanished as soon as I turned down the road toward Walloon Lake, which returned me to a more alert state of consciousness.

*Der Holzstapel*—"the woodpile" as my grandfather affectionately called it—was tucked away among the red pines on a peninsula known to my family as North Egg, where it has been for nearly a century. In Grundstein's day, the peninsula was all his; in modern times, our property was nestled among groomed lawns and multimillion-dollar new builds. Housing developers have long petitioned for our lot to be sold so they could remove the cabin and build another monstrosity, but they had yet to crack Tante.

"You can build your house *auf meinem Grabstein*," she would say. On my gravestone. (I am infinitely grateful for her resolve.

We own enough land to preserve the illusion of seclusion. To me, the cabin is the last true retreat on Earth.)

I eased Karmann down the winding two-track to the cabin. The poor automobile bottomed out at every bump. As soon as she was parked, I got out and urinated on the forest floor. I watched as my stream ran over the bed of dead-orange pine needles.

The cabin was exactly how I remembered it. The log walls darkened with dirt and grime, the gaps filled in with moss, and the stone chimney overgrown with Boston Ivy. The interior was dark and dry, smelled musty, and was covered in dust. There was a main room with a small kitchen and a round dining table and carved-wood chairs at the bay window that faced the lake—once Grundstein's favorite place to work (now mine). An oak bench by the wall accommodated additional seating if necessary. When the annex was added much later to make room for more beds and a bathroom, the loft over the kitchen was converted to storage space.

In the center of the main room was a large blue and green rug with curved lines and asymmetric shapes, nothing straight or perpendicular. Tante's mother, Ingrid Grundstein, made it by hand. It was another gift for Leonhard, for his beloved cabin. Wherever he was, he wanted to get back to *mein Holzstapel.*

I dropped my bag on the rug and drew back the curtains to let in some light. Gazing out the window at Walloon, I thought, *What were the chances that two of the greatest American novelists of that time period would meet as children on the shores of this remote lake in the middle of nowhere in northern Michigan?*

Sometime during my absence, another mansion had been constructed on the opposite bank—a great castle of white marble. Sunlight was already being obscured by the tree line, but my new neighbor's courtyard was lit as if it was day.

By contrast, the cabin had one working light. I tried the chain; the bulb was out.

I propped the door ajar and opened the windows in the annex to let fresh air through and to clear out the smell of varmints. A breeze came off of the water and blew through the room, delivering a familiar aura and throwing me back in time.

*Time to get to work.*

I took Daniels' copy of Grundstein's *The Timepiece* and my notebook with me and left the cabin to air out.

Just north of Walloon Lake, on the shore of Little Traverse Bay, there was a popular watering hole known as A.J.'s Lodge. It was an old barn that was converted into a restaurant and bar. Other than the addition of an electric sign flashing OPEN in neon, the exterior of the barn remained unchanged—the faded and chipped red paint authentic in disrepair. Over the bar, among the original beams, hung flat-screen televisions broadcasting images of sports games in competition with the bluegrass coming from the jukebox. For seats, a few, rustic picnic tables squared off the edges of a small dance floor; otherwise, you had to sit at the bar.

The smells of rotting wood, deep-fried food, and sweat made me smile. It'd been at least a decade since the last time my mother brought me there. (Now Emma and I go almost every night.)

A.J.'s wasn't busy, not Detroit busy, but it was alive and well. I took a seat at a picnic table near the bar—close enough to be social but not close enough to be roped into small talk. As I waited for the server, I read the description on the back of Daniels' copy of *The Timepiece*:

> Leonhard Grundstein's stunning debut novel, *The Timepiece* (1925), together with F. Scott Fitzgerald's *The Great Gatsby* (1925), published only a month apart, introduced America to a new literary era that would continue with Ernest Hemingway's *The Sun Also Rises* (1926).
>
> While Europe tries to reinvent itself in the wake

of a devastating war, Evert Heins searches for "experience." The murky times are muddied further when
he and his young bride, Sabine, fall in love with the
same woman—the dashing Hanne Remy. As it becomes clear that three is a crowd, Evert finds himself
grasping for love in the present while his past begins
to haunt him and his future seems increasingly uncertain.

Riddled with double entendres and driven by
complicated romance, *The Timepiece* draws a vivid
picture of love in a post-Great War world.

Leafing through the first few pages, I noticed Grundstein
dedicated the book to his first wife—"To Margarete with love"—
and the copyrights on the title page looked like this:

Copyright © 1925 by Leonhard Grundstein
Copyright © 1961 by Ingrid Grundstein
Copyright © 1987 by Gertrude Grundstein

*How odd is it*, I thought, *that his second wife inherited the rights to the
book dedicated to his first?* And I made a note: Talk to Tante about
the rights to Grundstein's literary estate.

Then, I saw an angel.

"My name is Beth," she said. "I'll be your server this evening."

I dropped *The Timepiece* to the floor. I'd been given a shot of
pure caffeine, enough to make ten cups of coffee, and my brain
was combusting. I scrambled to recover the book, and for the
first time, the graphic on the cover struck me as vulgar. There
was an image of a golden pocket watch, face-open, but all twelve
of the numbers were the Roman numeral III. On the face of
the watch, there were silhouettes of a man and two women, all
holding hands in a circle and dancing. The silhouettes, I now

noticed, were elaborately seductive. I put the book face-down on the table.

"I'm sorry. I didn't mean to startle you," Beth said. "Can I get you started with something to drink?"

I didn't process her words right. Instead, I pointed to the book and said, "It's research for a class."

"Cool." She waited.

"Grundstein's Lager?" I said. "Do you still have Grundstein's Lager?"

"You betcha," Beth said. She combed her ginger hair behind her ears.

"Grundstein's Lager, please," I said.

She said it again, this time with a friendly crescendo: "You betcha."

*You betcha. You betcha. You betcha.* The spell she held over me broke only once she disappeared into the kitchen.

Then, I thought of Alex. I shook my head and cursed, *God-damned, Grudge.*

There she was again—Beth. She had a tray resting on her shoulder supported with her left hand as she managed the kitchen door with her right.

"Grundstein's Lager." She said and slid the glass across the table.

I caught it—*thank, God.*

"Totally redeemed yourself." She spun off toward the bar.

I fought the urge to turn around and watch her go.

Tasting the beer reminded me, again, of Alex. She would say, "Tell me what it tastes like." And I would say, "It tastes fine." And she would say, "Fine isn't a flavor. Focus, Sam. What does it taste like? You're supposed to be an expert in analysis."

I had no intentions of performing a close reading of *The Timepiece*, not like I'd done for my graduate seminar. That would be too dangerous. I was reading only to remind myself of the tropes and themes, to highlight passages that smacked of modernist tendencies—things to discuss with my students. I wasn't going to conduct a scholarly hunt for leads and secret meanings. I wanted to avoid discovering anything that might disrupt my dissertation and give me reason to seek more answers to the questions Daniels had about Grundstein's work. I'd been told countless times that, even at the defense, dissertations were considered works in progress. The point at which a dissertation progressed enough for a doctorate to be conferred remained an abstract determination at best. I believed I was at that point; I'd progressed enough. All I wanted was to secure the doctorate and find out if a salary would be in my future.

"Confer or don't," I'd told Daniels, "but I won't defer my life any longer."

Reluctantly, Daniels, as the chair of the committee, accepted the final chapters of my dissertation as they were written and scheduled a firm date for the defense as Wednesday, June 24, 2009. I had eight weeks and one course to get through without finding good reason to rehash the text or without having to fib my way through the defense.

*Focus, Sam.*

I considered the first page. The first sentence read: "When the guns stopped firing, it was time for all sides to retreat to their corners of the Earth. It was time to go home." I scanned the rest of the page and turned to the next. There, I came upon a note written in the margin. I recognized Daniels' handwriting. The note read: TEMPTING OR TEMPTRESS? The paragraph next to the note read:

> I was waiting at the train station for the porter to find my luggage, and Sabine introduced me to her, Hanne Remy. They'd met previously at a café, Sabine explained. Hanne had brilliant blue eyes, and her short hair bounced about her shoulders as she talked, and she emphasized each word as they came

out of her pouting lips. "You can call me, Hanne," she said. And she smiled at me, and I knew, with her help, Fate would steal everything I'd ever possessed.

*Tempting or Temptress? What does it mean? The relationship between the one who desires and the one who is desired. The temptress preys upon desire. The tempted desires—willingly or mistakenly.*

I made a note: Who was tempting whom, here? How does temptation interact with fate? What role does consent and free will play? Possible discussion questions.

"How is it?" asked Beth, appearing at my table from no-where.

"Purgatory's the worst hell," I said. "Mine's barely gotten started."

"The beer," she said, laughing. "How's the beer?"

"It's great. Thank you."

"You Grundstein fans are all the same."

"What?"

"You come here, read Grundstein's books, drink Grund-stein's Lager, complain about Hemingway. We get visitors like you all the time—a disconnected cult of sorts. You guys should coordinate, form an association. Petoskey has a historical society. Maybe they can help."

"It's for a class," I said. "I worry I've lost interest in Grund-stein's ghost, but I have to get through it."

"I can spot one a mile away." She placed the check on the table. "I'll see you at the next tourist destination."

I downed the rest of my beer, paid the check by leaving a ten-dollar bill under the saltshaker, and made my way to the door.

At the cabin it was dark and cold, and the evening creatures were out calling for mates. By the light of an old oil lantern (I wasn't ready to replace the light bulb—my futile, little protest against the progress of time), I set a pot of coffee to boil and brought my bags into the annex. I unloaded them onto one of the bottom bunks next to a carved-wood ladder that led through a small door to the attic space above the kitchen. (When I was in the throes of my research, looking for anything and everything, I was sure I was going to find gold in there among the cobwebs and spiders and who-knows-what else, because that's what happens in the movies.)

On the way back to the cabin, I'd stopped at an all-night grocery and purchased, among other necessities, a Maglite and batteries. I loaded the flashlight and tested it against the wall. Then I poured a cup of coffee and topped it off with a healthy portion of Irish cream, centered the oil lantern on the kitchen table, and set the Maglite down next to it.

There was nothing left to do but read until sleep conquered me.

I thought of Grundstein. He was a man whose formative years took place during the Great War and whose prime adult years took place during World War II—times when men were expected to prove their manhood by fighting for their country.

*Your generation's a mass of dolts too scared to*— A bang in the attic overhead shot the thought dead.

In the annex, I changed into an old left-behind pair of jeans and an abused sweatshirt. With the hood up over my head, I drew the strings until it was securely in place, leaving only my eyes visible. I put on my socks and shoes and took one last pull from my spiked coffee.

*You'd be the first to die in a movie, Schurke.*

Armed with the Maglite, I ascended the ladder, flung open the door to the attic, and cast light inside. Something scampered across the particleboard flooring. I waved my light over every inch, and as far as I could tell, no eyes reflected back at me.

*And you'd be worthless in a war.*

I waited for my eyes to fully adjust. What I saw instead was the same old junk: unmarked boxes, stacks of old linens and blankets, and a variety of sporting equipment including a Croquet set, downhill and cross-country skis, and a tricycle. There was one clear path going straight from the door to the opposite wall of the cabin, where there was an octagonal window letting moonlight through at a harsh angle. The roof was too low for me to stand; I had to crawl.

*Prove me wrong, son.*

Sliding the flashlight in front of me, I inched my way into the attic, crawling down the center toward the octagonal window. I stopped at regular intervals to shine the flashlight on the whole attic from a new perspective. At each point, I found nothing but toys and holiday decorations. As I drew nearer to the opposite wall, I was ready to retreat.

*You're a coward.*

I clung to the wall. From the window, I could see the shoreline. The water was peaceful with the moonlight reflecting off of the lake and making the trees glow. The dock, unused for years, was stacked up behind the shed in eight-foot segments. The water would be frigid.

The shed was a family joke. Grundstein built it himself as a place to store his fishing gear and tools and such, but he didn't build it big enough to be useful. To any criticism, Grundstein would say, "If you can't stand the smell, stay out of *meinem Plumpsklo*"—my outhouse.

Buzzed, tired—I suddenly came by the idea that perhaps I didn't give *dem Plumpsklo* a proper search. With zeal, I whirled away from the window to go hunt through the shed. As I did so, my pant leg caught on the corner of a loose log along the wall just under my knee, and it ripped a line across my calf, grazing my flesh. I checked my leg through the slice in my pants and discovered a thin red line. The wood had scraped away a layer of skin, but nothing requiring medical attention.

The log, only loose enough to catch my leg and cause me pain, protruded about an inch. Shining my flashlight in the gap, it was now apparent that the log had been hollowed out and only a facade remained. I was onto something.

I wedged my foot in behind and leveraged it open as far as I could. The log cracked under the pressure. With about three inches of space, I could see the log below was hollowed out as well.

I plunged my hand into the gap up to my wrist. At the end of my fingertips, I could feel the frayed edges of paper. I put the flashlight down, and in the dark, pulled the wood back far enough to work my hand in another inch. I struggled at such a low angle, but managed to get a grip on the book and slip it out before getting my hand caught.

There, in the attic, I sat holding the treasure in my lap: a journal. It was made of tattered leather with a black ribbon running along the open edge of the cover—nothing special. I smelled, then, for the first time, the aged paper—organic, with notes of almond and vanilla (the aroma excites my nostrils even now as I write).

On the top, in ink, was the following inscription:

LG – July, 1961
F – HEM

I recognized the date immediately. That was the month and year in which my grandfather died. It looked to be written with a heavy hand, but it was, no doubt, Grundstein's.

"God, not now," I said. "Not yet."

In stunned disbelief, I brought the journal down to the kitchen and set it on the table in the fading glow of the oil lantern.

At first, I resisted it. I sat at the table drinking my coffee, now heavily spiked, from a shaky mug with clattering teeth. I wasn't ready to break the aged-leather seal. Whatever was in the journal was going to lead way on to way.

(*Oh, how things could've been different if I only could've had a moment to think clearly.*)

The journal put out a secretive aura that begged for it to be hidden as if having it out in the open was hazardous. I put the journal in the liquor cabinet, way in the back, behind the bottles of grappa and vermouth that were likely there when Grundstein was alive, and closed the door.

I put away the coffee, shut up the kitchen, brushed my teeth, climbed into bed, and tried to read more from *The Timepiece*, but the combination of excitement, caffeine, and alcohol refused to diminish. I was wired.

At last, I relented. At the liquor cabinet, unceremoniously clad in nothing but my boxer shorts and a white t-shirt, I removed Grundstein's journal, and at the table, by flashlight, I carefully untied the delicate ribbon.

# Journal of
# Leonhard Grundstein

May 29, 1961

A thought runs on repeat through my head: "Men can starve from a lack of self-realization as much as they can from a lack of bread," another novelist better than I.[1]

I am desperate not to starve.

Ingrid, bless her heart, after all I've done, feels my despair as much as I do. She's gone out after another forsaken journal. She believes deeply in the journaling. She also came home with a worn oak bench from the thrift shop to cover her shoddy work on the floorboards.

"Good," I told her jokingly. "Sit on that for a change."

She's making me a special breakfast and says she better not hear another peep from me before I produce a full page.

Apple pancakes with maple syrup, home fries, and bacon strips. The smell takes me back to my early days in these parts, when Hem and I were young bucks running all over town. One of our mothers would make us a hearty breakfast before we went out fishing or hunting.

Ingrid is afraid for my life. She's trying to save me with delicacies and memories. But if I think too much on it all, it only

---

1. Leonhard Grundstein references Richard Wright's *Native Son* here.

leads to regret. And guilt.

## MAY 30, 1961

It took my old body all day yesterday to digest the heavy breakfast Ingrid prepared for me. It left me sluggish and uncomfortable, struggling sleepily over the memories the feast brought to mind. There's a heavy price to pay for everything gratifying, even pancakes and maple syrup. God, as I see now, is a mighty capitalist who collects his debts to the full balance. How will I ever square up for all of it? The cost of overindulging on a warm breakfast is the least of what I owe.

Betz. Betz-with-a-Z. God, I can't do this today. Perhaps never.

## MAY 31, 1961

Couldn't sleep. It's four in the morning, and looking at the lake, I'm not convinced the sun will rise if I don't get this out.

I met Betz when I was fourteen. I was young, and stupid, and stupid because I was young. When I met her, she said, "My name is Betz with a 'Z'." I said, "Betz-with a-Z, my name is Leonhard with an 'H'." I thought that was funny. God knows she didn't.

If I ever had a grandson, I would've told him, "Women don't have the same sense of humor we do. Try to make her think you're strong or courageous. That'll do fine. But always make sure she thinks you're nice." It appears Gertie won't have a child, and I'll be gone before Ellie reaches an acceptable age.

Betz. I must get this down for Betz.

Hem and I would go to A.J.'s, and Betz would be there. Her dad made her help out at the lodge after school. She had sandy hair with golden highlights, and she was the golden highlight of Walloon. She wore an apron over this little blue dress. Drove me crazy. I couldn't ever come up with anything worthwhile to say to her. I placed my orders and said please and thank you. Hem did most of the talking.

Things were different though when Hem and I came back from the War. We were camping and fishing and doing whatever we always did, just with booze. Anything to try to untie the knot the War left inside us.

We were full grown then, and Betz was working at A.J.'s full time. Came back with my hair cut real short. She said, "Leonhard-with-an-H, your hair is missing." She even grabbed my head and rubbed it with her hands. I remember that feeling like it was yesterday.

"I like it," she said.

She made a point to tell me she lived in an apartment on her own. The apartment was above A.J.'s Lodge. She was paying rent to her parents.

An amber glow is creeping over the horizon, promising another chance at another day.

What was it? That summer? 1919? Hem and I lived the life—

—swimming and fishing—

—hunting, drinking—

—losing it now—

—tired now—

—a break.


JUNE 1, 1961

Betz. Betz. Betz.

I thought about Betz all night. I won't rest or die until this is off my chest.

Hem overstayed his welcome at Windemere and took off for Toronto. I stayed on *bei dem Holzstapel*. I was working on my first novel. Had an agreement with Pop to look after the place. Encouraged Hem to do the same and didn't understand why he couldn't. He was too big for his britches, always. Had wanderlust. Had to see, to conquer, the world.

I saw Betz often then. Had my eye on her, and believed she had her eye on me. In the fall of 1920 everything changed. Warm weather, deer camp, beer, the whole bit. That weekend I took home the biggest buck—a twelve-point. A meaty buck he was. Could barely hold that boy's head up for the picture.

I got back to town and headed to A.J.'s to celebrate. I bought beer by the pitcher for everybody in the place. Poor Betz could barely keep up. Later on, the drinking slowed down and patrons started to crawl back to their holes, and I spotted Betz sitting at end of the bar. She was counting cash. I was real tight.

After the War, I'd been down. Tried to carry myself with confidence like the others, those strutting around in uniform, but was a fake. Bringing home the buck pumped me up to feeling good.

I approached her from behind. Put my hands on her shoulders. She sat up, startled, but she relaxed. We talked about the deer. She seemed impressed.

I said something about how nice a night it was and something about going for a walk.

She said, "I'd like a walk." I remember that.

I waited at the door while she gathered her jacket from the kitchen. I helped her get it on. As we walked away from the lodge, I put my arm around her. Said something about being wounded from the War and needing a walking stick.

Clear out of sight, I stopped and pulled her to me. She didn't resist. I kissed her there. It was innocent, close-lipped. But illuminating. Could see the future, one in which Betz and I lived happily ever—

—but Betz didn't linger there—

—my vision blurring now—

—"I'd like to walk, Len"—

—propelled us forward—

—down the wood-path—

—near the lodge—
—momentum—
—trajectory—
—destiny—
—fate—
—end.

JUNE 2, 1961

The sunrise over Walloon is a dazzling orange this morning. My favorite part is when the colors split and the rainbow is visible. It's moments like that when I see clearly an Author behind the work.

I'm better and stronger today. Even the approach to confession is giving me strength.

At the time I wasn't a virgin, but Betz was my first kiss. During the war, I visited places with all the others, but you don't kiss. There's rules. One rule is you don't kiss.

Betz took my lips' virginity, and with it, a part of my heart—the part that kept the beat true.

We sat on the bank near Lake Michigan. The air was crisp and cool with an organic scent. The moon was full and bright and gave the incoming waves depth.

Like an eclipse, I avoided looking directly at her, but I sensed her. How far her legs and arms were from mine. Betz, she smelled of maple syrup.

God, everything could've been different.

We talked about life after the War. Had no idea where we wanted to go, what we wanted do, but we knew we wanted to go and do great things. Had no idea how to do anything.

It all seemed paralyzing at the time, but seems trivial now.

Ingrid is telling me to quit while I'm going. Says she should get some of what's left of my good mind today. I regret that I should have to listen to her.

• • •

JUNE 3, 1961

Exactly how it happened, I don't know. Am trying to remember. Want to get this right. Won't work if it's not right.

Betz was lying on my jacket on the ground on her back. I was on top of her. Kissing. Everything was slow.

Then I lost myself.

My hand on her bare leg. Up her blue dress. She said, "Lenny, I don't know."

More kissing. Up farther. Again, she said, "Lenny, I don't know."

The War flared in my mind. It's flaring again now.

Advancing lines, resistance. Establishing a position, retraction.

More advancing. Momentum. Surge.

Suddenly peace.

Relief came swiftly at the end.

She held on tight, her arms hugging my rib cage, her hands clinging to my shoulders.

I passed out on the dock, exposed.

When I came to in the dark, time was lost on me. She was in the water, knee deep, washing her dress like a frontier woman.

I awoke in the morning, and she was gone.

My jacket was tucked over my midsection. I stood up, put my pants back together, and staggered to the water's edge looking for evidence of—

—wobbled a moment—

—head spun—

—hurled—

—enough.

• • •

JUNE 4, 1961

Thought I would feel better, but I don't. This is the longest hangover.

At the time I was naïve enough to think only our friends knew. But word spreads around small towns like small pox. Her parents and my parents and other parents didn't show it, but they knew. Public silence, another small-town trait.

The word that got around had a bad feeling to it. Betz had a sterling reputation. Here it is: I got drunk, led her astray, and took advantage of her.

That wasn't my belief. I tried to talk things out with her, but she wasn't interested.

I could've tried harder.

Things seemed to be turning for the worst. There was a feeling about the town as if I was being watched and not in a good way. It was time for me to take leave.

Got the letter from Flechtheim in the winter. Must've been 1921. Wanted me to join him in Düsseldorf to start the new publication.

Here it is also: I fled like the coward I was.


JUNE 5, 1961

Up early again. Ingrid tells me I'm not done. She can sense it, too.

Met back up with Hem on the other side. He pressed me on the details. Heard about it in a letter from his mother. I was stunned the story had followed me across the Atlantic.

Can't hide from truth.

Hem seemed angry about it, demanded details. I thought maybe he had a thing for Betz I didn't know about.

Once I told him everything—much more than I can recount here—he seemed satisfied.

He wasn't interested in me or Betz. I know as much now. He

wanted the material. Showed me a story he drafted that "imag-ined the kind of thing," as he put it.

I was irate. Said it implicated me as a rapist.

He said it was fiction, wasn't about me. Said it was intended to be ambiguous.

I said, "Seems damn clear to me."

He got sore. Said I read the story wrong. Took that as an insult.

Was not the first time Hem and I threw fists at each other, but it was the last. We threw more punches in words, in letters, other ways.

I ended up with a broken nose; he ended up with a broken ego.

Even so. We were young then, early twenties. Didn't know any better. Not after the War.

Even then, we were drifting apart. For God's sake, the world wasn't big enough for the two of us.

But the world would sort us out.


JUNE 6, 1961

Must get back to Betz and do her justice, but I can tell I am wasting away again. Will be gone soon. Must finish.

Simply put: Betz's blood is on my hands—

—no, no, no, that will never do—

—this is getting away from me—

—can't think—

—can't write—

—can't.


JUNE 7, 1961

Here: I fear I raped Betz, and I fear it killed her. There it is in the most honest and true form.

• • •

JUNE 8, 1961

Slept hard last night. Best sleep I can remember. Fleeting though. Before I could even get out of the bed, the collective burdens of my mistakes have returned.

Betz became with child. My child. She, along with her parents, worked hard to keep it a secret. I didn't even know. But embarrassments are infectious diseases; they take on a life of their own. The rumors were unbearable.

JUNE 9, 1961

Can't today. Can't.

JUNE 10, 1961

Cruel irony. The words haunted me all night long. It's getting bad now—

After I sailed back to Germany as an American journalist—a guise Onkel Dieter had once suggested I take on during a particularly trying time.

How trouble chases the troubled—

While I wrote a letter home in December of 1921 about how going to Düsseldorf was the best thing, how Mr. Flechtheim had been accommodating and encouraging, how I was going good on a novel, how I'd met a girl, Margarete, who was giving me tours of the city, introducing me to the secrets of the locals, and how fine everything was going, Betz was pregnant and suffering.

There were complications with the delivery. Dr. Hemingway, Hem's father, was called in to help. He did all he could, but Betz was too—

—there, she was in trouble—

—above the lodge—

—in her apartment—
—bleeding out—
—I swear—
—I can't.


JUNE 11, 1961

I think I understand where all this is headed, and it will be over soon.

I found out about Betz through a letter sent to Hem from his mother. Hem gave it to me, and I still have it. Here:

> Ernie,
> The town's in mourning. A.J.'s poor girl Betz has passed on. We had suspected she was pregnant. Your father, called in too late, was unable to save her. You know as well as I do about the rumors regarding the father. I thank God you had nothing to do with it, although I do feel guilty for thinking on it that way. The loss has saddened your father terribly. It would be good of you to write to him.
> Always, G—

This, too, was my fault.


JUNE 12, 1961

In August of 1922, Marg and I took a trip to the Black Forest and met the Hemingways there. He was sore about his father being dragged into it though he never said it; you could see it in his actions.

Hem said he had begun work on a novel, too. The premise was built on a storyline I'd told him too much of at Walloon. Hem had the bravado to accuse me of stealing the idea from

<u>him</u>. The trip ended poorly. Marg and I packed up and returned to Düsseldorf. I know Hem thought he'd won that round.

JUNE 13, 1961

I'm ready to be done with all this unpleasantness.

Betz's death returned to me again when, years later, I received a personal message from Hemingway. The message arrived the same day the last installment of *A Farewell to Arms* was published in *Scribner's Magazine*. I received a typescript copy with a handwritten note:

> Grundstein,
>
> Tried like hell to end this book in a different way, but it had to be true. I'm sure you know by now my father chose the Hemingway death, one reason being his failure to save B— from delivering your bastard child. Know this is not for you. This is for me, and my father, and for her.
> —EH

I read the piece. Felt like I'd been lit on fire. I stormed around the cabin in a fury, and screamed, and cursed. And that night I sat down, and I penned an infinite number of responses as my feelings ebbed and flowed. One I remember. ~~I appreciate that you let Catherine die quickly.~~ But even that was too much of an admission of guilt to handle—

I never responded.

Couldn't.

JUNE 14, 1961

Later on, I received another letter from Hemingway:

Grundstein,

Take your silence to mean you didn't like the book. We both know there are a great many more details that have been hushed. Be glad I didn't go any further.

He didn't sign the letter—too big to sign a letter like that. Never responded to that one either.

This has all been too much for these old bones to bear.

I hope tomorrow will come in a better way.

# 9

I awoke at the table, shivering, with my head on the journal. A morning fog had seeped in through the open windows and was hovering about the cabin. I stood up, stretched, and tucked the journal back into the liquor cabinet. Putting on a fresh shirt, I packed up and headed into town to get breakfast.

My favorite hipster coffee spot was already bustling. Roaster's Toast served twenty flavors of coffee with pastries and sandwiches, but they were famous for their home-style toast—blackened, nearly burnt and softened with "fresh-from-the-farm butter."

I took a booth built for two near the bathroom, doubting the wait staff would even notice—

"You again," she said, giving me a start. Much like at A.J.'s Lodge, she was wearing an apron, but this time it was quilted with pastel patches, and the nametag read: BETH, ROASTER'S TOAST.

"Are you following me?" she asked.

"No," I said.

"Relax. This happens all the time. You're not the only visitor who goes to Roaster's to deal with their A.J.'s hangover. You might as well tell me your name if we're going to keep doing this dance."

"I'm Sam."

"Do you, Sam, know what kind of coffee you'd like?" Beth

said. "There's a list of our beans." She pointed to a carafe-shaped chalkboard on the wall behind me that featured a dizzying mess of handwritten words.

"What kind do you like best?" I said.

"I'm a purest, honey," she said in a way that sounded rehearsed. "House blend. Medium-bodied light roast."

"I'll take it."

"You betcha, Big Sam."

Beth came back with a coffee mug you'd expect to find at your grandmother's house. There was an advertisement for the Little Traverse Historical Museum on it. She said, "This is with one cream and one sugar. That's my favorite. If you don't like, I'll roast you."

"Thanks," I said, expecting her to whirl away as busy as the place was, but she waited, hands on her hips, while I took the first sip. I nodded my approval.

"What sights are you seeing today, Tourist Sam?"

I held up my mug and said, "The museum, actually, but it looks like it doesn't open until eleven. I'll probably hit the Petoskey District Library first then."

"The library? That's strange."

I pointed to Grundstein's *Timepiece* that was face-down on the table. "I read the papers."

"Alright, Uncle Sam, what can I get for you?"

"The home-style double, please."

"Jam?"

"Not necessary."

She smiled. "Man after my own heart."

My chest thumped as I watched her walk away.

("That's enough, Fabio," Emma's saying. "Move it along.")

I skimmed crusts of milk from the surface of the gray coffee with a spoon. Two baby-faced men in uniforms occupied the table next to me, bold in their camouflage, discussing training regimens.

At the dawn of a new day, and with a fresh cup of coffee and a warm breakfast in me, the revelations of the previous night seemed insignificant. Small town rumors. An old man's guilt. Grundstein's novels were notorious for sexually confused characters anyhow. Daniels and Grudge would be interested in the source material angle, but honestly, what value was there in that? To risk having Grundstein disgraced and discarded from the canon in time for me to be an expert on an author that academic departments wouldn't teach? I didn't think so. No, as a fan, it was disappointing. As a human, it was sad. As a scholar, it was nothing. *Thank God.*

(A woefully short-sighted understatement, of course.)

When I was finished, I thanked Beth and got up to leave.

"See you at A.J.'s tonight?" she asked.

"I'm sure you will."

I whistled as I walked toward the library, feeling pretty sly, and I called Alex.

ME: "Hey, it's me."

ALEX: "Who?"

ME: "Sam."

ALEX: "I'm sorry. I'm really tired. I stayed out too late last night, and when I got home, I was inspired to paint, so—"

ME: "Who did you go out with?"

ALEX: "Nobody in particular."

ME: "Give me a short list."

ALEX: "Tom. The whole crew from the indie he's doing right now."

ME: "Was Grudge there?"

ALEX: "..."

ME: "Did you get my note?"

ALEX: "Yes. Thanks for the invite."

ME: "I saw him at your house when I dropped it off."

ALEX: "Samuel, why did you leave without talking to me?"

ME: "I have lots of work to do. I needed to get started."

ALEX: "You know Monte and I are only friends, Samuel."

ME: "Do you think you'll come up?"

ALEX: "I don't know. You're getting good work done, aren't you? You need to focus."

ME: "Yes. I may have found a lead on something."

ALEX: "What is it?"

ME: "I'm not sure. I'm going to visit the museum today. I hope to have more soon, but it's not open yet. I'll stop by the library while I wait."

ALEX: "Thanks for calling, Sammy, okay? Call me later."

ME: "Okay."

The exuberance I felt moments before smoldered into mere coals, sizzling with confusion. I walked on with my head down, hardly noticing where I was going, hardly looking out for fellow pedestrians, hardly watching for cars as I crossed the street. I tried as hard as I could, forcing my memory to its full capacity, to remember the course of events that had happened over the past couple of days between Alex and I.

*We went to the gala together, did we not? Then, there was Grudge at the gala. At her house. I don't care for it. "Only friends," she said. There isn't reason for me to mistrust her, but when was the last time we had a clear connection, something intimate upon which I can hang my confidence? The New Year's Party? We'd kissed at midnight. Rushed, but passionate, wasn't it? That was nearly half a year ago. There've been more, haven't there? Over spring break, we held hands at the movies, didn't we? Briefly? Didn't we?*

For the life of me, I couldn't remember anything exactly.

Slipping into the library, something—the fluorescent lighting, the unstirred air, the overbearing quietness—just so happened to trigger a memory of visiting the library with my mother when I was a kid, and an image of the inscription on the journal, F – HEM, flared in my mind.

I went straight to the fiction stacks.

Sure enough, there was an end cap labeled: F – HEM. There was a generous selection of Hemingway's books. Nothing was out of the ordinary at first glance, but I was onto something; I could sense it.

(Emma's asking why I hadn't checked the library in the first place, during the height of my research. It never occurred to me to visit the public library, not with the resources I had at my fingertips at OPU. You see, university libraries use the Library of Congress classification system, which utilizes abstract alphanumeric codes to help manage large inventories. Many public libraries, however, are still on the more primitive Dewey Decimal System, or for small, rural libraries with limited collections, fiction/nonfiction organized by the author's last name— "Yeah, yeah, get to the point," she's saying. At first glance, the inscription didn't mean anything to me. But, now, I understood it to mean: Fiction – Hemingway.)

I closed my eyes. *What's here, Grundstein?* I waited. *Do I want to find it or should I leave it alone?*

Suddenly I felt nothing.

I ran my hands over the top of the books and underneath the shelves—nothing but three pieces of dried gum. I sat down and pulled Hemingway's books off the shelf one by one and scanned the covers, looking for something, anything—some kind of clue—maybe another inscription like the one on the journal.

Around me grew a scattered array of books on the floor.

A boy in a polo shirt and khaki pants with a lanyard around his neck stopped at the end of the aisle. "Can I help you?" There was a razor's edge in his voice.

"I'm only browsing," I said. "I'll put all these back when I'm finished."

"Just leave them," the boy said, grumbling. "They'll be easier to re-shelve if you just leave them."

"Okay," I said. "Thank you."

The boy rolled his eyes as he walked on.

Then, I spotted an unusual-looking copy of Hemingway's *The Sun Also Rises*; it was aged and worn. I checked the publisher's page. It appeared to be a special edition, printed in the 1930s. I looked it over quickly, flipped through a few pages. Nothing.

I stood back and looked at the shelf from a distance, thinking, *Maybe something will appear to me if I don't look directly at it like seeing the object behind a Magic Eye illustration.* Nothing.

I observed the shelf at a canted angle. Still nothing.

*Wrong library?* I thought. *Maybe there's another one in town.* But before I moved on, I recalled one of Grundstein's journal entries: *...sunrise over Walloon... ...a dazzling orange... ...the colors split... ...when I see clearly... ...an Author behind the work...*

I returned to the antiquated copy of Hemingway's breakthrough novel and examined it thoroughly, one page at a time. About a quarter of the way through I came across a note written in the same hand as the inscription on the journal. The note read:

Hemingstein,

Tried to write to you. Many times. Words give me trouble nowadays. Know your health has become a struggle too. Not alone. Age steals wits from the wisest.

I only feared you'd do it better. You were always better.

Odds are against this getting to you, but if this does, I've already perished, and I trust G— has sent me to the museum by now so I leave this for you in whatever hope is left.

Suspect maybe your snowy mind remembers too—

> *My Kinsmen do not Die - anon -*
> *There treading Opon the Grave -*
> *Oh, we Bretheren decry Grace -*
> *Our Place near the Dying - stone -*

—fossilized and deposited in my memory of northern Michigan like a Petoskey stone.

Immer,

Grundstein – May 30, 1961

Standing there, my hands shook as I read the note two, three, four more times. Written only one month before his death, Grundstein *left something* for Hemingway, and the note mentioned the museum. *But the curious poem—what were the clues?* I didn't see anything that would lead Hemingway to look in the attic of the cabin if that's where Grundstein had hoped his scavenger hunt would end. *Had they played in the attic as boys?* The annex and the storage space above the kitchen weren't complete until 1928, long after Hemingway and Grundstein had left to become men.

I desperately wanted the book, not to check it out—I had a library card—but I wanted it in my possession. It was stamped on the front and back covers with: **PROPERTY OF PETOSKEY DISTRICT LIBRARY.** *What would I say to that?* There were security scanners set up at the doors. *An alarm would surely go off.*

I held the book up at eye level with a cover in each hand, letting the pages dangle below, hoping something would shake out. As I did, a sliver of light passed through the gap in between the binding and the book cover. In the crest, there it was: the security tag.

I wedged my finger into the small gap and dislodged the tag with my fingernail. I shook the book vertically, and the tag fell to the floor. The tag was visible for only a moment before I scooped it up and stuffed it into the binding of *For Whom the Bell Tolls.*

Leaving the books on the floor as requested, I made my way back to the front of the library. At an open study table, I made a show of taking my own books out of my satchel and dumping them haphazardly about. I sat down and looked through my copy of *The Timepiece* for a while, and then put it down on top of the treasure. I spent nearly forty-five minutes plugging around on my phone, watching the library staff come and go, before I finally stuffed the two books, together, into my satchel, flung it over my shoulder, and marched toward the door.

("I won't approve of this," Emma's saying. "Tell me you get caught.")

I approached the exit with mock confidence; if an alarm went off: *It was an honest mistake. I meant to check the book out.* That was the plan.

I stepped in between the scanners. Nothing.

I opened the door. Still nothing.

Outside, free, I walked away with a nauseating cocktail of thrill and guilt brewing in my stomach and a personal note from Leonhard Grundstein to Ernest Hemingway in my satchel.

# 10

The Little Traverse Historical Museum sits in a beautiful park down by the marina on the bank of Little Traverse Bay in Petoskey, Michigan.

(As a kid, I went down to the park late in the year, when it was cold and all the leaves were on the ground, sometimes snowing, because the tourists were gone. I would run through the piles of leaves, kicking as much of them into the air as I could, as if my life depended on their flight.)

The museum used to be a railroad station. The train stopped running long ago, but in front of the museum, there still exists a strip of track to convince visitors the stories are true. (You see, histories are as difficult to keep up as leaves in the wind.)

I crossed the tracks and climbed the steps to the museum. To the right of the door there was a plaque titled: HEMINGWAY'S MICHIGAN. It described, among other things, how the building was built in 1892 and how Hemingway probably took the train from Petoskey to Charlevoix during his summers there. It always rubbed me the wrong way, of course. Hemingway overshadowed Grundstein at every turn. What bothered me the most about the description, other than the implication that Hemingway possessed this or any other region of Michigan, was the fact that Grundstein's relationship to Hemingway was reduced to vague "personal literary connections."

The displays inside were those common to small, local museums: pictures of the town and the town's people from ages ago with descriptions of dates and locations, and corresponding artifacts, furniture, letters, books, and clothes.

Hemingway's exhibit was, of course, the feature. There were pictures and descriptions of Hemingway's favorite places to visit when he spent time in Petoskey, all of which were blown up to ridiculous sizes. Ernest was only there when he was young, before he was *the* Hemingway. He never returned as the man we think of now. The most prized item in the entire museum was a note written by Hemingway to some nobody that just so happened to mention the town. (The museum must remove all doubts.)

There was one photograph of Hemingway as a young man standing on a sidewalk locking arms with another young man—both wearing fishing hats and dirty coveralls. Hemingway's teeth had a relaxed grip on the corncob pipe in his mouth. The two young fellows appeared to come straight from a lake or a river into town after a long morning of fishing. The caption read: ERNEST HEMINGWAY (RIGHT) ON MITCHELL STREET, PETOSKEY, IN FRONT OF FOCHTMAN'S DEPARTMENT STORE, 1920. The young man standing next to Hemingway, locking arms with the future famous American novelist, was my grandfather, Leonhard Grundstein. Even though Grundstein's own exhibit was only a few feet away, there was no mention of him in the caption.

Grundstein's exhibit was amateur at best. I scoffed at the idea of anything of real value existing within those walls. The most exciting piece of it was the old Underwood III typewriter on which Grundstein (according to the exhibit) started writing *The Timepiece*. Just looking at it, you could hear the *tick-tick tick-tick tick-tick* of it. The typewriter sat unceremoniously on an indistinct wooden desk as part of a replica bedroom. The exhibit was sectioned off by an orange felt rope. A sign dangling from the barrier read: LEONHARD GRUNDSTEIN (1900-1961),

GERMAN-AMERICAN NOVELIST.

I noticed a chest next to the bed that looked unfamiliar. It was closed and unlabeled. Curious, I leaned over the rope and attempted to open the chest, but the latch gave me trouble.

"Can I help you?" a woman asked, giving me a start.

I whirled around. "No, I was just looking."

She was a handsome woman—not alluring like Alex, nor transfixing like Beth, but she had her own charming quality—tom-boyish, yet distinctly feminine. Her dark-brown hair was high and tight.

"Looking for what?" she asked.

The words came out in a vomit of desperation: "My name is Dr. Samuel Schurke—" *Why? Why would I say 'doctor'?* "—from Oak Park University; I've been here before; I wrote my dissertation on Leonhard Grundstein; my aunt, Gertrude Grundstein, donated his belongings to the museum after his death." I pointed to the chest.

She said, "That's not Grundstein's."

"That explains why I haven't seen it before."

She extended her hand. "I'm sorry. What did you say your name was?"

I shook her hand. "I'm Dr. Samuel Leonhard Grundstein Schurke." *Why? Why? Why?* "Call me Samuel."

"Well, Dr. Samuel Leonhard Grundstein Schurke, my name is Bobbie Michaelson. I'm the new associate curator here. Most people come for Hemingway. I've lobbied to get Grundstein moved over by the Hemingway exhibit, but the curator is difficult. She doesn't like major changes."

"Trust me, I know. It's been more than a year since I poked around here," I said. "Has anything new emerged on Grundstein? Has anything been pulled out of storage, or has anything been misplaced that's been 're-discovered'?"

"Not that I'm aware of. What you see is what we have on Grundstein. We have some of his clothes in storage, but we have lots of clothes from that time period. His were not really anything we could use. All raggedy and worn. Pathetic, really. The stuff in the dresser is not even his."

"I see."

"Sorry," Bobbie said.

"I wasn't looking for anything in particular," I said quickly. "I went through it all thoroughly before, but I'm staying in the area for a little while, between semesters, so I thought I'd stop by."

"I'm more of a Hemingway scholar myself," Bobbie said. "My master's studies concentrated on Hemingway. That's how I got the job here."

"Where are you from?" I asked.

"Chicago. You said you were writing your dissertation on Grundstein?"

"*Wrote* my dissertation on Grundstein, yes. My defense is scheduled for the end of June. Beyond *Inferno*, in *Purgatorio*."

Bobbie looked at me sideways. "I thought you were *Dr.* Samuel Leonhard Grundstein Schurke?"

"Close," I admitted to the floor. "Very close. Technically 'all but dissertation.' But I'm currently faculty at OPU."

"Good luck to you, *Dr.* Schurke," Bobbie said. "Let me know if I can be of further assistance to you on your quest through hell."

"I'll need all the help I can get," I said, and I scurried toward the door.

For dinner, I was back at A.J.'s. Beth was there, and she made a joke about me stalking her. And again, I ate my meal in silence flipping through *The Timepiece* without being able to concentrate.

*If I table these leads until after the defense, I may never recover them. Then again, they've been cold this long; what harm is another month or two? And what have I found, really? The journal, I swear, is nothing. And, despite the reference to the museum in Grundstein's note, I'll take Bobbie's word for it that there's nothing new to find there. I've been over that place with a fine comb. As for the poem, I can't make heads or tails of it.*

Beth cleared my plate and brought me a cup of coffee.

"Did you visit *Holzstapel* today?" The way she said *Holzstapel* sounded like "holes topple," like she was making fun of the name.

I laughed.

"What's so funny?" she asked, deadpan.

"It's pronounced more like *hole*-schtah-ple. Emphasis on the first syllable."

"That's what I said, weirdo."

"I'm sorry. Yes, I've been there today."

"What did you think?"

I took a long sip from my coffee cup to delay, possibly avoid, discussion of the topic, but Beth seemed satisfied to wait. *Here goes. Cat out of the bag..* "It's quaint and rustic, but it gets a bit lonely at night, and the unreliable electricity and lack of Internet service is difficult to get used to."

"You're not staying there, are you?"

I nodded. "I'm family."

"Why didn't you say something? You just let me tell you about it, twice now, like some kind of rube?"

"I don't like to mention it. It draws attention. Do you really have tourists come through who go looking for the cabin?"

"All the time."

"And you tell them how to get there?"

"For a price." She shrugged. "Economy is small up here."

"That creeps me out," I said. "Have you been out there?"

"I've been there, but I've never seen inside."

I couldn't help myself. The door was open; I just walked through. "Would you like to see it sometime?"

"Of course I would."

"For a price," I said, smiling.

"Your coffee is on the house."

I gave her a look as if to say, *Come on.*

"For the duration of your stay," she added.

"Come out tomorrow night," I said, "and I'll give you a tour. What time do you get off work?"

"I can be there by eight."

"That'll do."

Suddenly her smile disappeared and her tone changed. "Would it be okay," she asked sheepishly, "if I brought a friend?"

I tried to bring the mood back up with a joke. "Is your friend a creepy stalker who lurks around my cabin at night?"

"I try to stay away from your kind, but I seem to attract them." Beth swiped my cash off the table. "We'll see you at eight o'clock tomorrow night."

# 11

I watched the sun rise over Walloon Lake. The hills looked like green porcupines clumping together for warmth. Over the horizon, a yellow glow grew steadily. Before my eyes, as the light fragmented, a rainbow of colors appeared as if by magic, but not for long before being replaced by a ribbon of blue sky.

(My notes show it was Tuesday, May 5, 2009—*Cinco de Mayo*—the 147th anniversary of Mexico's victory over the French at the *Batalla de Puebla* in 1862.)

I sensed what it must've been like to be Leonhard Grundstein, who often sat in the same spot at the kitchen table, scratching out ideas early in the morning.

I opened *The Sun Also Rises*, my contraband, to the site of my discovery, and I reread the note: "Age steals wits from the wisest. I simply feared you'd do it better. You were always better." And I reread the poem, trying to see it as a riddle. *What were the clues?*

*...kinsmen do not die anon...*

*...treading opon the grave...*

*"Upon" but with an "O"?*

*...bretheren... ...decry grace...*

*...place near the dying stone...*

*Was there or was there not nothing?*

Grundstein's annotations continued onto the next page where there was a large section bracketed in the left margin. In the right margin, Grundstein had scribbled the following:

> Café Suizo › Germany, March, 1923
> Brett › MS
> Barnes › Me
> Cohn › You

I rewrote a summary of the scene in my notes, making the appropriate substitutions as Grundstein's code dictated, which looked like this:

> In Germany, in March, 1923, Grundstein was fighting with Hemingway over MS (?). In the passage, Hemingway was seeking MS, and Grundstein wouldn't tell Hemingway where MS was. Grundstein said he didn't know where MS was, but then Hemingway knocked Grundstein out cold.

After reviewing the translation, I said aloud to the empty cabin, "My God, this is something."

I paced the room, trying to talk myself through it: "I know the inscription of the journal refers to this book, and I know the note in the book is from Grundstein. And the passage suggests, when read with Grundstein's code, that Hemingway used a fight between him and Grundstein as source material for the fight in *The Sun Also Rises*, which is consistent with the claims in Grundstein's journal that suggest Hemingway used Grundstein's encounter with Betz as the basis for his story 'Up in Michigan,' and used Betz's death as the basis for the ending to *A Farewell to Arms*. This is enough for an article at the very least—my God—enough to entirely change how one of Hemingway's famous short stories and one of his most famous endings are understood. Enough to put my name in large letters on a very crowded—"

I stopped.

"No. I'm not ready for an article. There are too many questions yet, important questions, questions I don't want some other scholar to fill in. Like goddamned Grudge. If I knew the specific topic of the fight—"

Pacing again.

"No. MS couldn't be—" *Don't say it.* "What's out there that Grundstein left behind for Hemingway by way of this note, this poem—" *Don't even think it.*

I flopped down onto the floor, onto the asymmetric rug Ingrid made for Grundstein, and stared at the ceiling. *Damn it, like it or not, this is big.* I took deep breaths to calm myself down, to sort out where to go next, and I came down hard and crashed—out.

When I came to, I was groggy and disoriented. It was nearly dark outside. Suddenly I snapped awake. In a panic, I collected my books and *The Sun Also Rises* with Grundstein's notes and hid them in the liquor cabinet along with the journal. I wouldn't have time for much more. Beth and her friend would be arriving shortly, and I was a wreck and the cabin was a mess.

Eight o'clock came upon me fast. I was mixing a pitcher of hot toddy as I watched a Jeep Wrangler bob and weave down the trail toward the cabin. The Jeep pulled up next to Karmann, and Beth climbed down from the passenger side. The friend got out and stepped around Beth to walk at her side. As they turned toward the cabin, I recognized the friend as Bobbie, the associate curator from the museum.

I stepped out the side door. "I'm sorry, Beth. You said you were bringing a friend, not a foe. Hemingway scholars are not welcome here."

"*Dr.* Schurke," Beth said. "I do believe you two have met."

"Are you driving Grundstein's Karmann Ghia?" Bobbie asked, looking at the car over her shoulder. "Shouldn't that be in a museum?"

"You want all of my inheritance, I see. Can you promise me it won't be stowed away in favor of a fishing pole that might have been used by Hemingway?"

"We'd probably get more patrons that way," Bobbie said.

"At ease, you two," Beth said. "May we come inside, please?"

Bobbie and I explained our chance meeting to Beth over our first glass of hot toddy as we stood in the kitchen. Then, I showed them about the cabin and told them what I knew about Grundstein's time there, Ingrid's rug, and Karmann.

"This is amazing," Bobbie said. "I've always wanted to see the inside. This reminds me of—"

"Windemere?" I finished her thought. "Yes, it's very similar."

"Thank you for the tour, *Dr.* Schurke," Beth said.

"The tour's not over," I said. "There's *s'more* if you want. No tour is complete without a campfire. What do you say?"

My guests sat together on one log while I prepared the fire.

"Are you thinking of getting your doctorate?" I asked Bobbie.

"No," she said. "I think the competitive nature of your world would destroy the magic of it for me. And I like where I'm at. Don't you find the work to be tedious?"

"On Hemingway, it would be tough."

"As far as I'm concerned, they're both dopes," Beth said, sandwiching a toasted marshmallow between two graham crackers. "Enough shop talk. Isn't the night sky grand up here? You can see so many stars, it's overwhelming."

"Orion's so clear," Bobbie said. "It's like he's hunting us."

"We can't have a campfire without a ghost story," Beth said. "What do you have, *Dr.* Schurke?"

"I don't know. I can't remember the last time I told a ghost story."

"Give us your best shot, doc," Bobbie said.

"Well, give me a premise, and I'll take it from there."

"How about this," Beth said. "Two men were chopping firewood in this forest. Okay, go."

"Okay. Two men were chopping firewood in this forest. George, let's say, who took great pride in the strength of his steady hands, offered to hold the rebel logs upright and still, so the other man, Chip, let's say, who took great pride in his accuracy with an ax, could split them. George and Chip chopped through the pile of wood without error, but on the final log, something went wrong. Did George slip? Did Chip miss? We'll never know, but what we do know is that Chip chopped George's hand clean off at the wrist. Blood gushed all over the forest floor as Chip tried to haul George to help. But poor George didn't make it. He died out here in these woods. And that's not all. The hand was never to be found. Rumor has it the hand lives out here somewhere, haunted by George's ghost."

"I don't believe it," Bobbie said.

"It's true. Apparently the hand lives under the floorboards of a cabin much like this one, and only comes out at night—" I ran my hand up Beth's back. "—to steal campers' s'mores!"

"Ahh!" Beth jumped into Bobbie's lap.

"Schurke," Bobbie scolded, stroking Beth's hair. "Do you have any idea how long it's going to take her to fall asleep tonight?"

"She asked for it," I said and downed the last of my toddy.


In the morning, the lake was like glass. I was ready to get to work and focus. In my pajamas, lacking all decorum for such a thing to do, I took the books out of the liquor cabinet and spread them out on the kitchen table. I thought of what it would've been like to be Hemingway in this situation, to have come here to Walloon Lake, to have found Grundstein's note, and to be looking for something Grundstein had left behind for him.

Page by page, I went through *The Sun Also Rises* again to make sure I didn't miss a thing. About halfway through, I was sure there was nothing left to find, but on the very last page of the text, there was another handwritten message. I ran my fingers over it, feeling the life of Grundstein's pen in the tips of my fingers.

> Hem, thought of you today. Understand now what Pablo was talking about in the good days, about the artist's dilemma, about copying and stealing. This was and remains a good book, your finest in my estimation. My work wouldn't have been half as good, nowhere near great, without having to compete with you.
> You won this round, friend. Looks like the next round will be in the next life.
> —Len, December 3, 1960

And, with that, it was official; I was on the hunt again, but for what, I wasn't yet ready to admit.

Over the next week, I became obsessed with keeping the line of inquiry open. I learned the journal and the book frontwards and backwards. At one point, I felt I'd gotten too close to them to see them clearly so I didn't look at them for a whole day, but the next day brought nothing new. I spent an entire day at the library looking over every page of every book they had on Hemingway and Grundstein. Under Bobbie's supervision, I re-inspected everything at the museum, too. Again, I went through box after box of Grundstein's old clothes, checking every pocket, every fold, every tag, for a forgotten note or an overlooked clue.

"You were right," I told Bobbie in a moment of frustration. "Throw these all out. They're worthless."

Also during the days—as I had promised Tante—I cleaned every inch of the cabin and the shed and found nothing. I took a hammer to every log in the attic without finding another treasure.

My only respite from the hunt was in the evenings. Every night that next week, Beth and Bobbie came over for a campfire, and we made up ghost stories.

(I wish I could expound on these nights probably as much or more than you wish I would, but I wasn't paying proper attention. You see, the events that lead to trouble are a good deal more memorable than the events that lead to pleasure.)

I remember, on the seventh night, we'd gotten so carried away talking and drinking that it became unsafe for Beth and Bobbie to drive home.

I remember telling them—dead serious—I wouldn't let them go and getting frustrated that they were laughing at me.

I remember them cuddling together for warmth as I put out the fire.

I remember struggling to get the woodstove started in the kitchen.

I remember Bobbie quipping, "I don't know who made the laws, but I know there ain't no law that you got to go hungry."

*What was she talking about?*

I remember there being a question of what they were going to wear to bed.

I remember there being a question of who would sleep on which bunk.

And I remember waking in the night under toasty covers shared by three naked people and shivering my ass off as I stepped out to pee, thinking, *Love is all the dirty little tricks you taught me that you probably got out of some book.*

("Don't skip over the details on account of me," Emma says. I say, "There is a time for everything, my dear.")

When I awoke the next morning, Bobbie was gone, and Beth was getting dressed. She had her jeans on and a red bra, and her back was turned to me as she worked to untangle her shirt.

"I'm sorry," I said. I didn't know what else to say. (I had no reason to be sorry.)

Beth appeared as if she was going to say something, but she said nothing. She pulled the shirt on over her head and flattened out the wrinkles with her hands. I watched, silently, as she put her shoes on, then her jacket. She turned to me and smiled.

I started to stutter. *Why? To explain? Explain what?*

"This has been a great week," she said. "I'm sad it's going to end." And she left without another word.

Then came a moment of insight: I'd neglected to thoroughly inspect the space *behind* the loose log where I'd found the journal. A mindless oversight.

In the attic, I proceeded to rip a hole in the wall and shined the Maglite into the darkness. There was something there, something glowing and reflecting like a nocturnal creature's eyes caught in headlights. With abandon, at the risk of getting bitten or injured, I crammed my arm down the hole up to my elbow to reach it. At my fingertips, I could feel a rectangular metal object. I secured it and retreated.

In my hand, I held a lighter. By design, it was clearly a precursor to the common gas station Zippo. Except for the dust, its silver was shiny and clean. A message was engraved on it. I angled the Maglite to dim the reflection. In a delicate script, it read: *SET IT ALL ABLAZE*. The only other markings were on the bottom: RONSON DE-LIGHT. NEW JERSEY, USA.

Looking at the lighter, I contrived to think up a million different scenarios in which the MS in the code or the clues in the poem could end there, but I couldn't shake the notion out of my head—*fine, I'll say it*—"I've caught the scent of Hemingway's lost manuscripts."

*Damn you, Daniels.*

# 12

My time up north was running out. I only had a few days left until I would have to head back to Oak Park and face another semester of classes. My shoulders and chest were wound tight. Anxiety. Nearly unbearable.

I drove to the museum one last time to find Bobbie. She was cleaning an exhibit on boats in Little Traverse Bay when I got there. It struck me, then, for the first time, that this might be awkward for her to see me after what had transpired between the three of us, but before I could reconsider, Bobbie sensed someone was behind her and turned to find me.

"Sam, my God, you scared me." Bobbie continued to clean the exhibit.

"I'm sorry, Bobbie. I need to speak with you."

"Sam," she said. "We don't need to talk about this. It was something that happened—"

"I know, I—"

"You don't need to feel bad about it, Sam. I don't."

"Bobbie, it's not about you."

"Beth? Yeah, I know. I'm concerned about her, too."

"No. I have something else I want to talk to you about before I have to leave. But about Beth? How do you mean?"

"I will go see her once I get out of work."

"I should go see her, too."

"No." Bobbie stopped working and faced me. She said, "Let me go see her first. I'll let you know how it goes."

I was confused, but I was on the scent. I was thinking of Hemingway, Grundstein, and the manuscripts. "But me and you, we're good?"

"Yes. I'm fine if you are."

"Bobbie, what do you know about Hemingway and lost manuscripts?"

"You mean the early writings, before *The Sun Also Rises*? You don't know about this?"

"I didn't really focus much on Hemingway—"

"It's okay, *Dr.* Schurke. I don't expect you to know everything about literature. Well, I know that, after Hemingway took some shrapnel in the leg on the Italian front, once he was healthy enough to travel, he was sent home. He spent about a year here in northern Michigan, recovering and writing and making trouble with some of the other rich kids, like Grundstein, who came back from the war. They acted like their service entitled them to behave however they wished. Eventually Hemingway's mom kicked him out of Windemere. He was like, 'If I can't stay here, then I'm going to Paris.' Sort of, but not really. I mean, he got married to Hadley and did some work for the *Toronto Star*, but the temptation to move to Paris, to live cheaply and to write, was too much for him. He and Hadley packed up and shipped out. The writings had something to do with Chicago or the Midwest. As legend has it, when Hemingway met Gertrude Stein and showed her, she told him something like, 'Start over and concentrate.' Probably did himself a favor by losing them anyhow."

"Do people in, I don't know, museum circles ever talk about where they might've ended up? Do you have any theories on where they went?"

"Gone. Never turned up. Won't ever turn up. Hemingway went crazy looking for those lost manuscripts. Some people say that was the downturn for his first marriage. He never forgave

Hadley for the loss. But, you know, there's a well-known professor who's made a career of making claims about leads on this. Haven't you heard of him?"

"Yes, of course. He's my advisor."

She studied my face. It was the first time she looked me directly in the eye that day. Then, she said, "Why?"

"Curiosity," I said. "I'm tired of thinking about Grundstein. I'm ready to think about something else."

She crossed her arms and looked at me sideways. "After all the help I've given you?"

I looked at my muddy shoes. "You're going to let me know how Beth's doing?"

She huffed, then began dusting an old photograph. "Fine."

"Thank you." I stepped out of the room.

"Sam?" Bobbie called after me.

I leaned back into the doorway.

"I think you should know," she said, "I've wanted to be with Beth for a long time."

"Oh?" (I can't remember saying anything more significant than that.)

"If you got caught up in something that I started, I'm sorry. I owe you that much."

"I see."

"That's what I want to talk to her about. Us, like, me and her. But I hope this doesn't make things awkward for us, like, you and I."

(My head was so cluttered.) I said, "I, too, have someone I've wanted to be with for a long time." (This all happened before I met Emma.)

Bobbie turned away, blushing.

"Good luck with Beth."


At the cabin my search hit more desperate lows.

*Hemingway went crazy looking for those lost manuscripts. Literally crazy.* (A joke, but not really.)

I took every item out the shed—all the tools, the lawnmower, the weed wacker, garbage cans, everything—and put them on the grass. I knocked on every inch of the shed's flooring, walls, and rafters looking for secret compartments. I searched for markings that would give me some indication of something. I stopped short of tearing the whole structure apart, and only because the sun had gone down.

The next day I did the same in the attic. I took everything out. I searched, scanned, scrutinized every inch. Again, I only quit due to nightfall.

The third day was an emotional rollercoaster. It began by systematically searching—re-searching—the rest of the entire cabin. At times, I would sink into the depths of despair, and I would curse away my human existence, the whole of it. Then, my adrenaline would pump up and energy returned.

At one point I got so frustrated, so frantic, so desperate to find the damn things, I investigated the stove. Once, I nearly got myself stuck in the chimney when I was examining the fireplace. I convinced myself that the manuscripts were hidden higher and higher up in the chimney until I shimmied all the way up to the top, but got nothing for my efforts but soot-covered hands and face. I thought for a moment Tante would have to hire a chimney sweep to come and extract my dead body. (Emma is laughing at me.)

Even though it would probably ruin my life, I couldn't help it; a force was compelling me forward. I was a man stuck on the open sea in a skiff with a fishing pole, a seafood allergy, and conundrum. I was exhausted, dirty, and I had barely eaten for the last three days. But I pressed on. I kept searching. There was nothing else I could do.

A realization: The woodpile—I'd been too focused on the library, and the museum, and the cabin, and the attic, and the shed; I forgot to check the woodpile next to the shed. I ran out to the woodpile and started heaving logs left and right until all of the logs were displaced and I was staring at the bare ground underneath. The moist mud was crawling with worms and decay. There was no sign of anything there. (Surprise.) I got down on my knees and dug with my hands, flinging dirt in every direction. And, there, as the sun set over Walloon Lake, I sat, on my knees, covered in soil, in the center of a chopped-wood massacre. (I'd gone crazy. Literally. No Joke.)

I went back inside and made a half-assed attempt to clean myself up. At the kitchen counter, I ate three pieces of plain bread and washed it down with beer—the most I'd eaten since before the incident with Beth and Bobbie, and I crawled in my bed.

Rest, real rest, was about to come at last, but there was a knock at the door. It was urgent and demanding. Forceful.

Three nights ago, I would've been scared to death—campfire stories running through my mind—but due to sleep deprivation, I opened the door that night ready for anything, good or bad, only hoping for rest.

There was Beth. She said, "I'm sorry, Sam."

Shaken by her unannounced arrival, I stepped aside as she rush in. *Whatever happened with Bobbie*, I thought, *must be serious.*

Beth said, "I've been thinking a lot."

"Did you talk to Bobbie?" I asked.

"I've been seeing a lot of Bobbie. We're fine. We're great."

"Good."

Without warning, she took my hand and led me to the annex.

(Emma has stepped outside. She said she doesn't want to hear this part. I asked her how this is different from the time with Bobbie, and she said she doesn't know, but she doesn't care for it.)

Beth pushed me down onto the bed. "I want one more night," she said. "That's all."

Next I knew, she had my sweat-stained shirt off and her hand down my pants.

"Beth, I don't know," I said, but she didn't seem to hear me.

In between breathes, she said, "Please don't take this personally—"

"—please don't feel—"

"—I just want—"

"—one last—"

And she mouthed—I was certain of it—*Oh, Bobbie!*

At dawn, alone, I did feel something. I tried to shake it off with a half-shot of whiskey chased by ten large gulps of water.

Then, another knock came at the door. This time, I wasn't in the mood to take any more nonsense. I flung the door wide open, standing there in nothing but my boxers, my hair greasy from four days without a shower and my body smelling of sex.

"It's Alex," I said. For there she was.

"Samuel, my God, what is wrong with you? You look like hell." Alex, too, entered without waiting for consent. "I have been trying to contact you for days. I was worried to death. My God, I thought I was coming up here to find a body."

"It's hard to get reception up here." *Dolt!*

"What's happened to you? You stink to the heavens. This place is destroyed, looks like World War III. You're a caveman. Didn't you bring anything to shave with? That stubble has got to go."

I felt my face, and the scruff was as rough as sand paper. "I've been a bit preoccupied."

"Sam, you're on your own for a week—"

"Nearly two weeks."

"—and you fall apart." She peeked into the annex, where items from the attic were strewn all about. "Samuel, there's wood all over the yard; there's boxes all over the bedroom. What is going on?'"

I shrugged. "At Woodlawn I heard the dead cry: This is my hard time." *Dolt. Dolt. Dolt!*

Alex rolled her eyes. "Are you ever coming home?"

"Of course."

"When?"

"I have to put this place back together yet, obviously."

"Your class starts on Monday, doesn't it?"

"Yes."

"Are you going to spend any of your remaining break with me?"

"Of course."

*Left, right. Left, right. I'm taking blows to the body and to the head.*

"I think you need to get cleaned up, pack your things, and come home. Today."

I was silent.

"I'm not even going to waste my time waiting for you," Alex continued. "I'm going back home. I can't stay here. The smell alone makes me want to puke, and I don't want to remember this look of yours." She poked a manicured fingernail into my furry chest. "Call me as soon as you've returned to civilization."

I did as I was told. I put the cabin back together and headed for home.

# 13

At the house, I had to park Karmann at the end of the driveway. Ashley was underneath a yellow Pontiac GTO Judge that was currently in my usual spot—a common problem. She had an underground network of people who needed their cars tended to—fender benders, glass repair—all off the grid. When people said, "I got a guy," or, "I know a guy who knows a guy," they were referring to Ashley. She was "the guy." Normally, I didn't mind. Ashley was my guy too, but to have this car parked in my spot was different. This was personal.

"Hey, creep," I said. "What's Grudge's POS doing in my spot?"

"Got a clicking issue. Goes *click-click click-click click-click*. The amateurs at the shop can't figure it out." Ashley rolled out from under the vehicle. "Nice beard."

I rubbed my chin. "Thinking of keeping it awhile."

She looked past my knees to the Karmann Ghia. "How's m'girl runnin'?"

"Like a deer. Up north and back. No problems. Probably time for an oil change, but I don't have the cash right now."

"I'll change it tonight." Ashley stood up. "Walk with me," she said. She went into the garage and clanked around one of her tool cribs.

Between her tools and her "rig"—an abused Taylor acoustic/electric and vintage VOX amp—Ashley had taken over the garage. Despite the hole picked through the wood where the pick guard should've been, Ashley's Taylor was new, bought for her by her father, Professor Stan Daniels. Ashley "broke it in" within weeks. The amp she got from a guy who needed door dings knocked out of his girlfriend's dad's Mercedes. Ashley could've gotten anything she wanted out of that guy. She took the amp.

"I'm playing some new songs at opening night at The Bullring. Nothing political this time, just poetry. Others won't appreciate it. I want you to come."

"Ah, I forgot. I got class on Monday, and I'm way behind as it is."

"Everybody's going. Alex's going to be there. And it's tradition."

"I've already got one gun to my head."

"You look ridiculous if you dance. You look ridiculous if you don't dance. So you might as well dance."

"Don't quote Stein at me," I said. "Not today."

Ashley pulled a wrench out of a toolbox. "I'm changing your oil for free."

"Okay, okay."

She smiled nefariously.

"Did Alex put you up to this?"

"Of course."


The opening night of bullfight season at The Bullring marked the beginning of the summer festivities. Young people emerged from the urban jungle, from all over the northern suburbs, to circle this watering hole like wildlife after a dry season. We weren't any different.

The Bullring had a mechanical bull in the center of a padded ring that was decorated to look Spanish, and every third Saturday from May to July, there were competitions. Opening night was the biggest fight of them all. The champion on opening night was the champion of champions.

For the bullfight, the host for the evening, referred to in Spanish as *Mayoral*, selected a female from the crowd. She was given a tight t-shirt to wear with a graphic of a bull on the front where the horns spread big and wide, cupping the bust. Across the horns read: TWO EARS. According to Spanish tradition, a successful bullfighter was awarded the two lopped-off ears of the defeated bull. According to this bastardized American version, the woman wearing the t-shirt was the prize. Prized participants of years past were invited to wear their t-shirts as proof and were treated like royalty and given front-row seats to the bullfights for life.

Once the prize-woman was selected, she had a chance to choose which two bullfighters could compete for her. The bullfighters had to chug a pint of sherry and then mount the mechanical bull. A bullfighter was allowed to fall off and remount the bull up to three times. If a bullfighter made it to two minutes, the operator ramped up the speed. If a bullfighter made it to five minutes, he won the fight. If neither of the contestants completed the fight, the longest combined time atop the bull won. If both bullfighters completed the fight, the prize-woman chose a winner. If a bullfighter puked, he was disqualified.

For the winner of the bullfight, the prize-woman performed a sensual *fandango*, which inevitably became nothing more than a raunchy lap dance.

After the *fandango*, the single ladies at the bar had a chance to "run with the bulls." The single ladies entered the bullring opposite the circle from the unselected bullfighters. The *Mayoral* waved a red *muleta* to initiate the chase. The men chased after the women until they were all wrangled into a pile of drunk and horny humans at the center of the ring.

To end the evening, the champion and the prize-woman performed a lively *jota*, an American interpretation of a Spanish waltz.

That night, the line to get in The Bullring extended around the corner.

From outside, I could tell Ashley hadn't started playing yet, which was a good sign. Ashley was a popular act. She played Bob Dylan-style folk music with an alt-punk flare. She would be accompanied by an accordion and a *vihuela* to play the music for the winning bullfighter.

Alex stood close to me and put my arm around her shoulders. We were holding a spot in line for Johnny. She was teasing Tom about something, some kind of inside joke between them, but they dropped it as soon as Johnny joined us.

"No Karla tonight?" Tom asked.

"No," Johnny said.

Inside, we found Gretchen standing at the cocktail table Ashley had reserved for us. By that time, Ashley was onstage, mid-song.

*No, no! Go from me. I have left her lately.*
*I will not spoil my sheath with lesser brightness,*
*For my surrounding air hath a new lightness;*
*Slight are her arms, yet they have bound me straitly...*[1]

"I love live music," Alex said. "It's in the moment. Art created right in front of your eyes and ears."

I was pleased to have her dancing at my side, occasionally bumping her hip into mine, and to see that Grudge was nowhere to be found.

*I make a pact with you, Walt Whitman—*
*I have detested you long enough...*

---

1. This quote comes not from Ashley's song, but from Ezra Pound's poem, "A Virginal." I can't remember the exact lyrics she sang that night, but the essence of the song reminds me of this poem.

*I am old enough now to make friends...*
*Let there be commerce between us.*[2]

Ashley announced she would be playing the final song before the bullfights would begin. The final song was the same every night of the bullfights. No matter what musical act was performing, they would play their own rendition of *"Marcha Real,"* the national anthem of Spain. Lacking official lyrics, the performers were expected to fill them in.

This was when the girls went crazy because the *Mayoral* would survey the dance floor and pluck the lucky prize-woman from the crowd before the end of the song. Alex abandoned me for the dance floor.

*Artists broken against her,*
*A-stray, lost in the villages,*
*Mistrusted, spoken-against,*
*Lovers of beauty, starved,*
*Thwarted with systems,*
*Helpless against the control...*[3]

The next time I saw Alex, the *Mayoral* was helping her onto the stage. The music stopped, and the *Mayoral* said, *"Tengo el placer de presentarles a Alejandría dos-orejas."*

The crowd cheered.

*"¿Qué torero le reclamarla?"* he added. That was the call to clear the dance floor except for aspiring bullfighters. I found myself being carried by way of the mob to the front of the ring, standing in line with four others.

The *Mayoral* sized up the bullfighters and repeated, *"¿Qué*

---

2. Again, these words come not from Ashley's song that night, but from Ezra Pound's poem, "A Pact."
3. And this quote comes from Pound's "The Rest."

*torero le reclamarla?*"

I, along with the other volunteer bullfighters, responded, "*Voy a! Voy a!*"

The *Mayoral* held his hand over the heads of the contenders ahead of me, whom Alex subsequently rejected with an elegant and dramatic shake of her head. Then, the *Mayoral* held his hand over my head. Alex smiled. For a brief moment, I believed she might not select me. At last, she nodded, and the crowd erupted with applause.

The *Mayoral* turned me toward the crowd and said, "*El Torero uno!*"

The crowd was pleased.

At that moment, I realized just how humiliating the next hour of my life would be regardless of the outcome of the fight.

The *Mayoral* shrugged and gestured to the last contender in line, and said, "*El Torero dos*, by default, I guess."

The crowd laughed.

Before the *Mayoral* could turn the man around and introduce him, a voice screamed over the crowd, "*Voy a! Voy a!*"

My heart sank as Grudge emerged from the crowd and stood at attention at the end of the line and repeated, "*Voy a!*"

The *Mayoral* appeared confused. He looked to Alex, and she said with a cunning smile, "I'll allow it."

The *Mayoral* held his hand over Grudge's fat head, and Alex nodded. The *Mayoral* dismissed the other contender, turned Grudge to face the crowd, and announced, "*El Torero dos!*"

So, there it was. The first bullfight of the season would be a showdown between me and Grudge over Alex.

Grudge went first. He chugged the sherry, spilling it generously onto his sweater vest, and he mounted the mechanical bull. Grudge fumbled with the strap, and the crowd heckled him for it.

I feared I would make the same mistake.

Grudge fell twice immediately, but seemed to gain some control with each attempt. On the third try, and through sheer determination, he maintained steady balance on top of the bucking and spinning machine. At two minutes, the operator cranked up the speed, and the bull bucked maniacally.

I willed Grudge to fall. Imminent. At any second.

The bull recoiled and caught Grudge in the chest. Lying flat across the top of the bull, Grudge hugged it tight. With each buck and turn, Grudge began to slide from side to side. But Grudge clung to the bull.

When the bell rang, signifying Grudge had completed the fight, he let go of the bull and flopped down onto the padding. The crowd went crazy for him.

My work was cut out for me. I would have three chances to ride the bull for the full five minutes. On my first attempted, at the first buck, I threw up in my mouth and tasted a mixture of regurgitated sherry and stomach acid. The first spin was more than I anticipated, and I flew backwards. Landing on the plastic padding felt like a slap on the back from God that knocked the soul out of my chest.

Feeling defeated already, I held onto the strap with both hands for the second attempt. *For Alex.*

Buck. Spin. Spin. Buck. Buck.

I braced for the speed increase, but nothing could've prepared me for it. My left hand flew free, but my right was caught in the strap. Somehow I managed to regain a hold with both hands, and I settled into the new speed, loosening my upper body to ebb and flow for balance and squeezing the bulk of the bull with my legs.

Each time the bull spun, I could see the clock. Time was declining rapidly.

...sixty seconds...

The crowd was so loud.

...thirty seconds...

...twenty seconds...

I swore I could hear Alex cheering for me.

...ten seconds...

...five seconds...

I had one more turn to survive, and I would be a champion bullfighter. I would win Alex for now, for tonight, for forever.

And, with two seconds left on the clock, I hurled red sherry all over the bull.

The crowd jeered in disgust. In the span of three seconds, I went from the edge of glory to the depths of disgrace.

I vaguely recall two bouncers wearing rubber gloves carrying me to the bathroom and dropping me off on the floor of a stall. Clinging to the rim of the toilet, the abrupt end to my state of motion made me queasy again, and I unloaded more sherry. I closed my eyes as I flushed; I couldn't bear to see the liquid swirl down the drain.

Feeling somewhat stable, I limped to the sink and rinsed out my mouth with the bar's metallic water. At some point, the bouncers draped a t-shirt embroidered with The Bullring's logo over my shoulder.

*Some consolation*, I thought.

I took off my soiled shirt, threw it into the trash, and put on the new one.

Clean again, I made my way back to the bar in time to see Grudge and Alex on the dance floor. I can still hear Ashley singing the song in my dreams.

> *By the gate now, the moss is grown, the different mosses,*
> *Too deep to clear them away!*
> *The leaves fall early this autumn, in wind.*
> *The paired butterflies are already yellow with August*
> *Over the grass in the West garden;*
> *They hurt me. I grow older.*[4]

---

4. This quote comes from Pound's "The River-Merchant's Wife: A Letter."

Johnny put his arm around me and said, "Sorry, dude. Not tonight."

"Feeling better?" Tom asked.

Watching Alex dancing with Grudge made me sicker than riding the bull. My failure felt like a brick in the bottom of my stomach; my embarrassment, flames burning in my cheeks. (I could be so dramatic.)

"You had a hold of that bull for a while," Gretchen said. "Too bad."

As soon as the dance was over, I led our group's migration to the patio in the back alley. Alex and Grudge walked over together, arm in arm.

"Wasn't that good?" Alex asked to no one in particular.

"Good enough," Johnny said.

"How are you feeling?" Alex said to Johnny. She pawed through her handbag. "I have some pills."

"No," said Johnny. "That won't do, but thanks."

Alex looked concerned, but she didn't pursue it.

"Are you feeling better?" Alex said to me.

"I'm fine," I said.

"You did well. You were so close. I was surprised."

*Thanks, I guess.*

"Where did you learn to ride a bull like that, Monte?" Tom chimed in. "I bet you have all kinds of hidden talents, don't you?"

"So hidden," Grudge said, "I'm not aware of them."

*Puke.*

A waiter came and took our drink orders, and that's when it happened. Alex placed an order for a glass of red wine called *Ménage á Trois*, and she kept saying the words, "*Ménage á trois, ménage á trois, ménage á trois...*" She was only playing with the words. Harmless. But it sparked a flame.

Tom said, "I have them all the time."

Grudge laughed nervously, shifting in his chair.

"Sure," Johnny said, "on a porno set with your dick in a sling doesn't count."

"Independent film set, thank you very much," Tom said.

"I'm sure it's a classy film," Grudge said, "with tasteful nudi-ty that's essential to the plot."

"Closest thing to a *ménage à trois* any of you will ever see," Tom said.

*Burning now.*

I lost it. "I have," I blurted. (I'm convinced the look on my face must've displayed as much astonishment as the looks on the faces of the rest of the Circle.)

Grudge rolled his eyes.

"And the one who wasn't the lesbian," I heard myself add, "came back three nights later for more."

(Emma's hitting me over the head and calling me a dog. She says I'm sleeping on the rug tonight.)

I leaned forward to slam my drink down on the table for emphasis, but wobbled and dropped the glass instead. I jolted forward to catch it. It splashed and spilled all over my hand. Em-barrassed, I heated up so quickly the sweat was like boiling water bubbling out of the pours on my forehead.

Alex canted her head. "That must've been some experience."

Ashley was singing again:

> *For I have known them all already, known them all—*
> *Have known the evenings, mornings, afternoons,*
> *I have measured out my life with coffee spoons;*
> *I know the voices dying with a dying fall*
> *Beneath the music from a farther room.*
> *So how should I presume?* [5]

By the time I wiped off my hands, dried my brow, and orient-

5. These words come from T.S. Eliot's poem, "The Love Song of J. Alfred Prufrock."

ed myself, Alex was gone. The wine-wash sobered me up quickly, and once the dust settled from Alex's exit, I found four pairs of eyes fixed on me.

"That was an exaggeration," I said quietly.

"Bullshit," Grudge snapped.

"You know you're going to have to tell us," said Johnny, taking a drink. "An experience like that, we're going to need to know all about it."

The waiter came, and I ordered another round.

"Okay," Tom said, "cut to the chase."

"Can't we simply enjoy the drinks and the night?"

"Seriously," Gretchen said, the way my mother did when she was disappointed in me.

"Some other time."

"That's enough for me." Grudge slammed his drink and slapped a ten-dollar bill onto the table. "Good night," he said as he stood.

Johnny raised his glass. "Good night, Monte."

Tom and Gretchen offered generic parting words as we watched Grudge leave.

"Okay, he's gone," Gretchen said. "Let's have it. Really, what's all this about?"

"As far as I can tell," said Johnny, "Alex wasn't involved so I'm clear to hear about it."

"It wasn't with students, was it?" Tom asked.

"God, no," I said. "It happened when I was up north. I met two women who wanted to see my grandfather's cabin. I invited them over. We had too much to drink. One thing led to another. Yada-yada. It turns out—"

"Sounds like a movie Tom's been in," Gretchen said.

"You're not going to yada-yada over this one," Tom said. "You know Johnny's going to write about it. Ashley's going to sing about it. And, if I ever play you in a movie, I'm going to need to draw on this."

Johnny added, "What's the point of all this if we're not going to pool our experiences for artistic inspiration?"

I cleared my throat. "They came to see the cabin. Then, they started coming over for campfires in the evenings. We drank. That explains a lot, actually. One night too much and too late. And, they stayed over and yada-yada.

"No," Gretchen said. "No more yada-yada."

"I was hammered. It wouldn't have happened without the alcohol. I was definitely interested in the one, and I know now, so was the other."

"This happened, like, last week?" Johnny asked in disbelief.

"Just happened. A lark. A plunge." I hadn't had time to fully unpack the episode yet. (Beth and Bobbie frequently visit us now, and Emma and I are best of friends with them. Who could've predicted it?)

Tight from taking in whiskey on an empty tank, I slouched in the wicker chair out on that patio with the taste of stomach acid in my throat and the scent of sherry in my nose begging still to be cleansed. I shot back the rest of my drink.

"Schurke," Johnny said, "you're my newest hero."

"So how should I presume?" I said.

# Part Two

"The lines of change are down. We, or at least I,
can have no conception of human life and human thought
in a hundred years or fifty years. Perhaps my greatest
wisdom is the knowledge that I do not know."
—John Steinbeck, *Travels with Charley in Search of America*

# 14

The morning would bring the first day of class. Nothing, it appeared, was going to stop it.

I poured myself a glass of Maker's Mark on the rocks, sat down at my computer, and opened an old syllabus for an Introduction to Literature course I'd taught countless times as an adjunct during my tenure as a graduate student.

The linear lines of text, ordered in time—left to right, top to bottom—were organized, structured, easy to understand. I shook my head.

Sipping on the whiskey, I opened a new, blank Word Document, and stared at the glaring emptiness of the page, begging for something to call its existence to order.

I typed:

> Dear Alex,
> Damn it: I'm sorry.
> Love, Sam

At the first keystroke, the blank-document abyss was confined to the draft of a confused love letter. Unsatisfied, I made a revision:

> ~~Dear~~ Alex,
> ~~Damn it: I'm sorry.~~ I should've told you—I know.

~~But, it never came up. But, the time was never right.~~
But, I haven't been able to make sense of it. Yet.
~~It just happened.~~ For some reason, when I think of
you, of us, I think of Clarissa Dalloway, and I know
what she's talking about when she says she's "far out
to sea" and how it's "very, very dangerous to live
even one day." If I could only find the way, the right
way, to say the right words.
    ~~Love~~, Sam.


Then, I typed: I love you, Alex.
Then, again: I love you, Alex. I love you, Alex.
Then, I copied and pasted it ten more times:

> I love you, Alex. I love you, Alex. I love you, Alex. I
> love you, Alex. I love you, Alex. I love you, Alex. I
> love you, Alex. I love you, Alex. I love you, Alex. I
> love you, Alex. I love you, Alex. I love you, Alex.

Then, again and again and again:

> I love you, Alex. I love you, Alex. I love you, Alex. I
> love you, Alex. I love you, Alex. I love you, Alex. I
> love you, Alex. I love you, Alex. I love you, Alex. I
> love you, Alex. I love you, Alex. I love you, Alex. I
> love you, Alex. I love you, Alex. I love you, Alex. I
> love you, Alex. I love you, Alex. I love you, Alex. I
> love you, Alex. I love you, Alex. I love you, Alex. I
> love you, Alex. I love you, Alex. I love you, Alex. I
> love you, Alex. I love you, Alex. I love you, Alex. I
> love you, Alex. I love you, Alex. I love you, Alex. I
> love you, Alex. I love you, Alex. I love you, Alex. I
> love you, Alex. I love you, Alex. I love you, Alex. I

love you, Alex. I love you, Alex. I love you, Alex. I
love you, Alex. I love you, Alex. I love you, Alex. I
love you, Alex. I love you, Alex. I love you, Alex. I
love you, Alex. I love you, Alex. I love you, Alex. I
love you, Alex. I love you, Alex. I love you, Alex. I
love you, Alex. I love you, Alex. I love you, Alex. I
love you, Alex.

It became a game. I watched the copied sentence snake
around and around in mesmerizing lines. The lines built pages
in rapid fire as long as I held down COMMAND + V.

Suddenly I became overwhelmed with frustration. I hit the
keys as fast as I could, waiting for something, anything, to signify
the end of this spiral. Some sign of completeness. And then, despair—the possibility, enabled by digital technology, to be able to
write endlessly into a Microsoft Word black hole. One could type
one's whole life away and not run out of blank page after blank
page—a serious hell.

Falling though digital space, I rashly decided to join Twitter.
I plugged in my university email address, selected a handle—
@ProfSchurke—and within seconds of my descent, I launched
two tweets:

@ProfSchurke: Damn it: Mistakes have been made.
9:03 PM – 17 May 2009

@ProfSchurke: Just set up twitter
9:02 PM – 17 May 2009

I felt better after transmitting my apology out into the Universe regardless of who would receive it, if anybody.

Without saving, I closed out of the Word Document, and as
quickly as it was something, it was nothing. Poof! Evaporated
into digital thin air.

Shaking the glass, I watched the half-melted cubes collide into each other, and chip, and crumble.

*Focus, for God's sake*, I commanded.

I began where I could; I changed the name of the course and the dates and times on the syllabus and saved the document as GD-GRUNDSTEIN-SYLLABUS-SPRING2009.docx. I kept everything as simple as possible, leaving the policies and procedures, even the grading scale and the assignments, the exact same as my previous class. I only changed the titles of the required texts to Grundstein's novels.

*"Read the books. Discuss them. Have the students write papers on them," Daniels had said.* Check-check.

I saved it and emailed it to the department's secretary, Rita, asking for copies. Done.

Satisfied, I called Alex, but she didn't answer. I hadn't heard from her since she left The Bullring incident. *How mad could she be, really?*

A minute later, I received a text message from her.

ALEX: Sorry. Can't talk now. Working with Tom on a project. Will call tomorrow.

*She didn't mention any new project to me. Neither did Tom.*

Disappointed, I checked my Twitter account. Thirteen new followers. Who: Gretchen and Ashley, of course, were among the first. I didn't recognize the others. What: Ashley was always "connecting with fans." Gretchen was always "following the news."

There was a notification from Gretchen, and I responded:

@GretchBreporting: @ProfSchurke More than 80k tweets have been published before you responded. Work on it.
9:54 PM – 17 May 2009

@ProfSchurke: @GretchBreporting I was actually procrastinating on prepping for class. Forced my hand.
9:53 PM – 17 May 2009

@GretchBreporting: @ProfSchurke About time you joined the rest of us @Earth
9:04 PM – 17 May 2009

I followed Gretchen and Ashley as well as the *Metro Detroit Journal*. Immediately, my feed began to populate with tweets and the sidebar filled with suggestions of more accounts to follow. Between scrolling through the feed and looking at the profiles of the suggested accounts, with the occasional click on an article or website, I dawdled on Twitter until well past midnight.

So there I was, again, standing at the front of a classroom, leaning up against the whiteboard, with seven pairs of eyes staring at me, begging for me to say, *Nice to meet you. Here's your assignment. I'll see you on Wednesday.*

To begin, I plowed through the syllabus like a lecture, then looked at the clock. *Only ten minutes?* "Any questions?"

Only one set of eyes was looking at me warmly: the big blues of Emma Stratford. (Emma tells me she felt sorry for me, as nervous as I appeared to be. She says I looked like a lost puppy. I shrug it off and tell her I found my way home eventually.)

"Alright, tell me your name," I said, yawning, "and something unique about yourself to help me remember you." I scratched my face; the beard was getting itchy. (Emma says she liked the bearded look until it got out of control.)

Emma's eyes were the magnetic kind that attract gazes, wanted and unwanted—a dangerous combination when paired with her friendly smile. Her sandy, shoulder-length hair was the right amount of careless to appear free-flowing, looking simultaneously unwieldy (she doesn't like the way I use "unwieldy") and intentional. All put together—I knew I was in trouble.

Along with Emma, we had three other females: Leslie, a Native American whose given name was actually Nita Barth, but she "went by Leslie in school"; Teagan Abbey, who dressed from hair to toe in jet black and "dated Dave Matthews every summer"; and Harmony Thyme, who was tall and thin with a long brown ponytail, who copped out and said, "I don't have anything unique about me to share." (Someone always does. As long as it's not the first person, introductions will go fine.)

We also had three males: Rowan Wilson, who was Harmony's boyfriend, who sat behind her and compulsively twirled her hair; Roy Glitterburg, a comedian wannabe, a real class clown, who said, "I like candle-lit dinners and long walks on the beach," and smiled at Emma (nobody laughed, thank God); and Eli Bony, who made rap music on his laptop under the name Bone-E, who was available "to disc jockey any party you need."

"Let me give you a brief introduction to literary modernism," I said, rubbing my chin.

*It would be a good time to go see Alex after class. Oxfords, khakis, shirt and tie, jacket—looking good.* (On what planet was I living?)

"No," I said. "Let me back up. I'm sure you've questioned why you're here. I bet some of you think, 'Why should we study literature? Isn't it a dying field?' With so much Internet to be read, other than scholars and nerds, who's reading literature anymore? Maybe you think, 'Everything written before the Internet is irrelevant to my existence.' "

*God, what was Alex doing with Tom?*

"Even if you don't or haven't thought this way, and you care to be a literate citizen in the twenty-first century, you're going to encounter these questions. English departments all over the country are dwindling, and this economic crisis is killing us under the demand for science and technology. Departments are being merged into broad 'General Education' or 'Liberal Studies' curricula so institutions can maintain their precious accreditation by getting students through their basic humanities requirements as quickly as possible and into major courses in 'more important' fields like engineering, mathematics, and health sciences. Some of you have probably already had to deal with these biases, fielding questions from your parents, relatives, maybe even advisors at this very university."

Emma was nodding along at every word.

"If you go on to study literature at the next level, maybe pursue it as a profession, you're going to have to face this question every day. You're going to have to justify course offerings to receive funding."

I was warming up, falling into the rhythm of the stump speech I'd delivered a dozen times before.

"I will argue that our collective English language studies matter as much today—if not more—than they've mattered for centuries. That's why there's so much cause for concern. The stakes are high. The English language is increasingly becoming the common denominator, not only for critical academic inquiry, but also for basic communications everywhere, every day, across the globe, for intercultural understanding.

"At this point, students, you might say, 'Come on, Professor Schurke. You're blowing this out of proportion.' But this is not a lofty rant. There's more being written and read in English on a daily basis than ever before, and by citizens of more nationalities than ever before. The need for highly effective communicators utilizing the English language is more important than ever before. I'd add that the need for effective communicators using the English language would at least remain the same or increase across all disciplines in higher education, across all industries in the nation, and across the globe."

I was in the zone, standing at the podium waving my arms for emphasis whenever appropriate.

"I hear you laughing at me back there, Glitterburg, but again, the stakes are high. As I mentioned, what's actually happening is that effective English language skills—not only reading and writing, but analysis, the ability to analyze text and extract meaning—are becoming so basic, so necessary, so essential to success in any career field that English is being further and further removed from a concentration and being pushed into a core discipline.

"This movement, despite what some believe, probably including the leaders of this very institution, corresponds with the push in higher education for 'practical' degrees. But I defy you to find any significant job posting, with decent pay, that wouldn't, in some form, require excellent written and verbal communication skills. Each and every one of them, *required*. And where else, but here, are the best of those abilities going to studied, learned, and practiced? How else would you want to study English, but to examine the works of the best ever to have been written?

"Think of it this way. If every single professional career opportunity required at its core a strong ability to play basketball, wouldn't you want to study with and learn from Michael Jordan? Wouldn't we as a nation seek to fund top-tier basketball programs at every institution, to try to develop as many Michael Jordans as we possibly could?

"To bring it back to our 'sport,' if you will, literature represents, in many ways, the epitome of civilization. Great works of literature are the physical incarnation of the pinnacle of human achievement—the loftiest of cultural relics."

I gestured to my head with gusto.

"Think of it—no other species on the planet has evolved enough to have any sort of written language, let alone the advanced psychological development to the point of being able to fabricate a story out of shear imagination. Think of what is the worst book on the shelf, in your opinion. Try to think of it objectively. That object is a remarkable achievement for the progress of the human race, thousands—tens of thousands—of years in the making. There's nothing in human civilization today more taken for granted than the common book."

I paused to let the point sink in and looked at my audience. Roy had his head down; Harmony was doodling; Rowan was twirling Harmony's hair absentmindedly; Leslie was looking out the window; and Eli was typing something unrelated to my lecture. Only two students, Emma and Teagan, probably out of manners more than interest, even seemed to notice that I was finished.

"Right on," Teagan said, then checked her watch.

"To put it simply, for those of you who might be pragmatists—admittedly, not the typical trait of students who major in English—'practical' degree programs often get you a job out of school quicker than, say, an English degree, but it's the strong background in humanities that's going to help you get your next promotion. These skills are going to help you reach the pinnacle of your human potential."

I shouldn't have expected applause in this lecture-room.

"At any rate," I said, "should we continue to teach and learn English at our colleges? Yes, of course. A time will soon come when the pendulum will swing back our way, when—"

The ticking sound of the Newton's cradle in Daniels' office rang in my head, and I forgot what I was saying. I shuffled through my notes, pleased to see my introduction to modernism would have to be short on time. My students looked weary already.

"Okay, modernism. Let's see, quickly, who? Americans that come to mind might include writers such as Ezra Pound, Gertrude Stein, T.S. Eliot, F. Scott Fitzgerald, William Faulkner, Sherwood Anderson, Wallace Stevens, William Carlos Williams, Richard Wright, e e cummings, Marianne Moore, Jean Toomer, Langston Hughes, John Dos Passos, and the like. And then there was, of course, Ernest Hemingway and Leonhard Grundstein— two legendary giants. And I would argue Grundstein was more of a modernist writer, at least early on, than Hemingway was.

"Okay, what? Modernism was a movement of thought that could be seen in culture, politics, philosophy, and literature, of course. For literature, it was simply—and not-so-simply—a breaking away from tradition. For culture in general, that meant re-thinking things like societal structures such as class, marriage conventions, romantic relationships entirely, and with the various forms of industrial revolution, notions of work and divisions of labor. Everything was changing dramatically, and the Great War expounded it all. After the war, all bets were off, for everything. For literature, that meant previous conventions of poetry and the novel, namely the styles that dominated what may be called the Victorian Era, would not suffice any longer, both in form and in content. This led to new approaches to writing, produced the stream-of-consciousness style—like Woolf's work for you Brit-lit fans and Grundstein's, as you'll see—a stark contrast to the kinds of novels people like Jane Austen wrote in the previous century. A good deal better, too, I might add. Modernists wanted litera-ture that more accurately represented life as they saw it, which meant more artistic and more abstract. Linear, structured nar-ratives took a backseat, and the inner workings of the mind—of thought—took a front seat. The previous forms didn't allow for that kind of content. Modernist trends also explored a new a sense of internationalism, the intersection between cultures, es-pecially after the Great War. This is somewhat evident in books you may have read in high school, like Fitzgerald's *The Great Gats-by* or Hemingway's *The Sun Also Rises* or *A Farewell to Arms*."

Even Emma stopped making regular eye contact with me. Daniels' voice came into my mind: *"Sex and Violence. When you're losing them, talk about the sex or the violence."*

"Modern romantic relationships," I said, "are complex, complicated in a different way than in the novels of previous generations. The institution of marriage, for example, becomes a slippery spot at the center of the vast, obscure, unfinished mas-terpiece of one's love life. People wanted to marry for love, unlike class-oriented marriages of the previous century. The modernist portrayal of love and marriage and romance—and *sex*—is closer to what we see in real life today than—"

A memory interrupted my train of thought. Bobbie was in front of me, her back nestled against my chest, my hands on her hips; both of us were on top of Beth swaying forward and backward, in sync. Bobbie had curled her arms around my back, leading the two of us, as if we were dancing and Beth was the music—on our way to love's summit, together.

(I see now how Bobbie had orchestrated it all.)

"Sex," I said, unsure of where to go next, but for the first time since class began, seven sets of eyes were on me. "A basic part of the human existence that can be and is often explored independently of marriage or even love. You'll see these in Grundstein's novels. That's a teaser for you."

I pressed on. "Okay, where? Well, modernism was in the air. It was a movement taking place all over the world. The more we study it, the more we find it was a widespread trend. Although, in literature, it's most commonly thought to be taking place in Europe, in Great Britain. Even the American modernists were blooming in France, mostly. Germany for Grundstein.

"And when? So-called 'high modernism' was, when?" It was intended to be a rhetorical question. I'd paused to think only for a brief moment, but Emma said, "From 1919 or 1920 until about, well, up to World War II, so 1939 or 1940."

The class seemed as surprised as I was to hear someone else's voice.

"Yes, exactly," I said. "Thank you, Emma. High modernism is considered to be, essentially, between the wars. Although the trends began well before the Great War, the peak is considered to be 1920s, and the trends continued—"

Again, like a recurring nightmare, Professor Stan Daniels stepped in the door at the back of the classroom. I stood at attention, serious now, lowering my voice. "I know that was a only a brief introduction to literary modernism and a whirlwind at best," I said, "but we'll get deeper into it over the next two weeks as we explore Grundstein's first novel, *The Timepiece*, from 1925, our first reading assignment. Read the first half by next Monday. That's one week from today."

Daniels leaned up against the back wall and folded his arms. He gave no nonverbal signals as to what he wanted or what he was doing there.

"Our second reading selection will be *West of Home* from 1932, which is considered Grundstein's masterpiece," I continued, "although many scholars, myself included, have made the case for Grundstein's last published novel, *The Son Down*, from 1952, as his best. It's a hard case to make because it was such a commercial failure at the time, but we'll get more into that when the time comes.

"As a reminder, you'll be responsible for the readings from week to week, and your attendance and participation with be crucial to your learning as well as your grade. The mid-term essay will be written on *The Timepiece* or *West of Home*—your choice. Being a truncated spring term, that's only three weeks away, so I recommend you keep up. We'll get to *The Sun Down* in the second half of our time together. The final essay will cover Grundstein's work as a whole and how it reflects modernist and/or, eventually, postmodernist tendencies. Any questions?"

My students didn't need another word; they understood the cue.

"For this coming Wednesday's class period, we'll get to know Leonhard Grundstein, the person, better. See you then."

The students packed up their books and made for the door in a mildly respectful hurry. Except for Emma. The last thing I wanted to do was deal with a student in front of Daniels. Students' questions were unpredictable.

"Professor Schurke," she said.

Normally I would've said, *Please, call me Sam*, but that didn't seem appropriate in front of Daniels. "Yes, Emma, what can I do for you?"

"I'm really looking forward to this class."

"Good," I said, watching Daniels out of the corner of my eye, who was eyeing me. "Me, too. It's going to be fun."

"I wanted to make sure I have the right copy of *The Time-piece*." (A very Emma-type thing to do, as I know now.) She was digging in her backpack. "I've taken literature courses before with a different text, and it's hard to follow if the page numbers don't line up right."

"Yes. I understand."

Emma drew the book out of her bag and handed it to me. The cover image—the silhouette of a man dancing on the open face of a pocket watch with two women who did not appear to be wearing anything—reminded me of that night at A.J.'s when I first met Beth. It felt as though Emma had pulled my pants down right in front of Daniels. I pushed the book away and said, "Yes. That's the one." My words were affirming, but my tone was repulsive, my action harsh—a mistake.

"Okay." Emma said, pouting a bit. (She says she doesn't pout, but she pouts.)

"Yes," I said, raising the pitch of my voice to sing-song, over-compensating. "That's the one I'll be using."

"Okay," she said again. "See you on Wednesday."

"I look forward to it."

Daniels shut the door behind Emma—a bad sign. He approached my desk where I was packing the remaining syllabi into my satchel, then stood and waited for me to give him my complete attention.

I closed my satchel and looked up.

"Welcome back. Good start to the term," Daniels said, smiling. "Now, how's the research going?"

"The research?" I asked.

"Getting ready for class and all."

"Oh, fine. Nothing unusual. Most of the course has come together. I mean, I have to craft a few lectures yet. Why?"

"Since you asked, Schurke, I'm curious how you're coming

on the loose ends of your dissertation? Found anything? Over the break, perhaps?"

"Nothing."

Daniels cocked his head.

"Yet," I added.

"Yes. Yet. That's how research goes, isn't it?"

I stared at Daniels unsure of how to proceed.

"Yes, that's how it goes," he said thoughtfully, gazing out the window. "You keep putting pieces together; you'll find something."

"Yes."

Daniels was acting strange even for him—distant, distracted, disturbed.

"You know," he said, "if you answered some of those questions, your dissertation would be a lot stronger and you'd have better career prospects."

"I know," I said. "Unfortunately."

Daniels patted me on the back a little too hard. "Keep looking." On his way out, he said over his shoulder, "And keep me in the loop."

In the empty classroom, I checked Twitter:

@GretchBreporting: A brighter story: Lithuania elects 1st female president with 68% of votes.
11:54 AM – 18 May 2009

@FluTrackerH1N1: 40 countries infected; 8,829 cases reported; 74 deaths confirmed.
11:53 AM – 18 May 2009

@GretchBreporting: Sad story from @News.USA: NY records 1st death from H1N1 "swine flu." Keep an eye on @FluTrackerH1N1 for updates.
11:52 AM – 18 May 2009

# 15

I didn't like lying to Daniels, but I hadn't really discovered anything. (I was lying to myself, too). The scent had gone cold. (A rationalization for inaction.) Every night, I reviewed my notes, the book, the journal, but each time my faith in them diminished.

Tante's was the only place I could think to even begin again. (Why couldn't I sit on my hands for six more weeks?)

Before I went to return the keys to the cabin, I made copies. I wasn't going to give up my access so I'd have to bother Tante again whenever, if ever, I uncovered the next clue and it led back to *dem Holzstapel*. I was heir to the cabin anyhow; I should have a set.

I invited Gretchen to come along with me. Having a third party present would improve Tante's attitude; she'd have to play the part of the host at least. And Gretchen, as a journalist, had instincts on people, knew how to ask questions, how to spot holes in a story.

Tante let us into her living room and asked Gretchen if she wanted a hefeweizen.

"No, thank you," Gretchen said. "It's not even noon, yet."

"*Aber gut für die Verdauung*," Tante replied, pointing to her stomach.

"I'll have one, Tante. *Bitte*. And, Gretchen will have *ein Radler. Danke*."

Tante passed through to the kitchen.

"What's a *Radler*?" Gretchen asked.

"Half beer, half lemonade. You'll like it."

Tante returned with a tray of drinks.

"What is it you're looking for this time?" Tante asked without further ado.

"I'm not looking for anything," I said. "I just came to return the keys to the cabin and to see you." I took the keys out of my pocket and handed them over.

Tante's eyes narrowed.

"My dissertation is complete as far as I'm concerned," I added defensively. "My defense is scheduled. We'll see what the committee says. For now, I'm trying to enjoy life a bit before judgment day arrives. I'm teaching a class on Opa this term." I took a sip from my beer.

"I'm curious about Leonhard Grundstein's involvement in the Great War," Getchen said, unprompted and ill-advised.

I nearly lost my beer through my nose.

She continued, "Sam says information on that period is slim to none. There must be something interesting you remember."

I didn't tell Gretchen why I'd invited her to come along other than to go to lunch afterwards, but she couldn't help herself. She's like a bloodhound.

"I don't think Leonhard was all that involved in that war," Tante said. "He was very young. He never talked about it."

"There's nothing of significance," I said in agreement, "to suggest he was involved in any way."

"*Richtig*," Tante said, looking at me. "Nothing of significance."

"Oh, there must be something," Gretchen said, pressing on.

"Most of Lenny's things are at the museum," Tante said. "Sam has gone through them enough."

"You must have some kind of relics or something of value."

"Gretchen," I said, as if to say, *This is not the time nor the place.*

Tante sighed. "I think I may have some newspaper clippings somewhere." She paused to think, then added, "Let me go see."

As soon as Tante was upstairs, Gretchen held up her hand for a high five.

*What?* I mouthed.

*You're welcome*, she mouthed back.

There was no time to waste. I tip-toed about the room, opening decorative boxes and shuffling through drawers.

"What are we looking for?" Gretchen whispered.

"I don't know yet, anything intriguing."

"I got this. Check the next room." Gretchen got down on her knees and looked under the sofa, sweeping her hand along the bottom.

Listening for a moment, I could hear Tante moving things around upstairs. I ducked into the dining room. Plain. Table and chairs. Didn't even look used. I could smell the textured wallpaper like it was decaying right where it was hanging. There were two pictures on the wall. One was a picture of Grundstein with Tante as a child. Grundstein was holding her hand, and Tante, who must've been about six years old, was using her other hand to shield the sun from her eyes. The other photograph took me by surprise. It was the same one I'd seen at the museum, the picture of Grundstein and Hemingway on the sidewalk in downtown Petoskey.

I took the picture off of the wall.

"Sam?" Gretchen whispered from the doorway.

"Is she coming?" I whispered over my shoulder.

"She's still upstairs. What do we got?"

"Go warn me if she's coming down, would you?" In my periphery, I could see Gretchen with her head cocked. She didn't take commands well.

"Please," I added. "I'll be right there."

Reluctantly she went back to the sofa.

I unhooked the back of the picture frame, and it popped out

and fell to the floor.

"What's that?" Gretchen asked, sticking her head around the corner.

"Nothing. Be right there."

"Whatever," she said. She returned to the sofa in the living room.

There was a small packet of papers folded tightly and tied with a thin ribbon. It had been jammed into the frame behind the photograph. I stuffed the packet in my pocket and swiped up the back of the frame.

"This drink is so delicious," Gretchen said, raising her voice. "You must give me the recipe."

Tante's voice was muffled, approaching.

I scrambled to re-assemble the frame.

"Where did Sam go?" Tante said.

"He went to the bathroom," Gretchen said.

The clasps on the back of the frame were stubborn.

"That's not the way to the bathroom." Her voice was dangerously close.

I forced the last clasp closed with my thumb and felt a slicing pain. The frame went back on the nail without trouble—*thank God*.

Tante turned the corner.

I shoved my throbbing thumb into my pocket, holding it firmly with my fingers, trying to shield the prized papers from any possible bloodstains that could ruin the evidence.

"Did you forget where the bathroom is?" Tante asked.

"Tante," I said, "I saw this photograph up at the museum."

"Yes. It's in the Hemingway exhibit."

"I know. Is this the original?" I adjusted the frame on the wall with my free hand.

"They have a print."

"That's neat," I said. "Were you able to find... what you were looking for?"

"I have one," Tante said, leaving for the living room.

I followed her and sat down next to Gretchen who shot me a scandalous glare.

Tante handed over an aged clipping from the *Berliner Morgenpost*. There was a profile picture of Dieter Grundstein, Leonhard's uncle from Munich. The English translation of the headline would be equal to: PEACEFUL RULER'S SON COMMITS SUICIDE, LINKED TO WILHELM'S DOWNFALL.

I sipped on my hefewiezen while I scanned the article. I knew the story, but I hadn't seen this clipping before. With inevitable defeat on the horizon, Dieter killed himself. Desperate times. Only one of many.

There wasn't any particularly revealing information, except the fact that there was potentially no limit to what Tante was hiding from me.

I asked Tante if I could make a copy of the article.

Tante took the clipping out of my hands and looked it over for a long time. "Take it. It's yours."

I took great care to secure it safely in my satchel.

"There is something else of Leonhard's you can have," Tante said thoughtfully. "I've wanted for a long time to get rid of it."

Tante went into the kitchen, opened and closed a drawer, and returned holding a polished Petoskey stone slightly bigger than a golf ball. It was a dull gray and freckled all over with dark brown eyes.

"Lenny's paperweight," she said.

I picked it up with my thumb and forefinger as if it was a bomb that could go off.

"You can't hurt it." Tante laughed.

I remembered the cut on my thumb and checked the stone to see if I'd stained it. There, I'd pressed a small smudge of red into an engraving. I quickly wiped the blood away and hid my thumb again.

"It's engraved," Tante said.

"What does it say?" Gretchen asked.

"*Unter dem Ruhestein*," I said.

"What does that mean?"

"Under the hearthstone," Tante and I said together.

"Buried, forgotten," I said. "Similar to, 'Let bygones be by-gones.' It's a family saying. *Danke*, Tante. *Danke*."

"*Bitte*." Tante's infamous seriousness returned, and she said, "Soon enough, you, Samuel, will be the keeper of the family line."

At the diner for lunch, Gretchen looked up from her steak and cheese and said, "What's this stuff with your Aunt Gertie all about, Sam?"

"That's just Tante's way," I said. "She's skittish. Makes ev-erybody nervous."

"No. Alex said you've been acting strange, said when she was up north, the whole cabin was torn apart in search of some-thing."

"The place was a wreck when I got there. I was supposed to pick it up; I promised Tante I would. I didn't make much prog-ress, obviously."

Gretchen looked me over.

"Honestly, I didn't find anything," I said.

She leaned in close enough that I could feel her breath on my nose when she whispered, "Sam, I'm on to you. You might as well spill it. Tell me what you make of the paperweight, Sam. And, the article."

"I'm not sure—"

"Not sure of what?"

"Okay," I said, pushing her back into her seat. "Will you promise not to tell anyone? I mean, *anyone*."

"Sam, I never turn on a source. What is it?"

"I'm being serious. My career could depend on this being a

secret until I'm ready."

"Strictly professional."

"I think I may have found evidence—" I hesitated.

"Out with it, Sam. Come on. It's me."

"I may have found evidence that Leonhard Grundstein's death may have been a suicide." I examined her face.

Gretchen stared back at me, stone-faced. "So, this clipping is a big deal then?"

"Potentially. Suicide does have a tendency to run in families, but it's a stretch. Dieter's death and Leonhard's death happened independently of each other."

"Your family doesn't already know how Grundstein died?"

"What I'm saying is, I suspect there may have been a cover-up."

"Why?"

"Gretchen, you saw my aunt back there. We're a very private people. We keep our dealings—"

"—*unter dem Ruhestein?*" Gretchen said.

"Very good. I'm impressed. Yes, *unter dem Ruhestein.*"

"So, what kind of evidence did you find?"

"Just hunches, really. I thought I might find something up at the cabin, where Grundstein spent his last days, but as you heard, it's a mess. I have yet to uncover anything of significance."

"What would happen if you did find something like that?"

"That would be good. I could publish a finding like that."

"Do you need my help with this, Sam?" Gretchen said. "Investigating these kinds of things is what I do."

"You've helped enough for now," I said. "Thank you. Off the record. You promised."

"I promise."


At the house, I went to my room and locked the door. In the closet, from under my dirty laundry, I removed my duffle bag, which contained the stolen library book, Grundstein's journal, and the Ronson lighter. I placed the items on my desk before me and added the pack of papers and the stone.

The inscription on the paperweight was in German: *UNTER DEM RUHESTEIN*. The inscription on the lighter was in English: *SET IT ALL ABLAZE*. The script was the same.

I shook the lighter, listening for fuel—no sound. Scratched the flint—no spark.

Next, I inspected the papers from the outside. It was a rectangle of folded paper about twice the size of business card. The paper had browned at the edges, and the folds were starting to wear. Other than the ribbon that held the packet closed in a delicate bow, there were no markings on the outside as far as I could tell.

My nerves began to fail me now that I was at another door and there was nothing left to do but open it. I shuddered before the idea of what I might find.

I got the whiskey out from the bottom drawer of my desk and took a swig directly from the bottle.

I closed my eyes and tugged at the ribbon. When the bow unlocked, the packet of papers flopped open on my desk lifelessly, like dead fish.

There were three letters—one big and two small, barely bigger than scraps. The letters read as follows:

> June 11, 1943
> My Dear Ingrid,
>
> I cannot write much for fear this won't reach you, but I'm hopeful. Do not despair. Spirits are low, but am fine. It's been one hell of a week. Send post to Ernest right away. Maybe he can help. All records are off here. It's as if I don't exist. Do your best in my absence. Send all my love to *mein kleines* Gertie.
> *Lieb Dich.* —LG

October 24, 1943

Ingrid,

Haven't heard from you in too long. Have even less confidence in any message from you reaching me as I do in mine reaching to you. Wake up every morning believing this will be the day I'll see you again. My hope wanes as each minute passes. By midnight (how could I possibly sleep), I'm at the edge of the abyss. Mind runs constantly, wishing to know how you are. How is *mein kleines* Gertie? How I love and miss you both so damn much. Some nights I can't bear to keep it in any longer and I shout to you *auf Deutsch*, but it only harms my state. Can't help it. Living creatures were not designed for cages. I hope to God this war will end swiftly. I cannot last much longer. I am <u>not</u> a Nazi. Never have been. Never will be. I don't even know a single member of our living family who is, but I have borne enough *für die Sünden der tausend*.

Oddly, I remain thankful in these dark days and nights, however unfortunate is the burden of my birthright, in this time and at this place, that father had the foresight to take the risk and move us here. Where would we have been had we stayed? Caught up in *die Welle der Gruppendenken*, no doubt. Even so, there is no Bill of Rights for me; I'm not considered an American in here. I am nobody.

I hope you're doing your best to support the homestead in my absence. Long to know what will be left upon the hour (if I ever see it) of my return.

*Lieb' euch beide für immer,*

—LG

December 16, 1944

    Losing all wits. Verge of complete surrender. Been gone so long. Gertie must be four by now. Won't even know me. Nothing they've done to me is greater than the knowledge that she would recognize me as a stranger. Desperation getting extreme. Considering options left. The end must be near—one way or another. —LG

I took another shot, and I sat for a long time, staring at the letters.

At last, I did my best, buzzed as I was at that point, to close the papers just as they were before. It would be best to return them to Tante's without her knowledge if possible, but that would have to wait until after my next class.

I hid my treasures and got ready for bed.

Lying there, wide awake, I thought of Alex. I hadn't heard from her since she dropped the Tom-bomb on me. As grueling as it was, I wasn't going to initiate the next communication. Eventually she would come seeking complete details of my exploits.

I checked my phone, and there it was, the long-awaited text.

ALEX: Can I see you tomorrow?

I didn't answer; it was nice being the hunted for a change.

I checked my Twitter feed instead:

@DetLionsLeak: Future looks bleak after unprecedented 0-16 season.
8:31 PM – 19 May 2009

@FluTrackerH1N1: 44-year-old Missouri man dies, swine flu confirmed, 7th in US.
8:27 PM – 19 May 2009

I was surprised to see a photo of Mr. Lawrence standing

outside of his company's building downtown Detroit waging his finger at a bouquet of microphones:

@MetroDetroitJournal: 'My company might not survive this,' top executive says in response to Obama Administration's new deal on fuel standards.
8:33 PM – 19 May 2009

# 16

I kept Grundstein's lighter and paperweight in my pocket. Whatever was going to come of this plot would inevitably involve them. The next day, when I was back in the classroom, I could feel their energy weighing in on me.

I was pleased to see everyone in their seats on time, because I was ready to go. Jumped right in: "To understand Leonhard Grundstein, we're going to start with his grandfather, Friedrich Grundstein. Because of Friedrich, Grundstein came from a wealthy Bavarian family. Friedrich was a savvy businessman who opened a small textile shop in the 1840s; by 1860, he'd diversified the family's financial interests by investing in other businesses—general stores, lumber yards, grocers, and my favorite, *Brezel und Brötchen*, a sandwich shop. He helped many families establish reliable businesses. As a result, in the 1860s, Friedrich's fortune grew as large as his popularity. Many referred to him as "*Der friedliche Herrscher*"—the peaceful ruler.

"Friedrich built the family a castle, literally a castle—on *Wörthsee*, a lake in the countryside. When Friedrich passed away in 1867, his son, Dieter—Grundstein's uncle—took over the estate, which began a period of steady decline for the entire family, from wealthy and prospering, to surviving, to uncertainty. Throughout the 1870s, Dieter sold much of the stock the family owned. By the 1880s, he nearly exhausted all of the money from the sales of Friedrich's investments as well. At the beginning of the 1890s, Dieter was on the verge of losing the castle.

"As a result of growing political strife and the family's insta-bility under Dieter's leadership, Paul—Grundstein's father—de-cided to collect what remained of his inheritance, sell his posses-sions, and buy tickets for him and his wife, Eleonora, to set sail for America in 1896. Four years later, Leonhard Grundstein was born, here, in Michigan. He was the first American-born mem-ber of his family, and he spent most of his life in an ambivalent space between his German heritage and his new American cul-tural identity, which had a lasting influence on his work, as you'll see. It would even get him into a bit of trouble that would impact his personal life and eventually, I will argue, his mental health, but we'll discuss that in more detail later in the term.

"At the turn of the century, when Leonhard Grundstein was born, an evolutionary century awaited him. The first half of the twentieth century would be as transformative and turbulent for Grundstein as it was for America and for the rest of the world—deeply changed, of course, by the World Wars.

"As a freshman in high school, Grundstein discovered not only the influential power of writing, but also his natural pro-clivity for it. For three years, he wrote fervent features for the school newspaper, including articles that challenged adminis-trative decisions regarding policies that were unpopular among his fellow students, like the food options in the cafeteria and the length of breaks between classes. In one article, Grundstein fa-mously described the school's dress code as 'anti-American.' Not two weeks later, the school's dress code was formally amended. Another tongue-in-cheek piece was entitled: TEN-MINUTE TAMMY. At that time, singing the National Anthem before sporting events was just becoming business as usual, the way we think of it today. At Oak Park High, the song was sung by a local woman named Tammy who bellowed, opera-style, all of the stanzas, including the ones you wouldn't even recognize. As the title illustrates, it took her ten minutes to finish. Grundstein suggested they cut the song in half and offered a chopped and

mashed-up version of the lyrics that didn't make any sense. Unfortunately, the youthful stunt was something FBI investigators
would later look upon without humor.

"Every summer, Grundstein's father, Paul, would take the
family on vacation to a cabin he built by hand on a small piece of
property at Walloon Lake in Petoskey, Michigan, where Grundstein and Ernest Hemingway became childhood friends. There,
the two future writers grew up as summer-time brothers. They
hunted and fished together, but they also fought with each other
as brothers do, sometimes bitterly. There were times when their
stand-offs would last for days. If the last week of the summer
went well, they'd be best of friends throughout the school year,
penning each other letters every week; if not, they'd go the whole
school year without corresponding at all.

"There was one fight in particular that was infamous around
Petoskey. The newspaper article on the incident led with the
headline: HEMINGWAY, GRUNDSTEIN BOYS BRAWL,
SPEND NIGHT IN SEPARATE CELLS. The article was poorly written and lacked significant details, but as the story goes,
Hemingway gave Grundstein a right hook to the jaw on the sidewalk in front of the general store. The two fought relentlessly until the sheriff came and took them both into custody. Both would
forever claim victory. It is unknown what caused that fight, but
rumors had it that they were fighting over a girl. Typical teenage
boys, right?"

"Right," Emma said, nodding. She'd been taking notes, writing down every word.

Rowan had stopped twirling Harmony's hair between his
fingers long ago and had put his head down instead. In the dead
air, his rhythmic breathing became unmistakable as that of a
sleeper.

Roy kicked his chair.

Rowan's head shot up. "I'm awake."

Roy snickered, while Harmony shook her head in embarrassment. Teagan and Leslie covered their mouths with their hands to hide their giggles.

Typing something into his laptop, Eli rapped, "We real cool. We diss school. We tweet late. We text-date."

"Yes. Thanks, Eli," I said. "We're almost done here. Just stay with me a bit longer. It was the coming of the war that reset their friendship. Although Grundstein lacked Hemingway's interest in war stories, he certainly shared the desire to demonstrate the kind of manliness that was romanticized by many of the young men of their generation. He also shared Hemingway's desire to see these major events firsthand with intent to write about them. We know, early in 1918, Hemingway set sail the Great War to serve as an ambulance driver on the Italian front. We know he suffered an injury over summer, was sent to Milan to recover through the fall, and was sent home in January of 1919. These events have been well chronicled, and Hemingway fictionalized the experience in his 1929 novel *A Farewell to Arms*. By contrast, we don't have similar accounts for Grundstein; we don't have records of his whereabouts from about 1917 to 1919. Although Grundstein never confirmed nor denied his involvement in the war, some choose to believe, since his alibi corresponds with U.S. involvement in the war, that he was a common soldier without a story to tell. Others say he served as a war correspondent under an alias for protection, although there's little-to-no evidence of journalism that could be traced to Grundstein. Some even suggest he was a traitor and fought for the Germans. The more farfetched claims see him as a spy, perhaps a double agent. Being fluent in both English and German, Grundstein's skills would've been useful, and there's some evidence suggesting Grundstein's long-forsaken uncle may have encouraged him to return to Germany to serve as a translator. As you'll see, some government officials may have had similar suspicions.

"But I think these are nothing more than conspiracy theories and legends with little merit and even less meaning. To borrow the words of the German novelist Erich Maria Remarque in the preface to what many consider the greatest Great War novel of all time, Hemingway and Grundstein were of, quote, 'a generation of men who, even though they may have escaped shells, were destroyed by the war,' unquote.

"I'll leave you with that parting thought. That should give you plenty of background for now."

Emma raised her hard. "I have a question, Professor Schurke. You mentioned Grundstein's German heritage got him into trouble. You haven't come back to that yet, what was that about?"

"We'll come back to that when we get to Grundstein's final novel, *The Son Down*. During World War II, as you know, many American citizens of various ancestries were treated as suspicious 'enemy aliens' on the home front under FDR's Executive Order 9066, Grundstein and his family included, and I have argued, as you'll see, that his last novel was a very thinly veiled critique of the American government, contributing of course to its commercial flop. Nobody wants to read a novel that criticizes your core beliefs, much less pay for it, but at times, that is the novelist's job."

A breeze smelling of fresh pollen blew through the open window and ruffled my lecture notes. Slapping my hands palms-down, I was able to prevent my papers from escaping. As I fumbled with the crumpled mess, Leslie sat up and asked, "Enemy aliens? What do you mean? What's Executive Order 9066?"

(In academia, it's easy to fall down a wormhole nobody cares about, but that tends to be the point at which one develops expertise on a niche subject.)

"Where to begin? Where to begin?" I said. "Well, are you familiar with the attack on Pearl Harbor? Tell me you've all heard of Pearl Harbor?"

(That also tends to be the point at which one becomes in danger of sounding like snooty prick.)

"On December 7, 1941, Japan attacked the American naval base at Pearl Harbor in Hawaii. The next day, President Franklin Delano Roosevelt gave the famous 'a date which will live in infamy speech' and declared war on Japan, thus representing the beginning of U.S. involvement in World War II. A mere seventy-four days later, on February 19, 1942, FDR signed Executive Order 9066, which enabled the Secretary of War to lawfully arrest and detain those considered 'enemy aliens.' Japanese and Japanese Americans, most notably, but also Italians, Italian Americans, Germans and, in Grundstein's case, German Americans, although proclamations made by FDR much earlier already allowed for their 'internment'."

(I was getting carried away.)

"For many years, scholars have been perplexed by Grundstein's activities during wartime. Speculations ran wild. Grundstein simply retreated from public life. Occasionally he was asked about his alibi for the missing periods, and he would say, 'If I felt there was air I needed to clear, I would.' When asked, 'What about your readers? What will you tell them?' He would say, 'If they enjoy reading my books, continue enjoying the books.'

"While researching my dissertation, I was able to uncovered, beyond a doubt, Grundstein's whereabouts during World War II, and it wasn't good. Not good for him, but less so for America. We'll cover all of this in a few weeks. I promise."

"You can't do that," Leslie said.

"What happened?" Teagan said.

"Don't leave us hanging like that," Roy added.

I checked my watch, still class period left. "Okay. Before February of 1942 was over, the national manhunt for 'enemy aliens' was already underway. Grundstein received a visit late at night at his home here in Oak Park, Michigan. Believe it or not, he didn't live where the National Historical Site is. That's a replica. His house was actually on the north end near where the golf course is today. His original home was one that was demolished for the construction of the expressway there. At any rate, four men came to his door—two police officers, one of whom Grundstein recognized as the Chief of Police, and two strange men in dark suits and sunglasses. You know what I'm talking about."

"G-men," Rowan said, nodding.

"Exactly. FBI. Hovers' men. These men asked my grandfather and his wife, Ingrid Grundstein, to sit at the kitchen table. The two police officers stood tall, legs spread, with hands on their guns, guarding both entryways to the kitchen, while the Grundsteins sat in silence—while my Aunt Gertrude, who was only a toddler, was sleeping in the next room—listening to the agents tearing up the house, going through everything—drawers, closets, cabinets, papers, files—overturning furniture—chairs, desks, mattresses. The men ransacked the whole house before they returned to the kitchen and grilled the Grundsteins with questions. They wanted to know about the incident that had led to Grundstein spending a night in jail as a young man after the foolish fistfight with Hemingway—a very dangerous thing to have on your record of course—and an absent paper trail for Grundstein's whereabouts during the Great War—a mystery still unsolved. They asked the Grundsteins about everything from what they bought at the store that morning to what their views of Hitler were. They threaten to arrest Grundstein for the so-called 'dissident articles' he wrote for his high school paper, but they only collected fingerprints from both Grundstein and his wife before evaporating into the night as mysteriously as they'd arrived.

"The Grundsteins were left to go about their daily business, living constantly under the fear of being arrested and taken away at any time. The horror stories were mounting in 'enemy alien' communities. Nearly a year later, in the spring of 1943, Grundstein was visited, again, in the night. Two officers dressed from head to toe in black riot gear ripped him out of bed. The figures put a burlap sack over his head and tied it painfully tight around his neck. They stripped him down to his underwear, and they dragged him out into the yard, beating him with bully clubs, all the while threatening to rape Ingrid if she alerted the neighbors. Ingrid watched helplessly as they threw Grundstein's limp body into the back of police cruiser with the numbers all covered up, and they drove away. The next day, Ingrid inquired at the station, but—big surprise—there was no report of an arrest. It wasn't until three weeks later that Ingrid finally heard of his whereabouts, when she received the first of what would become many letters from Grundstein as he sat in jail."

(With Tante's help, I was able to reconstruct the timeline of events using the letters and entries from Ingrid's diary.)

"Grundstein was taken to a jail in downtown Detroit and held, off the record, for more than two years. Since his name was never registered, Ingrid was unable to visit him, nor did he receive her letters. Ingrid expressed helplessness. Although Grundstein had apparently pressed for her to seek help from the highest government officials, she became deeply paranoid as news of 'enemy alien' arrests became more frequent. Grundstein begged her repeatedly to contact his old, celebrity friend, Ernest Hemingway. Ingrid sent countless letters to Hemingway, asking for his help, but there is no evidence to suggest Hemingway ever received the letters, something that only bolstered existing resentment between the two literary figures. Some more speculative scholars suspect Ingrid's letters were routinely intercepted if you tend to subscribe to conspiracy theories. In the fall of 1945, Grundstein was unceremoniously released and dropped off at his home as if at random.

"Can you imagine it? Having your husband beaten in front of your eyes and hauled away in the middle of the night? Not knowing where he was taken or by whom. Even worse, taken by people who were supposed to serve and protect. Held without recognition for two years. How despairing that would be. How powerless you would feel."

"I can," Leslie said somberly. "My people can. My people thought, by participating in the war, they'd feel more American.

And they did, during the war. But the feeling was only lent to them, and it would be taken away again."

"Washed in a river of make-believe," Eli added.

"Yes, and these groups had a hell of a time trying to re-establish their lives again after the war," I said. "That's why my reading of *The Son Down* is that of a scathing indictment of the American government, not as scholar's previously—and comfortably I might add—believed to be a criticism of the Third Reich."

The clock now showed ten minutes past the end of the class period. My voice was feeling hoarse, and my legs were sore from standing. But those rare moments when you had the students hooked on the line were what made you want to teach in the first place.

"Our assignment," Emma said, "is still to read the first half of *The Timepiece* for Monday? Do you want us to write up our thoughts or anything?"

Roy groaned.

"Yes," I said. "Same, same. But no writing necessary. Just do the reading. Have a good weekend."

I said to Emma, "Try not to read ahead. You'll confuse us all."

As they left, I spotted Daniels out in the hallway, looking over his glasses at me with a furrowed brow. He pointed two fingers at his eyes and then at me.

I busied myself by checking my Twitter feed:

@FluTrackerH1N1: Arizona patient dies, swine flu confirmed, 8th in US.
11:51 AM – 20 May 2009

@MetroDetroitJournal: GM to seek additional $4 billion in loans.
11:50 AM – 20 May 2009

# 17

After class, I stopped by the bookstore. I needed an excuse to go to Tante's again so I thought I'd bring her a new book. Though the lighter lacked fuel, I felt dangerous walking into a building full of kindling that was currently serving as rectangular sheets of human knowledge and thought.

First, I spent an hour sipping on a cappuccino from a house mug while I reread the beginning of Grundstein's *The Timepiece* for the tenth time in three weeks. At last, I engaged a saleswoman whose name, Ina, hung at the end of the lanyard around her neck. She said, "What kind of books does your aunt like?"

"Historical books, maybe. I don't really know."

"What kind of historical books? Historical fiction?" Ina wasn't even looking at me as she organized a shelf. "Historical nonfiction? Historical suspense? Historical thriller? Historical romance?"

"Historical romance, I guess," I said. "But nothing smutty."

"Historical romance, no smut." She walked away and gave me no indication whether or not to follow her. Soon, she returned with a hardcover book with a faded-yellow image on the front of a man and a woman hidden behind umbrellas standing on a pier looking out to a foggy bay. "*Hotel on the Corner of Bitter and Sweet*," she said. "I recommend this book."

"What's it about?" I said, pretending to read the description on the back while I looked for the price.

"A Chinese boy and a Japanese girl fall in love. Historical romance. No smut. It's what you want."

At the checkout, I was surprised to see Teagan, one of my students, behind the counter. I barely recognized her void of her black drab, now wearing a green polo shirt and khaki pants.

"Professor Schurke," she greeted me before—*thank God*—I had a chance to make a fool of myself, having seen her in my classroom not two hours prior. "I enjoyed your lecture today."

"It'll get better," I said. "I promise."

"This is so me, right?" She pointed to a bulge below her belt-line. "I look like a grandma in khaki."

"Do you get a good deal on books at least?" I asked.

"The discount is okay."

I set the book on the counter.

"Aha," she said. "Turns out the great professor's a sucker for pop romance."

"Historical romance."

Teagan smiled. "Somehow, I knew it."

"It's a gift for my aunt."

"Yeah, okay," she said, placing the book in a bag. "I bet you want a giftwrap then, too, eh?" She winked.

As I walked away, I heard her say into her headset, "Who sold this month's promotion to Elbow Patches? Ina? Nice. You only need three more to hit your goal for this shift."

@News.USA: $4 billion added to GM loan.
1:13 PM – 20 May 2009

@FluTrackerH1N1: 22-year-old Utah man dies, swine flu confirmed, 9th in US.
1:12 PM – 20 May 2009

Tante didn't like me parking in her driveway, and there were never enough spots on her street. I had to park Karmann around the corner and walk.

The lights were on at the house, but Tante didn't answer the doorbell. Unusual. Tante never left an unused light on. I checked the doorknob. Unlocked. Strange.

I cracked the door open.

"Tante? *Gutten Nachmittag*. Tante? It's me, Sam."

No response.

Competing scenarios illuminated my imagination: one where Tante was at some stage in the middle of completing a toilet, no point in which would be ideal to receive a visitor; and one where she was no longer in the middle of *anything*. Both scenarios caused me to proceed with extreme caution.

I stepped into the entryway. The air conditioning was humming. *Tante would never leave her house with it running if she could help it.*

"Tante? It's Sam."

No movement. No sound.

I crossed into the dining room. "Tante?"

The picture of Hemingway and Grundstein on the wall was perfectly centered in the frame, and the frame was level and flush against the wall.

I turned and listened. "Tante? *Gutten Nachmittag.* Tante?"

I slipped the frame off of its hook, cautious this time not to cut myself on the prongs—my thumb was still smarting from that mistake last time. I removed the back, replaced the letters, and returned it to the wall.

The picture was off somehow. I took up the frame again and shook it, trying to get the picture centered properly. Still wasn't right. The frame, too, looked different now, out of balance. Small adjustment. Still wasn't right.

A noise came from upstairs—a creek? A moan?

"*Tante, ist das dich? It's Sam.*"

Suddenly a new scenario emerged in my imagination: one

where Tante was in the middle, in the *process*, of becoming no more.

"Tante? Are you there?" I ascended the stairway at a moderate pace—a compromise between urgency and fear. "Tante? Is everything okay?"

At the top, the air felt unstirred. Tante's bedroom door was closed. No light was slipping through the crack at the floor. No sound.

I knocked.

No response.

"Tante?" I opened the door a sliver, only enough to see her bed was made and—*thank God*—unoccupied. *Where could she be?*

Just then, I got a text message from my mother.

MOM: Sammy, Gertrude and I are going to a late lunch by your campus. Care to join us?

ME: What are you two doing?

As soon as I pushed to send, I realized my mistake.

ME: Sorry, I can't. I'm not on campus right now.

MOM: We had to see the lawyer. Sorry we missed you. Call me later.

ME: Call me when you're done at the restaurant. Might be over by you by then.

MOM: Okay. :) Love you!

The silence had changed from eerie to empty, and it occurred to me that I'd never been in Tante's bedroom before. I'd never ventured, nor had I been invited, upstairs.

Daniels' voice: *Keep looking. Keep looking. Keep looking.*

It was a small bed—even for someone who had spent their entire life sharing their sleep with nobody. The blue quilted comforter looked handmade. I checked under the bed. Nothing. Not a single thing. Not even visible evidence of dust.

At the foot of the bed was an antique vanity. On it was only a small jewelry box containing a couple pairs of earrings and a necklace. Nothing of interest.

I avoided the dresser. I didn't need to open even one drawer too many.

Tante had a small closet. When I opened the door, I received a face full of Tante's signature perfume, which smelled like someone had spilled nutmeg all over clean linen; it made me gag. Her familiar, limited wardrobe hung all-too neatly, and there was one pair of black dress shoes on the floor. I closed the closet and scanned the room one more time looking, this time, for any evidence of my intrusion, and I left.

Tante had a guest room that was even more spare than her bedroom: a bed, an empty dresser, and an empty closet.

Looking behind the curtain of Tante's life made me feel inexplicably sad.

In the hallway, there was a linen closet. Nothing unusual. Just towels, various medicines, and a small stack of paper products.

*How did I get this far off track? What could I possibly find in Tante's linen closet?*

Other than the bedrooms, the second story boasted the house's only full bathroom.

I turned to leave, but something caught my attention. There was something in the magazine rack mounted on the wall next to the toilet. What stood out to me wasn't what appeared to be a recent issue of *Time*—Michelle Obama's face was on the cover with the caption: THE MEANING OF MICHELLE. It wasn't that Tante apparently took the time to read while she took care of her business that surprised me, either. It was the yellowish gold-colored paper behind the magazine. I recognized it as the same as the clipping that Tante had reluctantly offered me, oddly, after all these years.

I approached the rack as if it might contain infectious disease.

I carefully removed the old, rolled-up newspaper from its hiding place and, sure enough, there was an article missing, and the size of the cutout appeared to be a match for the article on

Dieter.

I checked my phone—no messages.

I took the paper out to the landing and spread it out flat. The front-page headline: THE WAR IS OVER. I scrutinized every inch of that delicate page, and the next, and the next.

*Why would Tante rather cut out the article and ruin this artifact than to give it to me whole?*

I didn't make sense. I looked for markings, for pages with excess wear. Nothing.

Disappointed, I rolled up the paper as I'd found it and brought it back to the rack, but for some reason, the paper refused to return to its hiding place behind the issue of *Time*. Something was blocking it.

(My heart still skips a beat when I think of that moment even now.)

As soon as my hand—down in the rack, behind the magazine, under the newspaper—felt the texture of the cover, I knew that it was another journal of Grundstein's. I knew, before I even saw it with my own eyes, that it was the same kind—small, black, edges gray with wear—as the one I found at the cabin.

I knew, also, as I sat there, on my knees, on the floor, looking at that journal dangling by my pinched fingers, if I opened that book, my life would take a turn. I'd found something. Something of great import to Grundstein. Something that would endanger my dissertation. Something that would make me look for more somethings. Inevitably.

I returned the newspaper and placed the journal on top of Tante's closed toilet and marveled at it for what seemed like an eternity.

An interruption: my cellphone rang.

It was a struggle to get it out of my pocket from that position.

"Mother?" I answered without looking at the caller ID.

"Schurke, we've been over this." It was Johnny. "I'm not your mother."

"Sorry," I said, speaking full-voice for the first time and hearing it ping-pong back and forth off of the bathroom tiles. "I was expecting a call."

"Where are you, Schurke? You sound like you're in a cell. Did they finally move your office to the basement?"

"Can I call you back in a few?"

"Fine," Johnny said. "Call me when you get out?"

I hung up and checked my inbox. Nothing. I checked the timestamp from my mother's last text; it'd been less than fifteen minutes. There was still time.

I picked up the journal and took a seat in its place—there, on Tante's throne—and I opened it, conscious to the core of my being of the importance of committing everything my senses could capture to memory. The cover both rough and brittle. The smell of an old library. The creek and moan of the aged spine, warning caution.

As I set my eyes upon the first entry, one single thought flared in my mind: *If Daniels gets his hands on this, Grundstein's legacy would be forever changed.*

The polarizing pulls between discovery and devastation stretched my feeble human brain to capacity, and whatever logic and reasoning it was once capable of was strained.

In that state of mind, I began to read.

# Journal of
# Leonhard Grundstein

May 21-28, 1961

May 21, 1961

I'm in despair. In fifteen more years, nothing has changed. The papers are full of suppression. The governor has officially declared martial law in Alabama.

I despair, too, that I am of no use to any cause any longer.

Ingrid wants me to start writing again. She's parked me at the table in front of another damned notebook, and she demands more words. Any words. She doesn't care how many or about what.

"This world has been cursed enough by my words," I say to her, half in jest. Only half.

She's busy repairing the old floorboards in the kitchen. She's having a hard time, but refuses to call a contractor.

She says I better have a full page written before she quits for the day. She's always been a bully.

I showed her what I've written here, and she smacked me over the head with the paper.

That's Ingie for you.

That's enough for today in my view.

. . .

MAY 22, 1961

In the night, I was visited by the Ghost of Christmas Past. Now, there is something I'm compelled to get down in writing. It has never been uttered, but as I near the end, it's time. The pen in my hand wants to argue with me even as I write.

The Grundsteins ~~come from a line of~~ are murderers.

Began, as far as I know, with Dieter. When I was in Germany, a particularly trying night sparked a conversation. Came home late. Dieter and I shared a beer in the study. Dieter was a man with little time left. As best as my memory allows, he said, "In the course of building and maintaining an empire, bad things can happen. There's dirty work to be done. A farm can't survive without killing a pig. Do you know what I mean?"

I said I did, but I would better in time.

Dieter said, "Before you were born, the family had some financial trouble. Your father always liked to blame me for it. I didn't have a knack for business the way my father did, the way your father did. I was doing my best, but as the eldest, it was my responsibility to run the family. When Wilhelm took over, many people looked to him to lead us to a new glory. Pompous, arrogant—sure—and perhaps unprepared for his position, but assertive. We liked that. And, at that time, I needed him to lead us, for the sake of our family and our estate. Of course, there was dissent—"

Ingrid is yelling at me now. It's nearly noon, and lunch is ready. My God, I used to be able to write a brilliant chapter in a single morning. At a half-day's struggle, I've barely cobbled together a worthwhile paragraph.

To finish: Dieter, the murderer, was telling me about dissenters. *Staatsfeinde.* He was referring to the Social Democratic Party. "The goddamn Marxists," Dieter said. "They were trying to ruin the empire with frivolous ideals. Something had to be done. One of Wilhelm's top men came to see me about dealing with the problem." I don't remember exactly how I reacted to what

Dieter was suggesting.

I remember saying, "How many have there been?" And Dieter the Murderer said to me, "Not nearly enough."

That's enough for today.


May 23, 1961

I dreamt about Dieter last night, and my memory seems to have kicked in. I remember he didn't care to remember them, but he said, "I was never able to shake the memory of my first—a short, little, bald man with a monocle. Snotty little bastard. Sad and lonely. Broke into his house and waited for him to come home. Made the mistake of talking too much. I knew of the plots he was suspected to be involved in, but I needed to hear it from him. The fat little man had nothing to lose. Threatening his life did nothing. He was so willing to die for his worthless cause. I told him so, and he took the opportunity to kick me in the shin. Didn't mean to kill him. Just threaten him. But I panicked. Chased him into the kitchen and took a swing at him with the butt of my rifle. Pinned his head between the gun and the bottom edge of a cupboard. He was down then, but not out. Took him too long to die. From then on I didn't talk. Just did the business. I was hired to take care of the pigs so the farm could survive. And I took care of pigs."

At that time, I took an opportunity to abandon Dieter and the War for good.

Dieter died on November 12, 1918. He lived only long enough to see the German Empire crumble. How's that for worthless?

Enough.


May 24, 1961

All night I dreamed of the War. The "Great War," as they

say. I suspect someone will find me out eventually, some report-
er, or journalist, or biographer—*die Blutegel*—will document my
participation. So let me begin my version—

I was disappointed as soon as I arrived in *Deutschland* and
discovered the assignment Onkel Dieter had promised me wasn't
going to be "an experience of a lifetime."

Father had warned me.

I was set up in a suite on the family estate and given the task
to translate British communications into *Deutsch* and told, if I
found anything "interesting" about British activities, to report it
to Dieter right away. What I was given to translate was nothing
of value—national newspapers, pop-culture magazines, personal letters.

I became disillusioned. I was far from the action. The British
and French fronts were far enough west of me that they may
as well have been a world away. While our army was making
headway, it seemed, against the Russians in the northeast, in the
southwest, there was little-to-no action of consequence.

The best outcome of the whole mess was that I met Al Flechtheim. Gravitated toward Flechtheim because he knew about art
as the finest of human endeavors, and we discussed starting a
cultural journal if the War ever ended. Was able to join him after
the War to help. Helped launch my career.

On summer nights in the tavern, belligerent, questions arose
about manhood. Flechtheim, who was older than me by twen-
ty-two years, told me I would never be a man because I would
never see real men in a real war until "I saw a man die." *Arschloch.*
Told me my writing would be impotent after the War. Nobody
would care about a man who had no war experience. One night
I got so tired of it, I knocked Flechtheim out cold with a right
hook and left the tavern in a rage.

History will forever put me on the wrong side, but that is neither here nor there: everybody was on the wrong side of the War.
*Eine tolle Debakel.* How can anybody justify anything they did for

any cause? It wasn't a holy war. Nobody liberated, or conquered, or accomplished anything.

And I was denied the chance to be on the right side of the second war. *Keine Chance auf Erlösung.*

I've digressed here. It's what I've done ever since returning from *Das Große Debakel.* I've placed blame elsewhere, and I can't any longer. I'll get it down right. Tomorrow, I'll focus.


MAY 25, 1961

I feel pressure, like my chest is sinking to the bottom of the ocean. Perhaps that's where I belong.

It was Sunday, the tenth of November, 1918. God forsake me if it wasn't exactly one day before the Armistice was signed. How was I to know?

I waited anxiously, every day, to find out if the War was going to be over, especially after I heard Hem was done and would be going home. Seemed like the wait was never going to end. There was talk of a revolution, too, to make matters more complicated. There was talk of a new republic.

Flechtheim had me going crazy thinking of *Das Große Deba-kel* ending without experiencing the War at all. I didn't want to return to all the stories without a story of my own. Young, of course. Hard headed, sure. But a fool.

I'd been a lieutenant since I arrived—or so I was told. Dieter wore a uniform like mine, but it was unranked, unmarked. His role was unknown to me at the time, but I knew he had power. And resources.

I found out later I was never there. I'd never been there as far as anyone knew. That was Dieter's doing. He was protecting me against myself. I'll be forever grateful for that.

I received burlap sack after sack of intercepted mail. It was all personal mail. Letters from family members to troops. Looked for patterns and codes. Never found anything.

Dieter gave me encouragement. Said all efforts equally helped the cause. Told me every day how important it was to find out there was nothing of relevance in those mail sacks. That way we knew we weren't missing something. So I kept on translating.

Ingrid is calling me again. My pen is as slow as my wits these days.

Enough.


MAY 26, 1961

I didn't mind, mostly. It was fascinating to see inside these relationships. The material would serve me well as a writer, better than anything anyone else brought home from the War.

Here it is again. My chest is sinking. Need to hurry.

On that Sunday evening, I needed to get out. I left on foot at dusk with my journal in hand, without a plan. Thought I might find a place to write down some ideas. If the War was going to end, it would be time to get back to writing seriously.

I went to the pub. The place was packed with men having drinks. It was tense. Some were sour over how the war was ending. Others couldn't care less anymore, were excited about surviving and returning to loved ones regardless. There, I met a second lieutenant, Robert, who was the latter type. He was headed home to his wife, who had a baby during the War—a boy he had yet to meet.

For years, I thought about looking up that boy, but the only information I had was his father's first name, Robert, his rank, and the date of his death.

Robert and I got to drinking. *Schnapps für Schnapps.* And to talking. Somehow our dissatisfactions came out—how I only saw the war through translated mail and how he was mostly a glorified errand boy. He drove packages and messages and weapons and bandages and such from here to there, after whatever request his superior had in mind at the time. None of it was worth missing his family and his boy for, he said.

Don't know how the thought came to me. Inclined to blame the schnapps, but I'm done with blaming. The thought came to me, somehow. I told Robert I had one final order to carry out, an important one. Told him I needed to deliver a top-secret intercepted message to the commanding officer at the front line to the south. Showed him my journal as if the message was inside.

Once I got going, my imagination ran away on me. There, I go again. No, I let my imagination run away.

Poor Robert listened with earnest while I told him I went to the pub that night to find a ride, to find a loyal, experienced driver to take me to the front.

Could tell Robert was getting worked up, and I pounced. Poured myself another shot, threw it back. Poured him another shot. Said, "I'm drinking to fortify my courage to ask one of these poor saps to take one last risk."

Robert cursed and slammed his fist down on the bar. He announced he'd do anything to leave the *Gott verdammt* War having contributed something of value. I pounded Robert on the back and told him he was the last hero left.

Ingrid is on my case, again. But, she'll have to wait. This has got to get down. Will work through lunch if need be.

*Zu betrunken.* Never should've made it to the truck. Robert got to cursing, and it propelled him forward. Walking ahead of me, he was tacking from side-to-side at 45-degree angles, on a crash course of cursing. I acted like a bumper on each side, redirecting him toward the truck. He cursed at me every time I bumped him.

Never should've gotten behind that wheel.

Never should've put him there.

At the time, I didn't care; I wanted to see that War or die. *Gott verdammt.* Not young enough or stupid enough not to know better.

We drove out of town for what seemed like forever. Vision

blurry. All I could see was blackness and winding road. Robert was a like bat; he sensed his way through the darkness without sight.

He was getting serious. Kept saying, "Look alive. We're getting close."

I was losing my will. Eyelids were heavy. Blacked out a couple of times.

Next I knew, Robert said, "Quiet."

I shot awake.

"A blockade straight ahead."

There was a truck parked halfway out into the road, blocking our way. Robert stopped the vehicle a football field short. Waited and listened.

Robert had a Bergmann-Bayard pistol hanging on the right side of his belt. I took it from him and said, "I'll take a look."

Robert said, "No. Stay in the truck. I haven't survived this long by getting off mission. I'll drive up as if we're going to stop, then we blow by. Keep your head low. We don't stop until we know we're safe."

I didn't listen. Got out of the truck.

In my sleep, I still hear his voice calling out to me to stop and get back.

Approached the blockade with the pistol in my right hand and the journal in my left. Two figures emerged. Couldn't identify them or their allegiance. The lights from their truck were too bright. All I could see were shadows.

Called out to them, "I have an important message to deliver. We need to get through."

One of the figures yelled back, "Turn around and go back."

The alcohol roared through my veins. I shouted, "I have an important message to deliver. We need to get through."

The second figure called back, "Turn around and go back."

I raised the pistol. "I have an important message to deliver."

The first froze; the second appeared to reach for a weapon.

I fired a shot into the air above. Shouted, "I need to get through." I waived to Robert. "Let's go."

Both figures now: "Stop! Turn around!"

I threw my journal into the window of the truck as it came upon me, jumped on the side railing, and hung on. "Don't stop, Robert," I commanded.

The truck lurched forward as another shot was fired, not by me.

Robert screamed.

I shot back. "Around to the left, Robert!"

The truck swerved off of the road. I took to two more shots. Screams. Gun shots seemed to come from every direction.

I shot back again before I was flung from the trunk into the air. The truck careened hard to the left, away from the road, toward the trees. Then, everything stopped.

When I came to, lying on my back in the brush, all I could hear was ringing and crickets.

Those sounds, too, haunt my sleep to this day.

I rose and wobbled, woozy. There was blood on my hand. Couldn't tell where it was coming from. My whole body was numb.

Behind me, I could see the tailgate of Robert's truck wedged in between trees.

On unsteady feet, I approached the light on the road. "Don't shoot. I'm unarmed."

I reached the road. "Don't shoot. I'm unarmed."

Braced myself on the truck as I moved to the side where I'd seen the figures. I could hear the engine running and the lights buzzing, and I could feel their warmth from going all night. At last, as I stepped out of the beam, I saw, in the middle of the road, two bodies—one on top of the other—forming one large lump.

Dead. I knew it was so.

The top man was face down with his arms around the bottom man's chest. Looked like a couple lying in bed together, asleep. I rolled the top man over with my foot. It was then that I recognized the uniforms. Münich Police.

My head cleared, and I recognized the road. Robert and I hadn't made it more than five miles from the pub. I was standing in the center of the road not two miles south of my uncle's castle. On a clear day, I would've been able to see it to the north from where I stood.

I hurried to Robert's truck. Front end was mangled up against a tree. Opened the driver-side door, and Robert's body spilled out. There was a bullet hole one inch above his right ear. Blood dripped from the left side of his head onto my boot.

Then, I ran.

I ran to the passenger side, collected my journal. Ran deep into the woods, followed the road from a distance, seeing only the gray moonlight through the gaps in the trees. Ran, non-stop, to the castle.

Entered my quarters through the back. Stripped naked. Placed each article of my clothing into burlap sack and buried the sack in the back of my wardrobe.

I washed up and discover the blood had come from a puncture wound on my right hand. The hammer of Robert's pistol must have caught my palm as I tumbled to the ground. Cleaned my wound as best I could; cauterized it with my Ronson—the most physical pain I have ever endured. Deserved every bit of it and more.

The smell of my burning flesh still stings my nostrils.

Didn't sleep that night. Haven't truly slept a night in my life since. Clutched my wounded hand, awake in bed, wondering what was going to happen to me—*ein Mörder*—the next morning.

Now that it's down, maybe I'll sleep. I'm so very tired.

• • •

MAY 27, 1961

Facts: Forty-two years ago, the Treaty of Versailles was signed. Forty-seven years ago, someone put an end to a privileged Austrian prick, instigating *Das Große Debakel* and ruining a whole generation of lives.

For me, there I was: a murderer.

The next day, November 11, 1918, the Armistice took effect, and it was a confusing time. Nobody ever came for me. The only world anybody had known for the last five years was gone, transformed in the night. By the time the crime scene was discovered—I can only assume—it was after the famous eleventh hour of the eleventh day of the eleventh month. In three days, power changed hands, and the new republic agreed to make peace. Nobody knew what exactly that all meant, but everybody was ready to leave the mess—including the deaths of the officers and Robert—to history.

Dieter and I set all traces of my involvement there—clothes, papers, receipts, evidence—ablaze.

As we watched it all burn, Dieter said to me, as somber as a confession, "Nobody but me knows exactly where you've been and what you've been doing. I took great caution. Travel back to America as an American. Don't talk about the War. Keep your head down until you get home. It'll be best to let people assume you fought for the other side. If you have to, act like it's too soon to discuss." He hugged me in a rare display of affection, kissed me on the crown of my head like a man saying his last words, and added, "Give my best regards to the rest of us. Tell your father I'm sorry for everything."

Dieter sent me to find the first train to Paris with nothing but the civilian clothes on my back and a small rucksack for my blood-spattered journal and my American passport. I parted while the flames were still roaring.

He never asked about the blood on the boots or the hole in my hand.

In France, I boarded a ship packed with American men my age. There were many men drinking heavily, distraught as hell; I fit right in. All that was chasing me was my secrets. *Ich werde auf wiedersehen, um alles schnell zu sagen.*

Enough.


MAY 28, 1961

Dieter was dead before I reached home. There was a letter waiting for me.

It was a tattered time. I hid out for the winter in my parent's basement. People didn't ask questions. They made statements: "Thank you for your service" and "You're a hero, son."

As instructed, I didn't say anything.

They'd give me a somber nod, but they knew nothing. They weren't in on it.

I was glad most people let me alone. Father refused to speak to me, but mother had seen what happened to her friends when their sons didn't return. She was glad to have me in the house.

I wrote most of the time. The material wasn't any good yet, but it helped me get through. Set my mind to something.

In the spring of 1919, I received a letter from Hem. The part of the letter I remember: "Have to walk with a cane, but could still beat you in a boxing match." Hem, how did it all go to hell? This wasn't supposed to be us. Not men like us.

Hem was going up to Windemere in Petoskey for the summer, "like ol' times." Invited me to join him if I "survived in any condition to be up for it." A Godsend. I would be there to greet him when he arrived.

Had we only known that was going to be the best time of our lives, we would've tried harder to enjoy it, fought harder to make it last, and worried less about everything that followed.

*Gott verdammt Rücksicht. Wertlos.*

I showed Ingrid the journal, how I've filled it.

I said, "Now it's finished."
She said, "There's three lines left."
I said, "There, now it's finished."

# 18

Grundstein only wrote on the right-hand pages with shaky, swirl-
ing cursive that inclined from the left to the right, but I noticed,
on the inside of the back cover in small, delicate numbers, in
fresh ink: 1 of 3?

It was in Tante's hand. Odd. The last date on this journal
aligned with the beginning date of the journal I found at the
cabin, but I didn't remember seeing a similar marking.

*Perhaps Tante didn't know about the other journal. But what would
make her believe there were three?*

My cellphone rang, destroying the silence.

I answered the call.

MOM: "Sammy? I'm on my way to drop Tante off. She's
feeling tired. Do you want me to meet you?"

ME: "You caught me at a bad time. I'm in the bathroom. I'll
call you back."

I jammed the journal back in the magazine rack. A shiver
scraped my spine as the newspaper crinkled. *Too fast. Slow down.* I
pulled the newspaper out, reset the journal, and covered it back
up. Everything looked normal, as far as I could tell.

I was out the front door when I remembered the book, *Hotel
on the Corner of Bitter and Sweet*. I ran through the living room to
the dining room. *Oh, thank God.* I swiped it from the table and
made my way back to the front door in time to see Mom pulling

her car into the driveway.

"Go to the side door," I said, trying to will my mother to pull the car around to the side of the house.

The car stopped at the walk to the front door long enough for me to start running through the story: *I saw this book. I thought of you. I stopped by to drop it off as a thank you for letting me use the cabin...*

The car moved forward, out of sight.

I stepped out onto the landing, hoping I could make my escape before Mom had a chance to help Tante out of the car. I locked the door from the inside.

*Tante probably forgot to lock it and finding it unlocked might raise more questions.*

I heard my mother's car door open and tried to shut the front door at the same moment she shut hers. I ducked behind the bushes and snuck away through the neighbor's yard.

Texted Mom: Sorry. Can't meet now. Will call back later.

At a safe distance from Tante's, with an idea forming in my mind, I pulled Karmann into a random driveway and took to Twitter:

@ProfSchurke: @askoakparkmi @GretchBreporting @AshleyDanielsBand Thanks!
2:16 PM – 20 May 2009

@AshleyDanielsBand: @ProfSchurke @GretchBreporting If Denny can't help, bring it over to the house. I'll see what I can do.
2:16 PM – 20 May 2009

@ProfSchurke: @GretchBreporting Want to see if it works.
2:15 PM – 20 May 2009

@GretchBreporting: @ProfSchurke Planning to get that antique lighter going?

2:15 PM – 20 May 2009

@askoakparkmi: @ProfSchurke Denny's Hardware on Coolidge & 11 Mile. Has everything. Will set you up.
2:14 PM – 20 May 2009

@ProfSchurke: Where would I go to get a Ronson #lighter repaired? @askoakparkmi
2:13 PM – 20 May 2009

I pocketed my phone and drove to Denny's Hardware.

At Denny's, I asked an associate at the front counter, a teenager with a mop for hair, if I could see Denny. I said it was suggested to me that Denny could fix my lighter. The boy laughed and said, "Emma, this customer says he's here to see Denny."

A voice came from somewhere within the maze of aisles: "Denny died like fifty years ago."

*We know what no other animal knows.*

"This must've been a joke," I said and hurried toward the door.

"Professor Schurke?"

*Dolt!*

I turned and faced her. "Hi, Emma."

"Was this the joke?" she said. "Did you know I work here?" She was wearing a construction-style vest that was highlighter yellow.

"No, I didn't."

The teenager snorted and walked away.

"Were you about to leave?" she said. "Don't you have a lighter that needs attention?"

"No. Well, yes, but—"

"Let me see it."

Emma extended a slender, tanned hand to me. Her fingernails were painted like lemon drops. "Moloch!" Emma exclaimed, snatching the lighter from me. "This is the oldest Ron-son I've ever seen."

"Good eye," I said. "You're familiar with this?"

"This is an early model. This is a collector's item." She looked at me. "I used to date a collector. Don't ask. I don't need to relive the details." She read the inscription. " 'Set it all ablaze.' That's odd. Where did you get this?"

"It was my grandfather's." I couldn't think of a lie, and the truth seemed sufficiently benign.

Emma's head snapped up, her beautiful eyes beaming. "This lighter, the one in my hands, belonged to *the* Leonhard Grund-stein." She placed it back in my hand. "That's probably worth thousands."

"Maybe," I said. "I'm curious as to whether or not it still works."

"They don't make lighters that tough anymore. A little fluid, it probably works fine. Let's see what we have."

Emma led me into the maze. "Fluid's in the back by the small motor oil." She picked out a small can with a cone-shaped spout. "This should do."

Her soft skin comforted my shaking hands as she helped me fill the lighter.

"Alright, here goes," I said. I clicked the lever. Nothing.

"Didn't see a spark," Emma said. "Harder."

At the second strike, a pillar of fire shot up.

"A flip," Emma said, "and it's lit." She smiled.

I bought the can.

@News.USA: Concern over H1N1 outbreaks in schools increas-es as unusually high number of cases are reported.
3:27 PM – 20 May 2009

@FluTrackerH1N1: 40 countries infected; 10,243 cases report-ed; 80 deaths confirmed.
3:25 PM – 20 May 2009

# 19

Breakfast at the diner was a tradition for the Circle; we convened on the fourth Saturday of every month. By the time I arrived on that occasion, Johnny, Ashley, and Gretchen were already there. They were standing near the cashier's counter talking with Montgomery Grudge. Johnny was saying something in his serious way, thrusting his head in the direction of his speech, eyebrows tenting upward to a point.

I liked seeing Johnny's serious head jabbing in Grudge's direction.

The conversation broke as a server at the counter held up a to-go bag and called, "Take out for Monte." Grudge left the circle, grabbed the bag, and headed for the door, directly at me. Grudge seemed surprised to see me.

I smiled at the sight of him. He was wearing a bow tie and a sweater vest, and his hair was all combed to one side, not a single follicle out of place.

"Looking dapper today, Grudge," I said.

"Piss off, Schurke," he said with a melody, as if he'd said, *Happy birthday*. Without breaking stride, he stepped around me and left.

I joined Johnny, Ashley, and Gretchen. "What did Grudge want?" I asked.

"Breakfast," Johnny said, putting his arm around me and

ruffling my hair.

"Is Tom coming?" I asked.

"Late, as usual," Gretchen said.

We sat down at a round table and turned over the mugs, including a fifth mug for Tom. The waitress came by and filled them.

Nobody turned over a mug for Alex. *I can turn off. Relax.*

Tom arrived while we fixed our caffeine with cream and sugar.

"Schurke," Johnny said, "Alex told me she found you, as she put it, in a 'state of disarray' up at the cabin? What, pray tell, does that mean?"

"The place was in 'a state of disarray' before I got there." I looked to Gretchen. "It needs TLC, but I was busy getting ready for class. Even my hygiene got away from me." With my mug, I gestured to the full beard taking shape on my face.

"It's getting away from you all right," Tom said.

The waitress returned and took our orders. When she left, Johnny changed his mood. "Gang," he said, "I'm glad everyone came today. I have something I need to share with you." It was strange for Johnny to take a cadence of defeat. He suddenly looked pale and weak—cheeks sunken with a faint green hue.

"Karla's sick," Johnny said. "Really sick. She's in the ICU now. That's all I know."

Ashley nodded. I'm sure she already knew about this. Gretchen, too, probably. Tom and I offered our condolences. Then, we sat in a somber silence, sipping on our coffees.

Collectively, we always assumed Johnny and Karla would end up together forever, once Johnny sowed his oats, but Johnny always seemed to have too many oats to sow.

The atmosphere of the moment triggered a truckload of similar memories—of family and death—in a single instant.

(Leonhard Grundstein's death was mysterious, abrupt—even if you account for a sharp decline in mental health. For a brief period when I was conducting my initial research, Daniels pressed me to uncover something more about it, but nothing had turned up, yet. Ingrid Grundstein—Leonhard's wife, and Tante's mother—died when I was five. She was a devout Lutheran. She passed quietly in her sleep one night. They said "unexpectedly," but it certainly should've been expected. She was of a generation on the brink of extinction. For the funeral, my mother dressed me up in a black turtleneck sweater. It was uncomfortable and hot as we sat in the balcony on unforgivingly hard oak pews. The preacher talked for an eternity, and when he would pause to take a breath, the congregation called out, "Lord, hear our prayer," jolting me awake each and every time. I remember seeing Tante down near the front with family members I didn't recognize and never saw again. She was middle-aged at the time, but she already seemed like an old woman to me. It seems like she's hardly aged a day since. Tante was stoic, emotionless. The whole family was that way. Congregants behind them sobbed, but not them. The whole row of immediate family was stone. Perhaps age makes death easier, but at five, it gave me the creeps. My mother hugged Tante in the reception line—a stiff, formal hug. Tante whispered something in her ear. Tante patted me on the head, said nothing, and we left, my mother leading me by hand back to the car. I asked my mother about it when I was older. Tante had thanked her, in not so many words, for sitting in the balcony, out of sight.)

"What are the doctors saying now?" Tom asked.

"They won't tell me anything," Johnny said. "I'm not family. Karla's parents make it clear they want me to stay away."

The waitress came for our food orders.

(My biological grandmother, Katerina Schurke, died of a heart attack, also "unexpectedly." She was working on her house. The doctors said it was too hot for a woman her age to be out in the heat working so hard, but that was Oma. She lived alone most of her life in a modest bungalow in town, supported by

Social Security and a meager share of the royalties from Grund-stein's bleak book, *The Son Down*. My mother couldn't get her to sit down a day her life, much less take assistance of any kind. On the day she died she was out painting the deck at seventy-three, for God's sake—less than half of a year from seeing the new century. She would've gotten a kick out of watching everyone collecting water in their basements in case computers crashed in Y2K. My mother was lucky she could get a hold of her by way of the rotary phone on her kitchen wall, which my mother paid for and told Oma the service was free. Oma would say, in German, "Would you look at that, a free service? My God, never in my life did I think I'd see the day in this country." She never took another man. Oma had a traditional Catholic mass for her funeral—incense, smoke, robes, and all that. I was eighteen. I stood next to mother in the reception line that time. *How are you holding up? How are you holding up?* Everyone asked my mother, *How are you holding up?*)

"How are you holding up?" I asked Johnny.

"Okay. Trying to stay busy. Waiting by my phone. I don't know what kind of call I'm waiting for though. I've been sitting at the diner across the street from the hospital every day. Waiting. I've actually been getting some writing done while I wait. It's the only appropriate thing I can think to do. What Karla would want. It's the only thing that's keeping me sane."

The waitress dropped off the food, but skipped over Johnny.

"Are you eating enough?" Tom asked.

"My appetite is unsettled. I'm drinking a lot of coffee."

"You have to eat," Gretchen said.

"Can we do anything for you?" Ashley said.

"No," Johnny said. "I appreciate it, but no. Send good thoughts."

"We'll do that," I said.

The five of us moved food around our plates, our heads hung low. The waitress circled the table and topped off our coffees.

Gretchen asked the question that was looming in the back of our minds: "Should we cancel the trip this year?"

We waited for Johnny to answer first. He thought about it, and then he said in a sad way, "No. Let's go. It's tradition. We need it."

"I know I'll need to get away for a while," I said, "assuming I survive this class."

"Agreed," Ashley said. "I'm tired of this country right now."

"Let's go camping," Johnny said. "Somewhere up north. No man's land. I need to get back to earth, to experience something on the ground. Get my hands dirty. Be rejuvenated."

I fingered Grundstein's paperweight in my pocket.

(What I remember of Oma was that she always—and maybe this only happened two or three times in my life, but I was a kid and I don't remember much else—but she always said to me, "Nothing in this world is simply this or that." There was only one story I ever heard about my grandfather directly from her. At the time she had been ill, and my mother took me to see her in the hospital. I remember the floor was too white, the lights over-head were too bright, and the air didn't move right as we walked through the hallways—you couldn't feel it on your cheeks when you moved. Her room smelled too much of flowers; it was hard to breathe. Oma asked me to crawl up and sit on the edge of her bed. I didn't want to, but Mom lifted me up. The bedsheets felt dry and lifeless on the pads of my fingers. Oma combed my hair with her hands. She said, "Do you remember seeing those little Petoskey stones on the shore of the lake at the cabin?" I shook my head, yes. "Petoskey stones. Do you know what they're made of?" I shook my head, no. "The stone is fossilized coral. It's special in that way. Both stone and coral." Oma made a half-circle shape with her fingers as if she was holding something, and she smiled weakly at it. "The surface was smoothed by giant, slow-moving sheets of ice that scattered them all over Michigan many years ago. Isn't it remarkable how many things had to happen to deliver these beautiful little stones to us?" Oma's oatmeal-colored face looked as though it was melting down to her neck. "My brain does barrel rolls just thinking of it." I shook my head, yes. "When your grandfather was a young man," she continued, "he was friends with Ernest Hemingway. Your grandfather once told me a story of a springtime when Mrs. Hemingway sent the two of them up to Petoskey on their own for two nights to clear a small plot of land to make way for a summer garden. He said, 'Digging up them Petoskey stones as big as footballs and heaving them into Walloon all day and staying up all night— that was the finest time of my life.' Oma looked at me with her cloudy eyes. "He told me that," she said, "during the finest time of my life." Oma pulled through and lived ten more years. I told Emma that story, and now she's convinced I need to put together a biography on my grandmother when this is done. I told her, "Do you know why serious writers are too serious about writing? Because the difference between worthwhile or worthless is more arbitrary in such a field than in any other." "What about Johnny?" she said. "Johnny's different," I said. "How so?" she asked. All I could do was shrug.)

Ashley got out her phone. "How about we leave on Friday, June twenty-sixth? We'll come home Sunday, July fifth. How does that sound?"

I looked at my calendar and counted the weeks. "That'll give me just enough time to submit the grades and take off for the holiday."

"I'm free whenever," Tom said. "I'll be in between projects."

"I can work on the road," Gretchen said.

"No working from the road," Johnny said.

Gretchen nodded, but we all knew she would.

Ashley held her fist out over the table. "In?" The rest of us bumped our fists to hers and said in unison, "In." Something we'd done since high school. None of us had ever broken a commitment agreed upon in this way in more than ten years.

Everybody queued up to hug Johnny before we left.

@FluTrackerH1N1: 43 countries infected; 12,022 cases reported; 86 deaths confirmed.
7:08 PM – 23 May 2009

Sunday was such a drag. It took me all day to put together a coherent lesson plan for Week Two, while all I could think about was Karla and Johnny. It seemed irrelevant to even worry about *The Timepiece* or the week ahead.

And Grundstein. *Could it be explained away sympathetically as another senseless incident of unfortunate circumstances? Another casualty of war? How would scholars react? God, can't this all wait until after my defense?*

I checked Twitter. Scrolling through the feed, a tweet caught my eye:

@latimes: Ex-president's suicide leaves S. Korea with questions about its leaders.
3:16 PM – 24 May 2009

I clicked on the link and read the story:

> "Roh Moo-hyun, known as Mr. Clean, was the target of a corruption inquiry. […] The suicide of former South Korean President Roh Moo-hyun on Saturday, days before he was expected to be indicted in an influence-peddling inquiry, left the nation grappling with new and troubling questions about the moral character of its elected leaders."[1]

---

1. See Glionna, John M. "Ex-president's suicide leaves S. Korea with questions about its leaders," *Los Angeles Times*, 24 May 2009.

*Suicide? Troubling questions about moral character? Would Grundstein really ly end a life as burdensome as death is?*

@GretchBreporting: @MetroDetroitJournal "Luxury auto sales plummet to 50% compared to previous year."
3:29 PM – 24 May 2009

It didn't help that it was beautifully warm and sunny. Sitting at my desk, I could see the neighbor's children throwing around a football in their backyard. It was one of the first days that truly felt like summer was coming.

@TheTomPeters: @AshleyDanielsBand @JohnnyLawJr So great. On repeat. Can't stop listening. Thinking of you and Karla. Cheers.
3:52 PM – 24 May 2009

@AshleyDanielsBand: @JohnnyLawJr Here's my latest song, "The New Lost Generation." Just for you.
3:49 PM – 24 May 2009

@JohnnyLawJr: "Sorrow is my own yard where the new grass flames as it has flamed often before but not with the cold fire that closes round me this year." —WC Williams
3:41 PM – 24 May 2009

I played Ashley's song.
Once Alex and I had spent a glorious day in Grand Haven. *A decade ago? Really?* Lying on the sand, Alex baked in her string bikini, and I, in Bermuda shorts, applied several layers of sunscreen on all of my exposed skin. At one point, Alex crossed her bare ankle over mine, left it there for a moment, then jerked it back. "You feel like slime," she said. Devastating. I remember reading Orwell's *1984* that day: *Who controls the past controls the fu-*

*ture. Who controls the present controls the past.* Ashley once thought that originated in a Rage Against the Machine song. A quick Google search settled the issue. On the ride home from the beach with Alex, the apprehension was enough to make my chest feel like it could explode—the anticipation, the "will we/won't we" of it all. What I wouldn't have given for only one more youthful day on that beach with her. I would've let myself fry in the sun like a dried chili pepper at the chance to get that single touch point back. (Not anymore. Emma and I enjoy the beach at Walloon almost every day.)

@News.USA: H1N1 confirmed activity spans multiple states.
8:19 PM – 24 May 2009

@EnterTUNEment: Rehearsal delays force start date for Michael Jackson's 'This Is It' Tour back 8 days.
8:13 PM – 24 May 2009

After an entire day of procrastination, by eight-thirty I was too tired to prepare for class, and Daniels' voice was clogging up my head: *"If you can't do this on autopilot by now, when will you ever?"*

# 20

I don't recall many details about how I survived the class period, but I do remember how I began with a writing prompt that I would've been ashamed to show Daniels: What did you like/dislike about the first half of *The Timepiece*?

"This isn't your mom's book club," Daniels would say.

I took attendance while everybody had their heads down, scribbling, then looked at the time on my cellphone. *Give them three more minutes.*

My eyes fell upon Emma. Her hair was gleaming gold in the morning light. I thought of her in her dorm room reading *The Timepiece* in her pajamas. *What would she be wearing? A bathrobe? Flannels and a tank top?* (She wears sweat pants and one of my t-shirts now.)

Roy, the clown, lifted his head, done in less than a minute.

I looked away from Emma.

Roy couldn't possibly have written anything constructive. Probably didn't even read the assignment.

A movement at the door caught my attention. Daniels was standing across the hallway, back against the opposite wall, making a note on legal pad. He shook his head, tucked the legal pad under his arm, and walked away.

Roy cackled like a villain. *What was he laughing at?*

"Finish the thought you're working on," I said with forced

authority. "Let's get started."

On my notes, I'd written: DISCUSS FRAGMENTED PER-CEPTION OF TIME. Now, that didn't make any sense.

*My God*, I thought, *I have got to get my act together and teach this course. This experience is how these students will forever think of Grundstein and his work. I must do him justice.*

Flipping from one dog-eared page to the next: "Turn to page three— No, four— There, you'll see— No— Page eight has the passage I'm looking— No—"

Rowan stopped twirling Harmony's hair and craned his neck to see the wreckage.

"Yes, Rowan? A question," I said.

"Oh, uh—" A deer in headlights. "Well, what's this Grundstein guy's problem anyway? Does he have brain issues or something?"

*Backfire.*

"First of all," I began too defensively, "we must be cautious when examining the life of an author. We must try to distinguish the author from the work as much as possible. Look at them objectively. Fitzgerald was no Gatsby if you get what I mean. At the same time, it's worth considering. Yes, sometimes we can draw important inferences based on biographical knowledge. But, what are you talking about, Rowan? What makes you say that?"

"He repeats himself all the time. At this, at that, at so-and-so's this, at so-and-so that. It's annoying. And, it never seems to go anywhere or mean anything. The narrator seems confused. It's unreadable."

I regained my footing. "Yes. At, at, at... Then, then, then... Et-cet-*tra*." Daniels was in my voice. "Good observation, Rowan. Some modernists rejected linear plots lines. They felt linear plots couldn't accurately represent the human experience. That timing was circular. The present is constantly being intruded upon by the past—by memories, emotions, lessons learned, perceptions, et-cet-*tra*." I shook my head. "What you're talking about,

Rowan, is actually something that gives Grundstein's work a distinctly modernist, perhaps even postmodernist, quality. How the past shapes—changes—the present. So much so, the present becomes unstable."

Pacing back in forth in front of the whiteboard, I needed this train of thought to last another hour.

"And, the future? Unfathomable, if not unbearable. What you're calling 'unreadable' is, in fact, the desired effect. Naturally, we need to hem consciousness in. Define it. Measure it. Science, theories, religion, relationships, romance—attempts to try to map our way. Otherwise, the human experience spins out of control. One needs routine, meals—breakfast, lunch, dinner— repeat. One needs anchors to hold things down.

"That's exactly what Grundstein is doing with all the repetition of 'at' and 'but, then.' They're landmarks marking time, organizing thoughts. Grundstein is playing with this experiential cycle. When Evert, our narrator, says 'at,' something in the present is instigating some kind of reversion into memory, the past, and just as the thread circles back, just about to lead toward some understanding of the future. 'Then—' The plot gets interrupted again. Evert desperately tries to confine and control time. But, Grundstein is also using this as a narrative device to give the reader some checkpoints, to help you get through the text itself."

On a Post-it Note sticking out of my book I'd written "timing" and circled it. I opened the book. "Let's take a look at a passage. Turn to page fifty-eight." It wasn't the passage I was expecting, but I had already announced the page number with such confidence I went with it. I asked Emma to read a paragraph aloud, but I let her go on for a page and a half, hoping something of use would emerge to riff on (she's socking me over the head right now, calling me an insensitive jerk), before I cut her off.

"Think of Evert, our narrator, and his timepiece," I said, forging forward. "Sabine and her drinks. Hanne and her cigarettes. All coping mechanisms. You'll see this magnified in Grundstein's *The Son Down* where this kind of consumerism explodes. On crack, literally. Where the protagonist is the only person left on Earth who's sober, who is incapable of becoming inebriated and is left in a terrible of hell." *Bring it back.* "But here, you see the time indicators. Time for the next drink order. Time for the next cigarette. Time to rewind the timepiece. If it doesn't get wound, time will be lost. Look for these as you read to the end. Their meaning changes from scene to scene, so think to ask yourself when you see them, 'What does this mean now, for this scene?' For the timepiece, ask, 'What does the timepiece tell us about Evert in this moment?' "

I remember asking Emma to read from one of the more famous scenes early in the book. The scene portrays a gory fight where Evert, Sabine, and Hanne watch a giant of a man take on two capable boxers at once. The giant punches, and punches, and punches the other two relentlessly, leaving one of them wounded and the other knocked out cold.

"Thank you, Emma," I said. "So what happened there?"

"One boxer kicked two boxers' asses," Rowan said.

"How is it relevant to our main characters?"

"They had a three way," Roy blurted.

"They had a three-way relationship, yes," I said, pointing at Roy, ignoring his lack of decorum.

A memory: *Bobbie. Rocking. On Beth. Soft and smooth.*

"A *ménage à trois*?" Eli said, in a French accent that sounded authentic.

"Yes, exactly," I managed. *Keep it together. Stay in the present.* "If we understand this battle to be representative—" An image: *Beth riding away in Bobbie's Jeep.* "—we can begin to construct an understanding—" *Her hair bouncing free in the wind.*

I don't recall what filled the time between that vision and the end of the period. I don't recall what I said or what was discussed. I remember closing the book, putting it on the podium, and saying, "Does that help, Rowan?"

Rowan shrugged.

*Good enough*, I thought. *Thank God it's over.*

I collected my notes, and without looking up, I added, "Hopefully you can at least get a better sense of what to look for as you work your way through to the end."

@FluTrackerH1N1: 46 countries infected; 12,515 cases reported; 91 deaths confirmed.
11:57 AM – 25 May 2009

I vividly remember walking down the hallway after class, humming that song by the Black Eyed Peas: *"I gotta feelin' that tonight's gonna be a good night, that tonight's gonna be a good, good—"*

Halt.

The door to my office was open and the light was on. Tuning my ears to the sounds coming from the office, I could hear voices speaking energetically in hushed tones. Trying not to make a sound, I moved closer to the door.

I heard Alex say, "They needed a female extra for the day. The person they had cast flaked. He asked me if I was available."

Grudge said something. Couldn't make it out.

"It's nothing. Really," Alex said. "Nobody will see it. I'm not much of an actress anyway."

Grudge scoffed.

"I'll be able to draw on this."

"When's it coming out?"

*What does this have to do with Grudge?*

"There won't be any red-carpet premieres or anything," Alex said.

"Will I get a chance to see it?"

"You'll have to ask Tom, but you shouldn't, Monte. Really.

You shouldn't. Look, you're overreacting. It's just acting."

"That only makes this worse," Grudge said.

*Why does he even care?*

"We're both artists. This is art we're talking about. It's different."

"Art can come at a cost."

"Monte."

"There are real-life consequences." Grudge was sniffling.

*Was he crying?*

"I know," Alex said softly, in a way I hadn't heard before.

"But, you know how I feel. Didn't that matter to you? Doesn't it matter?"

"I know, Monte. I know."

Then, nothing.

I eased away, then walked back toward the door as loudly as I could, humming— *"tonight's gonna be a good, good night"* — and twirling my keys again. Two steps away, I heard Alex, in full voice, say, "Montgomery, do you know if Sam's going to be returning any time soon?"

I stuck my head in the doorway. Alex was wearing a sun-bright yellow cocktail dress. The shimmer of her tanned and oiled chest and legs obscured my vision.

Alex turned to me with a broad smile. "Samuel, speak of the devil! I was looking for you." She greeted me with a warm embrace, and I melted into her arms and forgot everything I'd heard.

"Where have you been?" she asked.

"Class."

"How'd it go?" Grudge asked. His voice quivered.

"Fine."

"That's wonderful," Alex said.

I set my satchel down on top of the mountain of papers on my desk. I offered Alex a Jolly Rancher from my giant cut-glass candy jar in the likeness of Ignatius J. Reilly—the bumbling, mustachioed protagonist with the floppy-eared green hat from John Kennedy Toole's *A Confederacy of Dunces*.

"Sam dear, Jolly Ranchers? Are you five years old? Look at this place. Isn't it about time you cleaned out this mess you call an office?" Alex took me by my shoulders, my lips not six inches from hers. "Samuel, your dissertation is done. You're about to be a doctor, the University of Michigan could call for you any day now, and you're handing out little candies from a pile of trash? Even if you stay, don't you want to start fresh?"

I lifted a stack of books, papers, and files off of the chair in front of my desk and dumped it with a thud onto the floor to clear a spot for Alex to sit.

"I only keep things that might become useful to me throughout my career," I said. "It's hard to tell what scholarship might come out of the research I've done so far."

"I can tell you exactly how much," Grudge said.

Alex circled my desk. "What about this?" She picked up a box that was full of index cards decorated with my scribbles. "I can toss this in the trash on my way out the door; you'll never notice the difference."

"Those are ideas, or nuggets that could turn into ideas. Alex, did you come by to berate me about the state of my office?"

"No, of course not, silly." She dropped the box onto the open chair. "Come on. Let's do lunch."

I looked at my watch. "I have office hours."

"You have to eat, honey."

Grudge shifted uncomfortably behind his computer screen.

"I was going to grab a sandwich at the cafeteria."

"I'll come with you. Then, you can come back to your precious garbage heap, Mr. OCD Hoarder Weirdo."

"Soon to be doctor," I replied.

I grabbed the shoulder strap to my satchel, but Alex intercepted it.

"It'll all be here when you get back," she said. "We won't be long."

Alex took me by the arm and led me out the door; I was sailing now, having Grudge there to witness it.

"Ugh, Samuel," Alex said as we walked. "It's this government bailout of my father's company. He says the government's scrutinizing our spending. It's all very public. A mess at home, too. He has us all on a cash budget. Took my cards. I don't have any cash. How does anyone do anything without credit cards?"

At the cafeteria, I selected a pre-packaged turkey sandwich with wilted lettuce. "Can I buy you lunch?"

Her nose crinkled like a bunny rabbit. "I don't know how you're alive."

An unexpected voice crashed my party: "Professor Sam?"

I turned to see Roy.

"Taking your date to the food court?" he said, grinning mischievously.

I would've felt the same if I'd been leveled by a semi-truck.

"Honey," Alex said to Roy, "a date with me to the cafeteria is as good as a thousand dates with your girlfriend to the Ritz."

"Nice," Roy said, bobbing his head. "I'm impressed. See you in class, Prof."

"This is the caliber of my upperclassmen," I said as we took a spot in line. "Ashley's playing at The Bullring tonight. Do you want to go? I'll pay your cover."

"Maybe," she said.

I paid for my poor sandwich.

Alex's clutch purse vibrated; she checked her phone, then quickly put it away.

"Who was that?"

"It's nothing," she said. "Just did a favor for a friend who was mad at me and earned some petty cash at the same time." Then, suddenly, she became short with me and pushed the pace back to the office.

(I was too distracted at the time to pick up the clues.)

"Should I pick you up tonight?" I said.

"I'll let you know later."

"I can come by at seven unless I hear from you. How's that?"

"Fine," Alex said abruptly as we reached the office. She poked her head in. "Talk to you later, Monte." I didn't hear his response.

Alex turned and dissolved into the sea of students.

The song continued in my head, *I gotta feeling that tonight's gonna be a good, good night!*

I remember moving my satchel from my desk (which was conspicuously untouched) to the state of disorder on the floor. Nothing struck me as out of place.

(I was blissfully blind to all of it; however, from where I sit now, you see, with the benefit of hindsight, it's clear Alex was working with Daniels and Grudge even then. She told me right to my face, but I wasn't listening. Thank God I'd put Grundstein's letters back already.)

Feeling good, I was in no mood to deal with Grudge. I busied myself at my desk as I ate my sad lunch; I needed to get serious anyhow. Wednesday would be the last day we'd discuss *The Timepiece* in class, and we could hardly see it any better than an iceberg on a foggy night.

I read *The Timepiece* for the first time as a freshman in college. I had no idea, at that time, I would be on track to become a Grundstein scholar. To say the least, I didn't read it with a critical eye at the time; I read with as much focus as a horny college kid. My professor, Dr. Watson, dealt with the sex scenes with such indifference. That I remember—the sex scenes. Unfortunately, Dr. Watson was only concerned with the subtext. "The sex is merely an outward expression of something deeper for the characters," he would say. "What's *really* happening here?"

Now, it was my turn to play that part, and Emma, I'm sure, was the kind of student who listened very closely to what professors were talking about. I didn't need to make any more of a fool of myself.

I took the *Critical Companion to Leonhard Grundstein*, edited by Dr. Stanley P. Daniels, Ph.D., out of my satchel and scanned the introduction Daniels wrote for the edition. One paragraph stood out to me:

> Another reason for Grundstein's shortcomings is perhaps less obvious, but certainly as important. Hemingway was a public figure, a consummate celebrity. Grundstein was not—the opposite: a recluse. Grundstein was every bit as reclusive as Dickinson. He kept his life private, and his family continues to keep his life under lock and key. This not only contributes to the lack of attention that an author like Grundstein could and should attract, but it is also a great disservice to the advancement of the study literature. Unfortunately, by the time we know more about Grundstein the man, it will likely be too late to salvage the attention his work deserved.

*"Under lock and key,"* I thought. *Tante must know more. There's evidence in the journal that suggests the existence of at least one more journal. What else is she hiding, not just from the world, but from me as well? Even more concerning than the what is the why. Why is she hiding whatever she has? Why? Why? Why?*

Grudge was standing at the door now. "What do you have?"

I held up the book for Grudge to see the cover. "Just re-reading Daniels' introduction."

Grudge smiled. "I particularly enjoy the one passage—how does that go—'a great disservice to the advancement of the study of literature'? I helped him edit that line, you know. Brilliant."

"Funny, I don't see your name listed here."

"It's listed on my CV," Grudge said, "and I can back it up with a reference. That's all I need. Want me to come with you to talk to your precious *Tante*? Need a real scholar to get to the bottom of this?"

I held fast, not a twitch. "If she's holding information from me, she's certainly not going to give it *to you*."

Grudge shrugged. "We'll see."

"Especially not you," I repeated.

But he got the last word in. "Hey, if you get Alex out to The Bullring tonight," he said, "ask her what she's been working on with Tom. I'd love to be there to see your reaction."

"Why?" I said. "Are you going?"

Grudge turned off the light. "Ta ta, for now, Schurke."

*What is all this business with Alex and Tom? Why does it have anything to do with goddamned Grudge?*

# 21

Alex stood me up. She was nowhere to be found when I arrived at her house. She left me stuck in conversation with her pent-up, stressed-out mother who embraced me a bit too long and kissed me on the cheek a little too close to my mouth. She said, "This hideous beard has got to go, honey. It pricks me." At one point, I swear, she ran her hand across my crotch, but managed to make it seem as though it was all in my head.

So the next day I resolved to see Johnny. Grundstein was haunting me. Daniels and Grudge were stalking me. Tante was eluding me. And Alex was confusing me. I needed to get my feet back on the ground; I needed to see Johnny.

Johnny said he would be holed up at the diner across from the hospital, waiting for news. I went by at lunchtime. I spotted him at the end of the counter near the back. He had a notebook open on the counter, a plate to one side—fish and chips, uneaten—and a coffee mug to the other. He was writing with a flourish.

Johnny, the true impetus behind the Circle, was working in a white heat, ideas pouring out of him. Urgency.

I didn't feel right interrupting him. Whatever I would say, with my disillusioned notions of "problems" in my life, would only derail his work.

I took a booth near the door instead, and ordered a Rueben, extra sauerkraut, with coffee.

(As I sit here, now that Johnny's memoir has become a phenomenon, I wish like hell I could revisit that booth. I should've taken notes. A picture. Something to capture the moment. It was happening right there.)

I checked my Twitter feed:

@MetroDetroitJournal: GM set to receive additional $4 billion loan.
12:15 PM – 26 May 2009

@PubishersDaily: Publishing sales plunge 4.2% in the first quarter.
12:14 PM – 26 May 2009

@AshleyDanielsBand: I wish @nickelback's "If Today Was Your Last Day" was their last song. That'd be the path less traveled by.
12:14 PM – 26 May 2009

@FluTrackerH1N1: 46 countries infected; 12,954 cases reported; 92 deaths confirmed.
12:13 PM – 26 May 2009

"Samuel, son," Johnny said. He had his coffee mug in his hand and his notebook tucked under his arm. "How long have you been here?"

I lifted my mug in solidarity. "Long enough to take two sips and to place a sandwich order, but not long enough to get my food."

"Did you see me over at the bar?"

"No, I came all the way over to the hospital for the coffee. Of course. I didn't want to interrupt. What are you working on?"

"Some thoughts, you know," he said, taking a seat. "Everything's moving so fast and so slow right now."

"Have you heard anything from Karla's family?" I said.

"How's she doing?"

"It's hard to tell. Not good. The family doesn't tell me much. Did you know they never liked me?"

"Yeah, Johnny, everybody knew."

"What are you talking about?"

"Let's see, and I'm just spit-balling here, my guess would be that, since the first time they ever saw you, they got a front row seat to your bare ass as you were not only popping their fifteen-year-old daughter's cherry, you were also wrecking her waterbed. I know this might be hard for you to understand, but those aren't cheap."

"The cherry or the bed?" Johnny said, flashing his nefarious smirk.

"I'd say that hardly made a good first impression."

"I offered to pay for a new bed. Her dad refused."

"You didn't even use a condom; I'd say, they had bigger concerns at that point."

"I didn't impregnate her."

I gave him a look.

"Okay, okay. That was bad, but it makes for a fine story. I don't see why they should've held that against me all this time."

"How about when you convinced Karla not to go to Bryn Mawr, to live with you and be your personal housewife, instead? You think they liked that move?"

"She made that decision all on her own. I was being supportive."

"What about when you graduated from college and took off for two years traipsing all over Asia without sending anyone word as to your whereabouts."

"I begged her to come with me," Johnny said and looked out the window. He took a slow, deliberate sip from his mug.

The waiter brought my sandwich and topped off our coffees. The sauerkraut was piled so high it was falling out of the sandwich and onto the plate.

"You know you don't like it," Johnny said. "You can drive that ugly-ass, orange *folks vagon* and stuff yourself with that sour garbage all you want, but you'll never be any more German or less American."

I took a massive bite from my big, sloppy sandwich. With a mouthful, I said, "You know? That's exactly what my problem is. Thanks, Doc. I guess I won't need to pay for the sessions anymore."

I finished my sandwich while Johnny drank his coffee and watched people pass by the window.

"It's about time you got around to why you came," Johnny said at last.

I was knocked off center, somewhat, by his sternness. "Do you know if Tom and Alex are doing a film together? Do you know anything about that?"

Johnny looked surprised. "Tom's been working on some new project, yes, but I don't know how much Alex is involved. Why?"

"It's nothing. I just thought I overheard her say something to Grudge."

"You crazy academics," Johnny said. "If you two could learn to get along, instead of bitch-slapping each other all the time, maybe you'd both get something accomplished."

The air between us seemed to contract. I felt the need to say something, to change the subject. I said, "You know, I've been looking into Grundstein some more."

"Yeah?"

"As a writer, how much would you want people digging into your personal life? That kind of thing."

"You mean your kind of research? Academic stuff?"

"Academics and fans alike."

Johnny thought for several minutes. "Nothing is all good or all bad; it all depends."

"Let me try to be more specific. If I was your executor, let's say, just hypothetically, and it's my job to protect your life's work, and you die—God forbid—and I discover something bad about you unrelated to your work, and if the public knew, they'd disown you, take you out of the canon, ban your books from being taught in schools. Would you consider it my job to harbor that knowledge in order to protect the integrity of your work, or would you consider it my job to put that information out to the academy, to the public, to let them sort it all out? To see if the work could withstand it? That sort of thing."

"In other words, where's the line between a writer's life work," Johnny said, "and a damned cash grab?"

"It's something Grundstein's work, for all of its shortcomings, hasn't had to face. All his laundry, personal writings, and unfinished works have never surfaced."

"Yet, you mean," Johnny said, giving me a sideways look.

"I guess. Maybe, but if I ever found something, how would I know it wasn't just, as you say, 'a damned cash grab' of sorts? Wouldn't it be better to celebrate works we know to be finished and approved by the author? An 'ignorance is bliss' kind of thing. Or, err on the side of reveal all—a 'truth will set you free' kind of thing."

"What are we really talking about, Sam?" Johnny said.

"I just need to get through this dissertation business, but I feel like I'm approaching a car wreck—if I don't look, the road will continue to stretch out in front of me, but I'll be forever condemned to wondering if I should've stopped to help. Or, if I do look, the road will end, and I'll be launched off of a cliff."

"I see," Johnny said. "It's hard to say. If I was to produce something that only needed to be polished a little bit to be publishable, to give people a chance to appreciate what I've done, it'd be hard to say, 'Bury it.' We wouldn't have several great works with us today if we operated that way."

"Dickinson's poetry," I said, nodding.

"*A Confederacy of Dunces* won the Pulitzer for God's sake."

"The Nick Adams stories."

"Yeah, but, then," Johnny said, "one can never be sure how readership at large will react to any given work. Ask Rushdie how unpredictable that can get."

"Can you imagine?" I said. "And that was before Twitter."

"Trust me when I tell you, I wish I could help you with that question, but I can't."

"It would be better if authors wouldn't do crazy shit. No question about that."

"There's a fine line between madness and greatness." Johnny smiled. "For authors anyway."

I nodded. "Sorry for the interruption. Send Karla all my best."

Johnny patted my shoulder somberly, then got up and went back to the counter.

(An excerpt from Johnny's *The Lines of Change* comes to mind:

> After being hospitalized for four days and quarantined for seven, I was finally allowed to see Karla. She told me the tales about her sky-high fever, insufferable chills, and unforgiving vomiting, about her dangerous weight loss, and about her shrunken eye sockets and protruding cheekbones. But she looked good now. Her face was flush and rosy. Her eyes—big and full. Her weight—normal with soft curves over her thigh and hip bones.
>
> I asked her if she was contagious.
>
> She said, "If I was, you wouldn't be here right now."
>
> I was sitting at the island in her family's kitchen as she made herself a grilled cheese sandwich for lunch, as if the last two weeks had never happened to her. She told me, then, how the doctors suggested that she sequester herself until the outbreak was under control and public anxiety had calmed down. I

asked her if I could hug her and kiss her.

She smiled and said, "No, Johnny, you may not. But that has nothing to do with the swine flu."

I hugged her and kissed her anyway.

The next time I saw Karla was at Johnny's funeral.)

That night I went back to the house and holed up in my room. I didn't want to see or hear from anyone. I turned my cellphone off. I needed to think.

*Who cares? What's the matter with me? When did I get so far off track? Where did this get so out of control?*

I kicked a book across the floor—the book I'd bought for Tante as part of my ruse: *Hotel on the Corner of Bitter and Sweet*. I'd forgotten all about it. I sat down on the edge of my bed and started reading. A Chinese-American loses his wife. Japanese-Americans lose their homes. Their possessions. Internment. I thought of Grundstein, and a sentence made me stop: "Time dragged on, clock or no clock."

"Why? Why? Why?" I said, closing the book.

I pulled my tin trashcan over to the side of the bed and held the book overtop. I took Grundstein's lighter and stone out of my pocket and flipped them over and over in my hand. Then, I closed my eyes, tossed them into the air, and grasped at the darkness for a sign. To my surprise, one sank into my palm while the other tumbled to the floor. I opened my eyes to see the inscription: *UNTER DEM RUHESTEIN.*

Disappointed with the verdict, I collected the lighter and struck it up anyway. The flame produced was just as fair, perhaps having a better claim. "To wonder, 'Do I dare?' " I whispered. With the book in one hand and the change agent in the other: "Why not? Why not? Why not?" I tell of this with a sigh; I set the book unharmed aside.

# 22

I was only three minutes late for class. Roy, of course, had to make a comment. "Walk of shame, Schurke?"

I didn't expect Roy to get a legitimate laugh out of Emma. That threw me off.

"What would make you say that, Roy?" Terrible decision. *Please, let's spend a little more time on this topic!*

"You look like you slept in those clothes, and you could use a shave."

I rubbed my chin—into the bushy stage. "So, what?"

Eli said, "Talk the talk, you took the shameful walk."

"I can assure you, Mr. Glitterburg," I said to Roy, mocking my own professorial persona, "I'd perhaps feel less shame walking away from a one-night stand than waking up the way I did this morning."

Leslie: "Hung over?"

Rowan: "Doing drugs?"

Harmony turned around and slapped Rowan playfully.

"Thank you, Harmony. Let's get started," I said, taking my copy of *The Timepiece* out of my satchel. "So why is Evert obsessed with knowing the correct time, being 'on time'?"

Emma raised her hand.

"Yes, Emma?"

She ran her fingers down her notes looking for the right bullet point. I straightened up as I watched her, feeling as though her finger was tracing my spine. *Oh, Emma.*

I looked to the door. No Daniels. *Thank God.*

"Here," she said. "The present becomes unstable. We need to hem it in—define and measure it. Science."

"Very good, Emma. Thank you. Also, time, particularly mass distribution and standardization of time as we know it today, is a modern construct. It's as much a representation of how modern times, pun intended—" I paused smiling, but the joke didn't land. "—and modern technology is impacting the rapid change of the human psyche as much as anything else, as much as industrialization, as much as the changing power structures, the evolution of gender roles, the transformation of social norms. Thinking about that, if the timepiece is representative of Evert's mental state, it represents order among the chaos. In the first half of the novel, the timepiece appears at the precise moment when Evert is becoming unhinged, and it centers him, gets him refocused. How does that change in the second half?"

"He starts to lose it," Roy said.

"Lose what?"

"His mind," he added.

"Everything," Emma said. "Keeping track of the time becomes such an obsession while he loses track of everything else. His work. Sabine. And yes, his mind. What once stabilizes him becomes the epicenter of the earthquake."

"It's interesting, isn't it," I asked, "how the measuring and keeping of time has changed our psyches? How it's changed how we think about our world? Less than 200 years ago, keeping track of the time down to the second was unfathomable. Now, in the information age, what? Tweets update on my phone by the microsecond. Meanwhile, every other social construct seems to crumble with decay. It's madness. Let's think about this. What are some of the tools we use today to try to control our chaotic existence, things that would probably drive Evert equally, if not exponentially more, mad?"

"Google," Teagan said. "A Google search is like trying to see through the noise."

"Google Calendar," Emma said. "That's my timepiece. I'd go crazy without it."

"How long has Google been around?" I asked.

"Wikipedia says it was founded in 1998," Eli said, looking at his laptop.

Roy: "That's so last century."

Teagan: "Life without Google would suck."

"It's only existed for a decade," I said, "and now you can't imagine trying to get by without it."

Harmony: "Wikipedia's another good example."

Leslie: "Wikipedia knows more about my ancestry than I do. That makes me sad."

"I think Evert, and perhaps Grundstein, would agree with you, Leslie," I said. "After all, what happens to the timepiece in the end? Evert's late for the train that would take him back to Paris to make one last attempt at Sabine's heart. Since he's late, the train's getting away from him. As he rushes to climb aboard, the timepiece falls out of his pocket onto the tracks and gets flattened by the train. Now what might be significant about the fact that the train kills the timepiece?"

Leslie: "The train is a symbol for American expansion into the native territories."

"Yes, it is, but here, I think, it's one of the biggest symbols of innovation related to the industrial revolution. One of the largest advances in technology in the nineteenth century. Perhaps the only thing more foundational to the development of modern society than the timepiece. The advancement of modern time as we know it was, in many ways, driven by the need to keep the trains on schedule."

I checked my phone for the time.

"Alright, we have to begin our viewing of the 1932 film adaptation of *The Timepiece*; otherwise, we'll never get through. This film was directed by Lewis Milestone. I would be surprised if any of you are familiar with Milestone's work—" I wasn't. I didn't even screen the film before class. I merely conducted a few Google searches to collect some notes from the Internet. "—but he directed the original *Ocean's Eleven* in 1960 with Frank Sinatra as Danny Ocean instead of George Clooney. This guy was big-time Hollywood. He worked with Marlon Brando."

"Milestone was born in Bessarabia, now Moldova, raised in Odessa, Ukraine, and educated in Belgium and Germany, where he studied engineering. He was fluent in both German and English, and he was perhaps best known for his 1930 adaptation of the 1929 novel *All Quiet on the Western Front*, or as it was known in the original German, *Im Westen nichts Neues*. Erich Maria Remarque's novel about the Great War describes a German soldiers' extreme physical and mental stress during the war and the detachment from civilian life felt by many of these soldiers upon returning home from the front. For that film, Milestone took home the Academy Award for Best Directing.

"His German background and past success with the Remarque adaptation made him a natural choice to make Grundstein's bestselling and critically acclaimed debut novel into a film. He was again nominated for an Academy Award for Best Directing for *The Timepiece*. He lost that year to Frank Borzage's adaptation of Hemingway's *A Farewell to Arms*.

"An interesting anecdote, Clark Gable and Gary Cooper, two of the top actors of the time, had vied for the lead role in *The Timepiece*. At the prompting of Leonhard Grundstein, as the story goes, Milestone ultimately chose Gable. Grundstein apparently lobbied for Gable because of their shared Midwestern roots. Gable, as I understand, was from Ohio. Cooper went on to star in Borzage's *A Farewell to Arms*, of course.

"At any rate, Milestone was revered for authenticity in his adaptations—tight editing, clever dialog, and visual symbolism. He liked to use cameras on wooden tracks for more realistic shots. Look for those characteristics as we watch, not only similarities and differences from the novel, but also how Milestone captures the emotional essence of the novel throughout the film."

I was concerned my students, most of them not knowing what life was like before the Internet, would be disenchanted by a film that was in black and white and was closer to a century old than it was new. Five minutes into our viewing, however, I didn't see a single glow of a cellphone screen again.

I found myself as captivated as they were. When Clark Gable as Evert dropped the timepiece at the end, representing his shattered psyche, the shrieking, jolting montage of canted angles felt as though the train was crushing my heart.

A collective groan of outrage arose from my students.

"Absolutely stunning," I said, turning the lights back on. "One thing I do want to emphasize is how complicated romance becomes—" Alex, Veronica, Beth, Emma—all rolled through my head. "—as we move into the notions social mobility and independent sexuality, feminism, equality. Strictly in terms of sexual partners—" I didn't know where I was going with this thought. "—doesn't it seem like it would've been easier when your options were limited most likely to your parents' network of potential suitors?" *What was I saying?*

"Online dating can help, man," Roy said, and everybody laughed.

"Okay, okay," I said, checking my phone again. "That's enough for now. I have to discuss your mid-term assignment before we go. For next week, you're reading Grundstein's *West of Home*, and we'll be watching a portion of that film adaptation as well. You can focus on one of these two novels independently, or you can compare the two, or you can focus on the films, comparing one of the books to its adaptation. But, since this is a relatively small writing assignment, I wouldn't broaden your focus beyond those options."

Only Emma took notes as I went over the details of the writing assignment.

"And remember, this is not 'I liked this' or 'I didn't like that' kind of fluffy stuff. This isn't your mom's book club. I want to see a critical analysis of these narratives as representative of modernist ideals. If you have any questions or if you want to borrow the DVDs of the films, feel free to stop by my office hours. I'll see you all next week."

My students packed up and left. The class was finally up and running of its own volition.

*Only four weeks left*, I reminded myself as I peeked into the hallway. No Daniels in sight. *Just have to get through.*

@EnterTUNEment: King of Pop says he's, "Excited and ecstatic" about upcoming tour.
11:58 AM – 27 May 2009

@GretchBreporting: Oil prices reach six-month high.
11:57 AM – 27 May 2009

@TheTomPeters: Cutting out for a long weekend. #NeedARealVacationFromPretendingforaLiving
11:56 AM – 27 May 2009

# 23

*Thank God*, I thought, finding the office empty of Grudge on that particular Friday. There were limited course offerings on Fridays, and many students took the opportunity to disappear for the weekend, so I scheduled my office hours at that time to reduce the likelihood of an interruption.

(How did I not realize I was in the wrong field?)

Sharing the office with Grudge on such days was hit or miss, but if he wasn't at his desk already, it was unlikely I'd see him. It was unlikely I'd see a soul.

Before I got started, I shuffled through Facebook and found myself looking at photographs of Alex. She recently added a new album titled, "On location with Tom," which contained, as Alex's albums often did, many obscure images.

She was always snapping pictures "to capture an experience of a lifetime," as she would say.

There were several dark shots of stage lights at odd angles, creating silhouetted effects. There were images of the backs of peoples' heads, some of whom were wearing headsets, or getting their hair done—men and women—by stylists, or sitting in director's chairs, and in the fuzzy, unfocused background of all of them I could see the same bedroom set—lit up.

I could hear her: *This is wonderful. Look at this. What an inspiration!*

The bedroom set could've been found in the house on *The Simpsons*; with pastel pinks and purples, it had an innocent, untouched, eternal look. These images were followed by extreme close-ups of objects that were clearly part of the bedroom set: a torn corner of the purple bedspread with triangular-shaped embroidery, a pink vanity, a watch and a perfume flask in front of a cracked mirror, and a small clear bottle on the nightstand with the label blacked out.

My stomach was starting to turn, and I remembered Alex saying once, after I mentioned I'd found one of her paintings disturbing, "Good. That's what I was going for. An emotional provocation."

The last picture sent my head spinning. Alex was in a white bathrobe, nestled under Tom's arm with her hands around his midsection. And Tom, who was wearing jeans without a shirt, was, himself, nestled under an embracing arm—that of another man. A man I recognized.

It was the only photo Alex had captioned. It read: "Thomas and I with the ingenious, Rini Penders." Penders was a locally known independent film actor/director who wanted to be the next Tarantino.

A knock came at the door and startled me; I minimized the browser.

"Yes, hello," I said.

"Professor Schurke?" Emma peeked through the crack in the door.

I rose to my feet. "Yes, Emma. Hi."

"Hi," she said, remaining in the hallway.

"Come on in."

She opened the door, stepped in, and turned to reset the door to the nearly closed position.

Emma Stratford. In my office. Alone.

Her golden waves of hair—which I was used to seeing carelessly draped about her shoulders as she sat at her desk in class, lifted only occasionally as she'd run her left hand, beginning at her temples, through to her crown—was now pulled back with two free curls, one on each side, framing her face. She was wearing a spaghetti-strap tank top that left no room to cover a bra strap which was conspicuously missing, cut-off jean shorts with a higher waist than I was used to seeing on students her age, and flip-flops. She was smiling nervously, looking at me with those big, eager blue eyes. Her long nose and thin chin forced her full lips to form a V-shape, pointing on each end to her accentuated cheekbones.

"Could you leave the door open behind you, please?" I asked.

Emma's expression dropped. *Did she frown?* "Of course," she said.

"Sorry," I said, moving to clear books and papers for her to sit down. "I rarely get visitors on Fridays," as if that had anything to do with the clutter.

She said, "The staff doesn't clean your office?"

"Wouldn't that be dandy?" I said. *Dandy? Really? I never say "dandy."*

I offered Emma a Jolly Rancher.

"I'd love one," she said. "I don't think I've had one since I was a kid. Is that an Ignatius J. Reilly candy jar? That's amazing."

"When your brain begins to reel from your literary labors," I said, "you need an occasional Jolly Rancher."

She took off her backpack and set it on the floor between her legs as she sat down. "You really need to clean house, Professor Schurke."

"I know, I know," I said. "What can I do for you?"

"I have a few questions."

"About the assignment?"

"Sure," she said. She looked over her shoulder at the open door behind her. "I don't know what to write about."

"What did you think of *The Timepiece* film?"

"It was okay," she said. "Pretty good, I guess."

"It's really quite great. Did you like the book?"

"Sure." She shrugged. "I've read it before."

At that time, footsteps and voices came from the hallway. They were distant, but distinct—a group of boys. There were several conversations taking place at once. Occasionally the sound of shoes squealing on the waxed floor gave the impression that one boy had suddenly pushed another—friends probably, taking advantage of the mostly empty campus.

Emma and I waited for them to pass, but the group stopped, seemingly right outside the door.

"Do you want me to close the door?" Emma asked.

I thought for a moment, then said, "No, it's okay. About the assignment, there are limited options for a reason. You're probably overthinking it. You could start by writing out some ideas. It's early enough now that you could—"

"Hey!" a voice rose above the din in the hallway. Then, the sound of books falling to the floor. Shoes shuffling.

Emma's eyes pleaded with me, pouting, soulfully. (I recognize that look better now.)

"Just until they pass," I said, pointing at the door.

She was up and shutting the door before I even finished the sentence, then suddenly her demeanor changed. She bounced back to her seat.

"I heard some students call you Sam," she said, smiling—a broad, tooth-filled smile. "Can I call you Sam?"

I was off center already. "Sure." *Why not?*

"I think I know what I'm going to write about." Emma waved her slender hand dismissively.

"Oh?"

"Yeah, great suggestion. I'll try what you said."

"Oh," I said. "Yes. As I was saying, it's still early enough to change later if your first topic—"

"Yes, exactly," Emma said. She let her hair down to its full length.

*Was she flirting?*

"I have another question for you," she said.

*Was I going crazy?*

She wrapped her hair tie around her wrist.

"Is that so?" I said, hearing Daniels in my voice again.

"Your relationship status online says 'it's complicated.' "

"On Facebook?" *Hallucinating?*

"Some of the girls were wondering what that meant. I volunteered to ask."

*Girls? Which girls?*

"It's complicated, sure. As you know from class, in our times, it's all—" *Why was I turning this into a lecture?* "That's just a joke from a long time ago," I said. "I should change it."

"You're not currently involved?"

"Not really."

"You should probably change your privacy settings, too." She stood up unexpectedly. "You don't want to share everything with everybody, do you?"

"Do you want to see if those boys are gone?" I asked. "While you're up."

"That's okay." She moved closer to my desk.

(Emma's found an excuse to duck into the annex for this part. She's hiding.)

"They might be gone by now," I added.

"I can show you how to change your privacy settings." She put her left arm across the top of my chair and leaned over my computer, taking the mouse with her right hand.

I froze as her breast brushed against my shoulder. She smelled of strawberry shampoo and fine lotion. Her hair tickled the side of my face.

"You already have Facebook open, I see. Of course," she said. "Whoa. Who are they? Do you know them?" She looked down her nose at me. "Sammy, are you Face-stalking these people like a weirdo?"

"Those are friends of mine," I said. It sounded like anything but the truth. "That's Rini Penders, the director."

"Doesn't he make pornos?" she asked. She said the word *porno* naturally, comfortably.

"Independent films."

"Right," she continued, clicking in rapid-fire succession. "Profile. Settings. Privacy. Friends only. Friends only. Friends only." She stood up straight.

The zipper flap of her shorts was touching my wrist.

"I think," she said, "you should—"

Then, someone was at the door.

Emma stepped back.

I stood up.

The knob turned. Grudge walked in.

"Schurke?" Grudge said, looking at us with a sideways glance.

"Thank you, Sam—I mean, Professor," Emma said. "I'll get started on the essay right away. See you next week." She lifted her backpack and stepped around Grudge, who still had his hand on the doorknob. "Excuse me, sir."

"Have a nice weekend," I called after her.

Grudge looked out the door, then at me, and raised his eyebrows. "Meeting with a student, Schurke?"

"She had a question about the mid-term."

"I gather."

"Do you mind if I leave the door open?" Grudge asked, glaring at me.

"Sure," I said. "I'll be leaving soon anyway."

I turned back to my computer, closed out of Facebook, and scrolled through Twitter:

@JohnnyLawJr: No point in holding onto GM stocks any longer. 10:44 AM – 29 May 2009

@MetroDetroitJournal: General Motors headed for Chapter 11,

appears inevitable.
10:22 AM – 29 May 2009

@FluTrackerH1N1: 53 countries infected; 15,510 cases reported; 95 deaths confirmed.
9:15 AM – 29 May 2009

@News.USA: On this day in history: World War II memorial in
DC dedicated in 2004.
08:02 AM – 29 May 2009


The following morning, I received an email from Dr. Jean Bear,
the Dean of the College of Arts and Letters, with the subject:
TIME SENSTIVE, EXTERMELY CONFIDENTIAL, READ
IMMEDIATELY:

> If you are receiving this email, you are an em-
> ployee of the University. Please be aware the follow-
> ing message is for internal constituents ONLY.
> Yesterday, Friday, May 29, 2009, we received a
> report of an incident of alleged sexual abuse from a
> female student. The incident occurred at approxi-
> mately10:36 a.m. in the West Building.
> If anyone has information regarding this inci-
> dent, please come forward as soon as possible. And
> please remember, this is sensitive. Any breach in
> confidence may result in immediate termination.

My heart sank as if it'd dropped into my pants. I began craft-
ing an email right away:

> Dr. Bear,
> I was serving my office hours at that time in the

West Building. I was meeting with a student when we heard students fraternizing in the hallway quite raucously. Because of the noise, I had to shut the door to my office in order to better serve my student, Emma Stratford.

Unfortunately, as a result, I did not see or hear anything more, and I doubt Ms. Stratford did either. My colleague, Montgomery Grudge, joined us in my office shortly thereafter. He may know more, but he did not indicate so at the time, nor did he seem out of sorts.

Please let me know if I can be of further assistance with this.

Warm regards,

Samuel Schurke

Not five minutes later, I received a reply to my email, but it wasn't from Dr. Bear, as I'd expected. It was from Daniels, and it wasn't addressed to me:

Hi Jean,

I will remind Mr. Schurke of our preference for "open door" interactions with students, and I will inquire with Emma Stratford on that regard. Also, I will summon Mr. Schurke to my office first thing Monday morning to discuss further action. I will personally reach out to Mr. Grudge to find out if he knows more. I apologize for any inconvenience, and I'll be in touch.

Stan

Immediately after viewing that message, I received another email from Daniels addressed to me and copied to Grudge:

Sam and Monte,

My office. 8 a.m. Monday morning. Don't be late.

—SD

I felt sick. *God, if I could only survive one more month.*

# 24

When I got to Daniels' office, everyone was already seated—Daniels and Grudge—and two surprise guests, Emma and Dr. Bear. Two chairs had been pulled in from somewhere else; I sat down in the lone open one.

Dr. Bear was a former body builder with a curly mullet. She started in on me right away. "As you know, Mr. Schurke, although it is not a formal policy to maintain an open door when talking with students, particularly of the opposite sex, it is encouraged at all times."

"Yes," I said, "this was an extenuating circumstance—" A phrase I'd practiced. "—because the noise in the hallway was making our discourse—" A word I'd pre-selected. "—difficult."

"We'll get to that in a moment," Dr. Bear said. "Ms. Stratford, would you say Professor Schurke *invited* you into his office?"

"Sure," Emma said.

I sat up straight. "What?"

"Mr. Schurke, please," Daniels said in a surprisingly kind tone. He raised his hand to me to wait my turn.

I sat back in my chair.

"Please continue, Ms. Stratford," Dr. Bear said.

"He's very welcoming," she said. "He invites all of his students to his office."

"For office hours," I said.

"Yes," she said.

"Did he make a special effort to invite you individually?" Dr. Bear said.

"No."

"Did he insist on closing the door?" Dr. Bear added.

"No," said Emma. "Only because it was too noisy in the hallway."

I nodded.

Dr. Bear made a note.

"And, what were you discussing?" Grudge asked.

"Monte," Daniels said.

Dr. Bear nodded to Emma to proceed with her answer.

"I had questions about my midterm assignment," Emma said, "and Professor Schurke was very—" She smiled. "—helpful."

"Mr. Grudge," Dr. Bear said, turning to her left, "can you describe what you saw when you got to the office?"

"Yes. I entered the office at around ten-forty in the morning." Grudge was being so damn smug. "I saw the student standing at Mr. Schurke's desk. They both turned to me when I walked in. Mr. Schurke stood up. He was clearly startled by the interruption. The student said something quickly and left immediately."

"Oh, please," I said. "She's right here; her name is Emma. And how could you come to the conclusion she was—"

Daniels raised his hand to me again.

Dr. Bear said, "Ms. Stratford, did you feel startled, embarrassed?"

"No," she said.

"Was Mr. Schurke behaving in any way that could cause such a response?"

"No."

"What were you doing when Mr. Grudge arrived?"

"We were discussing romantic relationships in class—" My heart fell to the floor at the sound of 'romantic relationships.'

"—because of our reading, and we were looking at his Facebook profile—" Bounced and hit the floor again.

"Facebook?" Daniels said.

"What for?" asked Dr. Bear.

"We were talking about the 'it's complicated' Facebook status."

"Ms. Stratford," Dr. Bear said, "in the course of your discussions, has Mr. Schurke ever made any sort of romantic overture, explicit or implicit? And it's critically important that you respond honestly. I can promise you, your status as a student will not be negatively impacted as a result of behavior unbecoming of our faculty members. I am concerned about ensuring the learning environment, here, is safe for you and your fellow students."

"No," Emma said.

Dr. Bear waited, as if a sufficient pause was all Emma needed to come out with an incriminating answer.

"No," she repeated. "He has not."

"Mr. Grudge," Dr. Bear continued, "does what you saw contradict this statement?"

"Contradict it? No, I guess not."

Dr. Bear made several lengthy notes. "Mr. Schurke, would you like to add anything? Now is the time."

"No," I said. "Emma's account is accurate."

Dr. Bear looked over her glasses at me. "Open door, Mr. Schurke, from now on. In all circumstances. Yes?"

"Yes," I said.

"Then, as far as I'm concerned, this matter is history. Now, as to the incident in the hallway, you both said you heard noises in the West Building that made it difficult for you to talk. Did either of you see anyone or anything at that time?"

I said, "No. Nobody."

Emma said, "Nothing."

"Mr. Grudge?"

"Unfortunately, no."

Dr. Bear stood. "I trust you all will respect our mutual privacy in this regard. Ms. Stratford, thank you for your time; please don't hesitate to contact me if you have any—" She pointed at her notes. "—other concerns."

"Thank you," Emma said. She followed Dr. Bear out the door.

Grudge and I rose to leave.

"Sit," Daniels commanded. "Both of you." He waited for the sound of Dr. Bear's heavy footsteps to dissipate. "Damn it, Schurke. What's the matter with you?"

"Extenuating circumstances," I said again.

"Bullshit," Grudge said.

"Both of you—" Daniels rubbed his forehead. "Just go. Get out of my office."

(Emma has returned from the annex with a basket of dirty laundry to fold. "Is it over?" she wants to know. Yes. Yes, it is.)

I remember Twitter was blowing up with the news that day:

@MetroDetroitJournal: It's official. GM in bankruptcy, future of company, Detroit uncertain.
9:09 AM – 1 June 2009

@News.USA: Giant US automaker files for bankruptcy, shakes industry.
9:09 AM – 1 June 2009

@News.USA: GM bankruptcy largest in US history.
9:08 AM – 1 June 2009

I was concerned about Alex. I hadn't heard from her all weekend, and there was no further evidence of her on social media after she added that strange photo album to Facebook. By text, phone, Facebook messenger, Twitter direct message, and gchat, she was unreachable. Or unresponsive. And I was feeling so tired. Too tired to deal with anything. I spent the entire weekend stressing out about the meeting; now it was time for class to begin.

*Can I file for personal and career bankruptcy, please?*

I began class by lecturing: "If there's a definitive theme throughout Grundstein's 1932 novel *West of Home*, it's a dislocation of place and of identity—worldview. For the characters, the central conflict in *West of Home* is a pandemic of post-Great War schizophrenia, commonly referred to as 'shell shock'—what we might call PTSD. The characters are experiencing identity crises that would not be fully understood, explained, or solved. They are forced to try to find ways to merely cope, to get by. And they have to do so in a world where war shattered physical and metaphorical homes.

"The problem can be understood by what scholar Homi Bhabha, in the 1994 book *The Location of Culture*, demonstrates as 'unhomeliness'—an essentially postmodern trend. Here we see Grundstein's work begin to lean toward the postmodern. As Bhabha explains, the 'unhomely' is 'the condition of extra-territorial and cross-cultural initiations,' and 'it has a resonance that can be heard distinctly, if erratically, in fictions that negotiate the powers of cultural difference in a range of transhistorical sites.' Although Bhabha is mostly referring to post-colonial sites of the British Empire, the same concept could certainly be applied to expatriates of the German Empire, *die Deutsches Kaiserreich*, which fell as a result of the Great War.

"If we look at Grundstein's work through that lens, then *West of Home* is a perfect example of the kind of fiction to which Bhabha is referring. Ferdi Gerver, our protagonist, is involved in cross-cultural initiations in a political way in his role as mayor.

Christel Dahl, his love interest, on the other hand, is involved in an artistic way, as a novelist. Both characters attempt to navigate these new multi-cultural experiences. Both characters are located in foreign places as they are German ex-pats, Ferdi in Michigan and Christel in Paris. These places have histories of their own, and at certain points, those histories overlap and, to some extent, clash with their personal histories, specifically German history. It is in these cross-cultural engagements and transhistorical spaces where the 'unhomeliness' occurs, where these characters are constantly operating under the weight of *otherness*. This is beginning to happen on a large scale across the globe.

"Think of the saying, 'The sun never sets on the British Empire.' That's the scale we're talking about. As an example, Bhabha cites the stuttered words of S.S. 'Whisky' Sisodia from Salman Rushdie's *The Satanic Verses*: 'The trouble with the Engenglish is that their hiss hiss history happened overseas, so they dodo don't know what it means'."

Harmony and Leslie, who were drifting, snapped to attention at the sound of the stuttering.

"Obviously," I continued, "we know the sun does set on the British Empire now. That's the kind of massive shift Grundstein, and his characters by extension, were caught up in. A collective, global identity crisis. It manifests in Grundstein's characters in different ways because, according to Bhabha, 'the unhomely moment relates the traumatic ambivalences of a personal, psychic history to the wider disjunctions of political existence.' For Ferdi and Christel, as their personal histories correlate with regional and world histories, meanings and identities get lost without a defined home. Consequently, regardless of the global nature of it all, each individual must cope with their own crisis, *independently*.

"Traditions, you see—notions of citizenship, class, love and romance—become impractical to say the least.

"Ferdi copes by suppression, by constantly living in an intoxicated state of ambivalence. On page 114, Ferdi says, 'And as for accomplishing anything worth pride, between birth and death, one may just as effectively drink ten bottles of whiskey and stare at the sea and wait—the end result shall come out about the same.' Ferdi's ambivalence comes not only from that feeling of 'unhomeliness,' but also from a sense of futility working within the American political system. Instead of trying to swim any longer, he wants instead to submerge himself in a sea of alcohol.

"There is no doubt that Ferdi's drinking has an element of drowning sorrows, but it is more than that. We see this when he sends his assistant out to get him another drink, saying, 'No more Old Fashions. Old Fashions aren't going to get me anywhere. Just bring me the bottle.' That's the most famous line from this novel, which has been parodied so widely, you've probably heard it referenced and had no idea it was a reference to Grundstein's work. And Roy—"

Roy's head shot up, eyes red with sleep.

"—you can take that anecdote to the bar tonight to impress the ladies."

"I was just about to start taking notes," he said, looking about, confused.

"The use of alcohol is a response to the impact of a long history of cumulative wounds. He feels the full burden of his German identity. If Ferdi does not drink, as soon as he starts to sober up, he begins to feel that burden, again, too strongly. But his drinking is not a paradise; it's 'a never-ending hell.' In the letter he sends to Christel, he writes, 'Not even death can end the burden of my forefather's sins on my soul.'

"Christel, ironically, she copes with her sense of 'unhomeliness' by traveling. She leaves Germany, hops around Europe, and unsatisfied, returns to her favorite place, her hometown of Düsseldorf. It's clear that this mechanism worked as well for her as drinking does for Ferdi. Upon her return, it's apparent that nothing has been solved for her, and the only changes that have happened at all have been decay—the city is crumbling, her health is in decline, and her prior relationships are in shambles. 'This is not my home,' she keeps repeating. 'If only I could find my home.' She takes that strange trip to the farm in France because she holds this romantic notion that her problems can be solved by finding an oasis somewhere outside Germany that can take her back to her roots—a place where she and Ferdi can retire.

"But Ferdi knows better. He tells her, 'What would be the point?' Ferdi understands that the solution is not to leave Germany, even the promised land of America can't do anything for him, and by extension, for them. Their problem is internal; it will follow them wherever they might try to go.

"That's when Christel begins asking people the same question over and over, 'Do you think there's hope for Ferdi?' The question is not only about alcoholism, but it's also about the problem behind the drinking. The problem of constructing an identity, finding selfhood in a contemporary culture in which, to return to Bhabha, there is a 'displacement and disjunction that does not totalize experience.' We see this as Christel contemplates the order of the Universe in relation to her experience under the night sky, no doubt referring to Walt Whitman's 'When I Heard the Learn'd Astronomer,' she says, 'I am tired and sick. I am lost, by myself, and from time to time, I look at the stars and curse.' "

I looked at my students to see how they reacted to that.

"You wanna fly," Eli said, "you got to give up the shit that weighs you down."

"Yeah," Emma said vaguely as she put her notes away. It was the first time I heard her speak since the Dr. Bear Inquisition; it was such a relief to have her say anything at all.

"After journeying through the first half of *West of Home*," I hastened to add, "I always feel the need for a drink."

No response.

"Alright, in the second half, we'll see how these characters decide to move forward, into the future. Keep thinking about your topics for your midterms," I said, feeling something like a professor again, feeling like I knew what I was doing, and thinking, *Maybe—just maybe—I could do this for a living.* (Even though I already had a sense that the trajectory of my life was beating against it.) "The papers are due a week from today."

"That's what's going to make me drink," Leslie said smiling.

@JohnnyLawJr: @TheTomPeters How many balloons would it take to get the Renaissance Center off the ground? #UP
11:47 AM – 1 June 2009

@TheTomPeters: Just saw #UP last night. Fantastic.
11:23 AM – 1 June 2009

Daniels was in my office when I got back from class. He was leaning up against the wall behind my desk with folded arms. He said, "Montgomery paid me a visit last week."

*Grudge? What the—*

"He seems to think something's come up you haven't discussed with me."

"Look, you heard from Emma directly this morning. There's—"

"Not in regards to your... *conduct.* In regards to your recent research."

"With class and defense prep, I'm too busy for research."

"Let me be more specific," Daniels continued, "he says a little birdy told him you were aggressively searching Grundstein's cabin."

*Alex?* I shook my head. *Couldn't be.*

"I went up north over the break to work. You know that."

"Monte seems to think you've been *looking* for something.

Something big."

"I've not said nor done anything that should give anybody that kind of impression. Not intentionally."

"I know. I know," Daniels said. He picked at the corner of his beard. "I've been thinking a lot about the meeting we had this morning, Sam. I've been patient with you. But, I'm getting frustrated. And I thought of something. Remind me, what was that other student's name? She came to see me last semester."

"What?" I said.

"Don't. Not this Emma, but the other one? What was her name?"

"Veronica?"

"Yes. Veronica. After our meeting this morning, I realized, I don't think Dr. Bear knows about Veronica." Daniels evaluated my reaction. "You know, Sam, some people view our work like a competition. Some play for keeps. Montgomery, for example. But I didn't think you were like that. I thought you were different. I thought I'd trained you better than that."

"I'm not like Grudge." Defensive.

"You know, Sam, a lot has been made of Hemingway's lost manuscripts," Daniels said, uncrossing his arms, "but frankly, they wouldn't be worth much. Gertrude Stein had her work cut out for her with those young bucks like Hemingway and Grundstein flooding into her Parisian salon, asking for her attention. She gave both of them the same advice. To listen more closely to what one sees, what one hears. To pay attention to what causes emotion and to get that action down in the writing. Good advice. They needed it." Daniels stepped toward me. "She told Hemingway the manuscripts were no good, and I'm sure she was right. The only value would be sentimental, for guys like me—us—who, like the modernists, believe the modern world needs true literature."

"Yes. I agree," I said. *Too defensive.*

"I think losing the manuscripts were good for Hemingway.

It was good for us. It gave us *The Sun Also Rises*. One could argue that book wouldn't have happened if Hemingway was spending all his time trying to fix what was no good to begin with."

"Yes." *Stop.*

Daniels waited for me to say more. At last, he said, "You know, there's a time in the career of every scholar when he, for the first time, takes the backward view. To gain respect. To advance. To make some money. Whatever it might—"

"Make money?" I scoffed. "What, do you think I might buy stocks?" *Silence!*

Daniels clenched his jaw. "This isn't a political stance, Schurke. This isn't a game. My career is running out of time." He stepped too close. His breath was pregnant with bourbon. "Finding Hemingway's manuscripts—" He stopped suddenly, wobbled, then stepped back. "I would've thought the same-ay as you-en I was you-age. I would've tried to do-i-all on-y own."

"I haven't—"

"If ya-did," Daniels said, jabbing at my sternum with a firm finger, "ya'd know better-an ta-hide it fro-me. N't you?"

"Yes."

"Good." Daniels reached into the breast pocket of his sport coat and pulled out two pieces of paper. He unfolded them and showed them to me. "These-re two letters. This one, recommends immediate hire-to Assoc-Profess upon success'l completion of your disser'ation. And this, a consolation letter. 'Thank you for you-service, but unfortunately, we'n't have a position a'able for you at-is time.' That kind a'thing."

His penetrating eyes might as well have been guns pointed at my head as he took great care to fold the letters and return them to his pocket.

"I'm still-ciding whether-not you're goin-to fit in'ere, Schurke. Still wondering if you're goin-to be-a team-layer?"

I cleared my throat. "I. Haven't. Found. Anything."

Daniels sighed.

"If I do," I added, "you'll be the first to know."

"That-smart," Daniels said. "That-smart."

I nodded.

"Now-to this conver'ation," he said, "I would not-know any-thing abou-it. D'you?"

I didn't move.

"If ya-did know somethin-bout this conver'ation, I might also know somthin-bout a hissssstory of polissssy vio'ations on you-part—sexual missssconduct, inssssubord'nation. Is that un-derssssstood?"

"Yes."

"What's-at?" Daniels said.

"Understood."

"What'd'you understand?"

"I would not know."

Daniels cackled. "Good." He stepped around me. "Clean-is place up." He knocked a stack of papers to the floor, then looked them over. "Throw some-is worthlesss messss out. How's any-one suppposed to find a'thing in'ere?"


@GretchBreporting: GM will shed dead weight, including Sat-urn, Hummer, and Saab brands.
4:55 PM – 1 June 2009

# 25

I lost that Tuesday to paralyzing fear. Daniels had me paranoid. I didn't want to go anywhere in case I might see him, or Grudge, or Alex.

*Little birdy. Little birdy. Little birdy.*

Something was off.

I didn't prepare for class. I didn't examine my contraband. I didn't want more leads to fall into my lap. I wanted to press the pause button until I could get a better grip on it all.

I holed up in my room all day and did my best to do nothing but binge-watch old re-runs of *Seinfeld*.

"By the middle of the twentieth century," I said, beginning Wednesday's lecture, "several major, devastating events in history were complete. The emotional, psychological, and physical trauma that resulted from World War I and World War II initiated a disastrous rippling effect of cultural dissolution, of which, most notably, the decolonization of the British Empire was a tangible symbol. As these major events came to a close, a demanding question emerged: what's next? Moving into the latter part of century, it became increasingly clear that this rippling effect was not resolving but gathering steam, and it extended beyond Europe, beyond America, across the globe.

"This, in literary terms, has been somewhat classified, however ambiguously, as postmodernism. The American scholar, Fredric Jameson, in "Postmodernism and Consumer Society," set out to:

> 'Sketch a few of the ways in which the new postmodernism expresses the inner truth of that newly emergent social order of late capitalism, but will have to limit the description to only two of its significant features, which [he] will call pastiche and schizophrenia: they will give us a chance to sense the specificity of the postmodernist experience of space and time respectively.'

Jameson's conception of 'schizophrenia,' in this sense, reflects this disruption of temporal and cultural stability of the time. Grundstein's later novels, *West of Home*, and to an even greater extent, *The Son Down*—which we'll begin looking at next week—are, by Jameson's definition, examples of this postmodern literary schizophrenia.

"That is to say, the construction of space and time, meaning and experience, begins in language. The very way in which we conceive of and understand the human experience is filtered through, interpreted by, language—through the successful linking of miscellaneous signifiers. Meaning-effect. Sentences, paragraphs, books—all are organized by time, beginning to end. Textuality. This model of meaning is, then, applied to life in an attempt to better understand experience. Past, present, future. Hence, the experience of time. In fact, identifying with this linear model is *what constitutes a normal experience*. Therefore, the breakdown of language causes the 'schizophrenia.' The schizophrenic does not, or perhaps cannot, subscribe to a perpetual understanding of existence. Without this linked relationship between past and future, there's only the present. Infinite present."

Suddenly I was confused. *Language. Space. Time. Meaning.* New thoughts were intruding upon my remarks.

"Perhaps what is commonly thought to be a 'normal' experience is purely illusion," I added. "Perhaps the meaning that we normally understand to result from seemingly familiar combinations of signifiers, perhaps, signifies nothing."

*Nothing. Nothing. Nothing.* I felt the words as if they'd echoed throughout the classroom, but they hadn't.

Bracing myself against the podium, I looked to my notes for guidance. "Now, consider Grundstein's work. He was tuned into this trend early on, where we see the faulty, slippery nature of continuity, which, as we'll see here, destroy one's ability to predict a stable trajectory into the future."

*Schizophrenia. Postmodernity.*

"Let's take a look at page 213 of *West of Home*, where Ferdi's love interest, Christel, has the following realization:

> Ferdi couldn't trust. He doubted any concept of his past and rejected any thought of his future. He was condemned to obscurity—an abyss of ambivalence. He could see now the human experience was a misunderstanding. Life was not a path, as if you can look back and see exactly where you've been, and look forward and see exactly where you're going. It was a ball of dust floating out in the expanse of the Universe, pulled in every direction by gravities greater than its own, susceptible to an inevitable death in a million different ways, no matter how long it takes.

"Think, too, of Hanne in *The Timepiece*. She's the perfect image of attempting to maintain the conventions of her class, at this time, as much as possible. Christel, by contrast, desperately wants to break out of the same expectations of class, not for economic reasons, but for individual freedom. But Ferdi cannot bear to reflect nor project; he only thinks of himself in a perpetual present where expectations are inconceivable.

"To approach this in narrative in *West of Home*, Grundstein presents the reader with myriad endings. In doing so, the novel itself becomes its own schizophrenic fray—as unpredictable for the reader as for Ferdi himself. One ending of note is recognizable as traditional. Ferdi, unable to envision alternatives, accepts his inevitable duty to act according to the perceived path behind and before him—to marry Ursella and humbly accept her family money and business, whatever may come of it, and whatever personal ambitions may be sacrificed. In this scenario, Ferdi must cope with his feelings for and memory of Christel as a figment of his past:

> He works daily to not think of her, the other woman, a past love, and to speak of her nevermore, and through great effort, thinks only of Ursella.

"It's interesting to note, here, although Ferdi knows this is an issue for the greater human psyche, he cannot help but internalize the problem as an individual. Ironically, that's the only thought that enables Ferdi to put Christel in the past. The only way he can live is to make his dilemma responsible for his behavior. In this ending, the path becomes relatively simple: 'one must accept, however burdensome, the conundrum and uphold tradition in order to live peaceable as much as possible.' In this ending, 'Ferdi and Ursella weren't enthralled in blissful passion, the way a fairytale ends, but they were together—coping.'

"Another ending Grundstein presents is more complicated. Ferdi pursues Christel for love and will attempt to pursue his political career without Ursella and her family money. He sends Ursella a telegram, notifying her that his 'heart has been stolen by a damsel, for whom [he] has become much distressed.' In doing so, Ferdi moves into unpredictable territory—unknown step after unknown step. On this new course, Ferdi travels to Paris and hunts Christel down. When he finds her, he takes her into her apartment, imagining they will—"

"Get it on," Roy suggested.

"I prefer *romp*," I said over the laughter. "But I'm glad you're listening. See, Ferdi believes he can possess Christel, that she can now become his wife, but he underestimates how problematic the modern worldview has become and he misunderstands her intentions with him. Knowing the message is on its way and irrevocable, it's painful to watch Ferdi as he makes his desperate proposal, to which Christel responds, 'Oh, Ferdi, dear. It's so wonderful you're here. Let's not burden this moment by thinking ahead of it for a single minute.' We see that she, too, is unable to construct a picture of the future that contains love and marriage in the way that Ferdi hoped might be possible.

"For all the foresight and courage his realization afforded him to take this action, Ferdi was still blind to Christel's new understanding of love, one in which the very notion of marriage was unnecessary.

"In Grundstein's last ending, Ferdi, unsure how to proceed, keeps both Ursella and Christel at bay. After several months campaigning as a single man, he loses the next election in humbling fashion. He, then, finds that Christel has taken up residence with a female artist. She's managed to create a small niche for herself where she can be independent and free, with the constant companionship and the financial support of a roommate, but with the possibility of romantic deviations, whenever she pleases.

"Let's take a look at that important passage on page 256:

> 'I am not single,' Christel says, 'for I love and am loved by multitudes.'
>
> The door to Christel's room opens unexpectedly. A boy appears. He's thin and lanky with a frock of brown hair and a forward-leaning forehead. The

boy nestles in between her legs.

Ferdi looks to Christel, pleadingly.

'Oh, Ferdi,' she says, 'I wonder, if we were born a hundred years from now, could we have had the best of marriages—me as me, as I am now, and you as you, as you are now?'

'I should think so.' Ferdi says, standing to leave. 'I see now it was a mistake to bother you here. Pardon me.'

"Grundstein uses these endings as narrative disruptions to make the novel read schizophrenically, putting the reader right there, stuck in the present, with Ferdi.

"Ultimately, the reader is left to contemplate how best to envision the end of the novel, but that would be too concrete in Grundstein's view. The novel, like life in general, is much more complicated than that."

@MetroDetroitJournal: Obama Administration to issue $30.1 billion loan to GM, taking possession of largest US automaker. 11:19 PM – 3 June 2009

@FluTrackerH1N1: 66 countries infected; 19,273 cases reported; 117 deaths confirmed. 11:18 PM – 3 June 2009

I awoke the next morning in a cold sweat with someone knocking on my door. In a panic: "One moment, please."

"Open the door, Schurke." It was Grudge.

"What do you want?" I struggled to get my bare feet into tangled shorts.

"Tom let me in. We need to talk. I know everything."

I opened the door without finding a shirt and saw Grudge. His hair was cut short and his beard was gone, clean-shaven, smooth as the day he was born.

"My God," I said. "What happened to you?"

"It was time for a new look." His thin lips and absent jawline were now visible.

"I'm not sure you found the right one."

"Focus, Schurke. I'm here for the evidence." Grudge stepped into my room and shut the door. "I'm not leaving until I have it."

(He was standing not five feet away from the duffle bag in the bottom of my closet. *What a poor hiding place*, I think now. *How amateur.*)

"Ha, *viel Glück*," I said. "You know, Hemingway wouldn't approve of your new look. If he had something, he wouldn't have given anything to a guy who looked like you."

"Piss off, Schurke. I know you have evidence."

"Let's start there. What is it, exactly, that you know?"

"I want to know exactly what *you think* you know." There was that smugness again; I wanted to wipe the smirk off of his face with a swipe of my hand.

"If I found something, I would know what it is—"

"Come off it, Schurke," he said. "You know, you could use my help."

"That's generous of you."

Grudge laughed. "I spoke with Bobbie last night."

I nearly dropped dead at the mention of her name.

"Bobbie and I are colleagues," he continued. "Fellow scholars. We work together." Grudge paused as if he was being gracious enough to give me a chance to respond.

I said nothing.

"She told me all about it."

"About what?" I couldn't resist.

"She told me about your little trip to Petoskey."

I couldn't remember telling her about anything—nothing

250 •   K.M. Zahrt

about the journal or *The Sun Also Rises* I stole from the library, certainly not the lighter or the paperweight. But she knew a lot about my activities. I couldn't know for sure which pieces they'd be able to put together.

"Wasn't a state secret, Grudge," I said.

"Yes, I know. Alex told me, too."

*Why would she talk to goddamned Grudge about me?*

"That's right, Schurke," he said as if he could see my thoughts. "Your precious Alex tells me everything."

My insides were stewing.

"When I talked to Bobbie, she acted strange. She asked me all these questions about you. Gave me the impression that something happened that Alex might be interested to know more about."

"You think you can come over to my place and make demands, and I'm—"

"I'm trying to work with you, here."

"Why? Why would you? All of a sudden?"

"I'll find out what you're up to, one way or another. From Bobbie. From Alex. From you."

"Thanks, Grudge. I appreciate it. You're a gentleman and a scholar." I shoved him out into the hallway and shut the door in his face.

*What the—*

Feeling reckless. Like the desperate lawyers in the movies who clear the files from their desks in one sweep. I had to do something. I hit the whiskey hard.

Then, I called Bobbie at the museum.

BOBBIE: "This is... unexpected. If this is about Beth, I—"

ME: "This is about Montgomery Grudge."

I could hear Bobbie's breath catch on the other end of the line.

ME: "You know Grudge."

BOBBIE: "Yes."

ME: "What did you say to him about me?"

The line went silent again.

ME: "Bobbie, this is very important. What did you tell him?"

BOBBIE: "He asked me what you were doing up here."

ME: "What did you say?"

BOBBIE: "I said you came to the museum, and you looked around, but you didn't stay long."

ME: "..."

BOBBIE: "He asked me if you took an interest in anything in particular. I said you looked through Grundstein's clothes and asked me some questions about them. He seemed unsatisfied."

ME: "Did he ask you about... us?"

BOBBIE: "I said you showed me and a friend around the cabin. That's all. What's the problem, Sam?"

ME: "He's got my boss sniffing around me like a Doberman."

BOBBIE: "I thought you didn't have anything to worry about?"

ME: "I don't—"

BOBBIE: "Well, then, hang in there. I'm sure it'll all work—"

I hung up on Bobbie and took another shot. The taste of charred oak and alcohol lingered in my mouth.

*Grudge doesn't know anything; he's being a fool. And it wasn't Alex—*

Thinking of Alex. One day, she'd asked me to drive her to an estate sale. There, she'd found an unmarked box, and without looking inside, she'd negotiated to purchase the entire box. When I'd asked her why, she'd said, "For a painting. There's bound to be a gem inside." When we returned to her studio, she cut off the top of the box and dumped its contents out on a table. She didn't mess with the arrangement; she simply fixed a light on the table—"to give it depth"—and started painting.

I remember being stuck in my research, frustrated, at that point, and that was one of my favorite things to do—to watch her paint and think out loud.

"Focus more," Alex would say. "Think about something that can help you right now, today." She was painting a small portion of one corner of the canvas, painting several bullets that were spilled out onto the table. There was one used, empty shell in the middle of the pile. She pointed at it. "When I paint I have to draw a clear picture of something first, however small, before the larger picture will take shape."

*How much of Grundstein's life,* I thought, *will shape mine?*

@EnterTUNEment: Sources say Michael Jackson may be taking anesthetics intravenously to treat insomnia as King of Pop prepares for upcoming tour.
9:14 AM – 4 June 2009

@News.USA: 86% of influenza viruses reported to CDC resemble H1N1.
9:13 AM – 4 June 2009

# 26

I was surprised to see all my students were present except one. Emma was absent. That'd never happened before. Their midterm papers were stacked on the corner of my desk.

"Emma was here," Harmony said, noticing my confused glances toward Emma's empty chair. "She dropped off her essay."

"She said she wasn't feeling well," Leslie added, "was probably going to go to the hospital."

"Probably has the swine flu," Roy said, beaming a white smile.

"Not at a joke," Eli said. "Could kill lots."

*Swine flu? H1N1? Emma? No.*

"I'll look into it. Thank you," I said, sliding the papers into my satchel. "I'll have grades for these posted online before Wednesday's class. If you have any questions or would like specific feedback about your grade, you can see me after class or during my offices hours.

"Last week, we discussed the concept of schizophrenia in relationship to *West of Home*. Today, we're going to discuss pastiche to help you begin to understand what it is that Grundstein's doing in *The Son Down*."

Sometime over the weekend, I misplaced my copy of Fredric Jameson's "Postmodernism and Consumer Society," with my notes scattered all over the margins. Before class, I became frantic looking for it. Running out of time, I had to print off a new copy from the Internet, and instead of preparing my own thoughts, I merely highlighted the sections in which Jameson specifically referred to pastiche.

Without citing Jameson, I began reading through the high-lighted sections as if they were my own.

> " 'I must first explain this term, which people gener-
> ally tend to confuse with or assimilate to that relat-
> ed verbal phenomenon called parody. Both pastiche
> and parody involve the imitation or, better still, the
> mimicry of other styles and particularly of the man-
> nerisms and stylistic twitches of other styles. It is ob-
> vious that modern literature in general offers a very
> rich field for parody, since the great modern writers
> have all been defined by the invention or production
> of rather unique styles...'

"Think of master stylists, writers like Hemingway and Gr-undstein.

> " '...all of these styles, however different from each
> other, are comparable in this: each is quite unmis-
> takable; once one of them is learned, it is not likely
> to be confused with something else.
>     'Now parody capitalizes on the uniqueness of
> these styles and seizes on their idiosyncrasies and
> eccentricities to produce an imitation which mocks
> the original. I won't say that the satiric impulse is
> conscious in all forms of parody: in any case, a good
> or great parodist has to have some secret sympathy
> for the original, just as a great mimic has to have the
> capacity to put himself/herself in the place of the

person imitated. Still, the general effect of parody is—whether in sympathy or with malice—to cast ridicule on the private nature of these stylistic mannerisms and their excessiveness and eccentricity with respect to the way people normally speak or write. So there remains somewhere behind all parody the feeling that there is a linguistic norm in contrast to which the styles of the great modernists can be mocked.' "

As I read, a vision began to form in my mind, something illusive, yet unmistakable; something fragmented, yet complete: Grundstein. An old Grundstein—unlike the middle-aged man most commonly pictured. Disheveled white hair. Unkempt beard. Sitting at the table. At the cabin. Then, darkness. *What?*

" '...pastiche is, like parody, the imitation of a peculiar or unique style, the wearing of a stylistic mask, speech in a dead language: but it is a neutral practice of such mimicry, without parody's ulterior motive, without the satirical impulse, without laughter, without that still latent feeling that there exists something *normal* compared with which what is being imitated is rather comic. Pastiche is blank parody, parody that has lost its sense of humour...' "

Old Grundstein. Sitting at the table. Scribbling in a journal. Journal, gone. Darkness. *No. What?*

" 'But now we need to introduce a new piece into this puzzle, which may help explain why classical modernism is a thing of the past and why postmodernism should have taken its place. This new component is what is generally called the 'death of the subject' or, to say it in more conventional language, the end of individualism as such. The great modernisms were, as we have said, predicated on the invention of a personal, private style, as unmistakable as your fingerprint, as incomparable as your own body. But this means that the modernist aesthetic is in some way organically linked to the conception of a unique self and private identity, a unique personality and individuality, which can be expected to generate its own unique vision of the world and to forge its own unique, unmistakable style.' "

Grundstein. At the table. Darkness. *No. I need more—*

" '...the notion that this kind of individualism and personal identity is a thing of the past...' "

Gone. Cabin empty. Darkness. *No! I need more!*

" '...what we have to retain from all this is rather an aesthetic dilemma: because if the experience and the ideology of the unique self, an experience and ideology which informed the stylistic practice of classical modernism, is over and done with, then it is no longer clear what the artists and writers of the present period are supposed to be doing.' "

Standing. Outside cabin. Along shoreline. Gun. Rope. A Petoskey stone as big as a football. Darkness. *No!*

" 'And this is perhaps not merely a 'psychological' matter: we also have to take into account the immense weight of seventy or eighty years of classical modernism itself. There is another sense in which

the writers and artists of the present day will no longer be able to invent new styles and worlds—they've
already been invented; only a limited number of
combinations are possible; the most unique ones
have been thought of already.' "

I felt woozy; the room began to spin a clockwise orbit around
me. I clung to the podium and pressed on with an irrational determination to finish this counterfeit lecture as if that would get
me through.

" 'So the weight of the whole modernist aesthetic
tradition—now dead—also *weighs like a nightmare on
the brains of the living*, as Marx said in another context.' "

Grundstein again. Wading now. Knee deep. Rope around
the stone. Rope around waist. *No!* Darkness.

" 'Hence, once again, pastiche: in a world in which
stylistic innovation is no longer possible, all that is
left is to imitate dead styles, to speak through the
masks and with the voices of the styles in the imaginary museum.' "

My stomach now began to churn counterclockwise against
the spinning classroom. I held the essay close to my face, futilely
resisting the rotation.

" 'But this means that contemporary or postmodernist art is going to be about art itself in a new kind
of way; even more, it means that one of its essential
messages will involve the necessary failure of art...' "

Water. Neck deep. Rising. Gun. One inch above the right ear. *Don't!* Redness.

> " '...and the aesthetic, the failure of the new, the im-
> prisonment in the past.' "

The pressure on the back of my throat was welling up, about to overflow. *Get to the restroom!*

"That's all," I said. "For today."

Stuffed the notes in my satchel.

"Sorry. Not feeling well."

Threw the strap over my shoulder.

"Got to go."

Left.

Ran. Down the hall. Burst through door. Dropped satchel. Stormed stall. Heaved. Hurled. Smelled, tasted acid. Darkness—

When my stomach was somewhat settled and my vision was slightly less burred, I stood unsteadily and wiped the residue from the corners of my mouth with toilet paper. Flushed.

I looked about. I was in the Stall Pong stall again. It seemed like only moments before that I was there, but it was all so different now. The inside was awash with fresh, dull-yellow paint. The walls, a clean palette.

*Where are we going, Walt Whitman?* I thought, remembering. *The doors close in an hour. Which way does your beard point tonight?*

I patted my pockets for something to write with, but found Grundstein's lighter instead. I read the inscription: *SET IT ALL ABLAZE.* And I saw that it was good.

I closed my eyes, and with the bottom corner of the lighter, in scrawling letters, I began to scrape new words into the paint:

## RAPIST
## MURDERER

I lifted my eyes, and I saw that the words weren't anything, like nothing in my life. All was born again, and I knew there was something I ought to do. I added in one more word—COW-ARD—and thought: *Oh, Alexandria, faith is what someone knows to be true, whether they believe it or not.*

@News.USA: GM removed from Dow Jones Industrial Average.
2:52 PM – 8 June 2009

@TheTomPeters: 'The Hangover' is terrible. Not a damn thing funny about it. #lowestcommondenominator
2:51 PM – 8 June 2009

At the office, Grudge was at his desk chomping on baby carrots that he was pulling from a Ziploc baggy. My stomach wasn't in any kind of condition to watch or hear Grudge eat.

*The hangover is terrible*, I thought. I turned to leave.

"Schurke, where have you been?" Grudge said with the kind of sharp edge a parent uses when a child is in troubled. *Chomp.* His eyes were stuck on his computer screen. *Chomp.*

The passive look, the glaze over his eyes, and the random scrolling of his mouse told me he was on Facebook or Twitter.

"Your girlfriend came by looking for you," he added. *Chomp.*

At the thought, my chest fluttered.

"She left a note on your chair." *Chomp.*

There was a notepad on my desk chair, the only spot on my half of the office that would likely catch my attention. At first glance, I recognized Tante's handwriting, and the flutter changed to an unbearable pressure. To see evidence of Tante's presence in my office was an intrusion. From anxious to con-fused, the room began its orbit around me once again.

I held my stomach. *This is what life is*, I thought. *Ailments and intrusions.*

The note read:

> *Sam, mein Lieber,*
>> *Komm zu mir. Es ist Zeit, dass wir uns über deinen Großvater unterhalten.*
>>> *Immer, Tante*

Suddenly I didn't hear Grudge's chomping anymore. I felt compressed as if I was far under water.

Tante's voice rang in my head. *Sam, dear. Sam, dear. Sam, dear. It's time we discussed your Grandfather.*

*What in God's name for? And why now—so urgently, in fact, as to compel her to come all the way to campus and hunt me down? Why? Why? Why?*

I closed my eyes and rubbed the hair along my jawline with both hands. My beard was long and wiry now.

Grudge peeked over the divider that separated our desks. "Everything okay, Schurke?"

"Fine."

"You look—" *Chomp.* "—tired."

"I am. Been busy."

"Aren't you—" *Chomp.* "—only teaching—" *Chomp.* "—one class right now?" *Chomp.*

I rubbed my eyes.

"What else—" *Chomp.* "—has got you—" *Chomp.* "—so worked up?" *Chomp.*

"Cut out the damn carrots already, Grudge. For God's sake."

Grudge froze.

*Have to get out.* I snatched up the note and turned, but Grudge was stuck in my tracks, standing toe-to-toe.

"Carrot breath," I said. "I'm going to hurl if you don't get out of my face."

"You know what would make you feel better, Schurke?" Grudge said. "You need to tell us everything you know. And everything she knows."

I scoffed. "I know you read the note."

"Look at you," he said. "You're a mess. Look at this office. You can't do this alone. You need to clean yourself up. Trim that God-awful excuse for a beard. You're falling apart."

I snagged the bag of carrots off of his desk and dumped them in the garbage.

"What the hell, Schurke? Are you deranged?"

I brushed by him on my way out the door.

"You need help, Schurke," he called after me. "Let us help you."

@DetLionsLeak: Schwartz says Stafford will start in opener over veteran Culpepper, 'Not an experiment.'
3:48 PM – 8 June 2009

# 27

Grundstein, Grudge, Tante—an impairing cocktail.

On my way to Tante's, the road was racing under me like an arcade game at the movie theater lobby—the Earth tilting and spinning toward me—and I struggled, like a hamster running in a wheel, to keep Karmann, my life, my vision on the road. My hands, sweaty and weak, felt slippery on the wheel; my grip, tenuous. If I let go, I would career into the brush, and crash, and burn.

*All I want is one more day at the beach,* I thought. *At the movies. With Alex. To try again. To hope for a different outcome. With infinite sides to the dice, the chances of repeating any single sum would be endlessly improbable. Just one lean to the left or to the right. That's all. Is that so much to ask?*

(Of course, I would've forfeited everything that led me to Emma, and I wouldn't change that now, but one cannot know where it's all leading, except—)

When I walked in, Tante was setting the dinner table for two. "I knew you wouldn't be long," she said. "Take a seat. Dinner's ready. *Schweinsbraten und Klöße.*" A family recipe for braised pork pot roast with potato dumplings. (As a kid, it was the only meal I could keep down when I was sick. When I'm done here, I'll make it for Emma.)

As I sat down, Tante set a stein of beer in front of me.

"Thirsty?" she said.

"Yes." Hand shaking, I took two sips.

Tante finished setting the table without making conversation. I nursed the lager. When Tante sat down, she said, "*Lass uns essen.*"

"*Danke*, Tante."

We ate. When my lager was half gone, Tante got up to refill my stein without prompt, and she poured herself another as well.

As she did so, I took a peek at the picture on her wall of Grundstein and Hemingway standing in downtown Petoskey as boys.

Tante said, "This isn't about the letters."

My eyes snapped to hers, startled.

"You know about the letters, I know," Tante said, eyeing their location behind the picture on the wall. "After you and your *Freundin* came, I checked. They were gone. Two days later. Back. That's fine. Nothing you didn't already know." She set the steins down and returned to her seat. She took a sip of beer, held it on her tongue, and closed her eyes as she swallowed. "You were still looking for secrets. Fine. But how far were you willing to go without my consent?" She swirled her glass in front of her mouth, watching the golden liquid dance before her. "So I tested you. You need to learn how to properly fold a newspaper, *mein Lieber*. You now know about the journal, too, I know. I put it out like cheese for a mouse, to see if you would sniff it out. Then, there you were. The journal was in the rack facing in and to the east; you put it back facing out and to the west. Disappointing."

My jaw was ajar.

"Then, I waited a couple weeks to see what you'd do with it? *Zu spät für Ihr Buch. Ja?*"

"Yes," I said. "I'm done with the dissertation."

"*Gut.*"

I nodded.

"Samuel, families are foundational to society, don't you think? With a sovereignty all of its own, yes?"

"Sure," I said.

"Certain things should rightfully remain private. Don't you agree?"

"Family secrets. As in, not to be public."

"As in, should not be *veröffentlicht*."

"Yes. We agreed about the World War II years, too. I haven't included anything without your consent."

"I know."

I raised my mug and took a pull.

"Samuel," Tante said, "your grandfather was a man of his age, of depression, of war, of fear. I hope you can appreciate that."

"I do."

"It's not for us, privileged by the future, to—out of context, out of time, out of history—judge one's actions, yes?"

"Yeah, maybe."

Tante sighed, then contemplated something in silence for what could've lasted an entire generation, or two, or three.

"Samuel," she said, at last, "this is the fact: you are the end of the line. I've been debating a question for some time now. It's a question that plagued your grandfather at the end of his life. The question is whether or not I have the right to take certain information, unshared, to the grave. Your grandfather was not well at the end of his life. You know this, I know. He did not trust himself at the end. He waffled. One day, he'd think one thing; the next day, he'd think the opposite.

"He did his best to leave these decisions to someone else, someone trusted. Me. Now, I, too, have waited too long. I don't trust myself either. This—" She pointed to her temple. "—runs in the family, you know."

I shook my head.

"Samuel, *mein Lieber*, do you understand what I'm saying?"

"I think so."

"What am I saying, Samuel?"

"Opa had certain issues. I know."

"*Jawohl, viele Geheimnisse. Und?*"

"You believe the public has no rights to these secrets."

"No right and no business. I believe they should stay within the family."

"And, if you take them to the grave, the matter will forever be decided."

"Yes, but Papa was—" She paused. "—how to say, afraid to let this knowledge die." Tante studied me. "He didn't believe he had the authority to erase what he perceived as the debts of a sinner. But, I have even more trouble."

I thought for a moment, then said, "As one cannot judge what causes may have justified the actions of the past, one cannot predict the causes of the actions of the future."

"*Richtig.* I see your work," Tante said, her tone changing, lifting, lightening. "I've read your dissertation. Good scholarly work. Your reading of *The Son Down* is consistent with my own. It should help these so-called scholars better understand the book. It does a service to your grandfather. It's what I wanted to happen—was meant to happen—with it. Your grandfather would've been proud."

"Unfortunately," I said, "I doubt many will read it."

"That is not up to us. What is up to us is whether it's out there, available, alive. At times, I think Papa would've trusted you to make the right decision. Perhaps you are the person for whom he was waiting. But, at other times, I think of how your career could be... *erweiterte*... Perhaps the draw, the allure, for you would be too much. But then, I think of how hard this has all become for you. You've grown this beard. You're not eating—"

We averted our gazes, hiding behind our drinks. (We are of a line of cowards.)

"I've decided," Tante said, standing abruptly and walking out to the living room. She returned with two composition notebooks in her hands—*Two journals? Two!*—and a small stack of papers.

Tante set them down next to my plate and pointed to the papers. "Initial here, here, here. Sign here."

I complied. "What's this?"

"You are now the executor of Leonhard Grundstein's estate. Papa's legacy is yours, alone, to manage now."

I ran my forefinger down the center of the cover on the first journal, the one I'd discovered in Tante's bathroom. The material felt dry and rough, like a chalkboard.

"What's in here?" I asked, then frowned.

"You will understand it better than I do, I think."

"Are there more letters?"

"You've seen all the letters I know of. If you want them, you can have them, but I don't think you'll need them."

"No," I said.

"You will notice a small gap in dates. I suspect there's one or two journals missing. I don't have them, and I doubt they exist if you haven't found them yet."

I picked up the second journal—the one unknown to me—and leafed through the pages, which emitted a familiar aroma—notes of almond and vanilla. I closed my eyes and inhaled.

"Did Grundstein mention having anything else, something of Hemingway's, ever taking anything from him?"

"The lost manuscripts, you mean?"

"Yes. You know about them? Do you have them? Do you know where they are?"

"In there," Tante said, pointing to the last journal, "he refers to something that may be what you're looking for. But, let me be clear, he never, *nie*, spoke of such things."

A multitude of scenarios, both past and future, rushed through my head. *God, if only this could've waited three more weeks.*

"This is a pinch, I know," Tante said. "You'll have to decide if it's time to hold the family line, to maintain the discretion that has been decades in the making, or if it's time to disclose all and maintain the course of your career."

I downed the last of my beer and returned my mug to the table. "Tante, are you sure about this?"

"You, Samuel, are the last judge. Shut your ears to the roaring of the voices and do as you see fit."

# Part Three

"Smoke is soul returning to the Universe, to enlightenment;
set it all ablaze"
—Leonhard Grundstein, *The Mysterious Garden*

# Journal of
# Leonhard Grundstein

JUNE 15-JULY 2, 1961

JUNE 15, 1961

It was in the fall when I returned home, where I found that letter from Al Flechtheim. Letter was brief. He sent condolences to me and my family. Said Dieter "died with his dignity." Dignity? The Grundstein way? Flechtheim knew better. We all knew better. Dieter's situation was worse than I understood as a kid. Flechtheim wrote, "They've taken everything Dieter owned. For repercussions. For the best. I advise you and your family to leave the chapter closed."

Father said nothing of the letter. He burned it with my lighter.

That year, I worked in the sandwich shop by day. Spent my savings on a typewriter as soon as I could. Worked on a novel by night. That was the hardest I ever worked. Time of my life, too. I loved that typewriter—a brand new 1919 Underwood III. Lugged it all over town as if I was a painter with a portable easel. Should've taken it to Paris with me. Don't know where my original ended up. Didn't write *Timepiece* on it. Replica's on display at the museum.

So many regrets.

And nothing to show for it now. The novel is still in shards after all these years. Gertrude Stein once told me, when I was a young man, to dump it in the fire. Good advice. Started over, but couldn't dump it. Never could. Been chipping at it all these years. Can't get traction on it, but can't torch it either. Will be the death of me.

Off track. Time's running short. One last confession.

Late summer 1920. Received another letter from Flechtheim. Opened gallery in Düsseldorf, looking to start the magazine. *Der Querschnitt.* Was inquiring after help. Telegrammed him straight away with my response. Too eager. Must've looked like a buffoon who hadn't grown up a day in the War. He wired cash, told me to get on the first ship over.

That's how, only two years after I fled Germany—shrouded, anxious, guilty, disguised as an American journalist—I found myself on the next train to New York to retrace the exact route.

Mother begged me not to go, of course. Never saw father again.

Flechtheim was serious. Serious about everything, including parties. Put on soirées with the who's who. Pretended the War hadn't happened, or worked on forgetting it.

Under the fervor, soul-crushing despair.

We worked in the morning, drank and danced evenings. Atmosphere was intoxicating. Liberation.

Met Margarete, my first love. An artist. Mysterious. Magnetic. Saw her, swerving, a glass of wine at eye-level. Spoke in German. Flirted in English.

Can hear her now. *Oh, darling, you mustn't.*

Her saying.

Touched your forearm. *Really, you mustn't.*

Made me sore when she said it to other men. Knew how it felt.

She was all her own. Always would be.

Must've been 1921. Took her down to Paris by train. Hem and Hadley had arrived by then.

Was cold and raining when we got off. Paris in December.

Would become my recurring nightmare.

Hem said, "Man like you needs a damn good woman. This one is fine."

Brilliant? Or bullshit? That was Hem.

Talked on writing. I was working through *Timepiece* then. Hem was working, too. Was sending regular work to the *Toronto Star*. Told him about an idea for a novel. Told him it would be even better than *Timepiece* if I could get the fragments ordered right. He said he was working on a character, too, who lived in northern Michigan.

Hem bullied me with questions. Figured that was just Hem's way.

Hem got going on it, a few drinks in, like an avalanche. Wanted to dive deep, but I only had bones. No flesh. Needed time to think it all through, yet.

Hem said, "A lousy excuse for a writer makes fine excuses." Clear as glass.

Returning with Margarete on that late train is one of my fondest memories. Margie slept, her head on my shoulder, while I scribbled final notes for *Timepiece*.

A good place to stop. Must rest.


JUNE 16, 1961

Hopeful for today.

Hemingways in Paris. Thought we'd see each other more, but didn't. Me, on assignment for *Querschnitt*. Hem, for the *Star*.

August 1922. Hemingways took a vacation to Germany. Met them for a hike through the Black Forest. So lush. So alive. The rushing water, the flourishing greens. Could think there. Then.

One gets inspired.

Less than a month later, Margarete and I eloped. It was a Friday. August 25. In Triberg. Hemingways stood witness.

We fought that night, Ernest and I. *Timepiece* wasn't moving.

He was going well, writing on my story. Said he didn't remember it that way. Said the thing had evolved into its own story, into his story. Said it'd be published before I'd ever finish anything.

Hadley had to break us up. She said, "People write about similar topics all the time. It always turns out differently."

Hem added, "Don't be a damn coward. Go and do it better." Clear as glass.

Makes me mad even now. He could be such a bull.

But I would get him back.

Later.

I was headed to Paris for work on the magazine. Cabled ahead to Ernest to meet for drinks. Cabled back: "In Switzerland. On assignment."

No hard feelings.

The mischievous seed was growing even then.

The apartment—*rue de Vaugirard*. Empty? Such a small place, would be a quick search. Slip in and out. An idea only.

Wouldn't be necessary.

Muses were smiling down on me, saying, "What's yours is yours."


JUNE 17, 1961

Going now.

Was early December, 1922. To Paris by train. Late. Or early. Frigid night. Or morning. Condensation fogged the window. Could see a blurred likeness of Hadley. She was on the train platform. Bundled up. A porter with her bags.

Could barely believe my eyes. Can still smell the cold, damp air. The scent of winter.

Exited my train and stood there with her, behind her. Recognized the carry-all in the porter's hand. Ernest's travel case. Covered with stamps. He carried it carefully, anxiously. Contained his soul. His manuscripts.

At that intersection, ill-conceived misdeeds met opportunity. Hadley boarded the outbound train.

Watched her direct the porter where to load the bags.

Placed her scarf and a book on the seat. Tipped the porter. Didn't sit. Turned and followed the porter to the back of the car. Came out, stepped around him, walked straight toward me.

In my hat and overcoat, I was anybody waiting for the train.

She turned not six feet in front of me, down the stairs, into the station. "I only went for a harmless bottle of water," she told me later with tears in her eyes. A vision I'll continue to see in my grave.

The train was bare. Checked the schedule, checked my watch. Fifteen minutes before the boarding call.

Boarded. Packed my things in her seat. Looked over my expired ticket, rubbed my forehead, pretended to be confused. Then, collected everything, Hem's case included. Stormed off the train and slipped off into the night.

Henceforward, a villain.

JUNE 18, 1961

Guilt. So much guilt. All that's left. A million plots lead to divorce. Ernest's wanderlust, for one. Had suspicions, too. But he never forgave Hadley.

We were friends first, then contemporaries. Then on, I was the scoundrel to his scholar.

He became a charging bull, determined to produce better. And did.

JUNE 19, 1961

Both Hem and I could've been better. But now, here we are—old, tired, past prime, beyond ambition. What remains?

I'll play the fool no longer; I'll take my leave.

Only one more letter to write.

June 20, 1961

I must do the least foolish act since that December night in Paris. Post a letter to Hem. The first in years. An apology. A confession. A farewell. Then...

Can't.

May my work be remembered like a warm summer day.

Can't.

May I be forgotten as quickly as the rain.

Tomorrow.

June 21, 1961

Memory. Health. Slipping.

Doctor says I'm fine, but I'm ornery. A bull in a pen.

Can't write, stop living. *Wertlos.*

Poor Ingrid. With respite from me, she'd finally have peace.

*Wertlos. Wertlos. Wertlos.*

June 22, 1961

Hem and I. Summers up north. Not a worry. Hunting, fishing, working. Digging stones. Hard labor. Living.

Everything an opportunity for manhood.

Hemingstein

Grundstein.

That was us. Was.

June 23, 1961

Bad today. Scribbles. *Wertlos.*

• • •

JUNE 24, 1961

Rest. End soon.

Great War. Manhood. Inevitable.

Father knew. Dieter knew. I wouldn't have survived at the front.

Army wouldn't take Hem. Couldn't stop him.

Should've.

Must get it down.

Need rest.

Tomorrow.

JUNE 25, 1961

~~Dear Ernest,~~

Fallout my responsibility. ~~After Hadley lost it after it was lost after it was stolen~~ Everybody agreed that it was ridiculous. Hadley left them on the train.

JUNE 26, 1961

~~Dear Hemingway,~~

I want you to know it has haunted me. I can bear it no longer. ~~I want you to know.~~

JUNE 27, 1961

~~Hemingstein,~~

Was in Paris. Gertrude Stein. Collecting work. ~~Some of yours. Truth.~~

*~~Immer,~~*

JUNE 28, 1961

Hem, need to clear the air. I know. Not much time left.

My fault. Separated. Lost.

~~God knows. The godforsaken...~~

JUNE 29, 1961
*Wertlos. Wertlos.*

JUNE 30, 1961
HS,
Need to clear the air. No time left. I know.
Was in Paris. Gertrude Stein. Collecting work. Saw Hadley board train.
Unluckiest day of my life. Took the manuscripts.
Was wrong. I know.
Was afraid. You were better.
A museum now.
—LG

JULY 1, 1961
*Wertlos.*

JULY 2, 1961
*Nimmermehr.*

# 28

Reading in my room, behind the locked door I'd barricaded with a chair, I was up and pacing by the time I'd finished. "My God," I said aloud. Reality rocked my tired body and sad soul. It was too much for being so late in the night or so early in the morning. I crawled into bed and slept.

The next thing I remember definitively about that week was the swine flu. By Wednesday, the H1N1 scare was all anybody was talking about. It was taking over the news and social media:

@FluTrackerH1N1: 74 countries infected; 27,737 cases reported; 141 deaths confirmed.
8:03 AM – 10 June 2009

@News.Globe: WHO raises Pandemic Alert Level, cites significant transmissions of the virus.
8:03 AM – 10 June 2009

@News.USA: WHO officially declares H1N1 global pandemic.
8:02 AM – 10 June 2009

@GretchBreporting: #DoYourPart RT: Help prevent the spread

of swine flu: a comprehensive guide.
8:01 AM – 10 June 2009

@MetroDetroitJournal: Help prevent the spread of swine flu: a
comprehensive guide.
8:01 AM – 10 June 2009

I clicked on the link for the comprehensive guide, which took
me to a video. On screen, a blonde woman was shaking her head
in sync with the rise and fall of her inflection. She said, "Swine
flu occurs when a virus that commonly lives on pigs mutates to
be able to drill into human cells, allowing them to replicate and
explode throughout the human body. Cases have been reported
in nearly all fifty states, including here in Michigan. This map
of Michigan shows the locations of reported cases which, as you
can see, this strip along lower part of the state with the hottest
spots being Macomb, Oakland, and Wayne counties."

*That's us.*

"There are more than 600 confirmed cases of the swine flu
across the state with less than ten confirmed deaths. The first
confirmed death, I'm told, was a woman from the Warren area
who was suspected of having other health complications that
contributed to her death. Nationwide, there have been approxi-
mately 150 reported deaths so far. However, we don't know how
many cases are out there, so we don't know what the rate of
death actually looks like. This could be a very low rate of death.
As an example, thousands of people die every year from seasonal
flu."

*Karla? Emma? My God.*

(Emma says she wasn't sick at all. Her roommates were going to the mall. She ditched class. Never has an explanation for
an absence been so believable. She says she had no idea that it
would cause me such concern. So benign.)

"It's unclear if this is going to be a short scare or if it will have long-term effects. Flu strains tend to die out and then re-emerge with colder temperatures in the fall. We won't be able to get an accurate gauge of the problem until we see how many cases emerge next year. But, many are comparing this outbreak to the 1918 outbreak of Spanish influenza that took about fifty million lives. That's the fear we're dealing with. We simply don't know how dangerous this strain is going to be. We encourage everyone to take all the necessary precautions at this time. Wash your hands regularly. If you're feeling flu-like symptoms, remove yourself from public places—" I cut it off there.

*Remove yourself. Remove yourself. Remove yourself.*

I retrieved my students' essays from my satchel and brushed through the stack, checking (1) to confirm their existence, (2) to make sure they completed the minimum requirements of the assignment, and (3) to make sure, if challenged, I could make a legitimate case for a decent grade. Then, I logged into the university's online system and gave all seven of my students 100%. Next, I drafted and sent an email:

> Students,
>
> Due to the recent outbreak of the H1N1 global pandemic, and in order to put your safety first at the risk of being overly cautious, today's class is canceled. Please follow precautions such as washing your hands regularly and stay out of public spaces. If you're feeling ill, quarantine yourself and see a doctor as soon as possible. This is a public health emergency. For more information, follow this link to a comprehensive guide. Please pay attention to both local and university news for other updates and announcements.
>
> Please take this time to get ahead on your reading. Class will resume next Monday, hopefully, and we will continue our discussions of *The Son Down*.

Although you just turned in your mid-terms (grades have been posted online; please let me know if you have any comments or questions), it's time to begin thinking about a topic for your final paper. Finals are only two weeks away.

I wish you all well, and I hope to see you all happy and healthy in the classroom next week.

Take caution and stay safe,

Professor Schurke

I copied Rita, the department secretary, on the email and sent it. At the click of the button, I felt a pang that perhaps I was guilty of my own fear-mongering now, but the freedom was worth it; by noon, I was packed, in the Karmann Ghia, and on my way to *dem Holzstapel.*

(Why? I didn't know where else to go or what else to do, but in my effort to escape, I drove right into the storm. Everything would happen so rapidly over the next two weeks, my brain hadn't had the capacity to filter and analyze it all at the time. Even now, with the benefit of reflection, my memory truncates and expands inexplicably like an accordion noodled upon by a novice.)

All four lanes of northbound I-75 were nearly bare that morning. The sun was rising to my right giving the horizon a blazing titian hue. The supple curves of the landscape and the pale, flesh-colored fields were seducing me into a daze. I wished I could've stayed in that moment, maybe not forever, but for more than a flash. The very second the thought of trying to capture a mental copy became conscious, it was gone.

(I have been looking for moments like that ever since and may never find another; all the variables of a single, purely pleasant experience have to be just so.)

At the time of my arrival at the two-lane to the cabin, the weather had turned. Navy clouds covered the sky pouring rain down fast enough to drown Karmann's wiper blades. Visibility was dangerously low. I navigated by eyeing the side of the lane outside my window, and we bumped and splashed along.

At a slight curve where the lanes become particularly narrow, a poorly located puddle quaked the driver side at the front and at the rear. The muddy sludge on the road slid beneath us, just enough to force us to fishtail. We caught a small sapling along the back fender.

"Damn it," I cursed as I hit the brakes, sinking what hope of progress was left to a sliver as the mud worked swiftly to capture us.

Water beat against the windshield as if we were going through an automatic carwash. I begged the Universe to hold off enough to let us get to the cabin, but when I released the break and pressed the gas pedal, pleading with Karmann to go smoothly onward, she jerked and swayed. Something wasn't right. She wouldn't make it. I saw a vision of us being swept away in a flood.

I only had one choice. I took off my favorite corduroy sport coat and wrapped it around the duffle bag as best I could.

Wind resisted my efforts to open my door, but I managed to hold it in abeyance. I slipped out the door, shutting it firmly behind me, hoping the windows wouldn't leak as much as I knew they would. My shoes filled with dirty water as soon as my feet touched the ground. I ran as fast as the muck would allow about a quarter mile to the shelter of the cabin.

By the time I stripped clean, hung my wet clothing up to dry around the annex, cleaned up, started a fire in the woodstove, and got into warm, dry—*thank, God*—pajamas, it was too dark to attempt to save Karmann.

For dinner, stranded as I was, I had limited options. From some old cans in the cupboard, I boiled a soup of chicken broth, diced tomatoes, corn, and beans. *Thank God for the whiskey.*

(From time to time, I think of that night. There was something about that steaming hot concoction that felt right, though, as a complement to the sound of the rain and the wind and the woodstove, and the heat from the fire and the soup. Occasionally, on a rainy night, I feel compelled to make that soup, but I never do. It'll only serve to ruin the memory.)

I read Grundstein's *The Son Down* that night from cover to cover. It's a large book, nearly 400 pages, and it demands, page after page, to be consumed. That night, I read it as a reader and not as a scholar for the first time since my youth.

At the climax of the story—the moment critics find to be despairingly underwrought—that night and ever since, I've found it to be most satisfying.

The protagonist, Zug Kraeftig, enters the local watering hole after setting his warehouse and the warehouse of his nemesis, Henry, on fire with all their storerooms of products, branded with names, pristine and packaged, and he seeks out Henry at the bar and sits down at the next bar stool. After they drink, shot for shot, in begrudging silence for most of the night:

> "It's not instinctual for us to be competitors," Henry said at long last. "It was suggested to us, and that's all it took. We own the rest. I understand that now."
>
> "A tragedy," Zug suggested, "of living on the commons."
>
> "A State-issued, self-fulfilled prophesy," Henry added. "To buy. Buy in. Buy everything."
>
> "A State-issued, self-fulfilled heresy," Zug said.
>
> Henry offered a toast: "Let the world spin out from under us, I say. Let us not sell it at all; let us give it all away."
>
> Zug raised his shot glass to Henry's.
>
> As Zug and Henry left the bar together, the newest enemies of the State, the cries arose from within:

"Another round, barkeep!"
"Keep 'em comin'!"
"Another!"
"And another!"
"And another!"
"And another!"

As I sat there, alone, I could sense my orbit was on the verge of another redirection, and I wasn't for or against it. And, I fell asleep there, in the chair in front of the woodstove, head on my hands on the book, content.

In the morning, the world smelled of fish and worms. The sun shone through a fog, and rain drops plunged to their deaths from the roof without consciousness.

I got the waders from the shed. They hadn't been used since the last time I last took the dock out of the lake.

I was quite a sight marching down the road in those waders, still wearing the Oxford shirt I had intended to wear to class the day before, which was now ruined by the rain and the dirty shoulder straps of the waders.

Karmann was in worse shape than I'd expected. The sapling had done remarkable damage on her old body. The dented and cracked fender revealed years of rusting that was hidden just beneath the surface of the paint.

Ashley would be devastated.

The immediate problem: there was a gash in the rear tire— why I couldn't move in the mud.

The trunk opened without a fight, but I found the engine instead of a spare. The latch on the front hood was rusted out. I went to the shed for a hammer and a shovel. I used the fork of the hammer to pry it loose. In doing so, I scraped and dented the hood. At last, the hood creaked open to reveal a full-size spare and an old-fashioned jack—*thank God*. A puddle of rainwater had collected in the well of the wheel.

I was able to dig out enough mud to make room for two logs to serve as a makeshift foundation for the jack. When the flat tire was finally suspended an inch above the mud, I started in on the lug nuts, which were rusted out. I nearly threw my back out trying to get one started.

About the time the sun rose above the tree line, I stood back, covered in sweat and dirt. The car jacked, the flat removed—I admired my progress. The physical labor felt good and natural, though not without pain, like reuniting with an old friend.

But everything came to a halt when I went back for the spare. It was wedged in the nose of the vehicle in an angled compartment. By design it was snug, but over time, it had become stuck. Never in its life, not even in the course of Ashley's repairs, had the spare tire been required to be removed.

For more leverage, I worked the spade down along the side of the tire, trying desperately not to do the kind of damage to the grill that I'd done to the hood. I could feel something stuck underneath the tire that was making the snug space even tighter. Something had been jammed in between the spare and car's chassis.

I moved from the front of the car to the side and repositioned the shovel to the top the tire. As I applied force, I could get my hand in the space just enough to feel the edge of the object. I leaned onto the shovel and caused more dents and scrapes along the fender. There was nothing else I could've done to get enough space for my fingers to grasp the object in question. I could only get my fingertips around it. I squeezed as hard as I could and pulled. As the object popped free, my hand cut along the side of the shovel. The laceration was a shock to my system more than the bent tin box that was now in my hand.

I lumbered back to the cabin, holding the box in the injured hand and applying pressure to the cut with my other hand. Inside, I dropped the tin contraption onto the counter and began to wash my wound at the sink. The incision seemed to point toward the webbing between my thumb and forefinger.

*I'm going to need stitches*, I thought. *I'm going to have to walk to a hospital.*

I got the whiskey from its resting place atop the woodstove. I took a pull from the bottle, then splashed some on my hand, and my throat and my fleshed burned together.

Once I began to calm down, the pain became manageable. I wrapped my hand tightly in a washcloth and applied pressure for several minutes. When I worked up the nerve to check the wound, it appeared the blood was beginning to coagulate and the cut was adjoining reasonably well.

With an old white linen pillowcase from the annex I managed to cut into strips, I dressed the wound and avoided the emergency trip to the hospital.

I sat down at the kitchen table and set the bottle and the box in front of me. Naturally, I suspected the contents of the box would explain everything, but when I fumbled with the lid, I discovered it was locked with two, heavy-duty clasps. In between the clasps were four dials with the numbers zero to nine on each—like the locks found on briefcases and padlocks.

The right four-digit combination should spring the clasps open and solve everything. *Should.* There were only 10,000 different four-number combinations between answers and me.

There was an inscription on the top of the box: two four-digit combinations. I tried the first: 1961. Then the second: 3515. Both came up negative. I should've given Grundstein more credit than that. I studied the box for more clues, but there weren't any. It was simply a dull, gray metal box. I thought of trying to break the clasps, but the box seemed too brittle and I feared I would destroy *the* missing link. I set the dials to 0001 and tested the clasps. No luck.

0002. No luck.

0003. No luck.

0004. No luck.

I became obsessed with checking the next combination. I couldn't stop.

At 0184, no luck. *What if 0185 is the key?*

0185. No luck.

I sat there for what must have been three or maybe four hours, sipping on the whiskey and checking the next combination of numbers. By the time I reached 8000, I was drunk and despairing.

At 8867, my progress slowed as I rested my throbbing head and hand on the table in between each try. A hangover was coming on. I stood, woozy, for the first time in hours and wobbled to the sink where I drank several glasses of tap water. I was in desperate need of food. I found some old, uncooked noodles in the cupboard. What choice did I have? With blurred vision, I set them to boil on the woodstove. I nursed another glass of water while I tried the next thirty-three digits. Not one of them saved me.

At 8925, I strained the noodles and ate them plain. (That was the last time I ate spaghetti. It's never sounded appetizing since, and likely never will again.)

At 8950, I felt only somewhat better after eating. I was sobering up, but now I had a lump of old spaghetti noodles lodged like a stone in my stomach.

At 8975, I caught a second wind for the home stretch. Every click on dial seemed to echo throughout the cabin with infinite meaning as I slowly and deliberately tried the clasps, wholly believing that combination was, in fact, the one that would unlock all of Grundstein's mysteries, and by extension, my life, my future.

I set the dials to 8999 and sat staring at the box, thinking, *Whatever's inside this, Grundstein wouldn't trust to a simple combination like 8999.*

No luck.

In frustration, I switched the dials to 9000 in haste. I squared each of my thumbs on either side and said aloud, "One. Two. Three." And, I flicked clasps. Neither budged. I tried one clasp with both hands to see if it might just be stuck.

No luck.

By that time, it was beginning to get dark outside.

I checked for a keyhole. Anything.

Nothing.

Giving in, I slammed box down on edge of the table, trying in vain to break the clasps.

I shouted nonsense to nobody.

*You shout because it makes you brave or you want to announce your recklessness*, I thought.

At last, I stood up and kicked over my chair. "I've wasted another entire day and learned nothing."

*I shut my eyes and all the world dropped dead.*


Sometime later, I woke up in cold sweat, lying in the middle of the floor—again. A full moon provided the only light in the room. I couldn't tell how late it was. I couldn't make sense, at first, of where I was or what I was doing, but there was a vague number swimming in my head. Sitting up, I steadied myself, rubbed my hands over my closed eyes, and the number came into focus at the backs of my eyelids: *Nine. Zero. Six. Six.*

I set the chair on its legs and hoisted myself up to the table. At the sight of the little metal box, I remembered everything. And, I stopped.

"Nine. Zero. Six. Six," I repeated, adjusting the dials on the box. I flicked the clasps, and without pomp, without the pop of a fresh spring, they gave way.

"Behold the picturesque giant," I said, steadfast in my unbelief, slowly raising the lid with the rusty joints complaining of stiffness like the knees of an old man arising for another day.

Suddenly I stopped. Leaving the box on the table half-opened, I went to the sink and filled a glass with water, still wearing my soiled work shirt and waders, thinking, *This is the worst time for such a momentous breakthrough. I'm tired. I'm hungry. I'm hungover.*

I took off the waders—*how inappropriate, or perhaps appropriate, for the moment, whatever it would be*—and left them in the middle of the floor. I sat back down at the table.

I peered into the infinite darkness inside the box. "I do not stop there," I said and opened the lid.

There, inside, was a single sheet of paper, letter size, folded in half. Soiled. Somewhat tattered. Gently, with one fingertip on either side of the crease, I lifted the paper out of the box and set it on the table. The paper was once of good quality stock. Overall, well preserved.

With my left forefinger, I pinned down the bottom edge. I checked my right forefinger and thumb for dirt or blood before using them to pinch the top corner of the paper to unfold it.

I was surprised to see the name on the letterhead: LITTLE TRAVERSE HISTORICAL SOCIETY. The letter was dated May 24, 1961, and began:

> Dear Mr. Grundstein,
> The following is an inventory of the items and documents you have delivered to the Little Traverse Historical Society to preserve and protect as part of the rich history of Petoskey, our region, and our state. Thank you for entrusting this to us. It is our mission to steward these artifacts in accordance with your will.

There followed a long list of items, mostly clothes and small personal affects, most of which I recognized from my previous visits to the museum. The letter was signed by someone whose signature was an illegible flurry scribbled above the typed word "President." In the same hand, at the bottom of the page, was a handwritten note that read:

> Leonhard— You'll notice one item, in particular, has been withheld from this list. Please rest assured it's in good hands. Also, there's no copy of <u>this</u>, for your privacy. Thank you and best wishes. Yours, JJ

Now I was sober and alert.

# 29

It was late by the time I had the replacement wheel on Karmann and the tools put away. I changed into a clean shirt and drove straight into town, to A.J.'s Lodge.

As my luck would have it, Beth greeted me at the bar. "The cat must be getting desperate out there," she said.

I was stunned, silent.

"To drag you in. Nevermind. You're a mess."

"Thanks, Beth. It's good to see you."

Beth surprised me with a warm embrace. She said, "Tell me why you look like you struck oil in a swamp and smell like it too."

I looked down at my clean shirt.

"Your face is caked with dirt and grease," she said.

"Karmann had a flat," I said. "I got the doughnut on. Now I'm in desperate need to refuel."

"The grill's closed," Beth said, "but I'll see if there's anything in the back worth warming up."

The bar was occupied on one end by two men wearing a mix of camouflage, flannel, and denim and watching bull riding on the TV overhead. And there were two women shuffling doggedly in front of the jukebox holding hands and taking turns raising toasts.

Beth brought out a cold pulled-pork sandwich with chips and poured me a lager. "On the house," she said. "You've had a hard day."

I asked her for water and consumed it before the glass hit the counter.

"Strange day," I said with moisture on my lips. "Roller coaster day, actually."

"I heard about the low point, Greased Lightning. What about the high?"

I shook my head and looked away from Beth to my beer on the bar. "It's nothing," I said. "It's too early to tell."

"It's okay." She winked. "I know how you academics can get."

I bobbed my head in shame more than in agreement.

"How's Bobbie?" I asked.

"She's busy. At the museum a lot. I'm working a lot, too." Beth left to go wait on the other end of the bar. She chatted amicably with the men.

I ate the sandwich too quickly, but the chips only made me more thirsty. I sipped on the beer. My eyelids were dropping along with the level of the liquid.

I read some of the notes past customers had left on the bar. Mostly confessions of love and declarations of existence. *The joke is in your hands*, I thought. Then I spotted a penmanship that could've been Grundstein's. It read: MY SOUL IS CAPTIVE NOW. A MUSEUM. SET IN PETOSKEY STONE.

Like all the other secrets, it was unsigned, but the penmanship, the voice—it was Grundstein, no doubt.

I left a twenty on the bar. On my way out, I said, "I have to go. I'll see you again before I head back to Detroit."

To the regulars, Beth said, "There he goes. Greased Lightning."

I drove into town and parked behind Roaster's Toast. It was less than a mile to go from there to the museum. As I approached the pier, I could see the museum down below. It was a clear night with a bright, full moon and starlight glittering off of the rippling water in the nearby bay. A dreamy summer night—cool, fresh, breezy air.

I followed the shadows of the tree cover to the museum's overhanging roof and pinned myself up against the building.

I peered inside. No security cameras were visible. *Would a little backwoods museum need cameras?*

I used the bottom of my shirt to cover my fingerprints as I picked at the windows. Secure.

At the center of the building, where there was a small second story with a large, coned roof—the feature that gives the museum its recognizable character—there was a balcony with a low parapet. To access the second story, there was a door and row of windows. If there was ever going to be a lapse in security, I thought it'd be there.

At one end of the building, the old oak tree that provided my secure route to the museum grew overhead with thick branches that extended over the roof.

*A man goes far to find out what he is*, I thought. *Death of the self in a long, tearless night.*

And I was going for it.

The lowest branch was at least six feet off of the ground. I had to jump to get a good grip on it, and I was in no condition to hoist myself chin-up style. Somehow I managed, feet frantically kicking against the truck of the tree, to get myself atop that first branch—not, however, without torn pants and shin scrapes to show for it. The feat had barely begun and my hands were already raw.

Hugging the trunk like a scared bear cub, I climbed, one seemingly steady branch at a time, to a height above the roof. And the worst part was ahead—the trip out on the overhanging branch and the transfer down to the roof.

At the fattest branch, I centered myself on it and cursed the rough bark and dense foliage of the oak. I hung on for dear life, arms wrapped tightly around the branch, as I pushed myself forward with my feet, fearing the sound of my body scraping against the bark would give me away. At each movement, I wrapped my feet around the branch and reached, one arm at a time, to the next hold.

The recently consumed beer and warm meal were working against me, making me feel dizzy and sluggish.

I thought of the morning's headline: LEONARD GRUNDSTEIN'S GRANDSON FOUND DEAD AT MUSEUM, CAUSE UNCLEAR.

At that point, I was beyond return. The best way to get down would be via the roof.

I shimmied along, trying to get to a safe distance over the edge of the roof in case I, as I imagined I would, bungled the landing. As I made my way farther out on the branch, it began to bend downward, reducing the distance to the rooftop, but also increasing the recoil that would occur once I dropped. Not knowing what to do, I inched onward, preparing myself at any moment for a surprise landing if the old branch suddenly gave way.

At last, I could reach out and touch the shingles. The grainy grit was painful on my palms. *Why didn't I bring gloves? So amateur.*

I could begin to see a successful, safe transfer in my future. At the precise moment I was mentally prepared to make the leap, a flash of light cut across the darkness from the direction of the city.

I froze. The branch bobbed and weaved, swinging me around.

Two headlights were making their way through the shadows and the streetlights. I could see clearly enough to recognize it was, in fact, a police cruiser turning from the main road toward the museum.

I thought of a different headline: SCHOLAR CAUGHT ATTEMPTING TO BREAK INTO MUSEUM, INTENT UNCLEAR.

*Forget the police, Daniels and Grudge would be on my ass for sure.*

I held on tight, tried to breathe regularly, tried to slow my heartbeat.

The cop circled around the drive in front of the building and came straight toward me. *What the hell is happening? When did I become capable of this? Where could I possibly go from here? Why would I get myself so deep into this? Why? Why? Why?*

The light was suddenly upon me and the police car's engine was roaring. The cop was going to drive right through me and end it all right here.

Then, it was gone—the light, the noise—gone. I turned and watched the taillights disappear down the road.

At last, when the car was fully out of sight, I dropped to the roof, landing hard on my hands and knees, and I scurried to the balcony. I swung myself over the railing and sat, safely out of sight, waiting for it all to be a dream, hoping to wake up in my apartment with nothing but a clear schedule—no class to teach, no research to conduct, no leads to follow, no complicated questions about family history or future legacies, just waiting for my life to make sense, *to me.*

I pinched my arm. Nothing happened. *What other choice did I have but to continue?*

(The answer is many choices. As Emerson puts it, what "scares us from self-trust is our consistency. [...] A foolish consistency is the hobgoblin of little minds, adored by little statesmen and philosophers and divines." But I didn't believe that at the time. I allowed external forces to fill my sails. Now I'm a "zigzag line of a hundred tacks," insisting on myself "with the cumulative force of a whole life's cultivation." Emma says Emerson and I can insist all we want, but she'll be filling the sails around here.)

Without standing, I scooted over to the door on the balcony, tried the handle, and fell flat on my face as the door swung inward. No resistance. No alarms. I was in.

I crawled inside and shut the door behind me. There was

enough light coming in through the windows to see it was a storage room filled with boxes and signs from old exhibits, and file cabinets, and paintings propped up on easels and hidden under draped sheets.

I quickly scoured the room looking for anything. Along one wall, there were file cabinets labeled alphabetically. I opened the file cabinet labeled F-J, and sure enough, there was a file for Grundstein, Leonhard. I took the file over to the windows to leaf through it with more light. There were three documents. A gift agreement signed by Grundstein and the mysterious president "JJ," an itemized list that matched the copy Grundstein had, and a copy of a tax-deductible gift receipt made out to Grundstein for slightly more than $5,000—the apparent market value of his personal collection at the time.

I returned the file and was about to close the drawer when I noticed the name on the last file: Jarrett, James (Dr.), President. The file was packed with documents. I pulled it out and returned to the windows. I set the file down on top of a box and spread it out. The signature on the first letter confirmed it. Jarrett was, in fact, "JJ." Most of the documents were more than fifty years old and useless, stuff the museum could've thrown out decades ago.

At the back of the file was a group of papers clipped together. The first document was a letter to a donor thanking her for her contribution and letting her know her name would be etched in stone at the entrance of the building. Letter after letter was the same, only made out to different supporters. Only two documents in the packet were not thank-you letters. They were invoices. One was an invoice made out by Jarrett, the person, for a $2,500 donation to "name a stone." The second invoice was from a security company made out to Jarrett, the president, for the purchase of a "stone-front container." Detailed dimensions were listed.

Height: Six Inches.
Width: Twelve Inches.

Depth: Ten Inches.

*The perfect size to hold manuscripts*, I thought.

Listed on the line for engraving was: ANONYMOUS.

I returned the file.

A light flashed through the museum, nearly giving me another heart attack. It was the police cruiser again. I stood next to a mannequin and watched the car come down the drive, curve around the building, and disappear down the same road as before.

I decided to get out of there and return legally in the morning, showered and dress appropriately, to ask Bobbie about where the donors were recognized.

I slipped toward the door and snuck over the parapet on the balcony. It was too dangerous to try to jump for the tree branches. On my belly at the edge of the roof, I looked down. The lush green lawn appeared to be as inviting of a soft landing as any. I swung my feet over the edge, inching my way down to get my dangling feet as close to the ground as possible. As I made the move to hang from the roof, my hands gave way and I tumbled backward onto the grass, lucky to come away with only a tweaked ankle.

Limping, I started my trek back to Karmann. I rounded the front of the building and passed under the covered entryway. There, I stopped in my tracks. The stonework, engraved with names, lined the entryway.

*Unter dem Ruhestein.* The words scrolled through my head like an announcement on a digital marquee. *Unter dem Ruhestein.*

I crouched behind the stonework and looked toward town for any sign of the patrol.

Working quickly, I ran my fingers along the stones looking for an unmarked one. It was dark under the entryway and difficult to see the lettering. I came upon one that was different than the rest; it was made of polished Petoskey stone and had only a single word engraved in it. With my face not six inches from the stone, I could faintly make out the lettering: ANONYMOUS. About one foot long and six inches tall, it was the right size.

I picked at the edges with my fingers. The stone appeared to be loose, removable. Wiggling side-to-side, I made progress. Soon, I had enough room to grip it with my fingertips. With only two or three firm tugs, the stone dislodged and along with it came a rectangular black box.

I sat for a moment holding the box in my lap, stunned.

In the darkness, I could feel a seam around the sides. At the back, I wedged my thumbnails into the seam, prying the lip open. Inside was an old leather folio. The material was dry and cracked, but mostly undamaged.

Without missing a beat, I removed the folio, shut the box, returned the stone, and left, again, under the shadows of the trees.

In town, I walked at a brisk pace, but not fast enough to draw attention. My greasy, torn, grass-stained clothes would be enough to give me away. Luckily, I passed nobody. The town was asleep.

With the folio on Karmann's passenger seat, I drove inconspicuously over the speed limit, tense and alert, until I was safely parked next to the cabin.

# 30

At dawn I woke confused. The prior day's occurrences were as foggy as a harbor after rain. Even with the leather of the folio soft against my sore, dirty hands, I was convinced it was all a dream.

I set the folio down on the table and went about making a cup of coffee.

Then I stepped out the side door to the deck facing the lake. The chill of the crisp morning air and the warmth of the sun, now a thumb's distance above the horizon, felt pleasantly familiar. The water before me was harmonious, perfectly balanced, quiescent.

Work and class, Daniels and Grudge, Alex—for a fleeting instant, it was all far from my mind.

Gurgling sounds were coming from the kitchen now. The coffee was ready. I stepped back inside and refused to look at the folio, trying to protect this perfect morning as long as I could.

I poured myself a cup.

Confined again, I could smell my body odor. I took my mug to the bathroom and began to fill the tub. The steam from the fresh water arose and mingled with the steam from the earthy liquid in my hands.

When the tub was full, I stripped and slid into the water, thinking of nothing at first, then of Alex. *Will things ever be simple between us?*

("Never," Emma says, but she knows Alex holds no power over me now.)

I kicked my feet up over the edge and let myself slide to the bottom of the tub, like I'd seen in the movies.

Getting out at last, I took my time drying off. Putting on clean clothes felt more refreshing than the morning sun and the bath combined, like I was finally able to put myself together.

My beard was getting full and needed its own time to dry. I considered shaving it all off or at least trimming around the edges, but didn't.

By the time I checked my phone, it was noon, and I had two missed voicemails.

BETH: Sammy, it was great to see you last night. Since you're up, I was wondering, did you want to have lunch with us today? If not, it's fine. Just a thought. Okay? Let me know.

ALEX: Monte and I went by the house this morning to call on you, but the doctor wasn't in. You're in trouble now. Call me, a-sap.

*What was Alex doing? Why had she been acting so strange lately?*

I texted Beth.

ME: Sorry. I worked late last night. Just up now.

BETH: No problem. Can't anymore anyway.

I returned to the kitchen and stopped in the doorway. There the light was coming in through the windows at a certain slant, afflicting the skin of the leather folio.

I wondered about the inventory at the museum. I wondered who might know about this item that the mysterious JJ had been so kind as to leave off the list.

I refreshed my cup of coffee, sat down at the table, and centered the folio in front of me and was reminded of when I discovered that first journal. Pulse quick. Dizzy. Hands shaking.

The folio felt light and frail, and the leather was flimsy—nothing like how it seemed the night before. The thin tab of material that held the flap closed broke off under the slightest amount of stress and fell to the floor. The crease of the flap made its objections to my intrusion known.

Inside the folio was a plastic sheath providing additional protection for the contents, a stack only slightly thicker than an overly filled file folder. I removed the sheath, and an odor of wet shoes and old books escaped. On the plastic that entombed the treasure there was a faded-yellow graphic of a place setting—a plate in the middle, a knife and two spoons to the right, and two forks to the left. Lettering on the plate read: REUSABLE PLA-CEMATS, "cushion soft."

I thought of Ingrid buying them at the market, bringing them home to the cabin, serving Grundstein picnic lunches on the reusable plastic. It made me sad to think of it; so frugal she must have been, she even kept the plastic in which they came. And, what odd collection of circumstances had to accrue for this pile of papers to find its way into this placemat packaging, into Grundstein's folio, into that stone at the museum, and now, to me, in 2009, decades later, in front of my face?

One end of the plastic sheath was open and folded over. It was time to take the plunge; I plugged my hand in and carefully removed the contents. The front page felt different, smoother, than the back page, which was crisp and flakey, like sheets of dried seaweed. *The carbons*, I thought, but I was shocked to read what was typed on the title page:

The Mysterious Garden
by Leonhard Grundstein

I stood, papers in hand, knocking the chair to the floor be-hind me. My head swirled with questions: *An unfinished manuscript? Grundstein's unfinished manuscript? Not Hemingway's? Why would he want to keep it safe if he was just going to keep it a secret? What would Daniels do with this? Would he feast on this find like a vulture, leaving me in the lurch? Should I tell him? Would he make me rework the goddamn dissertation? Would Grundstein want me to? Why? Why? Why?*

All in an instant.

I sat down on the floor next to the tipped-over chair and leafed through several pages. It was in fact a manuscript for an unpublished novel. Nobody, *nobody*, maybe not even Ingrid, or Tante, or my mother, ever suggested Grundstein was working at the end of his life. But between the journals and the letters and this manuscript, it was clear that Grundstein had been. There must have been 150 pages there.

(I wish I paid more attention to that manuscript. I was too consumed, too focused on the object it self—the fact of its existence—to pay proper attention to the art of it, the life and soul of it: the language.)

The only part I remember was something of an epigraph, but not quite—more of a false start really. A sentence on the top of the first page read:

> Smoke is soul returning to the Universe, to enlightenment; set it all ablaze

The sentence wasn't punctuated, itself incomplete, as if the thought transformed into smoke before Grundstein had a chance to finish it.

After several empty lines, the novel began again.

> Adam lost the Book of Answers somewhere in the Mysterious Garden.

Stopped and started again.

> Basiliscus wouldn't let Adam out of his sight.

And again.

> Sarah, on her fragile hands and knees, pleaded
> with the dirt to produce, for her table was bare and
> had been for some time and she was with child.

The entire stack of papers was filled with fits and starts, fragments of narrative, some of which were as short as a sentence,
some of which were as long as twenty pages, but pieces none-
theless.

At that moment, a small, square fold of paper fell out of the
stack. I hoped I would find something useful, perhaps the treasure at the end of this hunt. *Where were Hemingway's papers?* There
were two separate letters, both written in Grundstein's hand:

> To Ingrid, my dearest: I'm sorry. Tell the rest I'm
> sorry. Life has been a wreck. Course derailed, fateful
> mistakes, youth... Never have recovered...
> Hope I haven't ruined you completely... Deserved
> better... All my love.
>
> To Hem: I'm sorry. What to say? Here I am, no bull-
> fighter, never had the art of it... My feet jittery be-
> fore the bull... You are Belmonte.
> I am the bull that doesn't charge properly... Nothing
> the bullfighter can do with me, no grace in the kill,
> no glory...

The letters were dated May 30, 1961—one month before
Grundstein's death. Neither were addressed nor signed. They
didn't appear to have been sent.

I turned to the carbons at the back of the stack. They weren't
copies. The voice was different, the tone, the language.

It wasn't Grundstein. It was Hemingway.

"My God," I said allowed. "This is it." With one hand, I

wiped any dirt, grime, and moisture from the table that might harm the documents. I arranged the folio and the plastic sheath side-by-side, set the stack down, and began tracing the papers backwards, putting Grundstein's pages to one side and Hemingway's to the other.

"Holy shit," I said aloud. "It's all here."

Once I had taken a proper accounting of the treasure, I was pacing, thinking. *What do I do? My God, what do I do?*

I took a seat on the oak bench by the sidewall, and that's when it occurred to me—Grundstein, the journals, the oak bench—the *loose floorboards*. I shoved the bench aside in one swoop, and the force of it rippled the loose boards as the bench's feet caught their edges and popped them up. I removed two, one with each hand. Less than two foot below was bare ground.

I peered down in the gap in the floor, and as far as I could see in all directions was nothing but dirt.

Packing the manuscripts back into the sheath and the folio, I decided I needed something more weather resistant. I went out to the shed where Grundstein kept his tackle box. I set it up on the tool bench and tried the latch.

*Locked? Oh, for God's sake.*

I examined the keyhole. The tainted brass looked familiar. I went back to the kitchen to get the copies I'd made of Tante's keys.

There was a small key that appeared to be a match. The key fit, but the old lock was stubborn. I could hear the friction of sand and metal fighting each other. At last, I was able to open the lid, which separated, stadium style, three tiers of tackle trays. I emptied the large compartment at the bottom—lures, spools of fishing line, an old pair of needle-nose pliers.

Tackle box and keys in hand, I ran back to the cabin. At the table, I put the folio containing the two manuscripts and the tin from Karmann containing the letters from the president of the museum in the bottom of the tackle box, closed and locked the lid. Picking it up and shaking it, I could hear the folio sliding from side to side. Something wasn't quite right.

I retrieved my bag from the bedroom and removed Grundstein's three journals, the purloined copy of *The Sun Also Rises* with Grundstein's note, the article about Dieter's death, the lighter, the can of lighter fluid, and the paperweight. I re-opened the tackle box and tucked everything under the folio.

I closed and shook the box again. I could only hear the hooks and lures jingling. Right and true.

Under the floorboards, I shifted the tackle box back and forth in the dirt until it settled into a secure position. I replaced the floorboards and the oak bench, and I swept and mopped the entire floor before I stood back and admired my work. No traces left behind.

The light coming in the kitchen had taken on a different hue. I looked out the window and saw the sun was high.

I checked my phone. There wasn't another word from Beth, but there were several text messages from Alex.

ALEX: Samuel, dear, where did you go?

ALEX: Are you ignoring me?

ALEX: Are mad at me?

ALEX: Are you okay?

I ignored her and replied to Beth.

ME: What are you up to?

BETH: Still at the museum. This day has sucked ass! omfg.

ME: Sorry to hear that! I need to head back down. I have class on Monday morning. Want to do dinner before I go?

BETH: I don't think I'll be able to. :(

ME: Catch you next time, for sure.

BETH: Drive safe!

Then, I texted Alex.

ME: I'm fine. Sorry. Been busy. I'll call you later.

ALEX: Schurke! Stop by when you can. I miss you.

*I miss you. I miss you. I miss you.*

I packed and locked up the cabin. I had to take Karmann slow on her bum wheel, but I didn't mind. Dusk was gorgeous that day with golden blades of light cutting through the pines. I rolled down the windows and let the warm, early summer air breeze by.

With Alexandria waiting for me on the other end of the drive, a lyric came into my mind:

> *Which of the young men does she like the best?*
> *Ah the homeliest of them is beautiful to her.*
>
> *Where are you off to, lady? for I see you.*
> *You splash in the water there, yet stay stock still in your room.* [1]

"For I see you, Alex," I said to the wind, "stock still in your room."

(I don't remember seeing Alex that weekend. I don't know what happened.)

---

1. See Walt Whitman, "Song of Myself."

# 31

I was late for class on that Monday. I unpacked my satchel at the front desk in a frenzy of huffs and sighs, avoiding eye contact and small talk with my students. I took roll robotically, not waiting for responses: "Eli. Emma. Harmony. Leslie. Roy. Rowan. Teagan. Okay." Emma was present and she looked healthy, and suddenly the swine flu seemed more like a nuisance than a pandemic.

Tucking the attendance sheet away, I said, "Let's begin." I took out my copy of *The Son Down*. The same copy I'd used in Daniels' graduate seminar, with the Post-It notes still sticking out the sides. My plan was simply to let my students drive the discussion. I didn't care where it went.

"So, what do we think of *The Son Down* so far?" I was looking at the ominous black and gray cover of my copy, with the words "The Son" on top, an illustration of a locomotive charging to the left and cutting through the word "Down" in large, industrial letters.

And, I realized just how long my beard had gotten. With my head down, the hairs were bent against my chest, curling out, making me look through a filter of hairs to see the name "Leonhard Grundstein" in small letters at the bottom.

*At the time I first grew the very tips of these hairs,* I thought, *what did I know about Grundstein?* I only knew about the jail time. I didn't know about the murder or the rape, and I certainly didn't know about the suicide or the manuscripts.

Suddenly I wanted to grow my beard forever. *How predictable my future used to be. How true my dissertation used to be. How enjoyable reading Grundstein's work used to be. How innocent I used to be. If I could only escape this, I'll never read Grundstein again.*

"I think I may have made a mistake," I said.

"It was a mistake to grow that thing in first place," Roy said. "Chicks like facial hair, not facial hairy."

I shook my head, and with each swing, the tension in the room wound tighter.

"Are you okay?" Emma asked at last.

"How many of you actually had a chance to begin reading the book?" I posed the question as if there was something in the story that would've explained my actions, had they read and understood the reference. "Emma? Not even you?"

"No," she said, looking way.

"Good, actually," I said. "Because, I made a mistake. I shouldn't have told you anything about this book, or anything about Grundstein specifically in regards to the book. If you know what I'm talking about, try to forget it. If you don't know what I'm talking about, don't worry. I want you to try to read this book as if you know nothing about the author. Just read it. Like the first time you've ever read a book. Try to forget everything you know. And just experience it.

"And for your final essay, I want you to write about that experience. In any way that you see fit. Has the experience impacted your life? For better? For worse? Completely freeform. First person. Personal essay. I want you to write uninhibited. Don't worry about length. Whatever you need to do to make it right, as you see fit."

I expected some push-back, but Emma was taking notes, and Roy and Rowan were nodding along. Teagan seemed indifferent, so normal. Harmony seemed a bit stoned. Her mouth was open, and she hadn't moved since class began.

"This is your final," I said. "It's all we have left. Just read the book and, through writing your final essay, contemplate the impact the experience has had on you. That's all I ask."

At last, Emma raised her hand.

"Yes?"

"So, what are we going to do with the remainder of our class periods then?"

Roy groaned. "Teacher, teacher, you forgot to give us homework," he said.

For a moment, Emma looked as though flames would shoot out of her eyes and cremate Roy once and for all, but she laughed, and the weight of the air in the room seemed to lighten. Even Harmony broke from her daze and chuckled.

"Alright, let's see," I said, beginning to loosen up myself. I circled around and sat on the front edge of the desk. "Wednesday's class will be an optional workshop for your final essays. If you want to stop in and workshop your ideas, something you have drafted, come on in. If you'd rather use the time to find a quiet place and read, fine. Do what you want with it. Just make sure your essays are ready by next Monday. That day, you can come in, drop off your essay, and you're done. Oh, well, except for the course survey. I'll collect your finals, then you'll take the survey, and we'll be done. How's that? Fair?"

Emma looked to Roy as everyone waited for one of them to say something.

Roy said, "Fair."

The students, even Emma, began to pack up their things. I looked up at the clock. Only thirty minutes had passed.

"I'm sure I'll see you all on Wednesday," I said.

On Wednesday, I sat in a student's desk at the front of the empty classroom with my feet up on the next desk, relaxing and reading *Hotel on the Corner of Bitter and Sweet*. It was the only thing that was keeping mind off of Grundstein, the manuscripts, the looming dissertation defense, and the decisions I would have to make. Just as I had asked my students to do, I was reading the book like I was reading for the first time, like I had never read more important books before, like a kid again, allowing myself to be taken along for the ride.

(I was so desperate to escape my time.)

A knock at the door startled me. "Professor Schurke? I'm sorry to bother you, but I heard from Roy that you'd be in here today."

"Jack?" I said, taking my feet down and standing up. The last time I saw Jack I was tearing his presentation on Michael Jackson to shreds in front of class. Jack was wearing a nice, collared shirt tucked into clean, unwrinkled jeans. His hair was cut and combed neatly. He stood in the entryway of the classroom with his hands together and his fingers interlocked, respectfully resting at his belt buckle in a formal way.

"I wanted to come by to thank you," he said quietly.

I shook my head, confused.

"Your course changed my life. I was bumming around, taking class after class, having my parents pay for everything, term after term. But, your course made me realize I needed to get my life together. I was embarrassed by my speech, and I want to apologize for that. Nobody's every called me out like that before. Most of the teachers here, in the classes I took anyway, were new. Pushovers. I spent so much time making them worry about how I would react to them, that they gave me decent grades for shitty work. You, obviously, were different. I needed that."

"Jack, I only—"

"You don't have to say anything. I just wanted to say thank you and tell you I'm sorry. I've changed."

I said the first thing that I could think of that someone more respectable than me might say: "I've seen a lot of untapped potential in you."

"Thanks," he said. "That means a lot to me coming from you. I won't bother you much longer, but I do have one favor to ask."

"What can I do for you?"

"I plan to go on to graduate school," he said, standing up to his full height, "I want to be a professor. Like you."

"What in God's name are you talking about?" A knee-jerk reaction.

"I was wondering if you would write a letter of recommendation for me, when the time comes."

"I don't know what to say."

"Ah," he said.

"Jack, this is a really tough career path. I'm not sure I can advise it. In fact, I'm thinking I would advise against it."

"Okay," he said, stepping toward the door. "I get it."

"No. I mean. It's just. It's very competitive. It's a lot of years and a lot of work. I'm nearly a decade in myself, and I still don't have a salary. Do you know what I mean?"

He was nodding at the floor. "If you don't want to, it's fine."

"I will. If you don't have anyone better than me, but—"

"Really?" he said, smiling.

"Of course I will. When the time comes. But I want you to think about this before you get too far—"

"Thank you, Professor Schurke. I truly appreciate it."

By the time I said, "I'm not sure it's worth it, Jack," he was already gone.

The course of the past two months was now rewinding through my head in a blur.

My first coherent thought: *Maybe making music people liked would be enough; that's something, a positive contribution, if only we could let it be that simple.*

Suddenly a knock came at the door. Daniels. Everything came to a dead stop.

"Schurke," he said, stretching his arms out wide, "where the hell's your class?"

"Today's a workshop day." A mistake.

"My God, it's worse than I thought. Tell me, since nobody's here, where the hell's the workshop taking place?"

"My students are working on their essays. This is a chance for them to come get some one-on-one— I mean, personal— Time with me to discuss their works in progress."

"Has anyone been here at all?"

"Yes—" *Thank God.* "—just had a student here. You missed him."

"Him?" he said. "Good."

"What can I do for you?" I asked.

Daniels moved to the front of the classroom and stood behind the teacher's desk, leaning on his knuckles. "There's been complaints about you this week."

"From whom? Roy?" *Why would I say that?*

"No." Daniels looked at me sideways. "There's no need for names here. Two separate complaints. One saying that you've been acting weird and one saying that your hygiene was suffering, and that she—or he, she or he—was worried about your health. I can see this beard is reaching unsanitary proportions. Schurke, is everything okay with you?"

"Everything's fine," I said.

"But then, I asked Rita if she's heard anything, and she shows me an email that says you canceled class because of the swine flu."

"Some of my students expressed concerns," I said, "so I canceled class as a precaution."

"You know the public health of this campus doesn't fall under your purview, right? You know people much, *much* smarter than you make the judgments about that, right?"

I nodded.

"Good. So, you're okay? Everything's fine? Your class is going smoothly?"

I nodded, again.

"No," Daniels said, slapping the desk. "I checked the records for your class. You gave all your students top grades on the midterm. What is that about?"

"I have a great, little section of students this term."

"Bullshit, Schurke. What's gotten you so bothered?"

"Nothing." (I've never felt so trapped in my life.)

"Monte tells me a little birdy told him that you might be hiding something. I've been trying to give you the benefit of the doubt." Daniels stood. "What are you hiding, Sam?"

*Grudge was a fool. Nice try, Daniels.*

"Damn it, Schurke. What do you have?"

"With this class and the defense coming up, I've done nothing but prepare and stress out. That's the truth."

Daniels came over and clasped his hand down on my shoulder. "Are you sure that's it?"

"Yes."

Daniels began pacing, hands on his hips, elbows out wide, talking to the floor. "For God's sake, Schurke, I told you not to worry about the class or the defense. You're supposed to be looking for what you've missed."

"I'm sorry," I said in a way that could have been confused with a question.

"I'm sorry too, Schurke," he said in a tone I was unaccustomed to hearing from him. "Just finish the damn class. For God's sake, Schurke, you damn millennials can't do a damn thing without someone holding your hand the whole damn time, can you?" He turned and marched out of the room.


I did as Daniels told me. I showed up on Monday, collected the finals and the course survey, registered the grades, and closed out the class. I did so before I even looked at any of the essays. *I'm giving these kids all "A" grades*, I thought. *If Daniels doesn't like it, he can suck it.*

I took a glance at the essays, skimming through the first page or two of each one. I was disappointed continually to see words like, "big government," "internment," and "illegal." (You simply cannot flip a switch and read something completely without bias.)

Feeling defeated, knowing I'd forever ruined *The Son Down* and perhaps Grundstein's books in general for my students, I turned to Emma's essay, hoping for something positive. It began:

> In Ernest Hemingway's foreword to the 1948 edition of *A Farewell to Arms*, he writes: "The fact the book was a tragic one did not make me unhappy since I believed that life was a tragedy and knew it could have only one end."

I read no further; I threw all the essays out.

# 32

With class behind me, there was only one more day before my dissertation defense, and an old maxim kept resonating in my head, *If you tell the truth, you don't have to remember anything.*

It had been more than a week since the damage to Karmann, but I had managed to keep her out of Ashley's sight. Fracturing at the seams, I didn't have the strength to face Ashley; I didn't want to answer her questions, nor did I want her to try to fix Karmann. Something didn't feel right about it. Like giving a dying dog hip surgery, it would cause more pain than it would be worth.

Ashley had left me a voicemail saying that everybody was going to The Bullring that evening. In need of a drink, I was compelled to go, but I decided to walk—turned out to be a good thing. I was nearly two blocks away when I first noticed the traffic was backed up. I couldn't see far, but the gaps in the leaves of the trees overhead were backlit by flashing red and blue lights. Something was off. As I got closer, traffic depressed from an occasional shift to stagnant, and I could see the cruisers were blocking the road near the entrance to The Bullring. Crowds had already gathered along the sidewalks and filled in the open spaces in the street between trapped vehicles.

Toward the back of the crowd, as I was able to zigzag my way through the bystanders, I maintained hope that I would be able to make my way through to the entrance of the bar.

Stepping around a smelly punk with shaggy hair dressed in a faded black Nickleback t-shirt with the words "Gotta Be Some-body" sketched across the back, I heard him say, "I think some-body's gettin' arrested."

"No way, dude," his buddy replied.

A few steps later, I was getting close to the scene. I weaved around a cuddly couple. The young man was rubbing the young woman's shoulder as if she was chilly, but it was far too warm of a night.

"God, I saw it happen," she said with a quiver in her voice. "I saw him get hit."

I looked back to see her staring dead ahead with red, puffy eyes.

"I'm sorry, babe," he said. "How awful."

When I turned forward, my face plunged into a sea of navy blue.

"Step back!" A female officer, tall and brawny, barked as she pushed me aside. She seemed willing to overlook the fact that I planted my face in her chest if I was willing to erase myself from her view. As I stepped back, I was swept up in the undertow of the crowd flowing into The Bullring, and I came to rest inadver-tently, like silt settling on the sea floor, at one end of a high-top table, at the other end of which happened to be Alex.

"Samuel, sweat heart," her voice chimed, ringing distinct-ly above the din of the club like Big Ben above London. She stepped around Johnny, Ashley, and Tom to wrap her slender arms around my neck.

"I was worried about you," she said. "Did you see the mess out in the street? God, it was awful."

"What happened?"

"Dumbass was trying to cross the road," Johnny said. "Cut it a bit close in front of a truck. Tripped. Truck got him with the bumper, impaled right in the chest."

"For God's sake, Johnny," said Alex. "That's a person you're talking about."

"That moron will probably survive relatively unharmed with the ability to multiply," Johnny said.

"Humans are impossibly fragile at times," Tom said, "and improbably resilient at others."

"That's the real tragedy," Johnny added, hanging his head over his drink.

It was clear from their somber philosophic tone that I was already a few rounds behind. I ordered a double shot of whiskey on the rocks.

"Did you already play your set?" I asked Ashley.

"Not tonight," she said. "Not playing tonight."

"Good," Alex said. "I'm in no mood to hear good music."

A waitress I didn't recognized—a rail-thin brunette with red lipstick—sidled up to Johnny and tugged on his shoulder. She said, "Your table's ready." She spoke so softly I couldn't be sure whether I heard her voice or I read her lips, and she looked deep into his eyes, with the intimacy of a lover, and then, she was gone.

Without a word, the group dispersed into the crowd and re-convened, as if by manifestation, on the patio. I had to track down the waitress to order my drink before I made my way out there, and somehow, in my brief absence, Grudge had shown up and taken my spot at the table.

"Take my seat," Alex said. "I'll take your lap."

*There is no pain that love will not overcome*, I thought that night as I endured for more than an hour with a numb leg for the plea-sure to be Alex's seat cushion. (Love is a fool.)

Somewhere along the line, in my moment of glory, I lost track of the conversation only to snap out of my trance and find Alex and Ashley in the middle of something serious. Really seri-ous. Serious enough to hold every other tongue around the table.

"I know what I agreed to," Ashley said, wiping the sweat

from her brow in vain, drunk as she was on that early summer night.

"Coitus," Alex said, apparently emphasizing part of the previous sentence I missed. "Passion, not romance."

"Jesus," Johnny said. "Have you all had sex with my sister?"

"It started that way," Ashley said to Alex unhindered by Johnny, "but now I feel too much. Don't you feel anything?"

"I've made a mistake," Alex said coldly, taking up her wine.

Ashley sat staring at Alex, stunned, as if she'd been stabbed. Alex was looking to Tom.

"First Tom, now Ashley," Johnny said to nobody in particular. "That leaves Gretchen. Gretchen, too, Alex? And, Sam?"

My head jolted up.

"Sam, have you also had sex with my sister?" Johnny asked more directly.

"No," I said limply, but how could he possibly believe the truth with Alex there, in a skimpy cocktail dress, all over my lap?

"That's it?" Ashley asked Alex.

Alex didn't look at her, nor did she speak. She took another swig of wine.

"Bye, Alex." Ashley said. Her chair screeched as she stood, ripping a tear through atmosphere on the patio, and she left. It would've been impossible to stop her before she disappeared into the crowd.

Awkward silence followed.

"It was nothing with Tom," Alex said to Johnny at last. "I was playing a part in a film."

Johnny's face turned visibly green, and his voice reached a depth I'd never heard before. "You made a porno with Tom. Alex, what the—"

"An indie film," Alex and Tom rebutted in unison.

"It was for art," Alex said, "and it was an *experience* of a lifetime."

Alex got up from my lap and sat down in Ashley's vacated

chair.

"It was the most authentic performance I've ever been a part of," Tom said, "and I stand by the work. I'm proud of it." He looked at Alex and then looked away. "But it doesn't change the facts."

"Why didn't you tell me, Alex?" I said, cutting Tom off, feeling sick.

"I didn't think you'd understand," Alex said.

"I wouldn't," I said. "And I don't."

"I'm leaving," Johnny said, getting up. "You girls sort this soap opera out on your own."

I got up, too, intending to follow Johnny.

"Sam, don't," Alex said.

I froze.

"Let me explain, first."

"I'm not sure I want to hear it," I said. "Not now."

Alex looked at Tom pleadingly, as if to say, *Please let me tell him.*

Tom shook his head.

"It was a performance, Samuel," Alex said. "It wasn't anything romantic."

"It's true," Tom said, alternating his gaze from the table to Grudge.

Alex tugged on my hand, begging me to sit.

I resisted. "What is this about Ashley? How's she involved?"

"It was just sex," Alex said. "Pure and simple."

"It's never pure and simple," I said. "Obviously Ashley didn't feel that way about it."

Alex waved her hand dismissively. "That's not how it started," she said. "I don't know when her feelings changed, but that wasn't our arrangement."

"Arrangement? How long has this been going on?"

"A year, maybe longer."

These words weren't helping; I couldn't breathe.

"I need space and time to think," I said, stepping around the railing at the edge of the patio.

"Samuel, please," Alex said. "Don't—"

"I can't do this right now."

(That was the last moment I saw Alex differently for the first time since seventh grade. No wind in her hair. No blue in her eyes. No sparkle in her smile. Just a rich girl who's never gotten anything but her own way. But I wouldn't know it in my heart until later that night, and I wouldn't actually see her again for two more days. Emma says I should cut this because she says it's not nice, but for Ashley, and for Johnny, I'll stick with the truth here.)

I crossed the lawn, not looking back, and I marched up the sidewalk, not thinking of direction. I walked for some time—sidewalk, intersection, sidewalk, intersection. I didn't stop long if I got held up at a light, crossing dangerously. Once, a car honked unnecessarily. Another time, a car honked fairly, surprising me how much brake the driver had to apply to allow me through. My head was swimming, and the tightness in my chest was all I could think of as I walked on.

I found myself heading for a destination: the office.

At that time of night, I had to dig my keycard out of my wallet to buzz myself in at the side entrance. The lights were dim in the abandoned hallways, and the only sounds were of my shoes on the waxed floor.

It felt good to be alone in the building, like having the sanctuary of a cathedral all to myself. Stopping by the maintenance room, I took a large green bin on wheels that was used to collect the recyclable waste, rolled it down to my door, and keyed into the office.

I sat down at my desk without turning on the lights. I didn't want the oppressive beam of the fluorescent lights. The sun was low enough to come nearly horizontally through the campus trees and into the window. I was off my feet for only a moment before my legs started to complain about the walk. If I rested any longer, I knew I would lose my resolve.

I opened the door all the way and took a thick book off of one of Grudge's shelves to use as a doorstop. The title was *Anthology of Marginalized Voices in American Literature*.

I paused as a new truth occurred to me: *Grudge and Tom. How did I not pick up on that before? There were a million clues I missed.* (I had been such a self-centered prick.)

I thought of the way Tom looked at Grudge earlier that evening when he said, *It didn't mean anything*. He was saying it to Grudge. Suddenly all the subtext became clear: Grudge and I were hit by the same shrapnel and suffered the same wounds, only from different directions.

Then I thought of Hemingway. *Why would Grudge be interested in a womanizer like Hemingway?*

I began throwing everything I'd accumulated into the bin. Books, files, papers, even office supplies. It all went quicker than I thought it would—all my work reduced to waste in a recycle bin in less than an hour.

When everything was packed up, I finally realized how absent personal affects had been from my workspace. The only evidence that I—Samuel Leonhard Grundstein Schurke—had been there at all, other than my name on the door, was the Ignatius J. Reilly candy dish full of uneaten Jolly Ranchers and the image on the university's computer desktop of me and Alex during our day at the beach. That was all.

I dumped the candies in the garbage and tucked the candy dish in the crook of my arm like a football. I wasn't going to waste the time to delete photo. My successor would take care of that; it would be the first thing to do.

At that, I kicked Grudge's book to the side and locked the door behind me. I wheeled the bin around back to the loading docks. I skipped the recycling bin and dumped the whole load of papers into the trash.

*All waste*, I thought. *I'm forging ahead—my life, my way—here for evermore.*

I looked at my phone. It was nearing eleven o'clock. My defense was less than twelve hours away, but I could only think of Alex, how I wanted to find her. I was ready, at last, to talk about how I thought we could still throw it all out and start over, how we could still commit to making an amazing, exclusive love together.

(What a dunce I was. An addict, really. I knew the dangers, but I wasn't prepared, yet, to thwart the desire.)

There was a shortcut we used to use as kids when Johnny and I would walk all the way to campus in the summertime to go to OPU's ice cream shop. The grass on the golf course was wet and blades of grass stuck to my shoes as I crossed. The sand traps glowed in the night as I imagined craters on the moon would. A small footpath took me through the brush from behind a tee box to the railroad tracks. Stepping from tie to tie, guided only by the light of the stars, it seemed reasonable to me that I could follow that railroad to a new existence with fresh, original experiences.

The ties were closer together than I remembered. When we were young, we could stride naturally as we imagined great adventures for ourselves as pirates, robber barons, and soldiers. Now, I had to take shortened, awkward steps.

I passed a section of track where the railway follows a bluff overlooking the road. Once, Johnny got it in his head that an enemy was approaching. He gathered rocks and filled his pockets. "Ammo," he said. When a car was close enough (I remember it like it was yesterday; it was a white Toyota Camry), Johnny took aim and threw the first stone. We watched in awe as it soared through the air. The windshield cracked. The tires screeched to a halt. We got the hell out of there. For weeks afterwards, every time someone knocked on the door, or the phone rang, or my mother called my name, I expected to be called to judgment. But it never came. (I suppose the guilt I've carried with me ever since is enough.)

I didn't continue on indefinitely. I exited the railway. It hardly took me any effort to hop the same low spot in the fence we'd always used. As kids, it was quite a feat; we felt as though we were scaling the Great Wall of China.

Over the hill, I crossed into the cemetery where, on the bleakest of December days, we used to go sledding on snowy evenings, doing our best to dodge the gravestones on our way down. I did my best to dodge the graves as I walked through, though I was beginning to feel weak and weary. My presence stirred the peaceful night of an ebony bird, and it fluttered and flew off into the darkness. I stood there, wondering—not fearing, not doubting—dreaming.

*Is there a balm in Gilead?* I thought. *Tell me, tell me, I implore!*

I left through the wrought-iron gate at the front of the cemetery and walked the block to the wrought-iron gate at the front of the Lawrence Estate. My personal code still worked. By the time I made it up the private drive, the lights were on in the entryway, and Ilsa was at the door.

"*Herr Schurke,*" she called out to me. "I see you."

"I came to see Alex," I said.

Ilsa closed the door.

I finished my approach.

She returned and said, "Ms. Lawrence is not in."

Mrs. Lawrence appeared on the stairwell behind Ilsa. She wore a blinding red robe made of shiny silk that ended too far above her knees to consider the view decent from where I was standing.

"Ilsa," Mrs. Lawrence said, "you've been a great help today. You may go." She looked at me. "Samuel, dear, do come in."

I stepped into the foyer.

Ilsa closed the door behind me. "Good evening," she said. She bowed to Mrs. Lawrence, then parted through the kitchen.

With only a thin layer of silk between me and Mrs. Lawrence, Ilsa's absence was regrettable.

"It's late, Samuel," Mrs. Lawrence said. "Don't you know what time it is?"

I looked at my cellphone. The battery must've died somewhere along the railroad tracks. "I don't," I said.

"My God, what is that monstrosity?"

"It's a candy dish. He's a character from a book. Ignatius J. Reilly. I was cleaning out my office tonight."

"It's hideous. Let's put it over here for now." Mrs. Lawrence took the candy dish and set it on a marble table near the door. "Don't forget to take it with you when you leave."

"I won't."

"You walked here from campus at this time of night? Is everything okay? You look a bit ruffled."

"Do you know where Alex is?" I said. "Will she be home soon?"

"I don't know, dear, but I'm glad you're here," she said, smiling. "I was becoming lonely this evening. Come to the living room. We can wait for Alex there." She left the foyer through the hallway, padding barefoot on the marble floor.

I turned and looked through the window to the driveway, hoping to see Alex approaching, wondering who might be dropping her off.

Feeling compelled by manners, I passed through to the living room. Mrs. Lawrence was sitting conspicuously to one side of a suede love seat. She was holding two chalices of red wine. Her long, slender legs were crossed, and the robe was draped in such a way that exposed everything up to the side of her hip.

"Samuel, dear," she said. "I thought you'd gotten lost." She raised a glass to me. As I reached to take it, she pulled it away. "Sit, dear."

I moved to sit in an adjacent chair.

"No," she said. "Next to me. Don't be shy."

I sat down on the love seat, facing forward. She made small

326  •  K.M. Zahrt

talk by making statements about Alex.

"Alex says you had fun at the gala."

"Alex says you have a cabin up north."

"Alex says you're almost through with your doctorate."

"Alex says you're hoping to get hired on at OPU full-time."

With each statement, she took a sip of wine, then adjusted in her seat, inching closer to me.

"Are you expecting Johnny home tonight?" I asked.

"How's your wine?" she said in response. "You've barely touched it."

I took a sip. Unnerved.

Mrs. Lawrence set her chalice down on the end table, then reached toward me. "Didn't I tell you to cut this beard?" She stroked my face. "You haven't trimmed it a bit." She leaned in close and brushed her lips across the edge of my facial hair, giving me goose bumps. "See how it pricks my lips."

"I'm sorry," I said. Confused.

"How do you expect anyone to want to kiss you?" She puckered and pressing her lips firmly into my cheek.

I took another sip of wine. Tipsy.

She kissed me again, closer to the jaw line. "See?" she said. "See how picky that is?" She let her hand fall from my beard to my chest, and she left it there.

"Where's Mr. Lawrence tonight?" I asked. Desperate.

"Oh, Samuel," she said, laughing. "It's just us here. Aren't you enjoying yourself?" Her hand descended across my stomach and rested at my belt buckle. "Don't you like spending time with me?"

"I—"

She interrupted me with a full kiss on the lips.

My mind began to spin, spitting out fragments of memories and thoughts that collided with my consciousness.

*...you've got a unique opportunity... ...the department has a need... ...help us fill it... ...et cet-tra... ...exploring... ...doesn't that sound like fun? ...keep*

*putting pieces together... ...you'll find something...*

She moved on top of me, spreading her legs to each side.

*...on top of her... ...Lenny, I don't know... ...lost... ...flashes of the War... ...lurched... ...shot back... ...swerved... ...screams... ...gun shots... ...everything stopped...*

She kissed me vigorously.

*...sounds of the night... ...blood dripped... ...cauterized... ...burning flesh... ...made quick work of it.... ...simple, easy... ...the train... ...the bag... ...fragments... ...darkness... ...wading... ...knee deep... ...rope... ...neck deep... ...gun... ...redness... ...Debakel...*

Everywhere—my beard, my chin, my ear, my forehead.

*...on top of Beth... ...Bobbie... ...grabbed me... ...controlled me... ...pulled me into Beth... ...arm around my back... ...dancing.. ...Beth... ...music... ...only using me...*

She unbuttoned the top of my shirt.

*...you get yourself cleaned up... ...I don't want to remember this... ...Alex... ...in a white bathrobe... ...nestled under Tom's arm... ...without a shirt... ...another man... ...that woman can be... ...ugh... ...tired... ...stressed... ...undersexed... ...out of control...*

She ran her tongue along my collarbone and up the side of my neck.

*...have you... ...with my sister?*

"I've wanted this for a long time, Samuel," she said.

*...with my mother? ...only using me...*

She grabbed my belt buckle.

*...The Timepiece... ...shrieking.. ...jolting.. ...canted angles... ...train... ...rolling.. ...collective groan... ...powerful... ...powerful... ...powerful..*

"No," I said at last, coming to my senses.

She didn't appear to hear me. She was moaning. My zipper was down and her hand was in my pants up to her wrist.

*...the joke is in your hands...*

"No," I said, again.

"What?" she said, still rubbing.

"Stop."

*...despair came over her...*

"What is the matter with you, Sam?" she said.

I hurried to put myself back together.

Mrs. Lawrence stood suddenly and wrapped her robe closed.

*...as you will when nobody around has any sexual relevance to you...*

"I've seen you staring. I've heard your comments. You've wanted this."

*...take thy beak from out of my heart.*

"I don't want this." I stood and straightened my clothes. "I'm leaving now, and as far as I'm concerned, I was never here."

I retrieved the candy dish and returned to the bluff where the railway overlooked the road.

*The joke is in your hands. The Joke is in your hands.*

And I heaved Ignatius J. Reilly down to the pavement and watched him shatter into shards. A car passed and ground the fragments further into dust.

*Nevermore. Nevermore. Nevermore.*

# 33

The day was upon me—Wednesday, June 24, 2009—dissertation defense day. There was nothing left to worry about. No more research to do. No more papers to write. No more courses to teach or essays to grade and submit. And no more waiting.

There was literally nothing left; the workers from the waste management company already came and cleared the dumpsters. All of my work for the past five years was done and gone, all except for that forsaken defense.

The grand finale or the anticlimactic dissolution of unfortunate events—my dissertation would either stand or crumble as it was written at the time it was submitted. It wouldn't be altered; I'd see to that.

Fully charged now, I turned my cellphone on for the first time since it died somewhere over the railroad tracks, and I tweeted:

@ProfSchurke: I've made mistakes, but #nevermore.
9:31 AM – 24 June 2009

As a gift, I promised myself I would spend the entire next day at the bookstore, splurge on an overpriced café beverage, finish reading *Hotel on the Corner of Bitter and Sweet*, and then aimlessly browse the stacks, reading whatever the hell I wanted, anything that would remind me what the magical allure of literature—

and freedom—once felt like.

I did everything I was told. I arrived early dressed in my best suit, freshly dry cleaned and ironed since the last time I wore it to the yacht club, and I set up the PowerPoint.

I looked out the window at the tree and remembered the last time I was in that classroom less than two months prior. Jack was giving his presentation, ruining another perfectly good class period, and I'd felt I was approaching the end of a chapter in my life, optimistic about the next. Then, Daniels had showed up and offered me the spring class that extended this chapter to include one hell of a conclusion. But it would end, one way or another.

I scratched my chin, admiring the great length of my beard. Thinking nothing of Alex.

"Schurke." Daniels was at the door.

"Good morning," I said, not taking my eyes off of the tree, hoping to catch a glimpse of the friendly squirrels, scurrying and jabbering onward, but they were gone.

"Are you ready for us?" Daniels asked.

"As ready as I'll ever be."

Daniels stepped into the hallway and invited the two other professors who made up my dissertation review committee to enter: Dr. Betsy Whittle, a woman with a constant scowl on her face, and Dr. Linda Ami-Peutetre, a petite middle-aged woman with a friendly smile that often contradicted her condescending airs.

The professors didn't greet me. *Perhaps Daniels had already gotten to them.* They selected their seats near the center of the room and began to unpack their belongings. I made a show of reviewing my notes.

I expected more people to come. The defense was open to fellow candidates as well as graduate and undergraduate English majors. All were welcome. I expected to see Grudge at least.

"Okay," Daniels said, looking at his watch. "Let's get on with it."

"Good morning," I said, cueing up the first slide.

I took a deep breath, about to launch into my introduction when Grudge entered.

"Sorry I'm late," he said to Daniels.

I could smell the scent of bar smoke on him from across the room. He took a seat in the back, noisily scraping his desk against the dusty tile floor with uncharacteristic abandon. He was wearing the same clothes that he had on at The Bullring the night before. His hair was noticeably unwashed and unkempt, nothing like his usual perfectly slicked wave.

"Walk of shame," I said with a grin, looking down at my notes.

Dr. Whittle scowled. Dr. Ami-Peutetre smiled.

"What was that?" Daniels asked.

"Sorry," I said. "Nothing."

"Would you begin?" Daniels was annoyed, like a father in public with two fighting sons.

I presented several crude slides of old material from my dissertation. "As I've outlined in writing, there seems to have been, among Grundstein's friends and family members, those close to him, a truly unwritten, unspoken, understood agreement that areas of Grundstein's past were unnecessary for public consumption, that despite any of Grundstein's own follies, his memory would be given every chance to stand in perpetuity, untainted. The family policy, if you will, was so ingrained that it was difficult to, even with connected dots, to finally locate any remaining letters, because even Grundstein's descendants, myself included, were unaware of their existence. This mysterious pact has left some significant gaps in our understanding of Grundstein's life and work. So I set out to try to fill in some of these voids. In the course of my research, I managed to uncover several letters to Grundstein from a variety of correspondents, contemporaries, and childhood friends." I could see Grudge gritting his teeth. "Most of the letters were received during the troubling period at the end of Grundstein's life, which he spent largely reclusively, with the exception of Ingrid, *bei dem Holzstapel*. The letters consisted almost entirely of kind words and well-wishes. In this collection were also several letters, or fragments of letters, drafted by Grundstein, which appear to have been left unsent. Unfortunately, although intriguing, these letters offer little-to-no insight into Grundstein's literary contributions. These letters occurred nearly a decade after Grundstein's last published novel, and there's no evidence to suggest he was actively working.

"What I was able to discover, by far the more valuable from a literary standpoint, was the journal of Ingrid Grundstein, Leonhard's second wife. The journal entries are sporadic, but they span most of the 1940s. In particular, I believe Ingrid Grundstein's journal gives us insight into that period of Grundstein's life, which I will elaborate on, here, shortly.

"With the help of a family member, I discovered these items that had been previously overlooked."

Grudge raised his hand like a schoolboy. "Question, Mr. Schurke."

"Yes, Montgomery," I said.

"You mean to suggest that they weren't hidden by your family, by you even, until such a convenient time. That's what we are to believe."

"Mr. Grudge," Daniels said, looking down his nose.

"I'm sorry, Professor," Grudge said to Daniels, "but I've been working with you to recover these kinds of documents for years now, and you've been working for decades. And there's nothing out there. Then, Schurke shows up, does a rudimentary search, and suddenly these documents appear, and nobody knew anything about them. I don't buy it. Why should we believe this fabrication?"

"It's possible that past curators at the museum could've been aware of them," I said. "That I cannot know. I cannot know how many historical society members were aware of them. Even so, their mission was and is to preserve them. If they had any reason to believe their release would jeopardize that mission, they could've contributed to their security, but this is all speculation. And worthless, too, I would add—"

"Can we cut the crap?"

Dr. Whittle and Dr. Ami-Peutetre turned and faced Grudge for the first time.

"Cut the crap, Schurke," Grudge said.

I looked to Daniels for direction.

"Dr. Whittle, Dr. Ami-Peutetre," Daniels said, ignoring Grudge, "do you have any remarks or questions for Mr. Schurke regarding his previously submitted scholarship on Grundstein at this time?"

Dr. Whittle waved her hand apathetically.

"I do have one question I'd like to pose to Mr. Schurke," Dr. Ami-Peutetre said, "perhaps more to the panel present." She picked up her copy of my dissertation. "The question at hand is, what does this add to the lexicon of Grundstein studies? What's the value in it? And, does it represent work worthy of conferring a doctorate?"

Grudge snickered.

"Mr. Schurke," Daniels said. "You may address Dr. Ami-Peutetre's concerns, then Dr. Whittle and I will have a chance to comment as well."

"I would say," I said, having rehearsed the answer to this question expecting Grudge to ask it, "what's been accomplished here is an exhaustive confirmation of several scholarly suspicions—some already adopted as leading views on Grundstein's work, others previously contested, and some new threads—particularly the now indisputable fact that Grundstein was illegally imprisoned as an enemy alien during World War II. Therefore, the conclusions outlined within form the most accurate, in my opinion, reading of Grundstein's *The Son Down* to date. In doing so, this represents a significant addition to, as you say, 'the lexicon of Grundstein studies.' I've defined, if I may be so bold, what should be the consensus on Grundstein's last published work of fiction."

Dr. Ami-Peutetre leaned forward, and I prepared myself to face a cutting follow-up question.

But, before she could say anything, Grudge said, "That's nothing but gobbledygook."

"Grudge," Daniels scolded. "Dr. Whittle, would you like to comment?"

*Thank God.*

"I accept Mr. Schurke's answer," Dr. Whittle said. "I see no further need for questions."

Grudge pounded his fist on the table. "Come on, Schurke, did you or did you not find something at Gertrude Grundstein's house just recently?"

Daniels raised his hand, then pulled it back, and folded his arms.

I waited hoping for an injunction from the other panel members, but their eyes stayed fixed on me.

I cleared my throat.

"Yes," I said at last, "I have discovered some additional letters from Leonhard Grundstein to Gertrude—"

Daniels stood suddenly, giving me a scathing look.

"—but, again, nothing of substantial literary value—" Truly on defense now. "—and the letters are a personal possession of Gertrude's, which she has chosen not to release, and I have chosen to respect that wish."

Daniels walked to the front of the room, wielding his copy of my dissertation. "Have you or have you not," he demanded, mirroring Grudge's syntax, "found anything else that's not documented here?"

I hung my head, thinking.

"Mr. Schurke?"

Randomly a thought emerged, salvation: *If you don't remember anything, you can tell the truth.*

"Did you or did you not," Daniels said, pressing on, "find evidence suggesting Grundstein had committed some kind of crime during World War I?"

A test: "I would not know."

Daniels looked confused, offended. "Did you or did you not find personal writings from the end of Grundstein's life, a diary of sorts?"

Steadfast now: "I would not know."

"Did you or did you not," Daniels continued, voice rising, "find evidence suggesting Grundstein may have been a Nazi sympathizer?"

"I would not know."

"Did you or did you not find evidence suggesting Leonhard Grundstein committed suicide?"

"I would not know."

"Within the past two weeks," Grudge offered, "I heard there was a mysterious break-in at the museum in Petoskey. Where were you on the night of July 12?"

"What, is this a criminal investigation now?" I said. "This is all getting derailed. Are we going to discuss my dissertation as it's written or not?"

"Answer the question," Daniels said. "It's simple enough. Where were you?"

"I would not know."

"What would you suspect the perpetrator was looking for?"

"I would not know."

"Schurke!" Daniels became enraged. "Did you or did you not find evidence suggesting Grundstein stole Hemingway's missing manuscripts? Did you or did you not find them at the museum? Do you or do you not have them in your possession?"

I smiled. "I would not know."

"That's enough, damn it," Daniels shouted. He turned to the committee. "If it pleases you both, I'd like to move to conclude the defense proceedings immediately."

"I second the motion," Dr. Whittle said.

"If you'll follow me to my office, we can deliberate there. This shouldn't take long."

Drs. Ami-Peutetre and Whittle stood to follow Daniels.

"Mr. Schurke," Daniels said, not making eye contact, "you'll be notified of our decision in the near future."

The committee left; Grudge remained.

"Leave me be, Grudge," I said. "Not another word. I swear. Go."

When Grudge was out of sight, my nerves crumbled—chills, goosebumps, shakes, shivers—but it was over. *Fertig.*

I checked Twitter. My latest tweet had been retweeted thirty-three times. *A sign.*

Late that evening, I received an email from Daniels. The subject line was: DEFENSE, FUTURE.

> Mr. Schurke,
>
> It is with regret that I inform you of the committee's decision. You did not pass. You are entitled to apply for reconsideration once more. I would not recommend it.
>
> Dr. Stanley P. Daniels

# 34

You may not remember the exact date or the exact time, but you remember where you were when you heard the news.

I was at the mall, at the bookstore, in casual clothes—a t-shirt and a baseball hat. My cargo shorts were saggy and loose. I felt like I was masquerading as a barely recognizable former self.

I sat in the café and drank a cup of coffee and ate a scone.

"A sample of espresso," the barista said, setting down the cup and pushing it toward me. "On me."

Without a single interrupting thought, I read to the end of *Hotel on the Corner of Bitter and Sweet.*

*...unique history...*

*...the circumstances of life...*

*...how horribly cruel...*

*...imperfect...*

*...it was enough...*

Finished, I returned the copy I'd bought for Tante to the store's fiction section for the next reader. I crossed over to the magazine racks and selected a periodical on the subject of re-modeling old cabins.

At that moment, a heavyset woman came into the café. She was out of breath and had her hands full of bags. She ditched her cargo at the nearest table and leaned on the back of a chair. Her chest heaved as her eyes darted about the café—desperate, searching.

Other than the barista and two old men sitting at a table in the corner, there was nobody to be found but me.

"Ain't you heard?" she said to me.

A thousand thoughts collided in my head: *A gunman's in the mall; someone's shot Barack Obama; another iconic landmark's been attacked; the H1N1 virus has mutated and the pandemic is out of control. What? Oh, God, What?*

"I would not know," I said and stepped back as if six more inches between us would save me.

She said, "Mi—" Then she choked as the levy finally broke and tears burst through. Somehow she managed to add, "Jackso—" That was it: *Mi— Jackso—* But that was enough; I knew the truth:

> Who:    Michael Jackson
>
> What:   Died
>
> When:   Thursday, June 25, 2009

I checked my phone for the where and the why, but nothing happened. The Google search was blocked. On Twitter, there was an image of a whale being lifted out of the ocean by several tweety birds. The message read: TWITTER IS CURRENTLY DOWN FOR UNPLANNED MAINTENANCE.

"How horribly cruel," I said. "Enough."

The woman put her head down and sobbed.

I sat with the sobbing woman for some time, maybe a half hour.

At last, I tried Twitter again. It was alive—*thank God*. An article came up on my feed. The headline read: FANS HOPE THE KING OF POP'S DEATH WILL LEAD TO ANSWERS ABOUT JACKSON'S TROUBLED PAST. The lead: "Fans gathered outside the King of Pop's mansion hope a posthumous examination of Michael Jackson's residence will uncover long-sought answers to troubling personal questions."

I scoffed and abandoned the article. Then, a compelling idea formed in my head, and I left the store with the intention to carry out one last act.

I ravaged my room, packing whatever was in sight that might be useful on the Fourth of July trip—shorts, pants, shirts, underwear. *Remember clean underwear.* The whiskey, the phone charger. *Remember the phone charger.* A book? *Remember a book.* The only one in my room that wasn't perverted by the studies of my past life was *The Screwtape Letters* by C.S. Lewis.

That was when Alex pulled Mr. Lawrence's nickel-colored Bentley convertible into the driveway. The green leather interior was as soft as the lushest of lawns. The car reminded me of Mrs. Lawrence.

Feeling irritable, I didn't want to see anybody, especially not Alex. She would only cloud my foggy judgment as I careening toward some kind of climax.

But she was already in the house.

I crammed whatever else I could into the bag as she ascended the stairs. I hardly had a chance to get it fully zipped before she was gracing my presence.

"Samuel, can we talk?" she said.

I picked up my bag vertically like a tired boxer hugging a punching bag. "I have to go," I said as I brushed by her as on my way out the door. She smelled of potpourri. "Shut my door, would you?" *The first time I'd ever requested anything of her!* I moved down the stairs.

Alex hurried to complete my request and catch up. "Where are you going?"

"Up north. I have to take care of something before the trip. I better have them pick me up at the cabin. Thanks for reminding me."

I dumped my bag on the kitchen table. She sat down and pulled on my shirtsleeve. "Will you sit down and talk to me for just one minute?"

I remained standing. "What is there to talk about?"

"Let's talk through everything."

"We both know there's nothing."

"Samuel."

I waited for more.

"Can't we put the past behind us?" she added.

"The past is as stubborn to kill as a prized bull."

"Sam, what are you talking about?"

"What am I talking to about? Fuck Ernest Hemingway. That's what I'm talking about."

Alex's face—mouth open, eyes wide, ears red, eyebrows cocked and loaded with judgment—conveyed an abject horror I'd never seen from her before. "Samuel Leonhard Grundstein Schurke," she scolded.

I nodded and added, "Fuck Grundstein, too."

Alex braced herself against the table, beginning to choke on air as if I had dumped a bucket full of water on her face. "Samuel— What are you—"

"And all the others like them." I was gaining momentum. "Fuck them."

"Samuel, my God, what are you even saying?"

Alex had me rattled—again. I was thinking so clearly before she stepped into my doorway. I turned to leave.

"For God's sake, what's wrong with you?" Alex begged, grabbing my hand with both of hers. "Sammy, you're upset. Talk to me, dear. What's the meaning of this—this vulgarity?"

(To this day, I don't know for sure. The meaning changes for me every time I think of it, even now. It's as slippery as marlin in the stream. What is meaning, after all, but abstract and meaningless?)

"Fuck meaning," I said at last. So basic. So fundamental.

There was truth in it. I paced the floor as the words came to me. "Who the hell were they to quit? For all their supposed greatness, their ability to look into the human experience—the psyche, the soul—"

Alex nearly fell out of her chair trying to reach out to me and pull me back.

"—when faced with the final decision concerning the string of the fleeting moments that comprise the present and lead to the future, these celebrated minds chose to end rather than to continue. They concluded, in that moment, 'I'm done.' Death instead of life. What can we learn from someone, no matter how great they were during their lifetime, who decided, once and for all, life wasn't worth continuing? What does that mean? That's the question."

I turned to her. "I don't know, Alex. Reasoning, rationale, explanation. I don't know. And to be certain, I no longer care. That's fact."

"I don't understand what you're saying, Sam?"

"These are people who seemed to embody the epitome of human potential," I said, laughing. "The Elvis-kind of people of the world. Now, Michael Jackson. But they couldn't stop dancing with the devil. What else can be done? What else is there to do? They're past."

Alex covered her ears with her hands, trembling.

I moved to her side and rubbed her shoulder until the room was silent.

At last, she said, "What does that have to do with us, Samuel?"

Crouching down to meet her eyeline, I took her hand in mine now. From that angle, I could see dust particles shimmering in the sunlight from the kitchen window—imperfections I couldn't see when I was standing.

"Is it possible, Alex, that they finally got it. That nothing means anything unless we make it so. It's hard, but it's right there. So basic. Fundamental. A freedom."

Together, we stared into each other's eyes. Hers—scared and searching—were an ocean of blue-green that had once captured my affection for too long. ·

I took her chin in my hands, thinking nothing of it, and I gave her a full kiss on the lips—a magical moment I'd once dreamed of, and now, nothing. (The Universe lets you know everything, if you only listen.)

"Samuel," she said. "We could be great again."

"I have to go," I said, feeling reckless. "I have a feeling this trip will change everything."

Then, from a distant place, I heard myself say, "It's Grundstein's last manuscript. An unfinished novel. *The Mysterious Garden*. I have it, and I'm going to put the final period on Grundstein and his work once and for all. As far as the world will know, it will be done."

I saw Alex looking as though I'd fired off a gun.

"How's it going to end?" I heard her say, and I saw tears dripping down her face were forced to detour around her feeble smile. "I'm worried you'll never see me, again."

I saw the tears had made lines, incongruous, through her make-up, and I knew, then, it would take an Earth-shattering event to realign our worlds with any semblance of synergy. (That event would happen, but I couldn't foresee it. Nobody could.)

"Are you sure you're okay, Samuel?" Alex asked in a shaky voice. "We can get help."

"You have to quit confusing a madness with a mission, Alex." I was feeling outside of my head. "We decide, now, what gets preserved and who gets hailed. Because we are here. Alive." (I will regret nothing.)

"Tell me what you are talking about, Samuel?" she said earnestly, rising and standing close at hand. "What are you going to do?"

"I'm going up north. You know this. Tell the others to pick

me up at the cabin tomorrow. After that? I would not know."

"Samuel, we could be so good together," she said, leaning toward me, lips first.

I didn't pull away, but I said, "It was nice to think so."

She stopped short and smacked my face where her kiss would've landed.

I looked at her only for a split second longer—*Oh, Alexandria!*—for I couldn't risk losing my mission, but the moment felt long enough for a million lightyears to shine between us and then flare out.

# 35

Once Alex drove away from the house, a sense of urgency forced me onward.

North I-75, again. A paved paradise. A certain slant of light. Amber waves.

Karmann resisted the center of the lane; she pulled toward the bum wheel. She screamed at me, *Away-way-way-way-way-way.*

"It's all falling indelibly into the past," I said to her. "You know this."

Her tires wailed. Her gauges flickered. I had to fight with her to keep her on the road the entire way.

The two-lane to the cabin was even more pothole-ridden from the recent rains. I worked Karmann surgically, navigating one blow at a time. At the first bump, the right rear hubcap was gone.

I spoke to her, "At ease, Karmann, at ease."

I could see the silhouette of the cabin through the trees. "We're almost there, old girl."

I patted the steering wheel like the neck of an exhausted horse. "Less than a mile to go before we can sleep."

At the second bump, the muffler went. Karmann let out a loud groan, then sputtered angrily.

I urged her onward. "Less than a mile to go——" I was now her matador, and each depression of the gas pedal was two *ban-*

*derillas* in between her shoulder blades. It was up to me to make our dance beautiful. "—before we can sleep."

At the last curve, the third bump dislodged the front bumper and did her in. Her tires tumbled over the amputated steel. The front right wheel blew completely as we bounced off the road and into the woods.

Slow motion. Karmann skirted along through the brush at five miles an hour. Decelerating. At ten yards, she met a pine that must've been more than 100 years old.

To my chest I took a firm blow from the steering wheel, but Karmann was already out of her misery. Smoke fled from her hood. The last clown—alcoholic and lonely—had finally driven the circus car into extinction.

Circling to the passenger's side, I checked my bag for the bottle of Maker's Mark. Still in tact. *Thank God.*

As I stood in the middle of the road, bottle in hand, paying my last respects, with the sun a half circle of red-orange fire burning behind me, I took a ceremonious drink. "This world is not yours, Karmann," I said, as she lay dying. "Meet Mr. White Pine."

> Who:   Karmann Ghia
> What:  Dead
> Where: *Der Holzstapel* at Walloon Lake, Michigan
> When:  Thursday, June 25, 2009
> Why:   ~~Because she fell apart and crashed.~~ ~~Because I~~
> ~~didn't take better care of her.~~ ~~Because it was her time~~.
> Because that's what happened.

(To this day, Karmann is still there, just a pile of rust and stardust.)

At the cabin, I moved as quickly as I could with my bag slung over my shoulder, which was anchored awkwardly by the bottle of whiskey inside. The old oak bench seemed more reluctant to be moved than I remembered. But I felt large; I contained the energy of multitudes. I moved it with a heave for the ages.

Floorboards aside, I extracted the tackle box and unlocked it. There they were, everything, unmoved. I took the letters out of the tin box I found in Karmann and the manuscripts out of the folio I found at the museum, and sandwiched them—along with the article on Dieter I got from Tante—in the copy of Hemingway's *The Sun Also Rises* annotated by Grundstein that I found at the library, and tucked it all—along with the can of lighter fluid that Emma helped me find—under my arm. I shoved Grundstein's Ronson lighter and Petoskey-stone paperweight in my pocket, restoring a sense of order I hadn't felt since I left them behind. The journals I stuck inside the leather folio and put them in the tackle box. I replaced the tackle box under the floorboards and returned the old bench to its place.

(For reasons I didn't understand, and still don't, I wasn't ready to include Grundstein's journals in the course of action I was about to pursue, even though the journals were, are, every bit as incriminating as the existence of the manuscripts, if not more so. But I wasn't thinking; I was being compelled by ideals. And, to this day, I regret nothing.)

I hurried to the shed with my pockets loaded, my arms full of priceless paper, feeling more unnerved than I'd ever felt in my life before (or since).

At the woodpile, I took out the manuscripts and pinned them down between two logs. I liked the look of the papers there; they seemed to be where they belonged. For now.

In my bag, I rummaged for the bottle of whiskey and took another pull. I held the bottle up to the sunset to see how much of the golden courage remained: a quarter bottle.

I shrugged. "That'll have to do."

The sun, at just a sliver, was a warning; I was running out of time.

At the fire pit, I ripped, unceremoniously, the letters to shreds and shaped them into a teepee over Hemingway's book at the center of the pit. I hurried to complete a log cabin-style fire before the light made its final retreat, creating an alter upon which my sacrifice would be made.

I rolled Dieter's article into a small torch and took another pull of the whiskey. The bottle shook as I raised it to my mouth, splashing alcohol down my beard.

It was time.

With the newspaper torch in one hand, I removed Grundstein's lighter from my pocket and drew confidence and assurance from the inscription. I flicked the flint with my thumb, and without hesitation, it came alive.

I lit the newspaper, returned the lighter to my pocket, watched the flame grow enough light to illuminate the scene all the way to the lakeshore, casting shadows among the trees.

The torch burned with haste. As way leads on to way. I tucked it in at the base of the teepee of shredded dreams.

I thought of Michael Jackson. I wondered if he would be cremated, like Grundstein, to try to hide something of the what and the why surrounding his death.

Part of me expected something paranormal to happen. Something symbolic. Something that would condemn or condone my course. But, nothing.

I held the torch to the base of the fire pit, and the flame worked from the paper to the book. The edges of the cover turned black first, then the flames grew. From the book to the wood, the fire came alive.

I stepped back to admire it. I listened to the snap and crackle and sipped on the whiskey as I watched.

The book soon withered into unrecognizable char, then crumbled away indistinguishable from the other coals and ashes. It burned no differently than a paper plate a child throws into a campfire.

Suddenly there was something in the distance, a disturbing

sound, a horrible clicking noise skipping across the surface of the water. I stepped to the shore and peered into the darkness. A dim light began to emerge from the trees along the opposite shore. Getting loser. Growing.

I picked at my ears. *Grudge's GTO? No, it can't be. My mind must be playing tricks on me, or the whiskey is. I've lost my wits at last.*

My head ached as I squinted to see better as the lights approached the clearing near the boat launch. A car appeared and stopped, but it didn't turn into the launch.

The clicking sound was distinct now, unmistakable.

I closed my eyes and covered my ears, but when I looked again, the car was still there. Accelerating, the sound of peeling rubber came to me across the lake, and the car turned up the road toward me.

Deep down, I knew Grudge—or Daniels, or both—would be coming to be the force that would act against my inertia. I knew it as soon as the existence of a manuscript was revealed to anyone beyond me—the inevitable reaction.

Under the pressure—transformation—I hurled the paperweight into the lake.

(I'm disappointed not to have it now. Emma and I have spent many summer mornings with goggles and snorkels, holding out hope it might turn up, but I suspect it found its rightful resting place.)

Through the trees, I could see the wide-spaced, double-circled headlights of Grudge's GTO bobbing and weaving down the drive to the cabin.

I ran to the woodpile and tore the manuscripts free. Then, I stood there, waiting, not acting. Somewhere deep down, I wanted, *needed*, an audience—this audience—for my next act, for the same reason one might fear hitting a hole-in-one without a witness. (So, there are two other living souls on this Earth who can verify the account that follows as true.)

The car stopped; doors opened.

"Sam?" cried Grudge. "Don't even start."

I was ready.

A booming voice: "Schurke, don't you dare."

It was Daniels.

"Where's Alex?" I shot back, already losing my nerve.

"We've gotten all we needed from her," Daniels said. (They'd been bribing her to work me. I should've known.)

"She's tired of all this, Sam," Grudge said. "We're all tired of your shit."

"Schurke," Daniels added in a stern voice. "Your grandfather would hate you for this, and you know it."

I fumbled through my pocket to produce the lighter as I watched the two shadowy figures move down the hill. I didn't look at the inscription, but I knew the truth of the message in my heart.

Two flicks. A flame.

It was all the threat I needed. Daniels halted and held out his arms to stop Grudge. (Even now, I take great pleasure thinking of Grudge tripping over himself trying to stop.)

I raised the papers for them to see and shouted, "Take one more step, and these manuscripts go up in flames."

"Hemingway's manuscripts?" Daniels asked.

"One of Grundstein's too. I have his last, unfinished, unseen novel right here."

"And Hemingway's?" Grudge wanted confirmation.

"You shut up, Grudge," I said. (Even though I understood he was no longer my nemesis, allegiance to our long-established attitudes toward one another persisted.)

"Sam, this isn't what you want to do," Daniels said, forcing a calm, measured tone.

"What do you know about what I want to do?"

"You want to leave academia, and that's fine."

I shook my head. "You're a tyrant, Daniels. And I've been your fool."

"You don't want to go to jail," Grudge said.

"Jail, Grudge, really?" I said, laughing. My voice ricocheted across the lake. "What law would I be breaking? These are mine. My inheritance. I'm the executor of Grundstein's estate, and I can burn them if I want to." I was becoming hysterical. "Oh, thank God for private enterprise and *freedom*! Long live capitalism! Even if there was a law, which there isn't, nobody cares about these papers, not enough to spend the money to prosecute the perpetrator of their destruction." Stomping back and forth, I yelled at the top of my lungs, "The papers you're after, even if I have them here, are already lost. The mystery of their whereabouts is more valuable than any scribblings of an egotistical brut with no training in writing. He's lucky, *you're* all lucky, Grundstein stole them."

I stopped and looked squarely at Daniels. "You once said it yourself, *professor*—as I recall—Hemingway never would've become your precious subject *without* Grundstein. So, let's leave it as it stands."

"Grundstein was—"

"Grudge, shut your mouth. You'll raise your hand and be called on before you talk again or else I'll burn these papers and smear the ashes all over your goddamned sweater vest."

"Sam, please," Daniels said.

"No," I said. "I won't bear to have these infantile stories from that Cretan published so everyone can drool over them and pretend the only reason they read like shit is because they're gushing with so much genius that we imbeciles couldn't possibly comprehend the greatness. I'm not going to live in that world. And, Hemingway doesn't get to either. He offed himself. He's done. He won't get one more day in the sun. Not with my help."

"What about Grundstein?" Daniels said. "What about your grandfather's legacy?"

"Legacy is a hoax, Daniels. Don't you get it? An unfinished manuscript from a dead writer isn't worth the paper it's printed on. I'm not going to let some publishing house assign a ghost-writer to it so they can brush it up, stick a price tag on it, and sell it like it's exactly what Grundstein would've done."

"We know you found more letters—" Grudge stopped as Daniels grabbed his shoulder.

"Please, Grudge," I said. "Tell me more about what you know."

"I was right all along." He sounded like a schoolboy on a playground. "And I know you found his letters, perhaps more."

"Please don't do this," Daniels said, ignoring Grudge.

"He won't," Grudge said, stepping forward, but Daniels pulled him back.

I waved the lighter dangerously close to the papers. "For the love of Moloch, there are no letters, you dolt!"

"There are no letters?" Daniels said. "There are no letters that you know of? Or there are no letters now?" He pointed at the fire.

"Cut the semantics, Daniels. And, stop acting like spending your life studying the work of a dead man is a worthy enterprise. Literature scholars are about as useless to the production of the present, the production of the future, as scoundrels. You've wasted your life. Don't waste another breath of mine." (Words elevated out of anger, not necessarily out of conviction.)

I paused, then continued, "Did you hear about Michael Jackson?"

"What the hell does that have to do with anything?" Grudge said.

"Shut up, Montgomery," Daniels said. "Sam, come on. What are you talking about?"

"Michael Jackson died today, and do you know what the first instinct was, the first thought anybody, everybody, had after checking Twitter, after gawking, shocked with self-centered grief they don't deserve? They thought about tearing his life apart, digging through all his shit, in the name of 'finding answers.' They're going to tear his home apart. They're going to go through all his things. They're going to look at every word the man ever wrote or said or sung. They're going to speculate about everything in between. They're going to write books about what they've found, and sell them at no benefit to him. They're going to cut open his body. Doctoral candidates will write worthless dissertations about it all. And, for whom? For him? For his family? No. For themselves. He's done. His work is finished. Whatever he did in his personal life is over, dead."

I felt good—powerful, in control.

"This is what I've learned from you, Daniels, after all of these years of working at your feet. I've learned that anybody's life, when examined, makes no sense. I've learned to leave it alone. Because what's the point? Nobody even knows. And nobody needs to know anything. If you like Michael Jackson's music, enjoy the music. Let the music stand and leave the rest alone. If you like Grundstein's books, enjoy the goddamned books. Listen. Read. That's it. Leave the dead fucking dead."

"Don't you dare, Schurke," Grudge said.

"They killed themselves," I said as a matter of fact. "That's the end of the line. That's when they gave up any right to the future. They can no longer grasp it with their dead hands."

"You know Hemingway was mentally ill at the end," Daniels said. (Such a worthless statement at such a time.)

"You can have Hemingway," I said, shaking the papers at him, "but Grundstein is mine."

"Grundstein was ill, too," Grudge said.

"No, enlightened," I said. "You know this: that we must die. That is the nature of plots. It was as true a quarter century ago as it is today, and it won't change."

"He's out of his mind," Grudge said to Daniels.

"Creeds and schools in abeyance, Grudge. You should know this, too. Won't you, of all people, sound the triumphal drums of the dead? Won't you fling the loudest music to them?"

"Screw you, Schurke," Grudge said.

"Turn back, Samuel," Daniels said. "Descend the stair. You're tampering with history."

"We're all tampering with history," I barked. "Every moment we're alive we're all complicit in the willful proliferation of lies by the false prophets and the deliberately selective memories of the masses. Nobody is free of it. The best among us harness this knowledge to advance their own agendas, and I will, too. I, too, will sing America, and you'll see how beautiful I am and be ashamed.

"*Vivas* to those who have failed," I said, pressing on ceaselessly, "and to those whose war-vessels sank in the sea—" I raised the manuscripts high over my head, and the firelight danced over the pages like an aurora in the night sky. "—and those themselves who sank in the sea—" I pounded my chest with my fist. "—and to all the generals that lost engagements, and all overcome heroes, and—*AND*—the numberless unknown heroes equal to the greatest heroes known."

In booming staccato notes that rang across Walloon Lake, I shouted:

"Smoke—

—is soul—

—returning to the Universe—"

"Don't do it," Daniels said. "Please, for God's sake."

"—to enlightenment—"

"Schurke, don't."

I wielded the manuscripts, aiming them at Daniels and Grudge like a gun:

"Set—

—it all—

—ABLAZE!"

I struck up the lighter again, and it produced a new, true flame. I lit the corner of the stack; the old papers became a pillar of fire. Then, abruptly, the roaring voices were silent at last. Everything became stuck in time except for the flames, which reached for the heavens.

Daniels and Grudge were wide-eyed. Aghast.

I looked at the manuscripts—Hemingway's lost and Grundstein's last—afire against the backdrop of the Universe. "It's funny, isn't it, how they burn all the same."

Even as the flames crept toward my hand, as I stood mesmerized by the sight, I could feel the heat singeing the hair on the backs of my fingers; it smelled of damnation.

I waved the torch over my head and called out to the sky:

"This—

—is the flag—

—of permanent defeat."

Daniels and Grudge came alive at last and ran toward me.

I flinched and the flames caught the edge of my beard and flared. I clapped furiously at my chin. Angry with pain, I dumped the papers into the pit and charged at the oncoming men.

Daniels swung at me, missed, and face-planted into the dirt. Grudge ran by me to the edge of the pit. I came upon him from behind and pushed him toward the fire. He jumped over and fell on the landing on the other side.

"Give it up," I said. "It's over."

Grudge arose and rounded the fire in my direction. I tried

to dodge him, but he managed to drive his shoulder into my gut. Taking his full weight to my midsection upon hitting the ground, I lost my wind and gagged for air. Grudge pinned me down at the neck.

I writhed from side-to-side trying, at once, to breathe and to see what was happening behind him.

Daniels limped to the edge of the pit. He was circling, searching for anything salvageable.

"Montgomery," Daniels called. "Let him up. It's over."

As Grudge got up, I gave him a swift kick to the back of his calf, and he stumbled toward the campfire light.

"He's lying," Grudge said. "He's got copies somewhere. We have to search the cabin."

"No," Daniels replied, not taking his eyes off of the fire.

"We have to do something. We have witnesses. We can punish him at least. Take legal action."

Daniels' silence was indignant.

"We have a responsibility," Grudge pleaded.

"Just shut the hell up, Monte," Daniels said. "It's done. What about that don't you understand?"

Grudge stepped backwards, feeling sucker-punched.

With regained breath, I made my way to the edge of the woods. The liquor, still warm in my veins, measured how little time had passed since the sun had set.

We stood in silence and watched the fire burn, witnessing years, a lifetime of work evaporate in seconds, minutes at the most, before our eyes.

*And the ages continued henceforward!*

"This is insanity." Grudge fell to his knees, limp.

After a long silence, Daniels said, "We've lost sight of our origins." The closest to an admission of guilt he was ready to offer.

Grudge arose. "I'm out of here," he said, turning up the hill.

"Don't you leave without me." Daniels followed, walking with his head bent low.

356 • K.M. ZAHRT

"Nobody will ever thank me," I called after them, "but I'm done with these lonely offices. Go off, get drunk, and float aimlessly in the pool you've made until your death comes for you. I'm done trying to go in everyone's way but my own."

It was getting cold; I sat down by the fire and looked into the coals and listened as the clicking of Grudge's GTO faded away into the night:

*click-click click-click click-click click-click click-click click-click*
*click-click click-click click-click click-click click-click*
*click-click click-click click-click click-click*
*click-click click-click click-click*
*click-click click-click*
*click-click...*

(To this day, from time to time, that clicking still rings in my dreams, and when I wake, the scar tissue on my chin itches.)

# 36

What will happen with Grundstein's legacy now that it's all accounted for? Its life is its own—not mine. I'll spend about as much more of my time and energy caring about that as a dead man can.

But then again, here I am. Why? (You see, the human existence is also a comedy.)

What about Alex? How far have our orbits diverged? Far enough for me to escape her gravity, to understand that our futures will never synchronize in the way I'd once predicted, the way I'd once hoped. (The next time I saw Alex was at Johnny's deathbed where the trajectories of our lives would be thrown wildly off course once again and the chaos of it all, alone, would remain steadfast.)

As for me, I was born. I'm alive. That's all I know for sure.

Free of Grundstein's skeletons, free of Alex's spells, and free of Daniels' curses, including my involvement with the university, I looked to live my life anew in Johnny's wake. My first act: I called upon Emma—something I never would've done before. Standing in the paint aisle of the hardware store, I told her everything I've written here, and then I told her I simply wanted to get to know her better, to see if we might enjoy some time together. ~~For the foreseeable future.~~ For now. Nothing more. No expectations. I won't be possessed, and I won't possess. She was open to the idea.

I took her to the beach. I didn't analyze every move she made, and I didn't measure constantly the distance between our physical bodies. No, I saw the blue sky and the glassy water for what it was—fragmented light and chemistry. I absorbed the warmth of the sun, and heard the soothing rhythms of the waves, and knew the joy of being alive.

Then, I took her to the movies. I didn't let the images of the silver screen dance unnoticed across my face while I wondered, *What will happen when this is over?* And I didn't critique the film either. Instead, I experienced the moment for what it was, and it was as glorious as any I'd ever had before.

Mr. Lawrence's former company—considered too big to fail—was restructured during bankruptcy, but he wasn't considered essential to the future of the new, more viable reincarnation. So, the Lawrence's got divorced, and Johnny's house was put up for sale. Moving day was the next time I saw Daniels; he came over to help Ashley move out. I took the opportunity to parade Emma right in front of Daniels.

*Sweet, sweet freedom.*

That day, Daniels said, "I had impossible visions of the papers on display under glass in our department at Oak Park University, and scholars from all over the country would come to interview me—us—about the contents and to get a glimpse of Hemingway's lost stories. But Hemingway's estate would claim the rights, or the Academy would take them. Or worse. They'd end up in Ann Arbor, where some pissant sitting in an endowed chair would lord over them. Everyone gets lost in Hemingway's giant shadow."

I accepted Daniels resignation with nothing more than a nod and carried onward.

To the point: Here I am, now, at the cabin with Emma. We're learning to practice Buddhism—*New loves! Mad generation!*—living deliberately off of my meager inheritance passed down to me from my grandfather, who was once a talented and celebrated novelist, who was also once a victim of crimes committed by his own government, who was also once a rapist, a murderer, and a thief, and who ultimately committed suicide—the perfectly complex character Johnny would've wanted to write about.

So, here's to you, Johnny, for whatever it's worth:

@SchurkeSings: Let us, the varied carols of America, unfurl. Let us, too, go then and sing, 'We are the ones who make a brighter day.'
11:59 AM – 8 Dec 2010

# THE SCHOLAR'S GAME

## Notes on Literary References

"Good artists copy, great artists steal."
—Pablo Picasso, presumably

"Hence, once again, pastiche: in a world in which stylistic
innovation is no longer possible, all that is left is to
imitate dead styles, to speak through the masks and with
the voices of the styles in the imaginary museum."
—Fredric Jameson, "Postmodernism and Consumer Society"

## ONE

## TWO

## THREE

• • •

# FOUR

30    **But I have been made so miserable by what has been kept hushed.** Djuna Barnes, *Nightwood*: I talk too much because I have been made so miserable by what you are keeping hushed.

31    **pressing ceaselessly against the current.** See F. Scott Fitzgerald, *The Great Gatsby*. See also reference on p. 5.

31    **No, I won't have my dreams mocked to death by time.** Zora Neale Hurston, *Their Eyes Were Watching God*: ...his dreams mocked to death by Time. That is the life of men.

# FIVE

34    **"Call me Samuel."** Herman Melville, *Moby Dick*: Call me Ishmael.

35    **Then, there she was.** Virginia Woolf, *Mrs. Dalloway*: It is Clarissa, he said. For there she was. (Woolf is an outlier in these references, but she was one of Johnny's favorites, and this is for him.)

40    **Finding myself alone...** Walt Whitman, "When I Heard the Learn'd Astronomer": Till rising and gliding out I wander'd off by myself, / In the mystical moist night-air, and from time to time, / Look'd up in perfect silence at the stars.

40    **"As if the dead really do persist," I said, "even in a glass of whiskey."** Thomas Pynchon, *The Crying of Lot 49*: As if the dead really do persist, even in a bottle of wine.

43    *This work, I thought, sags like a heavy load. And, Alex? Will it explode?* Langston Hughes, "Harlem": Maybe it just sags / like a heavy load. / Or does it explode?

# SIX

44    **"Here it is, another day."** See Ernest Hemingway, *The Sun Also Rises*.

45    **"We'll lose it," Johnny said, "if we talk about it."** Ernest Hemingway, "The Short Happy Life of Francis Macomber": Doesn't do to talk too much about all this. Talk the whole thing away. No pleasure in anything if you mouth it up too much.

46    **"It's their wealth," the driver added, "that allows them**

**to waste so."** Maya Angelou, *I Know Why the Caged Bird Sings*: But above all, their wealth that allowed them to waste was the most enviable.

47    **All my ideas of cathedrals come from the movies...** Raymond Carver, "Cathedral": Cathedrals. They're something to look at on late-night TV. That's all they are.

48    **I became tired and wandered off by myself. I went to a separate window, and leaned and loafed on the ledge...** See Walt Whitman, "When I Heard the Learn'd Astronomer." See also reference on p. 40.

48    **saw the freckled lights... And I was comfortable, and I didn't want to get up. I started to doze off when I heard— *BANG!*—and I rose up and listened, and heard it again. *BANG! BANG!* And I knew what was happening.** Mark Twain, *Adventures of Huckleberry Finn*: There was freckled places on the ground where the light sifted down through the leaves... I was powerful lazy and comfortable... "Boom!"... I knowed what was the matter, now... You see, they was firing cannons over the water, trying to make my carcass come to the top.

50    **See, two guys break into a farmhouse...** See Truman Capote, *In Cold Blood*.

55    **who don't look up to or down at nobody, who had dreams before debts, who'll survive this depression and will feel like people again."** John Steinbeck, *The Grapes of Wrath*: We're Joads. We don't look up to nobody. ... We was farm people till the debt. ... Why, I feel like people again.

## SEVEN

58    **the most dangerous game.** See Richard Connell, "The Most Dangerous Game."

61    **I had a delusional vision...** See Virginia Woolf, *To the Lighthouse*.

## EIGHT

65    **known to my family as North Egg...** F. Scott Fitzgerald, *The*

*Great Gatsby*: I lived at West Egg, the—well, the less fashionable of the two...

69    **There she was again—Beth**. See Virginia Woolf, *Mrs. Dalloway*. See also reference on p. 35.

72    **Your generation's a mass of dolts...** Ezra Pound, "To Whistler, American": You and Abe Lincoln from that mass of dolts / Show us there's chance at least of winning through.

73    **a thin red line.** See James Jones, *The Thin Red Line*.

75    **lead way on to way.** Robert Frost, "The Road Not Taken": Yet knowing how way leads on to way...

## JOURNAL – MAY 29-JUNE 14, 1961

76    **"Men can starve from a lack of self-realization as much as they can from a lack of bread"** Leonhard Grundstein references Richard Wright's *Native Son* here.

77-83    See Ernest Hemingway, "Up in Michigan."

84-7    See Ernest Hemingway, *A Farewell to Arms*.

## TEN

98    **"Call me Samuel."** Herman Melville, *Moby Dick*: Call me Ishmael.

99    **Beyond *Inferno*, in *Purgatorio*.** See Dante Alighieri, *The Divine Comedy*.

## ELEVEN

108    **"I don't know who made the laws, but I know there ain't no law that you got to go hungry."** See Ernest Hemingway, *To Have and Have Not*.

108    ***Love is all the dirty little tricks you taught me that you probably got out of some book.*** See Ernest Hemingway, *To Have and Have Not*.

108    **There is a time for everything...** Ecclesiastes 3:1 (New International Version).

• • •

## TWELVE

112    **"I, too, have someone I've wanted to be with for a long time."** Langston Hughes, "I, Too": I, too, am America.

113    **I was a man stuck on the open sea in a skiff with a fishing pole…** See Ernest Hemingway, *The old Man and the Sea.*

115    **"It's Alex," I said. For there she was.** See Virginia Woolf, *Mrs. Dalloway.* See also reference on p. 35.

116    **"At Woodlawn I heard the dead cry: This is my hard time**.**"** See Theodore Roethke, "The Lost Son."

## THIRTEEN

118    **"You look ridiculous if you dance. You look ridiculous if you don't dance. So you might as well dance."** See Gertrude Stein, *Three Lives.*

120    *No, no! Go from me…* See Ezra Pound, "A Virginal."

120-1    *I make a pact with you, Walt Whitman—* See Ezra Pound, "A Pact."

121    *Artists broken against her…* See Ezra Pound, "The Rest."

124    *By the gate now, the moss is grown…* See Ezra Pound, "The River-Merchant's Wife: A Letter."

126    *For I have known them all already…* See T.S. Eliot, "The Love Song of J. Alfred Prufrock."

128    **A lark. A plunge.** Virginia Woolf, *Mrs. Dalloway*: What a lark! What a plunge!

## FOURTEEN

132    **"far out to sea" … "very, very dangerous to live even one day."** See Virginia Woolf, *Mrs. Dalloway.*

139    **applause in this lecture-room.** Walt Whitman, "When I Heard the Learn'd Astronomer": …he lectured with much applause in the lecture-room.

## SIXTEEN

159    **We real cool…** See Gwendolyn Brooks, "We real cool."

160      **a generation of men...** See Erich Maria Remarque, *All Quiet on the Western Front*.

163-4    **My people thought...** Leslie Marmon Silko, *Ceremony*: ...feeling they belonged to America the way they felt during the war. ... They never saw that it was the white people who gave them that feeling and it was the white people who took it away again when the war was over.

164      **"Washed in a river of make-believe," Eli added.** Alice Walker, "Everyday Use": She washed us in a river of make-believe, burned us with a lot of knowledge we didn't necessarily need to know.

## EIGHTEEN

187      ***We know what no other animal knows.*** See Don DeLillo, *White Noise*. See also reference on p. 11.

187      **Moloch!** See Allen Ginsberg, "Howl."

## NINETEEN

196      **Sorrow is my own yard...** See William Carlos Williams, "The Widow's Lament in Springtime."

## TWENTY-ONE

212      **Nothing is all good or all bad; it all depends.** Leslie Marmon Silko, *Ceremony*: Nothing was all good or all bad either; it all depended.

215      **just as fair, perhaps having the better claim... I tell of this with a sigh...** See Robert Frost, "The Road Not Taken."

## TWENTY-THREE

224      **"When your brain begins to reel from your literary labors," I said, "you need an occasional Jolly Rancher."** John Kennedy Toole, *A Confederacy of Dunces*: When my brain begins to reel from my literary labors, I make an occasional cheese dip.

• • •

## TWENTY-FOUR

235-8   See Homi Bhabha, *The Location of Culture*.

236     **'The trouble with the Engenglish...** See Salman Rushdie, *The Satanic Verses*.

238     **'I am tired and sick...** See Walt Whitman, "When I Heard the Learn'd Astronomer."

238     **"You wanna fly," Eli said, "you got to give up the shit that weighs you down."** See Toni Morrison, *Song of Solomon*.

239     **beating against it.** See F. Scott Fitzgerald, *The Great Gatsby*. See also reference on p. 5.

241     **"What, do you think I might buy stocks?"** See John Dos Passos, *The Big Money*.

242     **I would not know.** See Ernest Hemingway, *A Farewell to Arms*. See also reference on p. 8.

## TWENTY-FIVE

244-8   See Fredric Jameson, "Postmodernism and Consumer Society," *The Cultural Turn*.

## TWENTY-SIX

253-8   See Fredric Jameson, "Postmodernism and Consumer Society," *The Cultural Turn*.

258     ***Where are we going, Walt Whitman? ... The doors close in an hour. Which way does your beard point tonight?*** See Allen Ginsberg, "A Supermarket in California."

258     **I lifted my eyes... All was born again...** Sylvia Plath, "Mad Girl's Love Song": I lift my lids and all is born again.

258     **I saw that the words weren't anything, like nothing in my life.** See Raymond Carver, "Cathedral."

259     **faith is what someone knows to be true, whether they believe it or not.** See Flannery O'Connor, *Wise Blood*.

## TWENTY-SEVEN

264     **a man of his age, of depression, of war, of fear.** Tillie Olsen,

"I Stand Here Ironing": She is a child of her age, of depression, of war, of fear.

267     **Shut your ears to the roaring of the voices...** See Sherwood Anderson, *Winesburg, Ohio*.

## JOURNAL – JUNE 15-JULY 2, 1961

278     *Nimmermehr.* It's possible Leonhard Grundstein was referencing Edgar Allan Poe's "The Raven."

## TWENTY-EIGHT

283     **to hold it in abeyance.** Walt Whitman, "Song of Myself": Creeds and schools in abeyance.

289     *You shout because it makes you brave or you want to announce your recklessness...* See Don Delillo, *Underworld*.

289     *I shut my eyes and all the world dropped dead.* See Sylvia Plath, "Mad Girl's Love Song."

## TWENTY-NINE

293     **It was less than a mile to go...** Robert Frost, "Stopping by a Wood on a Snowy Evening": And miles to go before I sleep.

294     *A man goes far to find out what he is,"* I thought. *"Death of the self in a long, tearless night.* See Theodore Roethke, "In a Dark Time."

296     **scares us from self-trust is our consistency...** See Ralph Waldo Emerson, "Self-Reliance."

## THIRTY

301     **There the light was coming in through the windows at a certain slant...** See Emily Dickinson, "There's a certain slant of light."

307     *Which of the young men does she like the best?* See Walt Whitman, "Song of Myself."

• • •

## THIRTY-ONE

315    **The fact the book was a tragic one...** See Ernest Hemingway's 1948 introduction to *A Farewell to Arms*.

## THIRTY-TWO

324    **...weak and weary... *Is there a balm in Gilead? ... Tell me, tell me, I implore!* See Edgar Allan Poe, "The Raven."

328    **...*despair came over her... ...as you will when nobody around has any sexual relevance to you...* See Thomas Pynchon, *The Crying of Lot 49*.

328    **...*take thy beak from out of my heart... Nevermore. Nevermore. Nevermore.* See Edgar Allan Poe, "The Raven."

## THIRTY-THREE

335    **...Daniels said, pressing on...** See F. Scott Fitzgeral, *The Great Gatsby*. See also reference on p. 5.

335    **I would not know.** See Ernest Hemingway, *A Farewell to Arms*. See also reference on p. 8.

## THIRTY-FOUR

337    **I felt like I was masquerading...** Ernest Hemingway, *A Farewell to Arms*: In civilian clothes I felt a masquerader. I had been in uniform a long time...

337    **I sat in the café and drank a cup of coffee and ate a scone.** Ernest Hemingway, *A Farewell to Arms*: I stood at the bar and drank a glass of coffee and ate a piece of bread.

338    **I would not know...** See Ernest Hemingway, *A Farewell to Arms*. See also reference on p. 8.

339    **That was when Alex pulled Mr. Lawrence's nickel-colored Bentley convertible into the driveway. The green leather interior was as soft as the lushest of lawns.** F. Scott Fitzgerald, *The Great Gatsby*: It was a rich cream color, bright with nickel [...] Sitting down behind many layers of glass in a sort of green leather conservatory, we started to town.

342 **"You have to quit confusing a madness with a mission."**
See Flannery O'Conner, *The Violent Bear It Away*.

343 **I would not know.** See Ernest Hemingway, *A Farewell to Arms*. See also reference on p. 8.

343 **"Samuel, we could be so good together," she said, leaning toward me, lips first. I didn't pull away, but I said, "It was nice to think so."** Ernest Hemingway, *The Sun Also Rises*: "Oh, Jake," Brett said, "we could have had such a damned good time together." … "Yes," I said. "Isn't it pretty to think so?"

## THIRTY-FIVE

344 **A paved paradise.** See Joni Mitchell, "Big Yellow Taxi."

344 **A certain slant of light.** See Emily Dickinson, "There's a certain slant of light."

344 **Amber waves.** See Katharine Lee Bates, "America the Beautiful."

344 **"It's all falling indelibly into the past," I said to her.** See Don DeLillo, *Underworld*.

344 **"You know this."** See Don DeLillo, *White Noise*. See also reference on p. 352.

344-5 **Less than a mile to go—before we can sleep.** See Robert Frost, "Stopping by a Wood on a Snowy Evening."

345 **"This world is not yours, Karmann," I said, as she lay dying. "Meet Mr. White Pine."** William Faulkner, *As I lay Dying*: This world is not his world; this life his life. … "Meet Mrs Bundren," he says.

345 **To this day, Karmann is still there, just a pile of rust and stardust.** Vladimir Nabokov, *Lolita*: And I shall be dumped where the weed decays, / And the rest is rust and stardust.

346 **But I felt large; I contained the energy of multitudes.** Walt Whitman, "Song of Myself": I am large, I contain multitudes.

347 **As way leads on to way.** Robert Frost, "The Road Not Taken": Yet knowing how way leads on to way...

349 **allegiance to our long-established attitudes...** Ralph Waldo Emerson, "Self-Reliance": ...a reverence for our past act...

351    **For the love of Moloch...** See Allen Ginsberg, "Howl."

352    **I've learned that anybody's life, when examined, makes no sense. I've learned to leave it alone.** Philip Roth, *American Pastoral*: He had learned the worst lesson that life can teach—that it makes no sense.

352    **"You know this: that we must die. That is the nature of plots...** Don DeLillo, *White Noise*: We know what no other animal knows, that we must die. ... All plots tend to move deathward. This is the nature of plots.

352    **Creeds and schools in abeyance.** See Walt Whitman, "Song of Myself."

353    **I, too, will sing America, and you'll see how beautiful I am and be ashamed.** Langston Hughes, "I, too": I, too, sing America. ... They'll see how beautiful I am / And be ashamed—

353    ***Vivas* to those who have failed ... to the greatest heroes known.** Walt Whitman, "Song of Myself": I sound triumphal drums for the dead... / I fling through my embouchures the / loudest and gayest music to them— / *Vivas* to those who have failed, and to those / whose war-vessels sank in the sea, and to / those themselves who sank in the sea. / And to all generals that lost engagements, / and to all overcome heroes, and the number- / less unknown heroes equal to the / greatest heroes known.

353    **pressing on ceaselessly.** F. Scott Fitzgeral, *The Great Gatsby*. See also reference on p. 5.

354    **the roaring voices were silent at last.** See Sherwood Anderson, *Winesburg, Ohio*. See also reference on p. 267.

354    **This—is the flag—of permanent defeat.** Ernest Hemingway, *The Old Man and the Sea*: The sail was patched with flour sacks and, furled, it looked like the flag of permanent defeat.

355    ***And the ages continued henceforward!*** See Walt Whitman, "To Think of Time."

356    **"Nobody will ever thank me. [...] I'm done with these lonely offices.** Robert Hayden, "Those Winter Sundays": No one ever thanked him. [...] What did I know, what did I know / of love's

austere and lonely offices?

356   **I'm done trying to go in everyone's way but my own.** Ralph Ellison, *Invisible Man*: And my problem was that I always tried to go in everyone's way but my own.

## THIRTY-SIX

357   **How far have our orbits diverged?** See Robert Frost, "The Road Not Taken": Two roads diverged in a yellow wood...

358   *New loves! Mad generation!* See Allen Ginsberg, "Howl."

358   **living deliberately...** Henry David Thoreau, *Walden*: I went to the woods because I wished to live deliberately, to front only the essential facts of life...

359   **Let us, the varied carols of America, unfurl. Let us, too, go then and sing, 'We are the ones who make a brighter day.'** T.S. Eliot, "The Love Song of J. Alfred Prufrock": Let us go then, you and I; Walt Whitman, "I hear America signing": I hear America singing, the varied carols I hear; Ernest Hemingway, *The Old Man and the Sea*: See also reference on p. 354; Langston Hughes, "I, too": I, too, sing America.; Michael Jackson/Lionel Richie, "We Are the World": We are the ones who make a brighter day.

# Acknowledgments

First and foremost, I want to thank you, Katie Zahrt, for your constant love and unwavering support for me and my writing, without which this book wouldn't have happened.

This book is also for Benjamin Orion and Tessa Kate; I hope you will be as proud of it as I am.

Thank you, Dr. Fredric Jameson, for permission to reprint the excerpts from your essay, "Postmodernism and Consumer Society." This book would not be the same without them.

Thank you, Dr. Bradley P. Romans, for your willingness to answer my countless questions about your experience completing a doctoral degree in literature as well as about literary modernism and many other ideas.

Thank you to Jeff Rice, Pardeep Toor, and Eve Vitale for our many conversations about literature and the craft of writing and, in particular, for your feedback on this book.

Thank you, Fabienne Gafner, for your guidance regarding the German language and for all the Swiss chocolate.

Last but not least, thank you to my parents, family members and friends, teachers and writers—too many to name—who have supported my writing over the years in a variety of ways.

It takes a village to raise a writer.

# About the Author

K.M. Zahrt is the author of *Odd Man Outlaw* and *Thanksgiving with Pop-Pop*. *The Nature of Plots* is his second novel. He lives in Michigan. For more information, visit www.kmzahrt.info or @KMZahrt on Twitter.

www.ingramcontent.com/pod-product-compliance
Lightning Source LLC
Chambersburg PA
CBHW030549260626
47157CB00006B/2237